MURDER BETWEEN FRIENDS

Recent Titles by Vivien Armstrong from Severn House

BIRD OF PREY
BEYOND THE PALE
CLOSE CALL
DEAD IN THE WATER
FLY IN AMBER
FOOL'S GOLD
NO BIRDS SINGING
REWIND
SMILE NOW, DIE LATER
THE WRONG ROAD

MURDER BETWEEN FRIENDS

Vivien Armstrong

This first world edition published in Great Britain 2004 by
SEVERN HOUSE PUBLISHERS LTD of
9–15 High Street, Sutton, Surrey SM1 1DF.
This first world edition published in the USA 2004 by
SEVERN HOUSE PUBLISHERS INC of
595 Madison Avenue, New York, N.Y. 10022.

British Library Cataloguing in Publication Data

Armstrong, Vivien
    Murder between friends. - (A Detective Inspector Hayes mystery)
    1. Police - Fiction
    2. Detective and mystery stories
    I. Title
    823.9'14 [F]

    ISBN 0-7278-6119-0

Typeset by Palimpsest Book Production Ltd.,
Polmont, Stirlingshire, Scotland.
Printed and bound in Great Britain by
MPG Books Ltd., Bodmin, Cornwall.

*For Charmian Taylor,
my locations expert,
with love.*

One

Stella Buckleigh decided that her life had sailed through childhood and two uneventful marriages like a royal barge, an unremarkable progress which, as she neared the white water of her fortieth birthday, called for some real excitement. It was Stella's idea to murder Charlie Hilton, a man she had never met, a celebrity whose adventures both on and off the screen were rarely out of the headlines.

It had all started on a Monday morning when she had strolled into her favourite boutique on Walton Street in Chelsea and discovered the usual salesgirl replaced by someone vaguely familiar. Katie? Yes! She smiled in triumph. Kate Barker. It could only be she; the plain skirt and white blouse were all too reminiscent of their old school uniform. Crikey! More than twenty years blown away in a moment.

Kate had hardly changed at all; her face devoid of make-up, her black bob, as always, brutally like a Japanese doll. Stella grabbed the astonished woman with both hands.

'Kate! It is you, isn't it? My God, I can't believe it. What on earth are you doing here? Where's Polly?'

She fell back, flushing with embarrassment. 'Sorry? I'm afraid I—'

'It's Stella. Stella Bower that was. Freemont Grange. You can't have forgotten.'

Recognition slowly dawned and, still reeling from this blast from the past, Kate stiffened as the door opened and a second customer burst in.

Stella drew back and, smiling, placed a finger to her lips. She turned to the rail of new season's garments flowering like exotic blooms on this showery April morning. The tiny shop

1

suddenly seemed crowded, the woman standing four-square in the doorway shutting out the meagre sunlight.

'Where's Polly?' she demanded. 'She promised to put some cruise-wear aside for me.'

'Polly's had an accident. Can I help you, madam? Your name? I'll look in the book,' said Kate.

'Strachey. Mirabel Strachey. Just look in the back room, girl.'

Kate cast a helpless glance at Stella, who leapt into the breach.

'Polly was saving some beach-wear for me, too. Utterly maddening. We shall have to be patient, shan't we? This new person is on her own and Polly left a message for us preferred clients to come back on Wednesday – she wants to show the new designs herself.'

This outrageous invention left Kate open-mouthed but Stella's grin mollified Mirabel Strachey, who nodded, then stalked out without another glance at Polly's stand-in.

'There you go. Simple. Don't let these old cows bully you, darling. You were always a pussy cat, Katie. Any chance of a lunch hour?'

'The manager's sending someone from the Kensington branch to help out. She should be here any minute but I can't get away before six. It's my first day,' she added, pushing back the heavy fringe from hazel eyes, pale as very expensive sherry.

'I'll pick you up at six then. We'll have supper at my place.' Stella squeezed her arm, grinning like the winner she had always been, never having become familiar with a rebuff.

Kate held open the door and watched her friend's smooth retreat with bemusement, hearing the sharp tick-tack of her stilettos on the damp pavement, recognizing the cut of a designer suit that contoured Stella's neat little bottom to perfection.

Two

The senior salesperson sent over to supervise the new girl proved to be a Frenchwoman called Nadine, fiftyish and formidably stylish in a black silk jersey sheath. She frowned at the taxi rudely hooting outside the shop twenty minutes before closing time and hurried out, expecting to greet an impatient customer. Kate blanched, fearing the inevitable.

Stella pulled down the window, all smiles.

'Hello there. I've come to collect Katie. Do tell her to buck up, would you? We're on double yellow lines here.'

Before Nadine could issue an icy Gallic riposte, Kate joined her at the kerb, her coat over her arm. 'It's Polly's special customer, Nadine. Mrs—'

'Stella Buckleigh. Kate's promised to give me a private rundown on the new season's collection. All right if we pop off now? Taxis are like gold dust in the rush hour.'

Allowing herself a tiny moue of exasperation, Nadine relented and watched the cab pull away. '*Merde.*'

Stella paid off the taxi and steered Kate up her front steps. In the square, white magnolias glowed like candle cups in the day's final burst of spring sunshine. The stuccoed terrace rose like a cliff against the washed-out skyline and as Kate waited for Stella to negotiate the double-locked front door, the strangeness of this unforeseen encounter made her smile.

Stella grabbed her arm and pushed her into a minute lift that brought them straight into the hallway of the top-floor flat. There was a pervading scent of lilies, but in fact the narrow foyer displayed no more than a console table heaped with a trough of yellow orchids – undoubtedly real, Kate recognized, herself something of a know-all in the house plant department – but nevertheless scentless.

Stella flung her bag and jacket on a chair and grinned, taking Kate's hands in her own and brushing a kiss on each cheek.

'There! What fun. Fancy finding you in that funny little dress shop. Serendipity.'

They moved into the living room, which overlooked the square, and Stella touched a master switch which threw the apartment into a glow of shaded lamps and concealed uplights.

'It's lovely up here, Stella. So quiet. Do you have family at home?'

'Just my daughter, Frances.'

'Lucky you. How old is she?'

'Fifteen and at that hideous stage of teenage angst. At school most of the time, which is just as well – we fight like alley cats over the stupidest things.'

Kate laughed. '*Plus ça change*. Surely you can't have forgotten our alliance against Miss Parker about the length of our skirts?'

'How about a drink? Gin, wine? No, champagne! A celebration of our reunion.'

Before Kate could answer, Stella rushed off to open a bottle of Bollinger and the next hour was spent reminiscing over times long past. They eventually settled on grilled trout and salad for supper and Kate set the table while Stella shouted from the kitchen, both now ridiculously giggly. They returned to the sitting room for coffee.

'Enough of all that. School was beastly, wasn't it? Only the three of us being such mates made it bearable.'

Kate nodded, suddenly serious. 'Fill me in. How come you ended up here?'

Stella stretched out on one of the sofas, a huge square coffee table piled high with magazines between them. She lit a cigarette and fell silent. Kate regarded the lean figure nervously dragging on her cigarette, her sun-bleached hair drawn into an untidy topknot, her sharp cheekbones gilded with the sort of tan never acquired in those grey Britist winter months that had only just blended into a late spring.

'We lost touch after our laughable stab at A levels, didn't we? Can't think how. The three of us linked like sisters through all those miserable years at that bloody boarding school, and then – poof!'

'We weren't the right material, were we? Congenital misfits.'

Stella laughed, closing her eyes, wondering how much she dare reveal to this rediscovered soulmate sitting cross-legged on the cushions like a plump 'momma san'. But Kate had always been a good listener, hadn't she? Perhaps that was the secret: Kate, the perfect foil. The third member of the clique had completed the alliance, the most intelligent of them all: Victoria, the thinker.

Stella coughed, stubbing out her cigarette as her voice, husky and at first barely audible, grew stronger as her narrative spooled out, the half-forgotten milestones of the past twenty-two years slipping past like hazy recollections of a dream.

'After leaving, I went back home for the holidays and had a bit of a barney over an abortive move on my part to swing a gap-year jolly to India. Dad stood firm and shoved me into a residential secretarial school in Oxford. I was pretty pissed off, as you can imagine, typing not being my idea of a way to the stars. But, as it happened, Oxford turned out to be lots of fun and my sex life leapt into overdrive. Like a fool I got pregnant, of course, and, being a real donkey, ran off with this lecturer, a married guy with children who lost his job and got to be a real pain in the neck. As luck would have it, I had a miscarriage and my parents tried to bully me into going back home. But I was no longer a kid and I got myself a job on a fashion magazine in London. Surprised myself by being quite good at it too, but then I made my next big mistake and fell in love with Monty Neville, a chancer like myself, but fun with it and a breath of fresh air after my stuffy academic romeo.'

'You married him?'

'Mmm.' Stella laughed. 'I was never too bright when it came to picking men, and it wasn't as if I had no choice. Trouble was, the fashion business was full of gays, so Monty's brand of passion knocked me for six. Hence my daughter, Fran.'

Kate's eyes widened. 'And he could afford all this?' she said, gesturing at their surroundings.

Stella laughed, a brittle sound which cut through the soft dusk like the rattle of hail against the window.

'Monty? In Eaton Square? Never. The marriage split soon after Frances was born. Monty was some sort of racecourse tipster for one of the dailies then, but he must have been lousy at it because his own bets seemed only to end up in a snow-storm of debts. I continued with the magazine job and was making good money, paid all the bills and managed to keep a nanny for the baby, but it was a losing battle and Monty's jokes got thinner and thinner.'

Kate murmured a sympathetic response. Stella smiled grimly and lit another cigarette.

'Ever read those dating columns in the weekend press, Katie? You know, lonely hearts, romance for losers? G.S.O.H. is a really popular requirement.'

'What's that?'

'Must have a good sense of humour. Utter tosh. My sense of humour ran out within a year of listening to Monty's excuses.'

'You left?'

'Pushed him out and filed for divorce.'

'But you still see him?'

'He's tried to touch me for a loan once or twice but mostly he focuses his charm on Frances these days, and naturally she's enchanted. But being the sole breadwinner, even on my salary, was not my idea of fun. I was never a stayer, was I, Katie?'

'But all this?'

'Sadly, not from my own efforts. I married again – a sensible move for once, probably the only calculated step I've ever taken. I married Anthony Buckleigh, the impresario theatre bloke. You never heard of him? Put on shows in the West End. Bankrolled movies.'

'Sorry. You've lost me now.'

'A darling man. Older than me, of course, but a generous

soul. Took over Frances as his own, pulled me off the tread-mill, and here I am, as you see, in clover.' This last was spoken with irony, Stella's fingers shaking as she stubbed out the cigarette.

Kate fell silent, unsure if Stella's interest in her listener had suddenly evaporated. But Stella had only stalled. 'He died,' she said at last. 'A helicopter crash in California. He was fixing up a deal with a film company and there was some sort of mechanical failure.'

'Oh, Stella. I'm so sorry.'

She shrugged. 'Two years ago now and the sweet man left me well provided for, as you can see. Except in the boredom department, of course.'

'You've met no one else?'

'Good God, no! There's a clause in the will. Marrying again would be financial suicide. Anyway, I'm rather off men just now – a few dates, a dalliance with a TV scriptwriter which will have to end. He's getting much too cosy here, and Frances hates him.'

'Poor you. Not that I've hit the jackpot, as you've guessed.'

'Heavens. Katie! You've let me ramble on in this maudlin way and I haven't let you get a word in. What happened? Why are you working in that crappy little boutique?'

'Simple. I need the money. I live in a very expensive house. I'm married to a rich man and I'm totally skint.'

'Sell up.'

'I can't. It's complicated. Charlie guards his reputation like the Pope, and a prenuptial agreement leaves me on the back foot.'

'You need a lawyer.'

'I've got one. A good man. But as I said, it's complicated.'

'What's his name, this prize shit you're married to?'

'He's an actor. Films mostly. You may even have met him through your husband. His name's Charlie Hilton.'

'Wow! You don't lark about, do you, Katie? The guy was recommended for an Oscar nomination for best supporting actor only three years ago.'

'Well, he's sure as hell not supporting me.'

Three

The smoke from Kate's bombshell disclosure had barely cleared when the lift doors opened and a schoolgirl burst in. Stella leapt to her feet.

'Fran! Sweetheart. What on earth are you doing here?' She crossed the room in long strides and pulled her into the circle of lamplight. Stella's mouth hardened. 'You've run away.'

Kate sat perfectly still like an innocent bystander likely to be caught in crossfire. Stella's daughter hardly seemed to resemble her at all, with dark hair and a chubby figure, but the obduracy was familiar, Kate's clear memory of Stella's dozens of similar stand-offs flooding her mind.

Stella was clearly attempting to damp down her exasperation, and stiffly took the girl in hand, pulling her into the room and introducing Kate.

'Kate, meet my daughter.'

Frances politely held out a grubby hand, but her stance remained mulish.

'Have you eaten, darling?'

'I'm not hungry.'

'Well, you had better join us and tell me all about it. Fetch a cup and pour yourself some coffee.'

'I'm off caffeine.'

'Vegetarian *and* abstemious. Good heavens, if it weren't for all my missing ciggies I would begin to wonder what ideas those stupid nuns have put into your head.'

Frances slumped on the couch beside Kate, her miniskirt riding up to reveal the thighs of thankfully a non-anorexic teenager.

'Have you run away?'

'I just left.'

'Does anyone at school know?'

She shook her head, her eyes suddenly brimming.

Stella relented and rounded the massive coffee table to hug her. 'I'll ring now. Say you've got a tummy bug and will be here for a couple of days. I'll drive you back on Thursday. Anything I should know?'

'I'd just had enough. The bickering, the bloody exams . . .'

'Sounds pretty normal to me. If you're not eating, why don't you pop upstairs and have a bath? I'll phone the school – we'll talk about it later after I've run Kate home.'

Kate rose to go but Stella closed the door after her daughter and resumed her seat.

'Don't go yet. Give her time to calm down. Where were we? Charlie Hilton. Fancy you marrying Charlie Hilton!'

Kate remained standing and insisted it was time to leave. 'Chaz will wonder where I am – he said he'd pop round this evening.'

'Chaz?'

'My stepson. Crashes out in the spare room from time to time. Charlie's boy from his first marriage. But, then, hardly a boy, twenty-four years old and if you think stroppy teenagers are a problem you should have a taste of Chaz. I'd better go, Stella. We'll get together another time – here, let me give you my phone number.'

Kate scrabbled in her bag and produced a sales receipt on which she jotted her address. 'As you can see, I only live a few streets away, no need for you to run me home.'

'Blast Frances. It's cut short our lovely gossip. We never even got round to Victoria, did we? Whatever happened to Tory, I wonder.' They moved into the hallway and Kate struggled into her raincoat.

'Funny you should say that. I traced her only a few weeks ago as it happens. Through the Internet. I was passing the time looking through that Friends Reunited website and a whole list of girls we used to know at school were listed.'

Stella laughed. 'Cripes! Your love life must be as skimpy as mine if you spend time fooling around on the Internet. And you say Tory was on it?'

Kate nodded. 'I phoned her straight away. She's living in

Suffolk, married to a GP, a chap called Stefan Blum. Or was. Sadly, the poor man died last week and I promised Tory I'd go to the funeral on Friday. Why don't you come too?'

'Won't she mind? A funeral's not exactly the ideal setting for an old girls' reunion.'

'Well, come anyway. I'll need some support and she seemed anxious I should go. I asked the manager at the shop for the day off – said my brother-in-law had died. Taking time off on my first week's chancing it, but Nadine said OK and Polly will probably be back by then; she only sprained her ankle.'

'Suffolk you say? How far's that? I'm not too hot on anywhere north of Oxford.'

'Takes a couple of hours by car if we leave early. The funeral's at noon. Say I pick you up at nine just to be on the safe side?'

'And you two haven't met in all these years?

'No.'

Stella looked dubious. 'I'll have to see how things pan out with Frances. She's been bullied at school lately, I expect that's the problem. Can I let you know?'

'Of course.'

'I'll see you out. Next time you come I'll show you the rest of the flat. It's got a wonderful roof garden. If the weather's fine we could have drinks up there – it's very sheltered.'

'Sounds wonderful.'

They parted under the grandiose portico, Kate scurrying off in the dusk like a rabbit down a hole. Stella watched her go, curiously dispirited by this strange encounter. And now Tory too? Did she really want to go back over all that old ground? But Charlie Hilton? Fancy that. It was intriguing. Kate wed to a bloody film star. Making up the trio at the funeral might even be worth it to hear the finer details of Kate's marriage to one of Hollywood's reputed bad boys.

But curiosity is a terrible thing. It killed the cat, didn't it?

10

Four

The drive to the funeral in Suffolk took longer than Kate planned and they arrived at the crematorium just as the coffin was gliding through the velvet drapes to the business end of the chapel. The sparse congregation was making a ragged effort at the final hymn as Kate and Stella crept in. Only the vicar noticed their arrival and they slipped into a back pew with not so much as a whisper from the late Doctor Blum's friends. Stella wore a black Armani suit, which, as she hastily glanced round, she guessed was a touch over the top. Kate blended in, her grey raincoat merging with the grim surroundings, the only bright spot being a mound of wild spring flowers untidily sprawling over the surface of the coffin. Stella struggled with a bubbling eruption of mirth as the heavy curtains snagged on this floral abundance that no florist in his right mind would own. She guessed it was Tory's idea. Probably Tory's determination to cover poor Stefan's cheap box with an idiosyncratic gesture – Tory, if she remembered correctly, being the arty type. A verger leapt forward and detached the offending briars and the casket continued its relentless progress.

Kate passed Stella a tissue, refusing to meet her eye, and Stella dabbed at her cheeks in what must have seemed a tender farewell.

They waited outside, eyeing each other with faint alarm. Would they recognize Tory after all these years? Were these people her relatives? Or Stefan's? Would there be some sort of lunch? Stella's mood plummeted. Coming here had been a terrible mistake. She touched Kate's arm ready to suggest a hasty retreat but then a distinguished-looking man in an old-

11

fashioned tweed suit raised his hat and presented himself.

'My name's Austen Rivers. You must be the London friends Victoria was expecting.'

Stella brightened and introduced Kate and herself, cheered by the old chap's smile.

'Victoria has organized drinks at the pub in the village. Shall I lead the way?'

Kate murmured something about waiting to speak to Tory but Stella insisted they followed their elderly charmer.

'We can talk to Tory later – I expect she's got to hang about here for a bit to speak to the rest.'

Kate reluctantly agreed and tailed Austen Rivers' Rover through lanes billowing with spring blossom.

The 'village' he had mentioned proved to be a mixture of smart houses and holiday cabins in various stages of disrepair. The Rover nosed its way towards the estuary where, across the water, a more built-up seaside town could be glimpsed. He stopped outside a pub and waited for them to join him.

'That's Southwold,' he explained. 'Much posher than Walberswick, and only a mile apart as the crow flies, but because of the river it is necessary to drive the long way round.'

'Victoria lives here in Walberswick?'

'I'd better explain, Mr Rivers,' Kate hastily put in. 'Stella and I haven't seen our friend for years.'

He seemed unperturbed and brushed away Kate's anxious interjection. 'Yes, yes, of course. Victoria mentioned something of it. Very good of you to come – poor Stefan made few friends himself. A very private person,' he added. 'Most of those at the service were ex-patients. He retired here from Colchester two years ago. A dicky heart, poor man. Got him in the end, didn't it? Stefan and I met on birdwatching excursions. I suggested they moved here and I believe everything was coming along splendidly. Poor Victoria. I'm glad you two young ladies are here – she needs bucking up.'

Stella was about to pump their new friend for more background information but just then several cars making up the main party pulled into the forecourt. She and Kate found themselves bundled inside and pushed into a side room where a buxom waitress was cheerfully directing the mourners towards a table laden with crab sandwiches, crisps and a generous selection of wine and spirits. Austen Rivers got caught up with a group of neighbours and the atmosphere visibly lifted, gales of laughter blending with a polite under-current of commiseration. Kate got drawn into a trio of locals and Stella scanned the room to see if she could spot the Ladies.

A low voice in her ear murmured, 'Hey you! I knew it was you. As bloody fancy as ever, I see.'

Stella spun round. The reed-thin woman with long brown hair and a darkish complexion could be no one else.

'Tory! You've hardly changed at all. For God's sake, let's get out of here before I burst into tears.'

Victoria Blum, as she now was, was more than a match for Stella and pulled a face. 'No way. I'd never be forgiven, chickening out on Stefan's do, though he wouldn't have hung about given the chance. Tell you what though, I've got Moses in the car. Come outside – I don't see why Moses can't join the party.'

'Moses?'

But Tory had slipped off, leaving Stella to follow, her mind buzzing with the sheer absurdity of the situation she had landed herself in.

Tory's ancient 2CV was parked between larger, shinier vehi-cles, the patina of its red-and-white paintwork dulled long since, the entire back seat occupied by the ugliest mutt Stella had seen outside Battersea Dogs' Home, a place she had been forced to visit during a series of school holidays when Frances had been passing through an animal rights phase. Tory whis-tled and opened the door.

'Out you come, Mo.' A lolloping beast all but fell out, its shaggy coat the matted texture of wire wool.

'Christ, Tory! What is it?'

'Full-blooded mongrel with a dash of Irish wolfhound and a possible seasoning of poodle somewhere in the past.'

'And it's going in the pub?'

'Of course. He's a regular! Gentle as a lamb. Stefan would never forgive me if Moses was left out in the cold.'

'Why Moses?'

'Stefan found him down by the river. Stashed in a plastic bin liner. Two puppies, just a few weeks old. Some cruel bugger must have tried to drown them but the bag got caught up in bulrushes. Stefan found a home for the bitch but kept the dog for himself. Moses went everywhere with him. I suppose I shall have to try to take him round with me, but heaven knows how the people at school will take it.'

'You're a teacher?'

'Sort of. When Stefan was working I used to man Reception and answer phones and so on. But I've taken a job at an adult education place two evenings a week, teaching calligraphy. For my own amusement really – no money in it of course.' Tory eyed Stella's designer suit as she attached Moses' leash. 'But you've done all right though, haven't you, Stella?' she chivvied. 'When the wake's broken up you and Kate must come back with me for supper. I've a house on the beach – don't look alarmed, I've asked no one else! Such a long way to come just to keep Kate company.' She smiled, a wicked grin which blew away the intervening years. 'But you couldn't resist it, could you, Stella? Shaking up the kaleidoscope to see what bits fit your own little scheme of things?'

Five

Tory stayed on till the bitter end and it was five o'clock before the last of the mourners departed. Stella and Kate had promptly retired to the pub garden to enjoy the unseasonal warm sunshine, but it would seem that in the backwoods, giving Doctor Stefan Blum a decent send-off was a serious undertaking. Moses padded about the back room hoovering up the crisps underfoot and making himself agreeable, but they found it impossible to have any sort of private conversation with Tory, and Kate was becoming increasingly restless.

'I suppose we shall have to go back to Tory's place for an hour or two, but we can't stay long, Stella. I've got to get back, I'm working tomorrow.'

'Play it by ear, sweetie. Tory's expecting us and I've been looking forward to our little get-together all week.'

Kate eyed Stella with considerable disquiet, wishing now that she had come alone, had been free to come and go as she pleased. But, having persuaded Stella to come, it would be tricky to bale out on Tory's do. The funny thing was, she mused, the grieving widow seemed to be thoroughly enjoying the party, even though, from the snippets of talk overheard in the bar, the Blums had apparently enjoyed a flawless relationship. Kate felt depressed and wondered if just one of Stella's cigarettes would re-ignite a craving barely under control.

'What's the rush? Even if we stay for supper you could be back in bed before midnight, Cinders.'

'I'm worried about Chaz moving in. He's always threatening to change the locks.'

'Bugger that! Change the locks yourself, Katie. This bloke needs a kick up the backside it seems to me. What's his problem?'

'Cocaine mostly, but anything mildly narcotic at a pinch. He's been spoiled, of course. Charlie was never around and Chaz had no regular base till I came on the scene.'

'When was that?'

'Nine years ago.'

'He's a big boy now, Kate. Throw him out; you've got troubles of your own without bankrolling his habit. Like I said, change the locks.'

'After a reassessment of Chaz's allowance, Charlie arranged that half the house was put in his name – it was some sort of tax dodge I think – but the lawyer insisted that it reverts fully to me if Chaz dies first. But if Charlie finds grounds for divorcing me, or if I die first, Chaz will take the lot. It seemed fair at the time, especially as I had the boy living with me then. But years have gone by and now Charlie's had a detec-

15

tive on my back for months trying to nail me down to something which would paint him "the white man" in court.'

'Can't you nail Charlie yourself? I'd bet my best Manolos that he's got starlets in and out of his bed all hours. Poor old sod probably needs a nubile wannabe to fan his flagging libido – he's all of fifty, isn't he?'

'Fifty-six.'

'Well then. What does this lawyer of yours say?'

'Rob Allinson's with a top firm but probably worries about his fees, knowing I'm all but washed up since Charlie stopped paying the bills and refuses to agree to a settlement.'

'Want me to put my solicitor on to it?'

Kate grabbed her arm. 'No! Rob's doing his best – he's just cautious. He reckons I've got a good case if Charlie tries to throw me out without a penny.'

Stella sighed and glanced at her watch as Moses ambled over and placed a slobbering jaw on her lap. She leapt up, spilling her gin on the grass as she shoved the dog away and dabbed at her skirt. Kate laughed, collaring Moses as Tory emerged into the fading afternoon to find them.

'Hi, you two. I thought you'd gone. Everyone's pushed off at last. Come on, let's go.'

They assembled in the car park and Kate reluctantly agreed to stay on for an hour or two while Stella, unaccountably eager, threw herself in the passenger seat and gazed around like a gobsmacked tourist as they followed Tory's old banger along the coast.

They had to park on a back lane and walk the last hundred yards along the beach, Stella teetering along behind in her suicidal heels.

Tory's house was a two-storeyed wooden construction built on a bluff overlooking dunes knitted together with marram grass. The tide was way out and the beach empty, wavelets lapping rock pools at the water's edge. Tory unlocked the door and led them straight upstairs, the living quarters commanding a panoramic view of the sea through high, uncurtained windows. The place was a shambles: books piled on every surface and waterproofs, presumably Stefan's, strewn in the corner.

Stella threw her ruined stilettos against the wall and collapsed on to a sofa, closing her eyes in utter surrender. Kate and Tory bustled about in the kitchen, shoving Moses on to a wide verandah where he could be heard noisily retching up the titbits scooped from the pub floor. Kate attempted to clear a space on the draining board to finish washing up dirty cups in the sink, while Tory made a pot of tea.

They rejoined Stella and Tory surveyed the two survivors from the wake with undisguised amusement. 'You should just see yourselves. Like people caught off-piste in an avalanche.'

Stella sipped her tea, letting her gaze wander around the room. 'All very well for you, ducky,' she muttered. 'Kate and I rose at dawn to come all this way and this is the first chance we've had to exchange more than formal condolences.'

'It wasn't as if we knew Stefan,' Kate softly put in. 'A pity. He seems to have been a lovely man. What happened?'

Stella lit up, relaxing against the cushions like an exhausted swimmer. No doubt about it, Tory had weathered a thin sort of marriage very well, hardly a wrinkle and no make-up at all. It could not have been easy though, strangely enough, Tory's life with the none-too-affluent Doctor Blum had probably been far less stressful than Kate's lot wed to a movie star.

'Stefan had heart trouble and had to retire early. Poor man was utterly floored by retirement – wandered around like a lost soul. We lived in Colchester then, a horrible town. One weekend he met up with Austen Rivers on some birdwatching jaunt and Austen persuaded him to forget about doctoring – Stefan was considering locum jobs at the time – and move here. Saved his sanity, if not his life. Stefan loved the wide skies of the east coast. One evening last week he came back after some birding expedition, made himself a cup of tea, and died. Just like that. I was on the beach with Moses, collecting shells, and when I walked in there he was, sitting in his chair, looking vaguely pleased with himself. It took me a moment or two to realize he was dead.'

Kate gasped.

Tory continued, her voice even. 'Perhaps it was all for the best. Even Moses and the birdwatching couldn't make up for what he'd lost. Not that Stefan was the world's most amazing practitioner, but he felt needed and perhaps that was it. Not feeling needed any more.'

Kate silently wept into a bunch of tissues, but Stella was transfixed by Tory's calm gaze through the window, out on to the darkening sea.

'I sat in here with him, holding his hand, and trying to make some sense of it all. I must have been in a sort of dream because by the time I came to my senses it was almost dark. I loved that man, and since we moved here we rubbed along like a pair of kids at the seaside. But it wasn't real, was it? And there was so much I meant to say, to tell him that he was the most wonderful man in the world. Not the most successful, not the handsomest, just the nicest companion one could wish for. Then I phoned Austen and he arranged everything for me – even the do at the Ringers this afternoon. I made up my mind not to be sad. Stefan would have seen the funny side of it, especially having a proper funeral with a vicar and hymns and all.' She laughed. 'Given a say in the matter, Stefan would have said, "Oh, just bung me in a hole on the beach, darling." But that wouldn't have been allowed, would it?'

Stella remained still but Kate rallied and went over to Tory to take her in her arms. 'Tory, I'm so sad for you. But I really must go. Shall we come up again when you've had a chance to settle?'

Stella jumped up. 'I'm staying. Is that all right, Tory? Have you got a spare bed? I can catch the train in the morning.'

Tory's mouth dropped, clearly astonished. 'Y–yes, of course. I'd love it. Must you go, Kate?'

''Fraid so.' She gathered her things and stood uncertainly by the door. 'Don't come out – I can find the car myself. I've got a torch in my pocket. Stella will explain my problem at home, the reason I'm bolting like this.'

They hugged all round and when Kate had vanished into the evening mist, Tory lit a fire with driftwood heaped in the hearth and reclaimed Moses from the verandah. The dog collapsed like a log into his basket and later, when Stella had changed into a pair of Tory's paint-spattered jeans and a

Guernsey sweater, they settled round the fire to pick up the threads of their tattered friendship. Stella dismissed Kate's troubles with frank disapproval, explaining the details of the divorce wrangle. 'I shall have to take the matter in hand. I think the best solution is that I kill Charlie Hilton myself.'

Six

Tory laughed, pushing Stella's homicidal threat into that ragbag of overblown eyewash Stella had always thrown over any impossible situation. It was just her way of solving a problem, wasn't it?

But what had originally occurred to Stella as a jokey short cut to help Kate slowly grew in her mind like magic mushrooms. She would have to think about it a bit more – something to ponder in the small hours, those white nights which had plagued her ever since Anthony had been killed. But the death of a spouse had been no solution for her or for Tory, had it? Merely exchanged one lifestyle for another. But consigning Charlie Hilton to a permanent la-la land in the sky would be a godsend for Kate.

Tory tossed a duvet on a couch in Stefan's study and unearthed a musty-smelling pillow from a cupboard choked with creased sheets and unused tablecloths. Stella threw Tory a playful grin as they made up the bed. 'You never made it to Tidy Monitor, did you, sweetie?' she said, glancing at Stefan's overflowing desk.

Tory surveyed the room with surprise, seeming only now to register the shambles. 'Yes, well . . . Luckily, Stefan was a disorganized bugger too, so we were like two bugs in a rug.'

'Look, darling, I know it's been a shock and you've not had a moment to consider your future, but have you any thoughts about what to do with this place? You can't spend the rest of your life beachcombing.'

'As a matter of fact, I have. I've made up my mind to sell up and move back to London. There's nothing for me here and I can get a job and set myself up with the money I'd get for this plus a little nest egg Stefan put aside for a rainy day. He never seemed to spend anything and we've been living the simple life here, as you can see.'

'You're serious?'

'Absolutely. I've already spoken to Austen about it and he agrees. Actually, he's already been approached by a couple of people to ask me if I'm considering putting the house on the market. I know it's not your cup of tea, Stella, but as a second home it's perfect and one of the blokes putting out feelers is the owner of a holiday letting company that could rent it out for huge sums practically all year round.'

'Why not let it yourself? It would give you a regular income.'

'I can't afford to bring it up to scratch – it needs doing up. And, frankly, I couldn't cope with the hassle of bookings.'

'Sure. OK. But don't rush into anything without professional advice. Get a proper valuation. In the morning we'll have a bit of a clear out, shall we? Just so the poor guy can see the potential.'

To anyone but Tory, Stella's bulldozing would have been offensive, but the years seemed to have evaporated like sea mist and Tory recognized an angel in disguise – even if the angel arrived in the unlikely guise of Stella Buckleigh.

Stella spent a restless night, tossing like the incoming tide, which was all too audible through Tory's rattling window frames. The wind had risen, causing the temperature to plummet. At dawn, unable to sleep, she threw in the towel, wrapped herself in Stefan's old cashmere dressing gown – which she found bundled on the window seat under a pile of pharmaceutical flyers – and made a start on the study.

On home ground Stella never needed to turn her hand to housework, so the task in hand had the flavour of playing house. Pearly, her Filipina maid, kept the flat as neat as a pin without so much as a suggestion from the boss lady, who was, it must be said, a demanding employer. But turning out the late doctor's study was in a category all of its own. Having never known the man, after an hour's sorting she felt like an old friend. Also, having never been burdened with a conscience when it came to nosing into other people's business, tipping out the contents of Stefan's desk was certainly an eye-opener.

Not that he had any embarrassing secrets – the folder of old letters and yellowing photographs being the closest to what one could call private papers – but Stella found herself fascinated to discover the shadowy image of the late doctor Blum emerging from the chaos. From Stella's limited command of German it would seem that in the mid-fifties, Frau Blum, presumably a German lady, and baby Stefan had escaped from Hungary only just in time, leaving Papa to tidy up his business affairs. The poor man had left it too late, it would seem, and after the family arrived safely in England the letters abruptly ceased, even to Stefan's relatives in Hamburg.

But Stella was no romantic and, having replaced the folder, turned her attention to a locked drawer. No keys anywhere. But she made short work of the problem with a pair of nail scissors.

The drawer was crammed to capacity with blank prescription pads, case notes, a pair of broken spectacles, dozens of half-full pill bottles and a quantity of sealed envelopes that rattled like dried peas. She laid her booty on the desk's scuffed leather surface and slowly emptied the contents of the envelopes on to a medical journal.

Stefan Blum was a hoarder, there was no question about it. But why amass all these drugs? She recognized most, being all too familiar with the uppers and downers of the theatrical crowd in which Anthony Buckleigh had moved. But even an eclectic habit could never require such variety – there was even a lump of crack cocaine hidden in a chocolate wrapper; a bonbon on which dreams go up in smoke.

21

Seven

Tory's bedroom was still dark, with heavy curtains shutting out the morning, cutting off the sound of waves crashing on to the beach.

'Hey, Tory! Wake up.'

Stella pulled back the bedclothes and a head sleepily emerged, dark hair stranded about her neck like wet seaweed, her white body naked as a Nereid.

Tory grabbed the covers, eyes widening in alarm. 'Christ, Stella! You gave me a bloody fright standing there in the half-light in Stefan's dressing gown – I thought he'd come back to haunt me.'

'As well he might. Did you know he was hoarding enough pills in there to put half the population of this God-awful village in dreamland?'

Tory yawned and fell back against the pillows, closing her eyes. 'Oh, you mean the drugs. I thought he'd locked them safely away. Why don't you put the kettle on, love? I'm not what you'd call a morning person.'

Stella strode across the room and yanked back the curtains. Light reflecting off the sea bounced into the room like a bumptious toddler.

'I'm serious, Tory. I thought Stefan had retired. Was he still prescribing for patients or just servicing his own habit? Or yours?'

'Don't be such a bore, Stella. Go and make a nice big pot of coffee like a good girl and I'll tell you all about it.'

Stella was not used to being bossed about, and at home there was always Pearly or, in the school holidays, Fran to make breakfast. She shrugged, tightened the cord of the stained dressing gown and withdrew without another word.

When she returned with the tray, Moses lolloped in behind and stretched out on the rug. Tory had put on a pink silk kimono and was in the process of climbing back into bed. A basket chair had been dragged to the bedside and she patted the cushions before taking the tray. 'Shall I be mother?' she said with a grin. From a near comatose state Tory had, in a matter of minutes, magically become as bright-eyed as the sparkling morning. The whole house was freezing.

'Don't you have any central heating?' Stella asked crossly, cradling the mug of steaming coffee with both hands.

Tory raised an eyebrow. 'We never seemed to notice. Why? Oh, poor you. You're cold. I'll light the fire, shall I?' She made a sudden move as if to leap out of bed on the instant.

'Hey, no. Stay put. You don't escape that easily. I want an answer to this business of Stefan's drug cache.'

Tory sipped her coffee, eyeing Stella with caution.

'It's all terribly simple. No mystery. Stefan volunteered to do two evenings a week at the addiction centre in Lowestoft. He was such a lovely man, Stella, a wonderful listener, ideal for the job really, especially with his medical background. There were all sorts, all ages, but Stefan struck up a rapport with the younger element, all that Hungarian charm in spades.'

'But he was brought up here, wasn't he?'

'Oh yes. His mother married again, Blum senior having died in prison after the Soviets took over – some sort of dissident, it seems, but Stefan was told very little about his family history. But "blood will out" as they say, although Stefan took absolutely no interest in politics. But you were asking about the class A drugs. Well, he got very chummy with some of the boys at the addiction clinic and persuaded some of them to share their secrets, the names of their dealers even.'

'And Stefan informed the police?'

'Of course not! But he did search out those dealers – utterly stupid of him, but that was Stefan all over – and warned them he would turn them in if they traded with any of his lads ever again. And by degrees he chivvied the boys to exchange the illicit lot for a prescription for something less harmful – probably bribed them with his own cash if I know Stefan. He had loads of charisma and getting them to trust him was a terrific achievement. Whether it worked in the long run, who knows? They could have got their stuff from another source and just strung him along for all I know. But they will miss him; he wasn't like the other counsellors. A couple of the ex-druggies turned up at the funeral, you know, were really shaken up by Stefan suddenly snuffing it like that.'

'But why did he keep the drugs at home?'

Tory grimaced. 'Never got round to disposing of them, I suppose. They should be handed in, shouldn't they? But I'd have to explain where I got them from. Simpler to flush the lot down the loo.'

'Leave it with me.' Stella finished her coffee and rose to go. 'Let's make a bit of a start, shall we? Are you prepared to let me get rid of the junk?'

Tory looked worried. 'I hardly know where to start.'

'I'll clear the study, shall I? Have you any boxes or bin liners? I'll put the private stuff back in the desk, but there's piles of rubbish, Tory. Sorry.'

Tory pushed back the covers and crossed to the window. She stared out to sea with the intensity of a girl shipwrecked. Stella moved to stand behind her, her hand on her shoulder. The tears fell silently, but when Tory spoke the words held a frisson of anger.

'He should never have gone like that! He never even said goodbye.'

Eight

'Hi, Kate. It's Stella. I'm back.'

'Hang on while I turn off the telly.'

Stella lit a cigarette and watched the rain course down the window pane.

'Fire away. How did it go?'

'OK. But Tory's no pushover, is she, Kate? That place of hers is an estate agent's nightmare, not helped by the fact that both of them hoarded stuff for ever. Getting Tory to let me bin the trash was a struggle but I stayed until late yesterday afternoon and in twenty-four hours a surface clear out made all the difference.'

'How's she coping?'

'Determined to stay cheerful and determined to move to London so I'm hoping it'll work out. I've invited her to stay at the cottage over Easter. Why don't you join us?'

'Heavens! Easter's looming, isn't it? Actually, the shop's closed from the Thursday till the Tuesday so I've got a long weekend. The smart set wouldn't be seen dead in town over Easter, so Polly tells me, so it's not worth hanging on for last-minute sales apparently. The customers hide behind closed curtains if they haven't got a luxury holiday option to boast about.'

'Don't be cynical, darling, it doesn't suit you. Well, how about it? Could be fun. Moses is coming too.'

'Where is this cottage of yours? I'm not into mud and wellies, Stella, and what makes you think I want to share my weekend with Tory's smelly hound?'

'Keep your hair on, ducky. For someone on her uppers you're a touchy cow. My little bolt hole is only a short dash along the M40 as it happens – just outside Renham.'

'That little town near Oxford? Really? That sounds more like it. And you say Tory's coming?'

'I suggested she moved out as soon as possible. Before the place silts up with more junk, to be honest. That friend of hers, Austen what's-his-name has got a buyer on the hook already. It looks like being a quick sale.'

'What about Stefan's things?'

'All gone apart from his birdwatching stuff, binoculars and so on, which Tory has a sentimental thing about. Austen's wife called in just as I was leaving and insisted Tory joined them for supper, so she's not short of friends, and the lovely lady piled all the bin bags into her Range Rover and whisked them off to the charity shop before Tory could have second thoughts.'

'I just can't imagine you doing all this spring cleaning, Stella.'

'Well, I read in this American magazine at the hairdresser's that housework's the new sex!'

Their laughter pealed out.

'Straight up. Can you believe it? Utter bosh. After a day's hard graft clearing Tory's house I was too knackered to consider as much as a nibble. Not that there was any on offer mind you – though, now you mention it, I've got a nice stack of invites on my mantelshelf. When I've had a manicure to remove the grime I shall sally forth on the party circuit and see if this housework lark leaves my libido in any better shape. Now, what about Easter?'

'Sounds lovely, Stella. Why don't you drop by for supper when your social diary has a chink and fill me in?'

'I usually go down a day or two early with the food and stuff and make sure Jimmy's got everything ready, and then—'

'Who's Jimmy?'

'Does the garden and looks after the house. Now there's a chap who shows the benefit of physical effort, sexy as they come, not your usual odd-job man but—'

'Not Lady Chatterley's Mellors I hope?'

'What?'

'Never mind. Just my little joke.'

'Jimmy's married. Lives in a council house in the village

and has the eyes of every nosy old biddy on his every move, so don't get any ideas, Katie.'

'Me? I'm right off men full stop. What with Chaz under my feet and Charlie threatening to throw me out, I'm hardly looking to complicate my life with your odd-job man.'

'Change the locks like I said. And if Chaz threatens you, call the police.'

'He's not the violent type – just a bloody nuisance. Steals money, pinches anything not actually nailed down and invites his spaced out mates to watch porno videos in my sitting room while I'm at work.'

'We'll have to sort this out, Kate. It can't go on.'

'Look, come round soon and I'll show you enough legal correspondence to fill a skip.'

'Best place for it.' Stella crossed the room and shuffled the half-dozen invitations Pearly had propped up along the mantelshelf. 'How about Thursday night? I've got a drinks party earlier but I can join you about eight. I've got something to tell you about Stefan's secret hoard.'

'Gold bricks under the bed?'

'Worse. Class A drugs.'

Katie gasped. 'Stefan was a user?'

'No, muggins. He was a bloody doctor. But he accumulated enough to make him a very popular man on the party scene. From what I could gather, the late Doctor Blum was a liberal type who crossed the line when it came to prescribing on the side. But don't mention any of this to Tory if you speak to her on the phone. I'll tell you all about it on Thursday night. Are you free?'

'Of course but—'

'Oh bugger! I've just remembered – Frances gets back from school for the Easter break on Thursday. Do you mind if she comes too? I don't like to leave her on her own her first night home.'

'No problem. Will you have eaten?'

'Mini bites at the cocktail party but don't worry about us. Frances is going through a funny phase lately, eats nothing but cornflakes and ice cream.'

'I'll have to go, Stella, there's someone at the door. Till

Thursday then. Oh, you didn't finish telling me about Stefan's drugs haul. Did Tory know about it?'

'Oh yes. But I dare not leave the pills in her house. Tory puts on a brave face, but Stefan dying suddenly like that has hit her hard. Who knows what she might do left alone in that glorified beach hut of hers with a selection of LSD and crack?'

'You don't think Stefan killed himself, do you?'

'No way. But apart from Tory's current sadness those two had a very casual attitude to security and the kids he counselled knew he kept stuff at hand. They might get the idea that it would be worthwhile breaking in, or threatening Tory even. Believe me, the contents of Stefan's desk would be worth a mint on the street, not to mention the blank prescription pads to sell on the open market. It's as easy as winking to falsify scrips for a few hundred doses of snow.'

'Oh, Stella. What did you do with the stuff?'

'I told Tory I'd hand it in to a pharmacist bloke I know – no need to drag Stefan's name into it.'

'You brought the drugs back with you!'

'It's OK. I'll deal with it as soon as I've got time.'

'You're mad, Stella. Why take the chance?'

'There wasn't time to dispose of the stuff before I left to catch the train home. Austen's wife was on the doorstep and so I simply stuffed the lot in a carrier bag, promised Tory I'd handle it and bolted. See you Thursday. Bye.'

Stella poured herself a glass of Chardonnay and checked the messages on her answerphone.

A final demand from her accountant about tax certificates. Oh, hell.

A reminder from the dental receptionist about Wednesday's check-up. 'Mrs Buckleigh, please call to confirm.'

A curt message from her ex, Monty Neville, to say that he was collecting Frances at 8 A.M. on Saturday to take her to Scotland for Easter. Poor kid – a week in the Highlands cooped up with Monty and that new girlfriend of his, the woman who, according to Fran, not only traps rabbits to feed to her ferrets but insists on loading the tea table with shop cakes containing enough additives to turn them all into hyperactive robots.

Stella lit a cigarette and settled to listen to the last message. It was Stanley Kerslake, the MD of the board running Bucks Theatre, the jewel in the crown of poor Anthony's holdings, a burden of which Stella, as major shareholder, dearly wished to divest herself. But Bucks had been Anthony's special baby, his means of bringing quality performers on to the London stage at a fraction of their normal take. The lure was the sheer kudos of being invited to perform at this offbeat venue that could set one up as a true artist, the chance for a has-been celebrity or comedy actor to prove something. The intimacy of Bucks Theatre, allied to the loyalty of its glitzy audience, was an irresistible opportunity, and Stan Kerslake had, so far, been able to sustain its reputation.

But Stella had her doubts and privately wondered if, since Anthony's death, the glamour had worn thin. It crossed her mind that the time had come to bow out gracefully and sell her shares before success, like Anthony's ghostly presence, simply floated away.

She came to with a jolt, realizing that Stan's voice had droned out without her. She deleted the first few messages and played Stan's over again.

'Stella, darling. You haven't forgotten our date, have you? The preview party after the show on Friday. You will come, won't you? I'll pick you up about seven, shall I? It will be a great performance – Shelley's pulling out all the stops. Oh, and I've got a special treat for you, Stella. I'm bringing a glamour boy along – he's bursting to be in a Chekhov revival with us next spring. Guess who? Charlie Hilton!'

Nine

The next few days were not the most comfortable for Stella as Pearly had decided to have a thorough spring clean. To add to the misery, the managing agents had decided to repaint the common parts and the outside of the building, which involved scaffolding and the leering attentions of the builders.

Stella tried to keep well out of it but Pearly moved from room to room like a typhoon and the windows grew darker as the scaffolding rose to the top floor. It occurred to her that Stefan's drugs cache would have to be moved to a safer hiding place until she got around to contacting Angus, her tame pharmacist, who lately had made subtle overtures hinting at a closer relationship.

She hurried into the bedroom to pull the offending carrier bag from under the bed and wondered if her sudden attraction for Angus came under the merry-widow heading or, as with the screenwriter she was in the process of dumping, a murkier appeal had drawn her to the attention of rogue males. Still, it would be sensible to go along with Angus's dinner invitations for the present, at least until she had decided how to explain the existence of her bag of goodies. Angus, fiftyish and horribly stuffy, was not her type at all, but a rebuff on the romantic front might make the legal disposal of Stefan's hoard very difficult once the pharmacist was in on the problem.

There was probably a reluctance on Stella's part to admit to herself that her prevarication had darker motives: had she really decided to get rid of the stuff, or was the secrecy of the little haul bringing some longed-for excitement into her humdrum existence? After all, there was no rush to dump it, was there? If she decided to leave Angus out of the equation she could easily just flush the tabs down the loo or even have a sniff or two herself, a naughtiness which had had to be jettisoned after marrying Anthony.

She pushed the decision to the back of her mind and locked the scruffy carrier bag into a weekend case just as Pearly pushed the vacuum cleaner into the room and stood stubbornly by the bed waiting for Stella to move.

She took the hint and hurried out just as the doorbell rang. She lifted the intercom. 'Hello. Who's that?'

'Stella, it's Monty. I need to talk to you.'

'OK, but I was just going out. I can't spare more than ten minutes; Fran's due back this afternoon.'

She let him in and he followed her into the kitchen, the only part of the apartment where Pearly's upheaval was yet to penetrate.

He moved straight to the kettle and, without so much as a nod in her direction, set about making coffee.

She grinned. 'Make yourself at home, do.'

He patted her cheek and hunted out sugar, milk and the finest bone china. Monty had never been one for roughing it. They sat at the kitchen table, their mutual wariness thinly overlaid with the politeness of a man and former wife with links neither wished to remember.

Monty was, Stella decided, holding up well, his well-toned body and lively attentiveness honed by years of necessity. Monty had had a rough ride, his successful spell as a tipster brought down to hacking it round the racing circuit being agreeable to trainers.

'How are things, Monty? You haven't come to borrow money again, have you?'

'Stella! You're a hard bitch. No, as a matter of fact I'm on a payroll now – a regular income after all these years. I can even see my pension in the bag.'

'Really? You're hitched up with a rich Arab owner, I bet.'

'No such luck. No, I've joined the winning side at last. I've got a place on the board of Holland's.'

'The bookmakers?'

'Yeah. Fancy that!'

Stella whistled. 'Good for you. Seriously, I'm glad for you

Monty – you've grown up at last.' She gave him a sharp re-appraisal, approving the fine linen shirt and hand-stitched shoes. 'Has this new girlfriend of yours pushed you on to the straight and narrow at last, something I never managed to do?'

'Morag? No way. To be honest, life on the tartan trail is a bit "claggy", as they say. But it suits me just now.'

'Is Easter at her place still on? I can take Fran to the cottage with me if you're pulling out.'

'No, I'm stuck with Easter – Morag's father's a big noise with the Jockey Club, so easing out will have to be smooth.'

'Smooth?' Stella laughed. 'That shouldn't be a problem for you, Monty, "smooth" being your middle name as I remember.' She sipped her coffee. 'Well, what's up?'

'It's Fran. I'm worried about her. I had this phone call – she wants to leave school. What's going on, Stella?'

She frowned. 'Usual stuff. Exams. And a fall-out with the in-crowd at a guess. She says she's being bullied.'

'Have you tried sorting it out?'

'Monty, it's really not serious. Fran's not a baby. She's got to learn to face up to shit like everyone else. She can't change schools just like that.'

His face darkened. 'She sounded pretty frantic to me. You sure you're on the right wavelength?'

'She's a teenager, Monty. It goes with the territory. Fifteen's a lousy age and Fran's just trying to jerk your chain. What did she think we would do? Whisk her home?'

'She could live with me for a bit – go to a day school in London. She's not the academic type. We can't just ignore a cry for help, she might just decide to run away.'

'She's absconded before and it took me half an hour to smooth it over so they'd take her back. The school has trouble with some of the girls – one even slit her wrists last term – and I reckon Fran's just out of step with the freaky lot. Anyway, how could she move in with you? You're never at home. And what about Morag?'

'Morag doesn't stay at the flat. She's at her father's place when she's in town.'

Stella rose and snatched up the crocks to pile in the sink. 'Listen, Monty. Believe me, kids of her age try it on all the time. Let her get it out of her system over Easter and I'm sure it will all blow over.'

'Have you considered boy trouble?'

'Boy trouble? Frances? She's boarding with girls all term and with me in the holidays. Where would she pick up a boyfriend, I ask you?'

'Get real, Stella. Sex isn't just for grown-ups, sweetheart. Meeting boys is a piece of cake. What about when she stays with her friends in the holidays? What about that Swiss ski instructor she got moony over at Christmas?'

Stella glanced at her watch. 'I've got to go, Monty. Nice to see you, but unless you change your mind I'll expect you to pick her up at eight on Saturday as you promised.'

He pushed back his chair and squeezed her shoulder as he moved to the door, his mood held strictly in check, his wariness of a quarrel with Stella over access to his daughter glazing over his disquiet. Stella was a great girl, he conceded, but having won sole custody her goodwill was an unfortunate necessity.

Monty gave a mock salute to the scaffolder whose face appeared at the drawing-room window as they moved into the hall.

'I hope you're burglar-proof, Stella. Leaving the place empty over Easter with scaffolding offering easy access is an open invitation to the bad guys.'

'Pearly's working half days while I'm away. She's determined to scour the whole apartment, God help us. Thank heavens I won't be here.'

'You're not alone at the cottage, are you?'

Stella grinned. 'Mind your own business. As a matter of fact it's going to be a girls-only weekend. I've invited some old chums over.'

'Not gone lezzie in your mature years, I hope!' he said with relish.

She grinned. 'Get out of here, Monty, before I push you out of the window.'

He left, the whiff of aftershave sending a frisson up her spine. Chucking Monty Neville out of her life was the best thing she ever did, wasn't it? Wasn't it?

She rushed to the shops and bought a sparkly top for Frances to wear to the cocktail party and hoped the girl would be in an amenable frame of mind. Being dragged to a cosmetics company publicity bash would have enchanted Stella at that age but Fran was, she had to admit, a shy and awkward kid and being propelled through a braying mob hell-bent on grabbing any freebies on offer was probably not first choice for the start of the school holidays.

As it happened Fran was in a quiet mood and, promised that a brief appearance at the promotion was merely a duty call prior to supper with Kate, the lack of option went down surprisingly well. She even wore the sparkly top with her jeans without demur.

'You like Kate, don't you, Fran?'

'She's OK, I suppose. The only friend of yours who doesn't look at me as if I crawled out from under a stone anyway.'

'Good. That's settled then. Oh, by the way, Daddy popped in today. He seemed worried about you.'

Frances spun round. 'What did he say?'

'Only that you were keen to leave at the end of term.'

'Daddy says I can move in with him.'

'You would like that?'

She turned away with a weary shrug as if the weight of the world was on her shoulders. Stella squeezed her hand and opened the lift door which precipitated them to the lobby. Dust sheets were already being laid up the main stairs and a painter moved aside as they passed, nodding briefly to the two smart birds clearly off out on the town.

'We'll talk about school after Easter, shall we, darling?'

'He's still taking me to Scotland on Saturday, isn't he?'

'Of course. Eight sharp. I'll set the alarm, though with these bloody builders peering in the windows from dawn to dusk we might as well forget about any sleep-ins for the next few weeks.'

34

Ten

The taxi pulled up outside Kate's house just after eight. Stella was impressed. Charlie Hilton had set his wife up in a smart terraced house just off Chelsea Square, presumably purchased before the honeymoon had waned. It was a pity about the prenuptial agreement, but at least Kate had had the sense to stick it out and not be bulldozed into divorce on Charlie's terms.

Stella had made a few enquiries about Charlie Hilton and the more she found out about her target the greater was her conviction that the world would be better off without him – though exactly how this murder was to be achieved she had yet to decide. This nefarious plan clung to her like an incubus, the first whimsical notion now forming into a possible scenario. Poisoning would be best, she decided, and Stefan's cache had fallen into her lap with perfect timing.

Kate opened the door, her comfortable frame cosily enveloped in a flowery kaftan which, Stella decided, placed her friend in the same box as a nice comfy sofa for two. Fran bounded out, her shyness seemingly taking a back seat once Kate appeared on the scene.

'Hello, you two. Lovely to see you. How was the party?'

They trooped into the narrow hall.

'Dreadful! But we scrounged a couple of goody bags for you, and I walked off with a bottle of champagne, so it was worth it. Here, put it in the fridge.'

'Stella! How could you!'

'Why not? We weren't staying and my baby here only had Coke so it was due to us, wasn't it?'

Two rooms had been knocked through to form a decent-sized drawing room with steps down to the garden, the former

35

parlour transformed into a formal dining room separated by double doors. A glowing sunset threw warm reflections on to rugs scattered across the parquet.

'The kitchen's in the basement. Come down, I'm making kedgeree in case you're peckish. OK?'

'My favourite,' chirped Fran, who looked happy for the first time since arriving home. Stella followed them down the steep staircase to the semi-basement, a replica Victorian range lending an impression of an old-fashioned kitchen, a notion that seemed out of sync as Charlie Hilton had clearly employed a plush interior designer to do over the whole house. But the effect was charming and Kate, who until then Stella had only seen awkwardly off-base, was obviously at home here.

Fran set the table and Kate lit candles along the high over-mantel above the range. The wine did its magic and, later, just as they were about to move upstairs with their coffee, footsteps sounded in the hall above.

Kate hurried out and called from the bottom of the stairs. 'Oh, it's you, Chaz. We're just on our way up. Hang on.'

Stella and Fran followed, both curious to meet this fabled bad boy.

He had lit the table lamps but was already heading out into the garden as they came into the living room. Kate called him back. He turned, a rangy figure in jeans and a striped rugger shirt, his black hair and dark complexion giving him an exotic air. Stella struggled to remember the name of Charlie Hilton's first wife. Ah, got it! Lola Lopez. Whatever happened to her? A vague recollection of a Spanish dancer with just one star-ring role surfaced and then submerged like flotsam in a murky pool.

'Come and meet my friend Stella.'

His smile lit up what had been a sullen reluctance that Stella had found all too familiar in Fran just lately.

'And this is my daughter, Frances Neville,' she said, pushing the girl forward.

'Fran. My friends call me Fran,' she said, holding out her hand and grinning, recognizing the boy's mood, warming to a fellow clearly as socially inept as herself.

Kate bustled about with the coffee cups. 'And to what do we owe this unexpected pleasure, Chaz?'

'It's my fucking birthday tomorrow, Kate. Or had you forgotten?'

She remained unperturbed, seemingly unfazed by a thrust from her stepson. 'Of course not. You said you'd pop in after I'd finished work and we'd go out for a bite to eat, if you recall. You've had a better offer?'

He winked. 'Actually,' he said, almost wheedling, 'I've had a great idea. How about if I get a few mates round here for a barbeque? I'll sort out the food and stuff myself. Promise. What do you say?'

She smiled – pretty generously, Stella thought, in view of the spikiness of Charlie Hilton's son and heir.

'OK. But not too many, Chaz, and definitely no fireworks. You had me on my bended knees to the neighbours at Christmas. They thought your lot were going to set the entire terrace ablaze.'

He grabbed her shoulders and plumped noisy kisses on the top of her head. A real chip off the old block in Stella's mind, a gesture worthy of Charlie in the days when he really was a heart-throb to set the pulses racing. He turned to Fran.

'You'll come, won't you? You can help with the bloody grill – girls are pretty good on the cooking front, aren't they?'

'Hey, hang about. Fran's not going to skivvy for you boys.'

The girl grinned. 'Actually, I'd like that. Sounds fun.'

Stella looked anxious, her mind filling with Kate's descriptions of the boy's drug habit. But perhaps they were out of touch, a few Es regarded by kids these days as no more than disco warm-ups. Maybe she and Kate exaggerated the danger, but, even so, Fran was too young – much too young – to join Chaz's birthday bash.

'It'll be all right, Stella. I'll be here – I wouldn't leave the house to the tender mercies of Chaz and has gang.'

'Stay the night, Fran,' he said with a winning enthusiasm. 'Kate turns into a Russian toilet attendant once I bring my friends round – stations herself on a chair in the telly room with her beady eye not missing a trick.'

'May I?' Fran pleaded.

'What do you think, Katie?'

'Oh, go on. Let the poor girl off the hook for once – you said she's got to endure two weeks in Scotland straight after. Might as well enjoy some company of her own age for one evening.'

'But she's only—' 'Fifteen,' Stella was about to insist, but instead Kate broke in.

'Come on, Stella, let's adjourn while these two get acquainted and you can tell me about Tory.'

Stella reluctantly followed her back down to the kitchen where they cracked a bottle of vodka and drew a sofa up to the kitchen range where they could toast their toes and feel fifteen themselves all over again.

Stella filled in the details of her stay at the beach house and later, in comfortable harmony, dared to ask about Charlie Hilton.

'Where did you meet him, Kate?'

'Oh, on a film set. Had to be, didn't it? Ten years ago Charlie was topping the cast lists and I was enjoying my first stint as a senior continuity girl on that film *Razzle Dazzle*. Do you remember it?'

'Vaguely. Where was Lola Lopez at that time?'

'Back in Europe with some French producer she naively thought was going to make her into a second Rita Hayworth.'

'Divorced?'

'Charlie got shot of her discreetly with the help of his studio lawyers, kept Chaz but hit the bottle big time. *Razzle Dazzle* was a flop and he turned to me for convenience, I thought at the time. He had Chaz at school in England, his agent trying to hush up his boozing and a stupid predilection for dressing up.'

'Dressing up? Charlie's a transvestite?'

'Not noticeably, as they say, but an embarrassing hobby he's managed to keep under wraps for years. I stumbled upon it – and for Christ's sake promise, Stella, that this is strictly girls' talk; never, never repeat this to a soul – and when Chaz came out to LA in the school holidays, Charlie persuaded me to fill in as a sort of watchdog. I felt sorry for the boy, and Charlie has bucketfuls of charm even now. We kind of fell into a cosy relationship and when the media latched on to it, Charlie announced to everyone's – not to mention *my* – astonishment that we were getting married in Vagas the following weekend. Big story, can't think how you missed it. Mind you, I was thinner then and Charlie made me go blonde so I looked the part.'

'Wow! Get you. And me just arm candy at that point with poor old Anthony.'

'You got to the finishing line intact though, didn't you, Stella? Charlie turned out to be a real bastard once the gilt rubbed off. His career hasn't recovered since he fluffed his chances with that Hemingway role in the nineties. Once I was no longer useful as a substitute mum for Chaz, and had no glamour to offer on the red carpet circuit, my chances of staying married to Charlie were negligible.'

'Poor you. Poor, poor Katie,' Stella murmured, the vodka settling woozily on top of the champagne cocktails at the launch party followed by the chilled Sauvignon with supper.

'I must go,' she said, rising unsteadily. Kate steered her towards the stairs, Stella's vertiginous stilettos clattering across the floor tiles like the ghostly echo of Lola Lopez's castanets. Kate steadied her ascent and they stood in the drawing room watching Chaz and Fran bustling about in the floodlit garden setting up amplifiers.

'What about this birthday party, Stella?'

'You think it'll be all right? You swear you will keep an eye on her?'

'Scouts' honour, Stell. You wouldn't recognize me in Wicked Stepmother mode – a real old spoilsport. Actually, Chaz's current friends are a decent crowd. I'm hoping they might even persuade him to get a job. Let Fran stay the night, they'll treat her like a kid sister and it'll probably shake her out of her current miseries about school. She can doss down in the twin bed in my room – a real virgins' bower, believe me. I'll bring her back early on Saturday morning and you can shunt her off to Scotland with Monty in a good mood.

39

I've got to be at work by eight-thirty so it'd be no trouble.'

'Well, if you're sure. In fact, I've got a press preview show to go to tomorrow night so Fran would have been on her own.'

The girl appeared at the French windows and Chaz charged off to flag down a cab in the street. They followed him out and watched him drape his arm around Kate's shoulder as the taxi drew away. Fran gazed thoughtfully out of the back window as the darkness dimmed the touching picture of the pair of them at the kerbside.

Later, lying in her bed, her mind fizzing, Stella crossed her fingers and wondered if omitting to tell Kate that she was to meet Charlie Hilton the following night was good luck or an ominous omission.

Eleven

Choosing what to wear to the preview of *Sweet Nothings* at Anthony's Bucks Theatre was something of a problem. As the major shareholder, Stella still wielded considerable clout and was reluctant to allow Stanley Kerslake, a nice enough bloke but ambitious as hell, to sideline her just yet. Maintaining her influence since Anthony's death had been important and until she, and she alone, decided to abandon the project, keeping a tight rein was essential. And looking the part was all in the game.

In the end she settled for a low-cut chiffon number with diamond drop earrings sparkling like chandeliers; no other jewellery, her hair drawn back in a chignon and a clutch bag only large enough to hold her secret – the bloody specs she needed to read the programme. Looking elegant was easy; the difficult part was upstaging the star of the show, Shelley McArthur, without apparent effort.

It was all getting a bit much, Stella privately conceded.

These celebrities Stanley insisted on 'giving a chance' were increasingly stealing the limelight. The paparazzi were no longer interested in the widow of the impresario who founded Bucks, the woman who, it must be said, could only contribute capital, whereas Anthony Buckleigh's instinctive theatrical genius had been the force which had brought Bucks the admiration of the critics and the envy of stars wishing to extend their professionalism even at the risk of falling flat on their fannies.

Stanley rang through on the intercom dead on seven. Stella told him to wait in the lobby and, after checking the windows, took the lift to the ground floor. Her mind was still anxiously mulling over Fran's invitation to Kate's for Chaz's birthday barbeque, the kid thrilled to be included in this, her first grown-up party. There had been an inevitable toe-to-toe unfairly fuelled by Stella's disquiet, the row starting when she pushed into the bathroom just as Fran was emerging from the shower.

'I wish you'd knock, Mum!'

Stella had stared open-mouthed as Fran grabbed a towel.

'Good God, Fran! When did you get that tattoo?'

She flushed but pushed past, pulling the towel around her. Stella freaked out. 'Answer me, Frances! When did you do this and why didn't you ask?'

'Ask? Why? It's my bum. Anyway I think it's lovely. Tiffany and I went into Oxford at Christmas while we were at the cottage. We were bored. I can't see what all the fuss is about. I could have got my nipples pierced at the same time but I chickened out. Tiffany got a belly button ring fixed while we were there but they wouldn't wear it at school so she'll probably have to get it done again in the hols.'

Her tone was polite but firm, a defiance Stella was not slow to acknowledge. She softened. 'Actually, it's quite pretty – just gave me a shock, that's all.'

Fran bundled quickly into a denim miniskirt and pink angora sweater which did seem to bulk her out, it had to be admitted. 'It's a wild rose – my favourite flower,' she said. 'I showed the tattoo bloke a sketch and Tiffany says it looks amazingly cool. She got him to do her boyfriend's initials on a heart

41

with an arrow through it at half term. Naff, I thought, but it was cheaper than mine.'

'Has your house mother seen it?'

'Crikey, no! Don't look so fierce, Mum, worse things happen at sea.'

As if on cue Stanley rang the doorbell and Stella reluctantly let it pass.

'Well, make sure you're back in time in the morning, darling. Daddy's picking you up at eight.'

'Kate's dropping me off on her way to work – I'll pack tonight before I go out.'

'Right . . . well, I'd better be off,' Stella murmured, her mumsy vibes zinging like overhead power lines. She stood at the door, regarding this newly confident daughter with apprehension. 'Well, have fun, sweetie, but for heaven's sake be sensible. Even Kate has reservations about Chaz, so watch out.'

Fran shrugged and turned away, frowning into the mirror as she pushed crystal studs into her rosy ear lobes, her cheeks burning with irritation.

'And don't forget to lock the service door. With all these workmen on the premises, who knows who's lurking on the back stairs.'

'Yeah, yeah, yeah.'

Stella hurried into the lift, yet another sharp encounter with Fran the last thing she needed. But a tattoo? On reflection it did occur to her on the way down that if the girl really was determined to leave school she could, instead of the tattoo, have made a proper job of it and had her hair dyed red, white and blue, thus ensuring immediate expulsion, no question.

'Stella, sweetheart, lovely as always.' Stanley greeted her in the lobby, a damp kiss brushing her cheek. 'The car's outside. Here, take my arm, we shall have to scoot.'

He propelled her – rather too brusquely, Stella thought – into his limo, his driver politely tipping his cap as she fell into her seat, the dark windows dimming the remains of the day to a grim twilight. Stanley's aftershave almost made her cough, but before she had time to shift aside, the car moved swiftly into the fast lane and was soon zig-zagging through the traffic towards Soho.

A smattering of celebrity gawpers lined the pavement as the car drew to a halt, the excited squeals of what could only be Charlie Hilton's fans dissolving into disappointment as Stanley handed her on to the red carpet. As Stella had to admit, Stanley's new PR girl had pulled out all the stops, flashing press cameras gratifyingly bursting like firecrackers all around.

'Is Charlie Hilton bringing anyone I should know? One of his starlets?' Stella said with a grin.

'Strictly bachelor these days, apparently. We're having a little drinks party in the green room before the curtain goes up. You've met Charlie before?'

'No, never.'

'He's angling for a role – play it cool, Stella.'

'Don't I always?'

The so-called green room had been Anthony's idea, but in reality it was merely a converted office suite backing on to the stage door. Anthony Buckleigh had planned every inch of his bijou theatre, imposing his considerable experience on the architects but especially on the electricians, to his mind of paramount importance in any venture. 'Don't worry about skimpy dressing rooms,' he would insist. 'What's important is clever lighting that makes everyone a star, and nice cool air conditioning in the auditorium so nobody goes to sleep.'

The green room was already full, the air scented with an avalanche of flowering bouquets.

'Heavens, Stanley, the place is festooned like the maternity wing at the Portland.'

'Shush now, be a good girl, Stella. Remember Shelley's the star. It's her big night. She's never done live theatre before.'

'I can hardly wait,' Stella drawled. Then, brightening, 'Hey, there's Charlie! Introduce me, Stanley – I'll leave Shelley McArthur to you.'

Stella literally swooped on Charlie Hilton who lurched to attention.

'Whoops – what a crush! Sorry to barge into you, darling, but I'm Stella Buckleigh – I've been dying to meet you.'

Twelve

Fran arrived early for the party, ostensibly to help move the furniture. Kate greeted her with a hug, an instinctive gesture which broke the ice, the girl's anxiety suddenly asserting itself as it dawned on her that Chaz was the only person she would know. Nervously she pictured the prospect of dozens of streetwise girls appraising this dumpy teenager's questionable inclusion in Chaz's clique.

But before she could hide herself in the loo, Kate pulled her into the garden where Chaz and a boy introduced as Rolf were strategically placing garden flares.

He grinned. 'Hey, come on, kid – we need an extra hand.'

Kate abandoned them and returned to the basement kitchen, keeping a wary eye through the barred window over the likely destruction of her spring border. Leaving the entire thing in Chaz's hands had been a gamble which appeared to be paying off, at least for Stella's daughter who seemed to have forgotten herself under the bossy instruction of the boys, who had her taped as gaffer in their struggles with the amplifiers and electrical cables snaking between impromptu lighting points and a creditable disc jockey's deck.

Much later, when a full moon hung like a Chinese lantern in the sky and the excited shrieks and babble of Chaz's gang was in full flood, Kate found herself dozing in front of the TV, her surveillance of the celebration reduced to locking her bedroom door and keeping her fingers crossed.

In all fairness there was little she could do. Chaz seemed to be behaving in an unusually gentlemanly way towards Stella's girl, steering her between the gaggle of noisy party-goers as if she were some sort of mascot, clearly impressing on his friends the special status of the kid in the fluffy pink jumper.

Kate woke with a start and looked at her watch. Three thirty! Jeez! She shoved her way through the semi-comatose couples draped about her sitting room and, now seriously panicked, sought Chaz. The music had dimmed to a bearable tide of sleepy background fuzz.

'Where's Fran?' she snarled, grabbing his arm. The birthday boy looked worryingly spaced out, his bloodshot eyes regarding his stepmother as if she had erupted on to the scene like a pantomime demon.

'Passed out – over there in the hammock.'

Kate flew across the garden all too aware that her promise to keep an eye on Stella's baby had gone horribly awry. But at least she was not locked in an embrace with one of Chaz's doubtful guests.

Fran was out for the count, the hammock gently swinging as she shifted in her sleep.

'She hasn't been on anything, has she?' Kate hissed.

'Not a sniff – why would I waste good stuff on an amateur?'

'You swear?'

He crossed his heart. 'Scouts' honour. Honestly. The kid had a great time. She even brought me a present.'

'What present?'

He laughed. 'A sort of IOU.'

Kate dismissed this with an impatient shake of the head, and between them they gently tipped Fran on to the grass. She woke with a start.

'Come on, sweetie, beddy-byes.' Kate pushed her ahead through the house and up the stairs, dumping her on a twin bed with a sigh of relief. Trusting Chaz was a stupid thing to do but the girl had triggered a latent protectiveness in him which, on balance, seemed to have done the trick. Kate's experience of Chaz's parties left her with the hope that little Frannie had imbibed nothing stronger than a dose from Chaz's poisonous punch bowl plus a strong whiff of weed, the scent of which hung on the air like holy smoke.

Fran slumped on the bed.

'Did you have a good time, darling?'

45

She grinned. 'Super. Absolutely super. Would you mind if I crash out in my undies, Kate? I forgot to bring a nightie.' She disappeared into the bathroom.

Kate sighed with relief, flopping out on her bed and switching on the alarm clock before putting out the light, barely hearing the continuing thump-thump rhythm from the garden below.

After the curtain came down on *Sweet Nothings*, a satisfactory number of cheers and applause brought Shelley McArthur to the edge of the footlights to repeatedly bow as the audience response swelled. Stella touched Stanley Kerslake's arm as he rose to give his current star a standing ovation.

'I think you've backed a winner, Stanley. That nude scene is a sure-fire headline grabber.'

'Yeah! Great tits, eh?' he whispered in her ear. 'We might even extend the run.'

After the final curtain calls, the audience slowly dispersed, Stella pausing to speak to friends who hung back to greet her.

'Do join us backstage, won't you?' she murmured. 'A small supper party. Shelley's wonderful, isn't she?'

Charlie Hilton left his group and insinuated himself between Stella and Stanley Kerslake. He bent down, his breath hot on her cheek, her diamond earrings jiggling under the house lights. 'You're not staying here long are you, Stella? I've got champagne on ice in my hotel suite – I'm at the Savoy. We need to talk.'

'We do?' she replied archly, her eyes dancing.

'Tell Stanley you won't need the limo. Half an hour backstage and then we can slip away. OK?'

Stella raised an eyebrow and moved off, leaving Charlie Hilton to the mercy of yet another fan. But she knew and he knew that a spark had ignited which no amount of rational response could defuse.

After a decent interval, she scribbled a note on her programme and asked a waiter to pass it to Charlie.

'I'll follow half an hour after you leave. Be discreet, I don't need any press attention.'

Thirteen

It was after 2 A.M. and well after Charlie's departure before Stella slipped away from Stanley's party and hailed a taxi to take her to his hotel. Stella believed in making a guy wait, but perhaps an hour and a half's grace was chancing it. He might even have dozed off!

The lobby was almost deserted but, as she presented herself at Reception, the night clerk immediately responded to her murmured 'Mr Hilton?' with, 'Ah, Mrs Buckleigh. Mr Hilton said he was expecting you – a late delivery of urgent legal papers he said. Shall I send them up to his room?'

'Er, no. I have to speak to Mr Hilton myself. Room?'

He summoned a bellhop to escort her and Stella arrived at Charlie's suite without encountering a single snooper, the lack of tabloid interest in admittedly a falling star in the Hollywood firmament either a credit to the discretion of the hotel or a worrying indication that Charlie Hilton was no longer of any great interest in the gossip columns.

He held open the door, his black tie still jauntily in place, his dinner jacket smooth and uncreased.

'Ah, Mrs Buckleigh – good of you to come over so late.'

They moved inside, Stella mentally applauding Charlie's diversionary tactics. But presumably smooth exits and entrances, especially via hotel suites, were his speciality.

The main room was attractively lit, a sofa and a couple of armchairs placed around a marble coffee table, fresh flowers cascading from a gilded pedestal.

'Sorry I'm late, Charlie. It's difficult to escape from Stanley's little soirées. You didn't miss much; it got a bit sad and boozy towards the end.'

'No problem. As it happens, Shelley McArthur's no fan of

mine. I'm sure she wasn't too happy to see me there at all.'

'Really?'

'A little misunderstanding. Years ago. Before she hit the big time.' He smiled, displaying a lot of very white teeth before fetching champagne from the fridge. He popped the cork with the neat twist of an expert, and passed a flute to Stella. She relaxed against the brocade cushions with a mischievous grin.

'Neat touch, Charlie, but what gives? Why me? Fishing for a role at Bucks at a guess, but you don't waste time, do you? And why at this time of night? Surely lunch would have been a safer bet.'

He dropped into one of the chairs opposite her and unbuttoned his jacket, an amused expression filming an underlying tension which flicked the corner of his eye like a warning note.

'You are too modest, Stella. I should have known that such a beautiful and intelligent woman is perfectly capable of seeing through my little stratagem. But that wasn't what prompted me to suggest this little tête-à-tête.' He raised his glass. 'A toast? To instant attraction.'

'Love at first sight?' she quipped.

'Call it what you will. But as soon as I saw you, I knew we were going to be special friends.'

Stella sipped her wine, unwilling to play his game.

'OK. As we're such buddies, tell me what's really on your mind.'

He fingered his tie and adjusted his approach.

'I need a stage role. Something light but classic. Something to take me into pastures new.'

Stella mentally winced, wondering how on earth her good friend Kate had been taken in by this buffoon.

'Shakespeare?' she suggested with a lift of the eyebrow.

'Er, no. Well, not yet. How about Chekhov? A chum of mine's produced a fantastic adaptation of *The Lady With the Dog*.'

She couldn't resist it. 'You're not taking the title role?'

'Now you're being unkind, Stella. I'm serious. You do know the story, I suppose. The lady and the lover. A classic romance.'

'A period piece?'

'In modern dress.'

'But of course. Silly me. Any nude scenes, Charlie? Stanley puts a whole lot of box office trust in nude scenes.'

'No – well, perhaps. I guess it could be rigged to fit in without spoiling the effect.'

Stella snorted, excusing herself with, 'Bubbles up my nose. Sorry, Charlie. Go on, I'm intrigued.'

'Shall I send you a copy of the script?'

'Why not? Post it to my cottage. I'm spending Easter with girlfriends and it will be the perfect opportunity to catch up with my reading.'

He topped up her glass, his jitters dissolving.

Stella stirred some conversational ripples. 'As a matter of interest, what did you think of Shelley's nude scene tonight? Brilliant, I thought, especially making her nipples stick out like that when the guy moved in for the clinch. Very professional. How do you think she does that?'

His jaw dropped. 'I didn't notice.'

She laughed.

He pulled a face. 'Hey, Stella, you're kidding, aren't you?'

'Sorry. Just couldn't resist it. Anthony – my late husband – would have been tickled pink if Shelley could have pulled off a trick like that. Seriously, Charlie, I have seen it done. One of our most revered theatrical dames "put out" in her nude scene in a play I saw at the Old Vic. Bloody marvellous – except nobody dared print it and all the short-sighted old buffers in the audience missed out. Did you know Bucks was previously a strip joint? Anthony redesigned it completely and imagined it would be a useful sort of smart cabaret club, but then changed his mind. Got this bee in his bonnet about bringing quality theatre to a small stage and persuading top-rank actors to appear. Worked like a charm.'

'Fantastic scheme! They tried to copy it in New York in the nineties but couldn't pull it off. No style.'

'Anthony had a magic touch. I'm not sure about Stanley's approach. Still, I must admit, the last three productions have wowed the critics, and, between you and me, Shelley was practically on her bended knees to get this part. It doesn't pay much – you realize that?'

He grinned, giving Stella a full octane blast of his beautiful dental work. 'Money's not everything, babe.'

She lowered her eyes. 'Really? I thought you were troubled by a big divorce settlement – that's what I heard anyway.'

He tossed this aside. 'An ongoing battle. My wife's a bloody witch. Wants my London house, a ridiculous settlement plus back payment for notional professional services in handling a family problem.'

'A problem? Your son?'

His lips tightened. 'You're awfully well informed, young lady.'

'Stanley makes it his business to foresee any possible bad publicity. Is Mrs Hilton likely to make a big stink about the final pay-out? Because if you lose your reputation as a decent guy and it gets splashed all over the media, Stanley could never bet on audience support for what the papers might dub a "love rat". This son of yours. Is it hers?'

'No. She just keeps an eye on him for me.'

'How old?'

'Old enough. No junior, believe me.'

'He's disabled?'

'Hell no! Just a fucking nuisance, health-wise. But don't fret, Stella. I can handle it. She could have dragged me through the courts a year ago but she's really just a stupid cow, a girl I met when I was on the rebound from Lola. It's all in hand, I promise you, no mileage there if that's all Stanley's worried about. I've got my lawyers on to it – Kate hasn't the leverage to make a public brawl.'

Stella grimaced, half rising to her feet. 'I must go.'

He leapt up, fearful that he'd blown it. 'You mentioned lunch? I'm only in London for the next few days, but I'll be working in Paris soon.' He pulled her close, his chin rough against her cheek. Charlie Hilton moved to Plan B. 'What about it? Paris? A bit of fun, Stella? My agent has a villa just outside Fontainebleau, a quiet backwater, all very discreet. We could really get to know each other, Stella, sweetheart.'

She gently pulled away. 'Let me think about it, Charlie. Send the script to my cottage and telephone me from Paris. Who's your agent?'

He reluctantly withdrew and riffled through a desk drawer, passing her a business card.

'And your country home is?'

'Percivals, Bramley Green near Renham, Bucks. Got that? The phone number's in the book.'

He nodded.

She swiftly made for the door. 'I'll see myself out, Charlie. And, please, no word of this to anyone, especially Stanley. It's a little private conversation between us, OK? I don't want anyone to think I'm pushing Stanley to sign you up for this Chekhov thing.'

'Sounds good though, doesn't it? You must admit it has class.'

She smiled, the Mona Lisa face which came in very useful when she wanted to do 'enigmatic', and hurried to the lift, her scheme to kill off Kate's terrible spouse suddenly less fanciful. Only she, Stella Buckleigh, could pull off such an apparently motiveless plot and get away with it.

Fourteen

Stella was enjoying a lie-in; Sunday without Pearly banging about with her vacuum cleaner and no builders out on the scaffolding peering in or shouting cheerfully to each other as they painted their way up the main staircase. Bliss.

The phone rang.

'Hi, Stella! It's Tory.'

'Hello, sweetie. How's it going?'

'I've accepted an offer on the house.'

'Excellent. Your friend Austen's contact?'

'Yes. Austen's been brilliant. Saved me the hassle of an agent and having browsers shuffling through the house like tourists.'

'I hope you got a good price.'

'Austen's satisfied and, frankly, I just want to get away as soon as possible.'

'I'm going down to the cottage in the morning. Why don't you drive down on Tuesday and stay a while after Easter? Kate's coming on Thursday – we could make a real weekend of it.'

'What about Moses?'

'No problem.'

'Sure?'

'Absolutely. Listen, I'll give you directions.'

They chatted on for a while, Stella promising to fill in the gaps later.

Tory rang off and Stella lay back on the pillows, bemused by the prospect of a girly weekend, an extraordinary departure from her usual leisure pursuits.

Never one for 'best friends', the appeal of this strange reunion was a puzzle. Why bother? But then, why not? On reappraising motives, Stella had to admit that reviving the alliance was partly curiosity, but mostly intrigue. The situation was deliciously dangerous, the temptation to stir up some excitement arguably the innate reaction to a comfortable, predictable life clouded with ennui. She relished the frisson of a scenario coloured by secrecy, the sheer unpleasantness of using her dearest friends as a means of putting some fireworks into her own boring existence never crossing her mind.

She spent the day making lists and tidying her closet. It was that time of year, the spring sunshine warm enough for her to take her breakfast tray on to the roof terrace where the sound of church bells filled the air with joyful promise of life everlasting. Not that Stella clung to a desire for long years or a heavenly afterlife. Quite definitely not. In fact, the prospect of growing old terrified her. Even Frances was no encouragement to look ahead. A child was one thing; a grown-up daughter bossing her about was a prospect to make one shudder.

The roof garden was entirely private, accessed via a narrow staircase set between the two bedrooms on the upper floor of the penthouse. It was paved with terracotta tiles and a small fountain splashed into a shallow basin creating sweet music. Stella left the water on all year, the mild temperatures of a London winter meaning no threat of frozen pipework. Pearly looked after the potted plants, disposing of the summer geraniums at the end of the year and prodding Stella into buying spring bulbs. The view over the chimney pots reminded her of Paris, and even the traffic was muted as if in respect for Sunday morning prayers.

She dragged the plastic cover off the garden seat and relaxed in the stillness of the terrace, which was sheltered from any breezes from the east by a trellis looped about with a defiantly early-flowering honeysuckle. A low wall overlooked the street and the square below, the dizzying drop masked by four small potted bay trees standing like soldiers on parade.

On Monday Stella loaded up her car with groceries and wine and drove down to the country in eager anticipation of the Easter break. The traffic gradually slowed down on the M40 but as she idled in the middle lane, a sudden thought made her laugh out loud. Three footloose women together was surely a recipe for mischief? Three voices tempting trouble from the gods? Three witches casting their age-old spells? What rubbish!

Stella was met at the gate by Jimmy Thompson, her odd-job man who was in the process of clearing away broken paling and the sawn-up logs from a heavy branch, which had fallen and seemingly demolished part of the back fence.

'What happened, Jimmy?'

'Half that bloody cedar crashed down last night. I warned you, Stella, when you was here at half-term. I told you it needed a proper tree surgeon to sort it out. Lucky it's not near the cottage.'

'Yes, well I'll phone someone tomorrow. No chance of getting the job done till after Easter though. No rush. I'm expecting friends to stay over the weekend; I don't want everything spoiled by the racket of workmen in the garden. Here, help me carry this shopping into the house.'

He threw down the chainsaw and followed her into the kitchen with the cardboard boxes.

'Any chance of a coffee?' he said with a grin. His tee shirt was ringed with underarm sweat, his tanned forearms muscled like a prize fighter.

Stella laughed. 'Cheeky devil! No, there isn't. You just get back outside and clear all that timber before I have second thoughts about overtime.'

He sauntered to the door, unfazed by Stella's cheerful rebuff. 'No Fran?'

'She's gone to Scotland with her father. Poor kid's stuck with some new horsy girlfriend of Monty's for a couple of weeks.'

'Fran's a country kid, Stell. Ever thought of buying her a horse? I know a bloke with a nice Welsh cob to sell. Kids her age go mad for that Pony Club circuit. Want me to ask round? You've got them stables at the back going begging. I could look after it for her.'

'Nice try, Jimmy, but no thanks. Just get back to work, sunshine; I've had enough backchat from the builders at the flat without coming down here to listen to the same old rattle from you.'

He mockingly raised his hand in a salute and clumped out, leaving a trail of moist earth across the kitchen floor.

Fifteen

According to Stella's directions, Percivals lay at the end of an unmarked lane about two miles south of the village. Tory had passed through Renham, the nearest market town, and found Bramley Green without a problem, but either 'south' was Stella's unique interpretation of the compass or she had missed the turning.

She pulled to the side of the road and almost decided to ring Stella's mobile and confess to being lost. But that would be to admit defeat, and keeping one's end up with Stella was, and always had been, wise. Moses rose up on the back seat, anticipating that the long drive from Suffolk was at an end. He licked her cheek as she pored over her scribbled notes, the long shaggy ears all but obscuring her view.

'Hey, get off, old boy. I can't see.'

A farm tractor stopped up ahead and a man climbed down to peer in at her through the side window.

'Need any help?'

He was a middle-aged rural type in filthy overalls and a tweed cap. Warm sunshine beat down and Moses pushed his head out, tongue lolling, clearly aroused by the rich aroma rising from the steaming ordure piled high in the trailer. Tory's smile broke out like an April shower from a cloudless sky.

'Would you? I'm sure I'm nearly there but,' she waved the directions like a flag of surrender, 'I must have gone wrong somewhere. I'm looking for a cottage called Percivals.'

'Mrs Buckleigh's place?'

'Yes! Oh good, you know it.'

'She rents out one of her fields for my sheep. With lambing

I've been to and fro to Percivals all spring. You ain't far off, lovey. Carry on up 'ere and turn off sharp-like after you seen a stile with a pointer to the mill. Percivals' lane runs 'longside. Can't miss it.'

'Oh great. You've been very kind. Stella told me to watch out for some sort of bridleway sign, now I come to think of it. Thanks a million. I'm just here for Easter.'

He touched his cap and gave a sly smile. 'Nice lady, Mrs Buckleigh.' Then he frowned. 'Nice little working farm Percivals used to be an' all. Wasted on weekenders if you ask me.'

He climbed back on to the tractor and moved off, leaving Tory with a suspicion that Stella, with her smart clothes and city friends, was probably not the most popular incomer to Bramley Green.

Percivals lay at the end of a single track banked by overgrown trees and ragged hedges with ditches either side. The car lurched drunkenly between furrows clearly the result of the tractor's frequent passing during the past three months. Tory took a deep breath, savouring the sweet scent of new grass and ploughed fields. It was different from the sea breezes she was used to, but the earthier, more claustrophobic atmosphere of Stella's bolt hole had a charm all of its own. Leaving the sad memories of her life with Stefan was a wrench, but Tory knew that it was the right time to break away, to make a fresh start.

The lane suddenly opened out revealing a red-brick house set in a field cleared to accommodate a rough lawn and beds of daffodils and budding tulips. Stella burst out of the door as she parked on a paved area flanking the cottage.

'Hooray! You made it.'

'No thanks to you, Stella. You should have emailed a map.'

'Email? You must be joking. I'd need Fran to do that. You weren't lost, were you?'

'One of your neighbours pointed me in the right direction.'

'Oh? Who was that?'

Tory leaned into the car to restrain Moses. 'A farmer type. Said he rented one of your fields for his sheep.'

'That'd be Frank Bossom.'

The dog leapt about at the end of a length of rope, the sheer bulk of the beast suddenly filling Stella with fearful foreboding. She backed away.

'It's OK. He's just overexcited after being cooped up all day. Have you a lock-up – a garage or something where I can put him while we unload?'

'There are stables round the back. I'll show you. Here, let me take your bags.'

Tory passed over an unzipped holdall brimming with her stuff. 'On second thoughts, I'll just give Moses a quick trot up the lane before bringing him in. Don't worry, he's very amiable. And so he should be, ugly mutt that he is.' She laughed, dragging her long dark hair into a ponytail and tightly belting a leather coat against the fading day. 'You go inside, Stell, it's starting to get cold.'

Supper warmed them through, the so-called 'cottage' bristling with mod cons: under-floor central heating, a mammoth freezer, plasma-screen TV and a stereo system piped to every room. Tory, being a very basic homemaker verging on hippy, was amused by Stella's idea of rural comfort but snuggled into the amenities like a hamster in a swansdown nest. It was terrific to get off the wheel for a while.

'Heavens, Stella, your friend Frank Bossom called this place a farmhouse.'

'So it was. Used to belong to an uncle of his, so I've heard. Anthony bought it ages ago, long before I came on the scene. He let the Bossom brothers farm the land for a few years but when I saw it I just flipped. Saw the potential straight away and got my designer friend, Priscilla, to remodel the whole set-up, make it habitable in a tasteful way. What do you think?'

'Oh, it's lovely. But why didn't you signpost the damned place and widen the lane?'

'Anthony's one stipulation: he wanted to keep it off the beaten track, a little place just for us. He hardly ever invited his friends down, though quite what Anthony's crowd made of a dead-and-alive hole like Bramley Green takes some imagination. It doesn't even have a pub. But Fran has always loved it. We spend at least a part of the school breaks here and I've got used to the quiet. Jimmy Thompson, the bloke I told you about, does the garden and keeps an eye on the place, and Bossom's up and down the lane every few days – all hours when they're lambing, though he leaves them to their own devices once the weather warms up. "Sheep don't need nothin'", as he so picturesquely puts it. Actually, I'm not so sure. I reported him to the RSPCA at Christmas – the poor bloody sheep were freezing and he's only got a ramshackle shelter for them.'

'But you don't know anything about keeping sheep.'

Stella bristled. 'I know there's nothing for the poor creatures to nibble on when the ground's covered in snow. Anyway, after the inspector came and had a look round, Jimmy told me Bossom soon came over with some feed. There was a dead animal lying in the field for days over Christmas and nobody came to drag it away. Crows were pecking at it. Horrible. Fran went frantic.'

'Well, he didn't seem to be harbouring any grudges, but I expect animal cruelty people have to guard the names of their informants – Bossom probably never knew it was you who shopped him. Anyway, he said to me, quote: "A very nice lady, Mrs Buckleigh."'

'Take no notice of what the locals say,' she said grimly. 'They're a cunning lot. Bossom's only biding his time, waiting to catch me on the hop so he can tip off his friend, the village bobby. As soon as I get the chance to cancel his lease I'll get shot of him.'

Tory bent down and stroked Moses, who lay supine in front of the flames of the fake log fire, felled by the heat and panting like a marathon also-ran.

Stella wore a long tartan skirt and black cashmere sweater, her blonde hair loose on her shoulders. She leaned across to pour fresh coffee. 'Would you like to see the news?'

Tory shook her head. 'Thanks, Stella, but I think I'll have an early night. Do you mind if I turn in soon? I'm feeling rather strange – leaving home upset me more than I thought.'

'Why don't you stay on here until the sale goes through? There's no need to hang about in Walberswick, is there? You can pop back to sign the final papers and in the meantime look around for somewhere to live. You mentioned you'd like to get a job. I shall be back in London once Fran returns from Scotland so you'll have the place to yourself. Give yourself time to relax. Think about it.'

Tory rose and stood holding Moses' collar, her slim, dark figure silhouetted in the firelight.

'I'll just trot down the lane with Moses before I settle him in the stables. I brought his dog bed, and he's not the sort to howl, even in strange surroundings.'

'OK. But you'll need a torch – it's black as Hades out there at night.'

'There's one in the car. Have you any wellies, Stella?'

'Yes, sure. Go on ahead. I'll bring them out to you.'

Stella fetched the boots from the scullery and followed outside. Tory had tied the dog to a tree while she searched under the dashboard for the torch, the interior light glowing brightly. She had decanted the contents of the glove compartment on to the passenger seat beside a large canister.

'Goodness, Tory! What's that – a bomb?'

Tory stroked the canister and straightened. 'I brought Stefan.'

'What?'

'Stefan's ashes. Poor chap. I couldn't leave him behind on his own. You don't mind, do you, Stella? I'll leave him in the car if you feel bad about it.'

Stella's response was hoarse with dismay. 'Er, no . . . of course not, sweetheart. Bring him into the warm.'

Tory's laughter pealed out, almost seeming to echo in the darkness. 'Bring him into the warm? Stella, you're absolutely priceless. Poor Stefan's been through the crematorium – I reckon he's been warm enough.' She put her arms around Stella, hugging her close. 'It's OK, I'll leave him out here.'

She untied the dog and strode off down the lane, the feeble light from her torch flickering between the trees like a firefly.

Stella stumbled back into the house, not sure whether to laugh or cry.

Sixteen

Kate arrived on Maundy Thursday with a man. Stella and Tory rushed outside to meet her, giggling as they tried to share a golf umbrella to shelter from a sudden heavy downpour. Kate emerged from an MG sports car with a rush, dragging her driver out and shouting for everyone to get out of the wet as the four bundled into the cottage. Suddenly Percivals seemed much smaller.

In the tiny hallway Kate hugged the others with gusto and, grabbing the arm of the fourth unwilling participant in this pantomime, pushed him forward. 'Stella, this is my friend and support, my regrettably unpaid solicitor, Rob Allinson.'

'Then he at least deserves lunch.' Stella shook his hand and introduced Tory, the eyes of the women focussing on the poor guy thrust into their crowded birds' nest. He was, in fact, not at all the theatre type she was familiar with, his three-piece city suit damp on the shoulders from the April shower, the tie askew, his darting glance that of a man unwillingly thrust into the spotlight. Stella was enchanted, the unexpected stranger in their midst bringing a pleasurable disharmony to their 'women only' weekend party.

'Rob came to my rescue. Chaz bunked off with my car last night without so much as a by-your-leave. Rob called in with some papers to sign as I was trying to book a cheap hire car – a fool's errand, of course, just before Easter with everyone on the move.' Kate brushed his damp jacket affectionately.

'Not really so gallant,' he put in, his smile brightening a face pale as only that of a man on the treadmill of long hours and scant leisure could be. 'I was driving down to Oxford anyway – my firm has a branch in the city and suggested I looked over it, the bait being a parking space right behind The High.'

They moved into the sitting room and Stella produced a bottle of wine.

'Rob can't stay,' Kate insisted, fearful that her prize would be eaten alive by Stella's avid glance. 'He's expected to lunch in Renham.'

'A friend of my sister's has set up a gardening school in an old manor house and I've promised to check his lease.'

'Pity. Never mind,' Stella said brightly. 'Come over this evening and I promise you a fabulous meal. Tory's a fantastic cook. Bring your gardening friend.'

He glanced at the tall girl smiling in the background and quickly looked away, drawn by her dark eyes, suddenly deciding to take up Stella's offer.

'Thank you. I'd love to.'

'Shall we say eight o'clock?'

'Perfect.' He shook hands all round, curiously formal, and hurried out, Kate at his heels.

Once his car had disappeared down the lane the three fell upon each other with whoops of delight.

'Clever old you, bagging a good-looking lawyer and a free ride.' Stella topped up their glasses and Moses was allowed into the room on licence of good behaviour.

Next morning Stella and Kate offered to do the dog walk, leaving Tory to finish some watercolours she was working on. They edged around Bossom's field, keeping a tight hold on the leash until they reached the bridleway, then headed for the mill, the ground underfoot sticky from the rain but the sky now rinsed a cloudless blue. Moses bounded ahead, intent on rabbits.

Stella linked arms with Kate and they stumbled across the uneven ground like drunks. 'Last night went well, don't you think?'

'Terrific fun,' Kate replied. The country air had brought a flush to her cheeks, the sharp bob now flying in the wind, her rounded features pretty as a porcelain doll's. 'Rob's such a nice bloke. I'm sure his boss would be dunning for a fee if he didn't fend him off for me.'

'He's no fool, Kate. Knows full well you've got a good case and, in the long run, like it or not, that swine you married will have to pay through the nose if he wants a divorce. You sure Charlie hasn't got some nymphet waiting in the wings?'

Her eyes widened. 'How would I know?'

'Hasn't Rob suggested you get yourself a private detective, shadow the bloody man?'

'I can't afford it. Anyway, Rob thinks I'll get a sympathetic hearing, especially as I've been financing his son for years – even paid for his last detox session from my own savings.'

'Silly you! Oh, bugger, Moses has caught something. Wait, I'll see if I can make him drop it.' Stella rushed off, calling him off in the sort of tone even a ragged mongrel would recognize as non-negotiable. Moses dropped a baby bunny, which scampered off into the undergrowth. Stella put the dog on the leash and rejoined Kate.

'To get back to last night. Tory put on a delicious spread, did she not? That girl has hidden talents your tame lawyer seemed unable to resist. Fancies her rotten, if you ask me.'

Kate burst into laughter. 'Stella, you see only the stuff you concoct out of your own head. Rob fancies Tory? You're mad.'

'And you're jealous.'

'Stella, why do you think he's moving to Oxford? He asked for that transfer to be near his pal, the gardening bloke. When the dust settles I bet he'll move in with Mervyn.'

'With Mervyn? The guy he brought with him last night?' Stella looked stunned.

'Yes, that Mervyn, who else?'

'You think Rob's gay?'

'Of course he is. He hinted as much on the way down. Tory guessed straight away or she wouldn't have been interested in Mervyn's proposal. Poor Stefan's not even cold; Tory wouldn't want any complications.'

'But working in a gardening school? Teaching botanical drawing? Is she serious?'

'We talked about it last night after you'd turned in. It's a decent offer and Mervyn was knocked sideways by the drawings she showed him after supper. She's been trained in computer design, you know. Having a nice young thing on the premises would be a winner for Mervyn's more mature clients. They only come for a month at a time, so there's a frequent turnover, no time to get bogged down with the no-hopers. I expect most of them are pensioners anyway, not serious students who need to make a career in horticulture. There are two big advantages: firstly, Mervyn says Tory can rent a cottage in the grounds, and secondly, he's mad enough to agree that Moses can join in the classes.'

Stella's murmured response of 'And Stefan?' was lost on Kate so she let it pass.

They wandered on past the watermill, making a detour through Bramley Green to buy some Easter eggs for Sunday morning.

'Have you heard from Fran?'

'I call her on her mobile – she seems never to be in the house. Monty says Morag's teaching her to ride.'

'Sounds great.'

'Mmm. Let's hope she doesn't want a pony of her own. I've already been propositioned in that direction by Jimmy, who's always on the make and has some plans to fill my stables with horseflesh – at a guess to amuse his own kids.'

'Doesn't look old enough to have kids.'

'Probably wooed his poor wife on her way home from school. Child bride, I bet, but frankly there's not much else to do down here if you cut out fornication and drink.'

Kate chuckled. 'What, no drugs?'

'Too pricey on an agricultural wage, silly. Did Tory really say she's serious about Mervyn's offer?'

'She's waiting till she's seen the set-up but it sounds ideal to me. Her idea of working in London isn't really practical – rents are high and Moses is not your average city pooch, is he?'

As if on cue Moses yanked sharply on the lead, alert to scuffling in the undergrowth.

Stella shouted a fearful 'Whoa!' and all but throttled the

poor beast to bring it to heel. 'No, Moses is no poodle, for sure,' she panted.

Breathless, the two of them hobbled back round Bossom's field and home to the downy comforts of Percivals.

Seventeen

On Saturday morning, Charlie Hilton's Chekhov script arrived, the parcel all dotted about with sealing wax like a top-secret dossier.

Tory brought it up to Stella's bedroom and dumped it on the bed. 'Pressie? Special delivery – must be something good. From some theatrical agency it says on the return label. I had to sign for it.'

Stella shot up, her hair a wild tangle about her ears, her eyes wide with alarm. 'Kate didn't see it, did she?'

'Kate's still in bed. I was in the lane taking Moses for a quick run before breakfast when the postman's van arrived. What's the mystery?'

'Well, if you promise to keep your mouth shut, it's a play Kate's ex wants to star in at Bucks – Anthony's theatre I told you about. His agent thinks I can swing it with Stanley, the producer. All rot, of course, but I couldn't refuse to read it.'

'You know Charlie personally?'

'Yes, but I don't want Kate to find out. Purely business, of course, but the whole thing is a sensitive issue right now. Just keep mum, Tory, and for heaven's sake don't say anything to Rob Allinson when you go to Mervyn's this afternoon.'

Tory shrugged, bemused by Stella's determination to pull strings – even at arm's length – for Charlie Hilton, a man she had made no secret of wishing to see dead and buried.

'You're a control freak, Stella, do you know that? You're playing with fire here. You can't interfere in Katie's life just to feed your own desire for a bit of drama. Are you hoping to bribe Charlie into caving in on a generous divorce settlement by holding out a chance to make it big on the London stage?'

Stella laughed, tearing at the parcel with her bare hands. 'Bribe Charlie? No chance. Blackmail sounds better; murder better still.' She put on her glasses and scanned the first few pages. There was no covering letter from the agent.

There was a ring at the front door and Tory turned to go.

'Wait! I'll be down straight away. We'll have breakfast together and let Katie have a lie-in. I think she partied too well at the restaurant last night, will undoubtedly have a real head-banger this morning.'

Tory bounced downstairs and Stella jumped out of bed to peer out of the window, surprised to see a police car parked outside. She hurried to dress, curious to see what had brought the fuzz at this ungodly hour. Tory had taken the caller into the kitchen and voices were muted. They turned as Stella came in and an attractive redhead, presumably a plain-clothes officer, abruptly stopped speaking. Tory looked extremely anxious and extended a shaking hand towards their unexpected visitor.

'This is Detective Constable Robbins. She was on her way back from a call-out and did a detour to warn us.'

Stella introduced herself. 'Warn us? Something wrong?'

The constable looked grave, her jeans and polo-necked sweater at odds with her formal manner.

'I'm afraid so, Mrs Buckleigh. We have received a serious complaint from a Mr Bossom, a local farmer. He says a strange dog has been seen at night worrying his sheep. One of the lambs has been savaged. He suspects the killer is a dog based here – I have a detailed description. You own a dog, Mrs Buckleigh?'

Tory visibly paled. 'Moses wouldn't hurt a fly!'

'There's some mistake, officer. Moses is shut up in the stables after dark.'

'Mr Bossom has not witnessed your dog worrying his sheep,

but as you are so isolated here and all the local dogs are known by sight, the chances of the strange dog described by his anonymous informant being yours cannot be ruled out. He's checked the boundary and says there is access from your garden through a broken fence.'

'That's possible. A tree crashed down a few days ago and broke a section which my man promised to repair straight after Easter. I'll see to it the gap is mended immediately. But, look, I know Bossom well; I'm sure he will accept compensation, though I strongly deny that our dog is the culprit – he's rarely out of sight. But I know how important it is to maintain fences around farmland and I wouldn't want Bossom to harbour misplaced grudges. He is, in fact, my tenant, and you will appreciate that it is imperative to keep on good terms with the neighbours – especially as my house is, as you point out, isolated and rarely occupied.'

The girl shrugged, clearly impatient to be off. 'Well, that's between you and Mr Bossom, madam, but harassing sheep – especially at this time of year – is a very serious business. If Mr Bossom catches your dog in his field he threatens to shoot it.'

Tory gasped. 'Oh no!'

Stella bit her lip. 'I'll speak with Mr Bossom directly – I'm sure we can come to some arrangement.'

'Where's the dog now?'

'In the scullery,' Tory said. 'I'll fetch him. You can see he's a lovely friendly dog.' She rushed out, leaving Stella to smile weakly at the stern-faced young detective who was much too pretty to have such a rotten job, Stella decided.

Tory brought him in, looking, DC Robbins had to admit, hardly the ferocious killer Bossom had described. Moses, sensing bad vibes, waved his tail in propitiation.

'Moses is unused to the country,' Stella explained. 'He's just here for a break; he's never seen sheep before.'

As a defence it sounded pretty feeble, but the policewoman was clearly intent on more important crimes than dead sheep, and, after a brief reiteration of the rules appertaining to animals harrying livestock, made a serious reassessment of Stella

Buckleigh in the light of the gossip in the village, and eventually drove off.

'Whew!'

Tory started to weep, flopping at the kitchen table, the picture of misery.

Stella affectionately squeezed her shoulder and gave Moses a swipe. 'Don't lose any sleep over it, Tory. Bossom's seen a chink in my armour. Bloody man knows full well it's probably a fox or, more likely, a stray from the village. Sees me as a likely target – no one else round here would stump up on the say-so of one of his pub cronies. Trouble is, once the police get a complaint they're obliged to follow up, to go through the motions at least.'

Tory looked up, eyes brimming. 'You really think so? Let me pay him, Stella. If you like, I'll go back to Suffolk and leave you in peace.'

Stella grimaced. 'Don't you dare! Honestly, it doesn't worry me for a moment. Bossom won't cause any bother – he's my tenant after all. He's just picking on a likely fool who'll compensate him for the loss of one miserable lamb. Lambs die all the time, especially with a skinflint like Bossom looking after the poor darlings. Anyway, you can't escape – you've got your appointment with Mervyn this afternoon. Do you know the way? I could drive you if you like; I've got some shopping to do in Renham. I might even call in at the cop shop while I'm there and have a word with a mate of mine, the chief inspector, our little ginger-haired constable's boss.'

'Is that necessary, Stella? Won't that just aggravate things?'

'No way. I like to keep in touch with our boys in blue – you never know when an ally on the force might come in useful. And my friend, DCI Roger Hayes, owes me a favour.'

Tory brightened. 'You bribe policemen too?'

'Not yet. Actually, Hayes is not your average copper. A fast-track detective well worth cultivating.'

'And he's beholden to you?'

'Not really. We got acquainted through Anthony's part sponsorship of a music festival in Oxford before Hayes got transferred to Renham. He studied at the Royal School of Music, would you believe! Plays the piano like a dream. Must be unique, a DCI who can breeze through a Beethoven sonata.'

Moses, bored by the lack of attention, started scratching at the kitchen door to be out. Tory leapt up and pushed him into the scullery with a marrow bone.

Stella was buttering fresh toast as Kate appeared, bleary-eyed, to join them.

'Did I hear voices? What time is it?'

'Here, take this coffee back to bed, sweetie. You look as if you need more shut-eye. It's only ten o'clock. We had a courtesy call from the cops, that's all, just to check we've not been attacked by the licentious locals, poor, unprotected women that we are. Tory and I are off with Moses shortly and later I'm taking her into Renham to buy a lovely new outfit to knock this Mervyn guy sideways. Can you get your own lunch?'

'It's my interview,' Tory explained.

Kate rose, juggling a mug of coffee and an enormous *pain au chocolat* on a tray. 'No lunch for me,' she said wanly, making her way unsteadily towards the door. 'Good luck with Mervyn, darling. And don't worry about Moses, he can spend the afternoon in bed with me.'

Moses started howling in the scullery, reinforcing Stella's determination to steer Tory and the horrible hound to accept the gardening school job without delay.

Eighteen

On Sunday morning Stella phoned Fran with Easter greetings. The girl was extraordinarily cheerful and gabbled on about Morag's house, Morag's stables and the pony Morag had handed over to her for the holiday.

She felt a stab of irritation and acidly retorted, 'Oh, that's wonderful, Fran. Fancy you taking to horses. I would have thought you were a bit old for that. Is Daddy there? Ask him to have a word, would you, darling?'

Monty came to the phone. 'Happy Easter, Stell. How goes it with your stagette weekend?'

'Don't be coarse, Monty. Actually, we're having a lovely time – as, I gather, is Fran.'

'Yeah. Surprise, surprise, she's taken a real shine to Morag. Morag wonders if Fran could stay on for a bit? I could bring her back to London before term starts if that's OK.'

'Fran wants to stay in Scotland?'

'As it happens, Morag and I are going back to her father's place; he's got this small stud farm near Lingfield and there's a foal Fran wants to see.'

'Listen to me, Monty Neville. I don't like dogs and I certainly don't want Frances to get mixed up in your bloody horsy set, so please don't encourage her to think I'm going to buy a pony. She's a teenager, for God's sake. Whims come and go like Christmas – next week she'll be wanting to go clubbing!'

'Keep your hair on, Stella. I thought you'd be glad of a break. You've done nothing but complain about the kid lately, running away from school and being moody.'

'Moody! That's not the half of it, let me tell you. She was suspended from school for a whole week last term and sent home with a nasty letter from the head.'

'What for?'

'Oh, nothing serious. Swearing at her maths teacher. They overreacted if you ask me, but I suppose they could have expelled her. I had to go on my bended knees, promised Fran's angelic behaviour in future and jabbed in a plea in respect of her impending exams just to sweeten the abject apology.'

'Well, I've always thought your own bad language wasn't exactly ladylike – she picks it up at home.'

'Hell, you're one to talk! Anyway, I took her down to the cottage for the week to cool things down and she went back to school straight after with her module, or whatever you call it, up to date after working in the Renham library for days like a real little swot. I could have done without her being at home just then, I can tell you – I had to cancel my booking at Champneys.'

'Poor you,' Monty sarcastically retorted. 'But seriously, Stella, Morag's done wonders. Fran's as happy as a cricket, though I admit it's probably more to do with the boyfriend.'

'Boyfriend? She hasn't got a boyfriend!'

'That's what you think. Some little toerag's been ringing her daily ever since she got here. Sends her text messages, the lot.'

'What's his name?'

'Morag teased it out of her. A spotty sixth-former I imagine. A boy called Chaz.'

'Chaz! Monty, that's no spotty teenager. Chaz is twenty-four years old and as dangerous as a sack of scorpions. Thank goodness she's out of range in Scotland. If you keep her for the rest of the holidays and I rush her back to school straight after, the whole thing will have blown over before half term at Whitsun.'

'You know this chap?'

'He's the son of a friend of mine – one of the girls staying with me here as a matter of fact. I don't want to fall out with Kate over this, and obviously no harm's done, just a few lovey-dovey phone calls, the sort of thing to turn her head.'

Monty laughed. 'You old witch. Let the poor kid have a bit of space. You're overreacting, Stella. Never thought you'd come across all "mother hen" or I wouldn't have mentioned it.'

Stella sighed. 'I expect you're right. I'm a bit tense just now. Keeping my two house guests amused is more difficult than I thought – not to mention Tory's dog, which has probably got a taste for attacking sheep.'

Monty tried not to laugh, picturing Stella, normally so in control, losing the reins. 'The thing is, Fran wants to ask a girl from school to join us for a few days. To show off her new riding skills I expect. A girl called Tiffany – now does this kid pass your suitability test?'

'Oh, yes, Tiffany's OK. She's her best friend.'

'Well, what do you say? I'll phone you when we get to Lingfield, shall I? I gather term starts the weekend after next, Easter being so late this year. OK by you?'

Stella paused, juggling her options. 'Sure. Incidentally, I may go to Paris for a few days straight after and possibly to the States as soon as Fran's back at school. May I give the school your mobile number in case Fran absconds again? I'm visiting friends but shall be on the move, so it would be helpful if I could promise that you will be available to deal with any emergency.'

'Fine by me. Do you want to have a word with Morag before you ring off?'

'No thanks. Anyway, I got the impression Morag was, as far as you're concerned, just a fill-in. No point in me wasting my breath being chummy with a passing fancy, is there?'

'Well, don't bank on it. Morag's the only girlfriend I've had who's been decent enough to make an effort with our daughter. I may change my spots, Stella, get married again. Never too late. Even for you, sweetheart.'

'What does that mean?' she snapped, but Monty had already rung off.

It had been arranged that the three women would join Mervyn and Rob Allinson for a farewell supper at a pub

71

in Thame that night. Stella had to admit that the weekend would have been dull without the company of Kate's lawyer and his gardening friend. The girls-only party she had envisaged had distinct limitations and, even in her newly widowed state, Tory looked forward to some augmentation of the 'coven', as they had started to call it. Not that they disagreed, but time had moved on, and the people boxed up together in a remote country cottage were no longer the ingénue school friends who had bonded so well all those years ago.

Mervyn was the perfect foil to Rob; a gregarious man, stocky and bearded, his fund of wicked jokes that set off the noisy hilarity at their table attracting the frowns of several twosomes hoping to enjoy a romantic candlelit supper *à deux*.

While coffee was being served, Stella slipped off to the cloakroom, steering a path between the crowded tables subtly lit by old-fashioned standard lamps stationed like sentries at the corners of the room. On her way back she felt a hand on her arm and spun round to encounter a familiar face. The man jumped to his feet, clutching his napkin to his chest, his head almost brushing the low beams.

'Hey – Inspector Hayes! What a nice surprise.'

'Mrs Buckleigh, I saw you with your friends and hoped to have a quiet word. But may I introduce Pippa Cooper? Pippa works for the Oxford Festival which your husband so generously supported.'

Stella shook hands and, after a few words with them both, turned to rejoin her party. Roger Hayes resolutely stood his ground. 'Would you excuse us for a moment, Pippa? Perhaps a quick drink at the bar, Mrs Buckleigh?'

Stella shrugged, hoping that her pay-off to Bossom had not breached any rules of engagement as far as police complaints went. 'Yes, of course, Inspector.' She smiled apologetically at Hayes' date, an intelligent-looking girl with eyes alert with interest. Roger Hayes must be quite a catch, Stella decided, and their mutual interest in the music festival probably oiled the wheels.

Roger steered her to the bar and ordered two brandies.

'Such attention, Roger. What's all this about? Not that bloody sheep business surely?'

His gaze wandered to Stella's low-cut cashmere sweater before quickly resuming eye contact. 'Oh, you mean Robbins' report – your dog harassing sheep?'

'*Allegedly* harassing sheep. And for the record, it's not my dog. Moses is just visiting, as I explained to the constable. And Bossom was, last time we spoke, perfectly satisfied with a financial apology.'

'Forget that. No, it's something else. A quiet warning. Three attractive ladies all alone at that cottage of yours. It's pretty remote, isn't it? Suitably alarmed, I assume?'

Stella sipped her brandy. 'Of course. Not that there's anything to steal apart from the stereo equipment and the telly. My handyman keeps an eye on things when I'm away.'

'Jimmy Thompson?'

Stella gripped the edge of the bar, startled by his response. 'Yes. You know Jimmy?'

'Strictly between ourselves Thompson has a record you ought to know about. He features on a certain register.'

'He's a flasher?'

Hayes glanced around the bar before continuing, his voice barely a whisper. 'This is strictly off the record, Mrs Buckleigh, but your isolated location gives me cause for concern.' He briefly outlined a series of enquiries involving Thompson, only one of which had ended up in court, resulting in a short custodial sentence for stalking.

Stella downed her drink impatiently. These people were all the same, she decided. Talk about give a dog a bad name . . . 'I've found Jimmy perfectly satisfactory, thank you.' She rose to go.

He stood, eyeing her with equal impatience. 'I can't go into details, Mrs Buckleigh, but he's not a man to trust too far, believe me. Just a friendly warning, take it or leave it.' He took her arm and steered her back to her table, quickly retreating before Mervyn could draw him into the group.

'Didn't know you were so matey with the police, Stella,' he quipped. 'Our chief inspector's made quite a name for himself round here. Not exactly a ladies' man, but he has that dangerous look that women find irresistible, so I hear.'

She brushed this aside, refusing to elaborate on her tête-à-tête with Hayes. The rest of the evening passed cordially, despite arrangements for Rob to pick up Kate for the return to London putting a damper on a jolly occasion.

Back at the cottage the three of them kicked off their shoes and relit the fake log fire. Moses ambled in to join them, his fur giving off a strong whiff of fox as he settled on the hearthrug.

'You're going to love working with Mervyn,' Kate said. 'You see if you don't. Coming here for Easter was fate.'

Tory curled up on the sofa looking pensive.

'Well, if it doesn't work out I can always pull out. The lodge Mervyn's letting me have is lovely. It's well away from the main house and has a spare room that I can turn into a studio.'

'What about the work? I bet ninety per cent of Mervyn's clients can't draw for toffee.'

'I'm not expecting scientific diagrams, just teaching them enough to make decent botanical notes. And there's the design work too.'

Stella giggled. 'God help you, Tory. Still, Mervyn's got a waiting list through to next spring and a regular ad in *Country Life*, so he must be doing well. A decent cook's the thing, of course. After a day's digging the poor things will have worked up an appetite.'

'Talking about tasty morsels,' Kate insisted, 'how did you get so chummy with that dishy policeman? I presume that was his wife with him tonight.'

'Divorced. The girlfriend is something to do with the music festival, apparently. Actually, he was putting down the poison about Jimmy.'

'Jimmy? Your gardener? Not a mad axe man I hope. I saw him out at the back this morning chopping away at the fence.'

Stella grimaced. 'Nothing serious. Just a word in my ear about his record.'

'He's been in prison?'

'A couple of years ago he escaped a rape charge through lack of evidence, it seems. Before I took him on, but then I'm the last to catch up with village gossip, of course. No, Roger just thought we should watch it, poor naive creatures that we are.'

'Are you going to sack him, Stella?'

'No. He's a saucy bastard but I'm rarely here alone and, frankly, I'm probably cheek by jowl with muggers and rapists all the time in London, especially since the painters moved into the building.'

Tory yawned. 'On that happy note, Moses and I will leave you,' she said, and dragged Moses off outside. Kate poured herself a nightcap and leaned across to hug Stella.

'I'll be off at ten o'clock in the morning. It's been a super weekend, Stella – a real break. You've been an angel putting up with us.' She raised her glass. 'Thank you. Thank you for everything. We won't lose touch again, will we?'

Nineteen

Stella phoned Tory from the flat before leaving for the airport.

'I'm just off to Paris for a few days. Be back Saturday. Everything all right at the cottage?'

'Absolute bliss. The weather's perfect and I've been finishing some drawings for reference for the new job. The library in Renham's pretty good, isn't it?'

'Really? Can't say I've ever been there, but Fran uses their IT equipment when she's stuck at the cottage. She spent days there finishing some school project when she had an unexpected week off last term.'

'Yes, well, I've been researching stuff for background info and it's been great being able to use their photocopier until I bring down my own stuff from home. Mervyn wants me to start as soon as I can.'

'The gardening school continues through the summer?'

'Not August, but there's a six-week break after New Year when he and Rob go skiing, so it's seasonal but still adds up to nearly twelve weeks off a year in total. Sounds good, doesn't it? And the rent on the lodge is very reasonable so, thanks to you, Stella, Moses and I seem to have fallen on our feet.'

'And Moses is being a good boy?' Stella pointedly enquired.

'Saintly. And that grumpy old farmer, Bossom, has been politeness itself since Jimmy mended the fence.'

'No leering attentions from the locals then?'

'No such luck. Oh, just one thing before you ring off. A really big favour, Stella.'

'A loan?' The jokey response sounded a little brittle, Stella's sensitivities since being married to Monty Neville having never really hardened.

'No, of course not! No, it's Stefan. I've been thinking. It is a bit mawkish hauling poor Stefan about with me; he would have laughed himself sick if he'd heard of anyone clutching a tin of ashes to her breast like I've been doing. Would you mind terribly if I scattered the bits round your garden? Under the apple trees in the orchard, say?'

Stella sighed. 'Tory, darling, are you sure? Why not bury the urn or whatever it is? Then, if you have second thoughts you can always dig him up again. Scattering's so final.'

'No, I've thought about it. Moses might dig Stefan up again if he sees me burying something – you know what he's like with his marrow bones.'

'OK, you know best. I think under the apple trees sounds perfect – we can remember him each year when the blossom looks so beautiful each spring. Why not do a watercolour of the orchard as a sort of memento?'

'Stella, I knew you'd understand. Oh, before I forget, I took a phone call for you from "a friend". Wouldn't give his name but I'm sure it was Charlie, I recognized his voice from all his old films they keep repeating on TV.'

'Charlie Hilton?'

'Yes. But don't worry, I won't mention it to Kate. Have you seen her since you got back?'

76

'No chance, but tell me quickly, did Charlie leave a message?'

'No, rang off smartish when I said you'd gone back to London.'

'When was this?'

'Tuesday night.'

'Oh, that's all right then, I've spoken to him since then.'

A flash of intuition projected Tory to ask the sixty-four-thousand dollar question. 'Stella, you're not meeting him in Paris, are you? You're not still angling to persuade him into a quicky divorce, surely? I thought you were joking, all those wild words about death being too good for the guy.'

'Tory, it's not what you think. I have Charlie Hilton in my grasp – he's gagging to do this Chekhov play at Bucks, and, one way or another, I'm going to force him into a deal: to let poor Kate go on decent terms. I was married to a mean bastard in Monty Neville and I know from experience what it's like to have the bailiffs knocking at the door. Kate deserves better and I'm going to see she gets it.'

'Stella, it's not your business. Be sensible; Charlie Hilton's no pushover – he'll turn on you like a cornered rat if you put the screws on the man. I've heard it from Kate; he can be vicious – beat her up more than once – and he has a devil of a temper. If he finds out you're setting a trap he'll turn extremely nasty, I warn you.'

'Oh, that's just wife-beating – he wouldn't dare lay a hand on me.'

'But you *are* meeting him in Paris?'

'Well, yes, but I'll be home on Saturday. Monty's bringing Fran back to London at the weekend so I can run her back to school. How long are you staying at the cottage?'

'Oh, only until Friday or Saturday. Is that all right with you? Shall I take the laundry into Renham? I found the laundry book in the kitchen.'

'No, just bundle it up and leave it on the kitchen table for Jimmy. He's got a key. He clears up after my weekends and does all the chores. Quite the little housewife, in fact; he can turn his hand to anything, even a bit of flashing if he takes a fancy to you, so watch out.'

They arranged to meet up as soon as Tory had settled the house sale and set herself up at Mervyn's. Stella rang off, anxiously gauging the time it would take to get to Heathrow. Stefan's drugs were still hidden in the suitcase under the bed and she toyed with the idea of flushing them down the loo before she left. But temptation was too great to resist – who knew when a few 'sweeteners' would come in handy? On impulse she ran into the bedroom and retrieved the case, unscrambling the fancy combination lock with her favourite code – treble three, the only combination which, with her desperate lack of numeracy, covered every eventuality. Fran considered this basic limitation in her mother's battery of accomplishments endearing, one of the few traits which they shared. Stella excused Fran's problems in the maths class as stemming from some genetic fault and not stupidity at all.

Stella sorted through Stefan's little haul and extracted a quantity of cocaine to take with her to Paris, concealing it in the false bottom of a jewellery case which had served the same purpose before her promise to Anthony that her 'uppers and downers' were a thing of the past. She wrapped the remaining cache in a ski hat and jammed up the case with winter woollies before spinning the combination lock again and thrusting the suitcase back under the bed beneath the spare duvet from the airing cupboard. Luckily, Pearly was a very incurious housekeeper and, even in manic spring-cleaning mode, was willing to admit that the vagaries of her short-tempered employer were best left undisturbed.

Charlie sent a driver to meet her at Arrivals. Stella relaxed as the limo cut through the early-evening traffic, speeding her, behind tinted windows, to her unknown destination, excited by the frisson of an assignation with, she had to admit, a man she barely knew – a man she planned to damage not just on behalf of her friend Kate, but because it was in her power to pull the strings, to control the scenario as never before.

Twenty

The 'villa' proved to be a former eighteenth-century hunting lodge, tastefully brought up to date by Charlie's agent, who probably used it for business entertaining as well as his own leisure. The reception rooms were decorated in period but the plumbing was brutally twenty-first century. Stella felt a Marie Antoinette moment coming on, though the complete dearth of staff made this hard to maintain.

Charlie greeted her formally, handing her from the Mercedes with the flourish of a French grandee. He kissed her cheek and led her into the house, leaving the driver obsequiously to place her suitcase in the hall and back out. The door closed behind him and the subtle purr of the limousine was heard to diminish into the dark.

Stella smiled, hoping that the rich ambiance of the place had not dampened his style, temporarily rubbing off the rough edges of the real Charlie Hilton. She supposed he was in a quandary as to how to play it. In his mind had Stella accepted the invitation as a normal guest? His recollection of their ambiguous relationship in the London hotel room was probably hazy. If the woman had arrived assuming it was no more than a secret discussion about the Chekhov script, he would have to magic up the staff pronto. But Charlie, being Charlie, would assume his charm had done the trick, the smile that fans had hyperventilated over for years fascinating even to a sophisticated madam like Mrs Buckleigh. A rich widow with valuable contacts? Well, why not? Why, Stella surmised, would Charlie Hilton not assume she would fall for him even now that his teeth were capped and his biceps sagging?

The bedroom chosen for her had all the trappings of a French farce, including a connecting door to the master bedroom.

Stella kept a straight face, allowing Charlie to show her round like an anxious estate agent.

'Your friend must be doing well, Charlie. Is all this tax deductible?'

'Probably, but who cares? We've got it to ourselves for as long as we like.'

'You know I can't stay after Saturday, don't you? I have to take my daughter back to school.'

'Pity. But a few days alone together will be just terrific, won't it? I gave the staff leave till Sunday – we didn't want them hanging round, did we? You did say you wanted to be discreet, didn't you, babe?'

Stella squeezed his arm. 'Sounds wonderful to me. But what about food and so on? We could starve. I warn you, Charlie I'm a lousy housekeeper.'

'Then you've picked the right guy. Everything's prepared, and an unmade bed is just too sexy, eh?'

She looked doubtful but Charlie was right – having servants peeping through the keyholes was the last thing she wanted.

'There is one snag, Stella. I've got to drive into Paris tomorrow morning for a fitting. Would you like to come? We can use my car, no need to bother with the driver. Lunch in the Rue de Rivoli?'

'Sounds perfect. How long will you be?'

'It's a Victorian outfit for my next film. It shouldn't take long – you might like to do some shopping, perhaps? The wardrobe company has a place in the ninth *arrondissement*. I said I'd be there about midday; couldn't waste time driving out to the set.'

'Where's that?'

'Way out beyond La Défense. Not a fun place at all, you know what these locations are like.'

'I'm easy. I'll give you my mobile number and we can meet at the restaurant. Nothing ritzy, a nice quiet little bistro sounds just the thing for springtime in Paris, doesn't it?' she simpered, a difficult thing for Stella, but Charlie seemed vastly encouraged, grinning like a matinee idol.

'Leave it to me, sweetheart,' he said. She busied herself in the bathroom and, when she emerged, found that her suitcase had been whisked unseen to her dressing room, presumably by Charlie. Suddenly Stella felt a quiver of fear. The emptiness of the house was unnerving. It was as if the place had eyes – ghosts who had seen such secret assignations many times before.

'I need a shower and a little rest, Charlie dear. I'll join you downstairs in half an hour, shall I?'

'I'll have the champagne on ice. Isn't this fun? It's such a treat to have an utterly relaxing few days with a lady like you, Stella. A real lady. Oh my.' He stood in the doorway looking every bit the part; his velvet dinner jacket smooth as sealskin, his eyes bright with anticipation. He closed the door without a sound and she lay on the bed gazing up at cherubs frisking in a painted roundel on the ceiling.

Charlie was as good as his word: dinner was perfection, a buffet laid on a low table before the fire – a real fire, for God's sake – a fire which only a boy scout could have rigged up so quickly. Candles burned in gilt sconces along the wall and the rose damask sofas glimmered with a flickering metallic sheen in the firelight.

Stella had changed into a long chiffon dress, a midnight-blue confection patterned with a shadowy design like skaters' trails, which twirled with her every movement. Charlie brought two glasses of champagne and they sat side by side in front of the blaze. The house had every luxurious refinement but draughts seemed to swirl about for no apparent reason, causing the fire to send out unexpected gusts of smoke, the old house clearly having hidden currents that no amount of determined modernization could overcome.

Charlie had put some mood music on somewhere, the melody wafting through the rococo plasterwork like a carefully crafted soundtrack. Stella relaxed, her anxious feelings forgotten, revived by the confirmation of her control of the situation. Charlie Hilton she could handle, no problem. And a few days in a lovely place like this would, she must agree with Charlie, be fun.

Twenty-One

The canopied bed in what could only be termed the love nest was soft as a cloud and, after the flight plus the drive to the villa, Stella slept like an angel. She awoke with a start, the room already glimmering despite the morning light being all but shut out by heavy drapes. Someone was knocking at the door. She glanced at her watch, astonished to find she had slept undisturbed right through the night, amazed that her fabled Lothario had stayed on his side of the communicating door. Stella felt a little piqued, wondering if Charlie had toyed with the idea of seduction and decided, on balance, not to bother.

She called out, 'Is that you, Charlie?' and adjusted the silk nightgown off one shoulder, content with the knowledge that the room was still in semi-darkness.

The door opened and Charlie sidled in bearing a silver tray like a room-service waiter. He wore a very short Japanese kimono, loosely belted, revealing a forest of chest hair and an expanse of tanned thigh that, even in the half-light, looked very appealing. Stella plumped up the pillows and moved across, making a space for him. He grinned and slid the breakfast tray – laid for two, Stella noted – on to the painted chest at the side of the bed.

'Good morning, gorgeous. You slept well?' he murmured, hoisting himself on to the coverlet with alacrity.

She kissed his cheek, freshly shaved and nicely buffed up with some sort of moisturizer – smooth as a baby's bottom in fact. He nuzzled her ear and, despite Stella's guarded response, his lips brushed her eyebrows, her nose and her bare shoulder. Stella found herself softening despite her plans to delay the capitulation until later – later that evening perhaps, after she had teased him a little. But Charlie Hilton was no amateur when it came to the classic love scene, and his practised routine was, to his satisfaction, paying off even with a sophisticated lady like Stella.

He slid his hands under the sheet and began kissing her in earnest, the removal of the bedclothes, her negligee and finally his kimono culminating in what Stella had to admit was the shag of the century. Whatever Charlie's failings in the acting department, his technique in the bedroom was spot on.

When the encounter – for that was how she was determined to regard it – finally petered out, the hour was well advanced and the coffee barely lukewarm. She shivered and, recovering her negligee from the tumble of bed sheets, pulled it about her in an anxious desire to regain her aplomb. Charlie pinched her cheek and slid off the bed to place the tray between them. He poured two tumblers of what appeared to be orange juice from a flask and they clinked glasses in a mute toast.

'You've topped it up with champagne, Charlie. Bad boy.'

He laughed and moved away to open the curtains. 'We deserve a little celebration, don't we?'

Stella sipped her juice, knowing all too well that Charlie had planned all this, probably deciding even the evening before that a too-urgent assault might not persuade a woman like Stella Buckleigh, whereas a dawn skirmish would certainly find his quarry in a relaxed frame of mind after an untroubled night in a setting simply made for love.

They gazed at each other, both aglow with a sense of achievement. Nevertheless, Stella acknowledged that Charlie Hilton had beaten her to it, had won the first round hands down. A sense of foreboding flickered at the edge of her mind like a ticking clock. She thrust these thoughts aside and clung to her tattered self-confidence. She was in control and Charlie was her target. All these sexual hurdles were unavoidable, but, in a strange way, her moment of weakness had reinforced her determination to make Charlie Hilton – and all the other mean bastards out there – pay their dues.

She nibbled a croissant and watched Charlie range about the room with his coffee cup, parading his naked charms in no unconsidered circuit. He was slim-hipped and of only average height, but really in very good shape for a man of his age.

'What's the plan for today, Charlie?'

'Well, if you're agreeable, shall we make an early start? It will take an hour to drive in, possibly longer depending on the traffic. I could drop you off on the Right Bank, or would you like to explore the designer discount stores? Mendes Saint Laurent is quite near where I'm going, and I don't have to tell you, darling, that you have the most beautiful body just made for stuff from the collections.'

'Leftovers, you mean,' she said with a grimace. 'No thanks. You don't have to worry about me, sweetie, I know my way about Paris practically blindfold. Anthony liked drifting around his favourite haunts and a morning gadding about on my own will be bliss. You'll ring me when you're through with the wardrobe department? You have my mobile number.'

They dawdled over a fresh pot of coffee in the kitchen and were eventually on the road, the sparkling air dispelling Stella's latent misgivings about this dubious escapade. So far he hadn't even mentioned the Chekhov project, but she was not so beguiled with the man's attentions to assume that only one of them had an ulterior motive.

They parted near the Place d'Alma and Charlie's little Renault disappeared into the traffic. Stella made a beeline for her favourite beauty salon and spent the next two hours luxuriating in a massage and a facial.

She emerged feeling utterly wonderful, and stepped out towards the Avenue Montaigne, her eye focussed on an aperitif in the Bar Théâtre, a place Anthony had had a weakness for, especially for late-night snacks after they had been to a show. It all seemed so long ago. Stella felt a stab of guilt, knowing all too well how her husband would have rated a woman hell-bent on seducing her friend's husband, for whatever reason, which in Stella's case was a nefarious desire to see him brought to his knees. Was she quite, quite mad? Or just plain wicked?

They lunched at a Moroccan bistro, clearly very much *à la mode* and peopled with models wiggling to the African music.

The scene enchanted Stella, who awarded Charlie a whole bundle of brownie points for organizing such an unexpected delight. They arrived back late and Charlie insisted on hauling a large suitcase from the car to bring inside without delay.

'A little surprise for later, my darling,' he whispered, puffing with the effort of supporting Stella on one side and the mysterious luggage on the other. They were both a little drunk.

They fell into bed like exhausted Channel swimmers and awoke hours later to the chimes of the clock above the stable block. Charlie rallied like a man on speed and left her in the shower while he prepared the 'cabaret', as he called it. Stella wondered what else Charlie had in his repertoire and hoped it did not comprise a full *tour de force* in the kitchen department, as the late lunch and too much wine had left her feeling distinctly jaded.

When she appeared from the shower she found a be-ribboned dress box on the bed. She perched on the edge and cut the bows, wondering if Charlie had gone overboard in the gift stakes, wondering if things were getting out of hand. She removed the lid. But the masses of tissue paper concealed a whole bloody outfit: a shapely pair of riding breeches, a black jacket and hard hat plus – not altogether surprisingly – an elegant little whip. Oh, la, la!

Being a good sport, Stella decided that the least she could do would be to play along with Charlie's little pantomime, and pulled on the gear. The boots were a bit tight but everything else fitted perfectly. She glanced at her reflection and tweaked her ponytail into place. The poor sod's spent a bundle on this, she guessed, but then, on second thoughts, examined the dress box more carefully.

In small gold letters, the purveyor of Charlie's fantasy was clear to see: GARNIER ET CIE, COSTUMIERS. She relaxed. Not such a big spender after all; she might have known. He had borrowed the whole outfit from the theatrical costumiers he had been with all morning. She felt better about that and bounced downstairs full of *joie de vivre*, happy to take up her role in Charlie's dream scenario just as long as she was the one with the whip.

He was waiting in the salon, the music now much louder,

a fulsome rendering of something from the thirties – Noel Coward or Ivor Novello. Oh dear. She hurried in brandishing her riding crop, teetering on the edge of a desperate desire to giggle. Her smile froze. She stared at him in total disbelief. Charlie Hilton was togged up in what one could only guess was his idea of Greta Garbo in her heyday. He wore a dazzling gold lamé gown, long gloves and a flaxen wig. His manly chest was plumped up in what must be the last word in transvestite underpinnings, the décolletage hidden under a bunch of silk poppies. The smooth cheeks had taken on a hectic glow, his ears and throat aglimmer with *diamanté* baubles too gross to contemplate.

'Oh, Charlie . . .' she said weakly.

'Isn't this fun, Stella? I knew you would love it. Let's dance.'

He took her in one swooning gesture and they circled the room in what Stella's dazed confusion imagined must be a slow foxtrot.

Twenty-Two

The last full day with Charlie went smooth as silk, with them both relaxed about the clear limits of a flexible relationship based on sex, booze and lines of Stella's cocaine.

The villa had lost its strange vibes for her along with its gradual dishevelment. The house was like a duchess who had loosened her stays, the dressing-up games that seemed to fire Charlie's libido casting a louche fog over what had been a very formal arrangement of rooms.

Stella was, in fact, beginning to enjoy herself, the sheer novelty of Charlie's weird demands throwing her calculated plans on hold. Once or twice things got a little rough, but Stella enjoyed the frisson of fear and dismissed Tory's warning that Kate's husband had been violent. Charlie Hilton was, in some ways, the sort of character she thought she knew: a narcissistic actor living in a dream world, utterly selfish, ambitious and committed to achieving his own desires at any cost. But she had to admit the guy was fun with it.

'Charlie, you haven't forgotten I'm leaving in the morning? I have to be at the airport by eleven. Would you fix it with your driver? A nine thirty pick-up at the latest?'

'Sure, sweetie. But don't let's spoil tonight, I'll drive you myself, I promise.'

True to his word, Charlie was up and chirpy by eight and already deep in phone calls in the library. Stella had packed her overnight bag and left the last of the coke in his silver stud box in the dressing room. He swiftly cut off his caller and took her in his arms, nuzzling her ear in what she now recognized as move number one in Charlie's love routine. She pulled away.

'Not now, darling, there's no time.'

His mouth took a comical downturn and he drew back. 'But, sweetheart, we haven't even had time to discuss the Chekhov, and you're all ready to fly the coop. You've hit me hard, babe; I feel as if I've been KO'd in a birdstrike. What are my chances?'

'Your chances? With what?'

His mouth hardened. 'With the Chekhov, of course. You did read it, didn't you?'

'Absolutely riveted, Charlie, couldn't put it down. But these things are not set up overnight, you know. We must play it carefully. I've got to woo Stanley, and there's the question of a leading lady. Someone on the way up, I'd say. One of those cool beauties who haven't logged up any bad publicity so far. Someone with great tits, the acting doesn't come top of the list – after all, you're the top billing, Charlie, the box office draw. But Stanley has to decide, I did tell you that.'

'And that's your last word? After all we've been to each other?'

'Charlie, dear, be patient. I've told you I'll work on it but, hell, we're only just beginning to know each other, aren't we? I tell you what. Why don't you come and stay with me for a few days so we can talk about it? And later I'll wangle a meeting with Stanley and let him think it's all his idea. But we can't present it as a fait accompli, and to give it the right angles we need to have a proper plan. My country cottage would be best – it's way off the beaten track and we can enjoy a few more nights like we've had here,' she wheedled.

They walked to the car, Charlie deep in thought. But he knew, deep down, that using Stella Buckleigh's influence to attain his only chance to star in a prestigious London production was his trump card.

He dropped her off by the airport entrance, refusing to go through to the check-in, despite his belief that his sunglasses and baseball cap rendered him invisible to any hawk-eyed pressmen who he confidently imagined were still alert to any gossip surrounding a Hollywood star such as Charlie Hilton. Stella strode off without a backward glance, trailing the bait that she knew he would be powerless to ignore. Sure enough, he phoned her that evening promising to be with her at Percivals the following weekend, the sweet talk a little fuzzy from either booze or the last of the cocaine.

She spent the next few hours restructuring her plan. There was really no need to *kill* Charlie, and she had to admit that the disposal of a dead body had been the bit she had not quite thought through. No, blackmailing the grasping devil into settling with Kate in full would be much easier. Charlie thought he was calling the shots, that he had Stella Buckleigh in the palm of his hand, the man's ego being his fatal flaw. The new plan was brilliant. But she would have to get a move on, the shared weekend at the cottage needing preparation – not least the hire of the indispensable fancy dress.

Monty arrived at the flat at teatime bringing Fran and her friend Tiffany, who said, 'Mum's picking me up at half past four outside Peter Jones. She's got some shopping to pick up, and I said Fran and I would be there if that's OK with you, Mrs Buckleigh.'

'I'll drop them off now, shall I?' Monty proposed. 'I'll treat you to a blowout, girls. How's that?'

Fran looked tanned and less stressed, her wild-rose colouring in contrast to Tiffany's freckled cheeks and ginger hair. She hugged Stella with affection and Stella winked at Monty over the girl's shoulder, glad that things were less combative between them. The break had done them good, but it was a pity that they would have so little time to be together before Fran went back to school, assuming she had buckled down to the idea that at least one more term was unavoidable.

'No need for Daddy to take us,' Fran chipped in. 'We can walk, it's only up the road.'

Stella nodded and Monty slipped Fran a tenner and stepped back. Like a flash the girls were off down the service stairs, the lift seeming to have developed a mind of its own since the builders moved in.

'A drink, Monty?'

'Great. Whisky, no ice.'

Stella poured Coke for herself and they plumped down like a pair of comfortable slippers at the fireside.

'Everything went well in Scotland then? And afterwards? At Morag's father's place in Kent, wasn't it? Or Surrey somewhere?'

'Lingfield. Near the racecourse, but close enough to London for the girls to fit in a bit of shopping midweek, so it wasn't all mucking out.'

Stella stiffened. 'They came into town on their own?'

He laughed. 'Yeah, sure. On the train. Stella, these kids are fifteen years old, they're quite capable of looking after themselves.'

'I don't doubt it. But the two together spell trouble. When Tiffany came down to the cottage for a few days at Christmas they got themselves tattooed.'

'Big deal.'

'It's not funny, Monty. They didn't stay late, did they?'

He patted her hand. 'No, of course not. Back by six and both unravished.'

89

'How would you know? Anyway, what were they after?'

'Tiffany needed some new jeans – she'd torn hers at the stables – and Fran wanted to pick up some stuff from home. But keep your hair on, Stella, your cleaner – Pearly? – was here, they said, so they couldn't have trashed anything.'

Stella, mollified, lit a cigarette, wondering if Monty was right, that she was being too protective.

'Actually, there was one thing I ought to mention. Morag found a pregnancy testing kit in their bathroom.'

'What!'

'She confronted both girls and took a fierce line but it was OK. Tiffany roared with laughter and said they were having us on – a joke, see?'

'And Fran went along with this? That bloody Tiffany's bad news, believe me. I should try to split them up, but Fran seems so short of friends at school that Tiffany is her lifeline.'

'Morag believes it. Says it's just the sort of stuff she'd pull on her dad at that age. But I thought you ought to know in case Fran complains about Morag coming the heavy.'

Stella took a drag on her cigarette and smiled weakly. 'I suppose she's right. Morag sounds nice, Monty. You're lucky.'

'Well, I might as well come clean. I've asked her to marry me.'

'Good God! I thought I'd cured you of that.'

He looked crestfallen. 'Yeah, well, congratulations would have been nice, Stell.'

'She accepted?'

'Yes. Wonders will never cease.' He gave a nervous laugh. 'I had to ask her bloody father too.'

'On your bended knees?'

'All but. He's a crusty old buffer and obviously disappointed that Morag hadn't flown higher but, anyway, the wedding's to be in October. We told Fran.'

'She's pleased?'

'Delighted. Probably thinks it's her best bet to get that horse she's hankering after.' He emptied his glass and rose, holding Stella in a bear-like hug. 'Be glad for me, Stell, I'm doing my best but it's not going to be easy.'

Twenty-Three

'Hi, Stanley, I'm home – I've been away for a few days. How's the show going?'

'Didn't you see the reviews? Terrific. Best yet. Absolute sell-out.'

'Shelley holding up well?'

'A real trooper.'

'Great. You're a genius, Stanley. But I have a little problem. Nothing serious, but the police have been on to me to boost the security at the cottage.'

'Trouble?'

'Not yet. But I'm advised to get things updated. That electrician of ours, Billy, does that sort of stuff, doesn't he? I'd rather use someone I know, someone I can trust. You remember the cottage, don't you? Anthony loved it and I've been spending more time there lately.'

'Hang on there, Stella, I'll get the file. Billy Truelove's your man, absolutely tip-top. Shall I give him a ring?'

'Just read out his number, Stanley, and I'll talk to him myself.'

Within the hour she had arranged for Truelove to join her at the cottage the next day. 'It's urgent, Billy, or I wouldn't ask you to drop everything just for me.'

Truelove was Anthony's find, a quiet man with a wide expertise that he certainly needed in the theatre business. Stella concluded her arrangements with Billy and strolled through to the kitchen where Pearly was clearing out the cabinets, the final onslaught on the spring clean. She turned to face Stella, her bland features unusually irritated by the interruption.

'Coffee, ma'am?'

Stella had given up trying to explain to Pearly that the 'madam' bit was very old-fashioned and 'Stella' would do, but Pearly only seemed to run on familiar lines and these newfangled ideas of domestic service left her confused.

'I'll get it, Pearly, don't let me stop you. I shall be going down to the country this afternoon and I'm not sure whether I'll be back until the weekend. I wanted to ask you something.'

Pearly patiently downed tools and climbed off the kitchen steps. 'Yes, ma'am?'

'While I was away, I understand Frances came back one day to collect some things.'

'That's right, ma'am. With her friend, Tiffany. Thursday it was, my day for sweeping the roof terrace.'

'Don't look worried, Pearly, I just wondered if she asked you for anything.'

The Filipina shook her head. 'No, nothing. She and her friends dropped by for a while and I made them some sandwiches and coffee.'

'Them? There were others?'

'Just Tiffany and a boy.'

Stella stiffened. 'A boy?'

'Tall young man, nice manners. I didn't get his name. Then Tiffany went off to the shops and the other two came up to the roof terrace to watch me water the plants. They stayed up there about an hour, then started playing some computer game in the study. I had to leave to catch my bus, but Frances said she would lock up. Was there a problem?'

'Oh no, I was just surprised when Mr Neville told me they'd come up to town from the country on their own.'

'I checked round next morning, ma'am, and everything was in order.'

'Of course. Fran is very careful. I'm just extra cautious while the builders are here in the building. I expect they make a lot of extra work for you.'

Pearly sighed. 'Dust gets everywhere, even with all the doors and windows closed. How much longer will they be, ma'am? The lift is often out of order, and I had to carry the trash down all those stairs on Monday.'

'Oh dear. I'll see what I can find out from the managing agents' office. It really is very inconvenient having the scaffolding blocking out the light and men peering in at every turn.'

Stella left Pearly to it, turning over in her mind the question of Fran bringing Tiffany and the mysterious boy back to the apartment. It could only have been Chaz – nothing wrong with that, surely? But it was as well Fran was back at school; it was impossible to keep tabs on a teenager all hours.

Billy Truelove drove up to the cottage in his white van bang on time on Tuesday morning. Stella greeted him with real pleasure, remembering how Anthony had enthused about the technical genius of 'young Billy', who could turn his hand to anything and was utterly reliable.

Billy was a serious cove, fortyish and very thin, a cigarette permanently clamped between his lips, his words slow and barely audible. Stella assumed he had a family somewhere but personal details never enlivened his sparse conversation, though his manner was friendly enough. The sterling quality that Stella revered was Billy's discretion, loose talk backstage being something which clearly passed him as unheeded as the smoke from his inevitable fag end.

He trooped into the cottage behind her, his eyes missing nothing. She explained her difficulty.

'I particularly wanted you to do this job, Billy, because I need confidentiality. The police have warned me to boost the security here, so CCTV outside is the first requirement as I explained on the phone. You've brought the gear?'

He nodded.

'Good. Now the other problem is thieving. I think I know who's doing it, or at least who is opening up the place to his mates, and as I'm away such a lot the cottage is a perfect target. One or two things have gone missing lately, and, as I told you, I need evidence. Hence the video cameras in this room and the bedrooms upstairs. Is that possible? Something undetectable which can play for hours if necessary?'

'Standard equipment, Mrs Buckleigh. I had a word with a friend who runs this surveillance business and he's supplied me with the latest stuff. Expensive, but you knew that, didn't you?'

Stella smiled weakly. 'I want the best, Billy, at any cost. I have my daughter to worry about; she's already mentioned she's not keen on coming down here these days. Wouldn't say why, but you know what these young girls are like once they get a bee in their bonnet.'

'I'll do a thorough recce, shall I? You show me round and then just leave it to me.'

'Will it take long?'

'I'll be finished by four or five o'clock and show you how it works. OK if I run some cables behind these books? I may have to move some stuff about to get the cameras out of sight. I brought my sandwiches, so don't you worry about me, Mrs Buckleigh. You push off and enjoy yourself.'

Stella took him round, pointing out the spots she wanted to focus on, and left him to it. As she was reversing out, Jimmy Thompson appeared in the drive. She wound down the window.

'No need for you to work inside today, Jimmy. I've got an electrician renewing the old wiring. I shall be back later – just sort out all that fallen timber, will you? Saw it up and take it away. I don't want rotten wood lying about. Mrs Blum will be back shortly and she'll be sketching in the orchard. I want all the rough grass under the apple trees neatened up – no briars, OK?'

'Get rid of all them wild roses? That's a shame – my favourite flower,' he said with a sly grin. 'You reckon Tory's coming back to stay? The lady with the dog?'

For a second Stella's brain clicked back to Charlie's obsession with the Chekhov story, *The Lady With the Dog*, which obviously meant nothing to her odd-job man. Her mind was playing tricks.

'Yes. "Mrs Blum" to you, Jimmy – don't think you can sweet-talk my friends when I'm not here.'

He laughed. 'That dog of hers'd put me off damn quick. Never liked dogs meself and that bloody Moses is a wicked beast.'

'Just get on with the outside work, Jimmy, and leave my

electrician to get on with his job. Mr Truelove's a man of few words so he won't be interested in any gossip, I warn you.'

She drove into Oxford and located the fancy dress hire shop listed in the Yellow Pages. As she emerged from the shop she all but collided with a tall guy on his way in. 'Hey, Inspector Hayes! Surprise, surprise. What brings you here?'

'Just checking up on some disappearing police uniforms. And you, Mrs Buckleigh?' he said, indicating the bulky bags she was struggling to tote back to the car.

'A party. For my daughter,' she said, nervously clutching the props which were hopefully going to spark Charlie Hilton's notion of partying.

'Let me help you.'

Stella reluctantly relinquished the bags, which he tossed into the boot. 'Can you wait a few minutes while I have a word with the owner here? I thought you might like some tea. At the Randolph?'

'Er, yes, OK, but I can't stay long. I have to see my electrician before he leaves. I took your advice, I'm getting some security cameras installed at the cottage.'

'Good for you. Hang on and I'll drive us in. We can pick up your car later.'

Stella stood at the kerb trying to decide whether all this cosy talk with a detective chief inspector was wise, but, on balance, she thought it was probably better to act natural and be gracious about it. Roger Hayes was not the usual flatfoot after all; he was an intelligent man with interesting connections in the city. Stella wondered why he had been shunted into Renham. In Anthony's time, when they had first met, the handsome DCI seemed on fast-forward to the top, but perhaps he had blotted his copy book, upset the top brass along the way, the police establishment presumably being subject to rivalry and petty jealousies like any other profession.

He came out of the hire shop after a few minutes and they drove into the city, her anxieties about this unexpected involvement deepened by his apparently innocuous questioning about, of all people, Tory Blum.

Twenty-Four

When she got back to the cottage, dark clouds had gathered and Billy Truelove had all the lights on. There was no sign of Jimmy but piles of logs were stacked at the side of the drive beside slashed rose bushes, their flowers now drooping like scraps of paper on the torn branches.

Billy had made himself a mug of tea and was all packed up ready to go. The place was as orderly as before, the furniture and bookshelves neatly in place, not a sign of any disturbance.

'Sorry I'm late, Billy. I got waylaid.'

'No sweat. I've only just finished. Cup of tea, Mrs Buckleigh? The kettle's still hot.'

'Actually, I had tea in Oxford, thanks. I don't want to delay you; the traffic builds up like crazy at this time, though, luckily, it's mostly coming out of London so you should be OK. Shall we do the rounds?'

'Let's start outside.'

They went through the back door where a CCTV camera was sited above the kitchen door.

'It's a bit obvious, isn't it, Billy?'

'Meant to be, Mrs Buckleigh. Frightens the life out of burglars to see stuff like that likely to clock them before they've even got inside. There's another at the front so you're pretty well covered.'

'Automatic?'

He nodded. 'You'll get a few unwanted nature shots, foxes and the like prowling about and setting it off, but it's the best deterrent I can recommend.'

'But I can switch it off when I don't need it? I have a friend coming to stay and her dog's in and out all the time.

When we're here the dog's more of a put-off than any alarm.'

He lit a cigarette, reluctantly agreeing with this cavalier attitude to modern technology.

'And inside?' Stella persisted.

They trooped back in, Stella shivering with anticipation.

Billy took a drag on his cigarette and got into his stride. 'Well, inside's a different kettle of fish altogether. If someone's got inside – and don't discount your regulars, the cleaning woman for instance – you need something sneaky, Mrs Buckleigh, something the bastards don't know about. Any decent video picture of thieving will back up other evidence these days.'

'Right. Now, I'm not too clever with technical stuff – my daughter's the one who's computer-savvy – so you will have to be patient with me, Billy. This surveillance stuff is top of the range, you said. Complicated I bet.'

'Not at all. My mate sorted out the best for you, but it's easy as winking.' He disclosed the hidden camera in the sitting room. 'Timer, see? Or manual or twenty-four hour. Suit yourself.'

'That seems simple enough even for me,' she quipped, her nervousness evident only by shaking fingers as she handled the equipment. 'It's on now. What does it show?'

'If we do a little try-out with me as the villain, I'll show you how to replay it through your telly. It's got a wide range and, believe me, no thicko will be searching the shelves before he nicks your other stuff. Them gold snuff boxes on the side here would catch his eye and be in his bag quick as a flash.' Billy did a swift circuit of the room, snatching bits and pieces on the way.

Then he showed her how to test the equipment and a vignette of Billy Truelove playing burglar appeared on the TV clear as a screen test.

Stella burst out laughing. 'Billy, you're wasted in this business! Get Stanley to give you a walk-on in his next production. One more thing. How do I make a copy?'

He looked surprised but explained in the simplest terms how she could do it, even if that clever daughter of hers wasn't around to effect the magic. Indeed, to Stella it did seem a little like magic, but she was quick to learn and got the hang of it after some initial bungling.

He lit another cigarette and stood aside while she led him upstairs. The cameras were all but invisible in the bedrooms. 'Could I move them about? Vary the angles?' she asked.

'Just as you like, but crafty, see. You don't want the buggers to catch on. What setting do you want?'

'While I'm here I'll stick with manual,' she replied, her confidence restored now that the simplicity of the plan was clear.

'Well, that's it, Mrs Buckleigh. You satisfied?'

'Absolutely, Billy. Your bill – do you want cash now?'

'I'll have to tot it all up and get a firm price from my supplier. He gave me a selection of stuff to try out on sale or return so it'll take me an hour or two to get a total. In the post? Here, or at your London address, Mrs Buckleigh?'

'Oh, here I think. I shall be down here quite often once my friend starts work in Renham. She's recently widowed; moving down here from Suffolk and starting a new job will be unsettling for her at first.'

He eyed her with a scrutiny she found a little off-putting but nothing more was said and after a few pleasantries Billy Truelove picked up his bag and moved to take his leave. As he was about to go he said the words which Stella guessed had been on the tip of his tongue upstairs.

'I'm glad you've got a friend moving down here, Mrs Buckleigh. If you don't mind me saying so, this was a nice weekend place when your hubby was around, but it's a lonely old spot for a lady on her own. That odd-job man was hanging about all day, thinks himself something of a smooth talker, tried to suss out what I was doin'. I wouldn't let him inside. But I've no time for tattooed louts like that, seen too many of 'em in London to be impressed by what a country bumpkin like that thinks is clever chat.'

'But tattoos? It's all the rage these days, Billy. You and I are out of touch, even my fifteen-year-old daughter has a tattoo, I'm sorry to say.'

He shook his head and climbed into the van. 'You take care of yourself, Mrs Buckleigh. Nice seeing you again. Any time you have any more little jobs you know where to find me.'

She waved him off, the lane now almost dark, the warmth and light inside the cottage as welcoming as a cosy nest. She brought in the bags from the boot of the car and dumped them inside before closing the curtains and emptying the contents on the dining-room table.

There were three outfits and a selection of what were popularly called 'fuck-me' shoes. Gambling on Charlie's size had been tricky, but the bloke in the hire shop seemed unfazed by her order: two full-length gowns, one red and one black lace, a wig, a pair of long sequinned gloves and a selection of undies in jumbo sizes fitted with appropriate fillers such as Charlie had displayed in Paris.

Her own outfit was much more frisky, standard S & M in fact, and, according to the sales man, very much in demand, especially in May Week. She hired tight black lederhosen, fishnet stockings with frilly suspenders, a Venetian mask and, best of all, a leather bustier. Never having shopped for such frivolities before, it was necessary to take the advice of the po-faced salesman who added an assortment of flashy restraints including jewelled handcuffs and a wicked-looking switch not dissimilar to the riding whip Charlie had provided for her before. As he totted up the bill he had whispered encouragingly, 'Much in demand, miss, especially this time of the year.'

The stuff was nowhere near the same class as Charlie's theatrical costumiers' professional supply, but it made one blink to think that transvestite gear was clearly popular, even in Oxford. Perhaps especially in Oxford? It was a world previously a mystery to her, but, all the same, part of life's rich tapestry, it would appear. Maybe it would have been wiser to have hired some quality stuff in London, but there was a need to play it cool and a small-time hire shop on the Cowley Road was as far as she was prepared to go. She had booked the stuff for the whole week, an unusual request, it seemed, the average partygoer reserving his fancy dress for one-night stands as a rule.

Stella poured herself a stiff gin and tonic and mentally

totted up the cost of entertaining Charlie Hilton for the weekend. Apart from the extortionate cost of the security equipment – of which only the CCTV would be of any lasting use – there were gourmet takeaways to stock up on, not to mention the supply of cocaine for the bloody man. Luckily she had kept Stefan Blum's illicit stash under the bed in London; the cost of buying in drugs for Charlie would have been the limit, and might even have put her off the whole idea, even if she knew a supplier these days, and that would have meant a dangerous shopping spree. Even her tame pharmacist would blanch at such a request from a seemingly respectable Belgravia matron. She giggled, running through a list of possible drug dealers currently in her circle of acquaintances. She drew a blank, all such excursions well into her past, before her reincarnation as a widow with a teenage daughter and credit at all the most exclusive designer boutiques.

Her best bet would be the builders working on the building, she mused – builders were always in the know, and ever ready for a quick buck. Fortunately, she had no need to tap these limited options. Stefan Blum, a man she had never met, had provided a cache of drugs worth a bloody fortune and all at no cost at all. At least that little expense could be crossed off her requirements for a rerun of Charlie's idea of a weekend frolic.

Before she slept, a niggling doubt refused to go away. Why was she doing all this? To force Charlie to come to a settlement with poor Kate? It hardly seemed a reasonable answer. For kicks? Maybe. The most likely answer was the least palatable: that her life was so boring, so lacking in excitement, that the prospect of being in control, utterly in control, was a sweet revenge on men like Monty Neville, whose blight on her life with his wretched debts and demands had scarred her for ever.

Twenty-Five

On Wednesday morning Stella got a call from Tory. 'Just checking to see if you were about,' she said.

'I'm staying at the cottage for a few days but I'm expecting a heavy date for the weekend. He's arriving Friday night.'

'Really?' Tory squeaked, her grasp of Stella's lifestyle hazy, the long gap in their friendship resulting in acres of uncharted terrain.

'Where are you, Tory?'

'At a service station on the A11. The house sale is all taken care of and Mervyn suggested I move in straight away. I managed to squeeze all my stuff into the car, decided to make a clean break. The buyer seems keen to keep or dispose of my furniture between his various holiday lets.'

'I still think you should have hung on to that beach house of yours, Tory. This bloke who's buying you out is clearly no fool, and a place like that could earn a fortune rented out to holiday visitors. It's not as if you need the capital right now.'

'No, but I didn't know I was going to get a furnished place with the new job when I agreed to sell, did I? Anyway, it's too late now. Oh hell, my battery's running low. I was hoping to drop in to see you – don't worry, I won't be a gooseberry on your weekend. Would this evening be all right? I need to sprinkle poor Stefan under the trees.'

'Yes, sure. Is Moses with you?'

'Of course. But Mervyn's arranged a booking with a local kennels until after the weekend to give me a chance to settle in. I'm dropping him off on my way through. Poor love's going to hate it.'

'Do him good, and do you good too – a chance to relax and find your feet. Come for supper, OK?'

The line went dead and Stella guessed that Tory's mobile had packed in. She replaced the receiver and decided to run into Renham to stock up on some wine.

Tory arrived in a rush that evening, presumably the first victim of the CCTV set-up at the front. Stella decided to say nothing to Tory about the surveillance equipment, as one little remark could lead to another and Tory was already suspicious of Stella's activities.

They settled in front of the fire and spent a cosy hour filling in the blanks. Stella admitted to a nagging anxiety about Fran's association with Chaz.

'He seems to have hit on the kid straight away, phoning her in Scotland, meeting her at the flat while I was in Paris. I tell you, Tory, I'm worried.'

'I met him once. He seemed a nice boy; I'm sure Kate's on his case.'

'He's twenty-four years old, Tory, no spotty teenager! And Fran's just at the age to get a crush on an older guy.'

'Well, she's back at school now, isn't she? Forget it, Stella, these little romances come and go. Fran probably needed something to brag about at school. Remember how we were? At least she's not gone moony over one of the teachers.'

Stella laughed. 'Actually, in one way she's true to form – her latest craze is horses. Classic for a teenager. Monty's been egging her on. My ex has a new fiancée whose papa is a big noise in the racehorse business, which is a huge attraction to Monty who has, at long last, got himself a regular salary with a big bookmaking firm. Morag, the girlfriend, is very popular with Fran just now, so maybe the bribe of a pony will turn her off sex.'

'Go easy, Stella. Fran may have more than a crush on the chap and if you show mumsy disapproval it'll only make her keener. Play it cool. Believe me, it's the only way.'

Later they moved out into the garden with torches lighting the way. A full moon supervised their excursion like a curious bystander, beaming down on them as they tramped through the orchard to choose a place under the blossoming apple trees.

'How about here?' Stella suggested. 'It's a nice open space. I got Jimmy to tidy up.'

The urn was remarkably full and Tory was becoming tearful. Stella thanked her lucky stars the bloody dog wasn't there to complicate things.

Tory hesitated, looking to Stella for a prompt.

'Do we say anything, Tory? A prayer? A poem or something? What would Stefan have wanted?'

Tory sniffled, and quickly unscrewed the top. 'Nothing. Stefan wouldn't want anything like that. Shall I just toss it around? We don't have to dig a hole or anything, do we?'

'Here, give it to me,' Stella said gently, taking the urn and making a slow circuit of the small glade, shaking out the dust which fell in a steady stream, immediately disappearing between the stalks of the rough grass.

Tory stood motionless in the moonlight, silently weeping, the tears flopping on to her jumper to vanish as effectively as Stefan's ashes.

Stella hid the um behind a tree, promising herself to dump it in the morning, and took Tory in her arms.

'All done now, sweetie. Let's go back inside and pour ourselves two large brandies. It's getting cold, you're shivering.'

They hurried back to the cottage and Stella persuaded Tory to stay the night. Next day Tory made a hearty breakfast, her composure restored.

Stella sighed. Being able to shut off the past like that – even a happy past with Stefan – was a wonderful way to live. She wished she could shake herself down like that, move on without regrets. But soon her reverie was brutally interrupted.

'Tell me. Who's the bloke you're expecting on Friday?'

Stella turned away to refill the kettle. 'Oh, no one you know. A man I met at a party.'

'You're lying, Stella. I know you. It's Charlie Hilton, isn't it? I warned you to steer clear of that situation, didn't I? Why put yourself in the middle of Kate's troubles? She won't thank you for it, and the chances are you're kidding yourself if you think you can make him change tactics.'

'Oh, but I can. He's a mean bastard, Tory, and on the skids as a film actor. Having a starring role on the London stage could put him right back on top. I intend to make him pay up before he runs out of cash. Kate need never know I manoeuvred him into a settlement. Believe me, keeping his macho image publicly intact is vital – Charlie will be the last person to want any scandal to hit the headlines.'

'Scandal? You mean a whisper to the film moguls that Charlie's having an affair with you? That's no scandal for a man like Charlie, a man long separated from his wife. Anyway, you wouldn't want any shit like that to be bandied about, would you?'

'Let it be, Tory. I know what I'm doing. There will be no bad publicity, Charlie won't want that and I can probably persuade my partner in the theatre to give him a short run. He's not such a terrible actor and I've seen the script. With the right sort of co-star, Stanley will fall in with it – especially as Charlie Hilton is desperate enough to do the play for peanuts.'

Tory rose to go, buttoning her lip, hugging Stella in a warm farewell before surging off down the lane in her horrible wreck of a car.

As Stella closed the door, the phone starting ringing.

'Hello?'

'Stella, it's Monty. I must see you. It's urgent. The school rang me. They weren't able to get hold of you in London. Fran's in the sanatorium.'

'What happened?'

He gave a nervous laugh. 'Serious hangover. Apparently she got into a gin binge with Tiffany. They're both pretty groggy. Fran's much worse than the other kid but the school want them out. Pronto.'

'Christ!'

'I said you were abroad. Touring. And I couldn't take responsibility. I'd better come down and tell you all about it. I thought you'd probably prefer to keep out of it for as long as possible. When the dust settles you may be able to persuade the school not to expel her. The stupid thing is she made no attempt to lie low. It almost looks like a deliberate attempt to get herself thrown out.'

'Thanks, Monty. I can't possibly collect her before Monday. Spin it out for me, will you? Come down here tomorrow and we'll concoct a plan. It's exam time. Fran's been busting to leave for weeks and it looks as if she's finally pulled it off. What time can you get away?'

'Be with you about three. I had to tell Morag what's going on but she's not too worried. Says girls at her school got drunk most weekends, and chances are the head will be open to persuasion – it's not as if she got herself pregnant, is it?'

Her heart turned to ice. In a moment of pique she decided to test out the video scam on Monty.

Twenty-Six

Stella kept Jimmy out of the cottage, sending him off to borrow the tractor from old man Bossom to cart off the sawn timber. It kept him busy all morning, giving her a chance to fill the house with flowers and test the video equipment. When Jimmy finished clearing up the logs he appeared at the back door.

'Coffee?'

'Yes, sure. I'll be with you in a couple of ticks. Just make a bonfire of those rose bushes, will you, and I'll bring it out to you. Now you're here, may I borrow your keys? Mrs Blum's moving to Renham and I need to get a spare set cut so she can come and go here when I'm away.'

His face darkened. 'Can't you use your own?'

'Actually, no, Jimmy. I'm really busy and I don't intend to hang about in Renham while the job's done,' she said tersely.

'She's moving in permanent like?'

'No, of course not. But we're old friends and I'd like to offer her use of the cottage for a break now and then. She's got a tied house with her new job, but it's a bit like living over the shop. It's nice to be able to get away sometimes.'

He swallowed this with ill grace, handing over the keys as if he were relinquishing the crown jewels. Stella wondered if Jimmy had been using her house for his own extramarital shagging, his reputation with the local talent no secret in the post office. She tensed. The awful possibility of Jimmy Thompson rolling about in her bed had never occurred to her before. Perhaps DCI Hayes had been right. Perhaps it was time she made other arrangements. Possibly a cleaning woman from the village. And another gardener wouldn't be hard to find in these depressed times. She shook her head and decided to worry about all that later; there was enough on her plate for now.

Monty arrived just after four, his stylish black Range Rover liberally spattered with mud from the lane. He was familiar with the cottage, though normally only on flying visits collecting or depositing Fran in the holidays.

Stella produced some hot snacks and a pot of coffee which he topped up with a splash from the decanter. The man was a bag of nerves, his usually smooth manner seriously undermined. Surely an overreaction to the Frances drama, Stella thought.

'Well, Monty, what's the current situation?'

He sipped his coffee, regarding her with bloodshot eyes. 'I got that harridan of a headmistress calmed down. Tiffany's parents blame Fran and I think it's probably true. Anyway, Tiffany's been whisked off back to London, but as far as the school is concerned, I said you would deal with it when you got back next week.'

'Did you see Fran?'

'Briefly. She looked shagged out but by no means remorseful. Quite cocky in fact. Admits she bought the gin intending to scoff it herself, but Tiffany found out and got in on the act. They were found in the bathroom, Fran steaming in the tub and Tiffany throwing up in the loo.'

Stella winced. 'Oh dear. What happens if they won't take her back?'

'She'll have to go to day school in London and live at home.'

'Good God, Monty, you don't know what you're asking. I'd have to employ a live-in of some sort, I'm out all hours and, like I said, I've plans for a holiday in the States.'

He shrugged. 'With us then? Morag's easy. Her father's buying us a London house as a wedding present, so there'll be plenty of room once we move in, and in the meantime we could squeeze her into my flat. Getting Fran into another school shouldn't be difficult – at worst she could go to a secretarial college, couldn't she? Or a crammer?'

Stella looked utterly dismayed by the ramifications of this total rethink regarding arrangements for their daughter.

'Actually, that's not my only problem,' he muttered, helping himself to a second tot of whisky.

'There's more?'

'Stella, I know I've been a pain in the arse over the years, but I'm on the verge of making it at last.'

'By marrying into the racing hierarchy?' she acidly retorted.

'Well, yes. I told you I'd landed a spot on the board at Holland's, didn't I? Well, it's all been going like a bloody train, no trouble at all, and me being hooked up with old McDermott's daughter made their eyes light up in the directors' dining room.'

'Bully for you.'

He paused, eyeing her from under knitted brows. The silence grew.

Stella stiffened. 'Bloody hell, Monty. You haven't got the sack, have you? Not now, with everything coming up roses.'

He swallowed hard. 'Well, not yet.'

'Don't tell me. You've been fiddling your expenses.'

'Worse. Look, I'd better come clean. Morag knows nothing about this, of course, but we're old mates, Stell. Through good times and bad . . . ?'

'Mostly bad from my recollection,' she countered.

He struggled on, the words coming in short bursts like the staccato rattle of a machine gun. 'Truth is I got in a bit of a panic when things got serious with Morag – used my betting accounts to back too many losers, even tried the casino in Monte Carlo where nobody would recognize me. Now the roof's about to fall in. Holland's have read the riot act, and I've got to clean up the mess damn quick or all hell will break loose.'

'And Morag can't help?'

'I dare not tell her, Stella. She's not like you; she's a bloody virgin when it comes to trouble and her father doesn't need a stick to beat me with. Glad to see the back of me given the chance. It would be a loan, Stella. I swear I can pay you back in six months at the latest. With interest,' he added hopefully.

She leaned back against the cushions, the overpowering scent of too many lilies decking out the cottage now making her nauseous.

'Well, what do you say, Stell? For old times' sake?'

'For old times' sake I should wring your sodding neck! How much?'

'Twenty thou. Well, twenty-two to be exact, but a round figure would do. You wouldn't want to see me banged up, would you, Stell?'

She laughed, an ugly gurgle bubbling up in her throat like bile. He waited. At last she pulled herself together.

'Monty, who do you think I am? The Queen of Diamonds?'

'You can afford it.'

'How do you know?'

'I saw your name on the Rich List.'

'Oh, did you? Well, it was right down the bloody list, and I don't have money like that hanging about like ripe fruit reading for picking.'

'But you will help me out? It's the last time, I promise. Once I get married there'll be no problem. Old man McDermott's only got one daughter and he's not wanting to see her name dragged through the mud over racing debts.'

'You do love this girl, don't you, Monty?'

He shrugged. 'It's about time I settled down, and I don't suppose you'd marry me again, would you, Stella?' This last sally was spoken without a hint of irony.

'You've got a nerve, Monty Neville. I'm still bleeding from the trauma of being married to you before.'

He grinned. 'But you got Fran out of it. That makes it worthwhile, doesn't it? Come on, Stella, be a sport. I've no one else to ask and I'm really desperate.' His hands shook as he tossed back the coffee.

She steeled herself to send him packing, but the ghastly business of Fran being forced into the equation hung between them.

'Let me see what I can do,' she parried. 'It'll take a few days. I'll ring you next week. Just keep the lid on the school fiasco, will you? I'll sort everything out after the weekend.'

'Everything? Promise?' he said, squeezing her hand.

She pushed him away, anger suddenly flaring, the sheer affront of the man striking her like a blow.

'No, I won't promise. I'll think about it. Why should I bale you out yet again, Monty? Try this trick once more and I'll spell it out to that poor cow Morag like she'd never believe. I've saved your skin a dozen times and I'm getting tired of it. When will you learn? Betting's no answer for you – you were a lousy racing tout and the poor punters who put their hard-earned cash on the nags you swore would romp home have mostly gone bust and will cheer when you go down the tubes too.'

Monty leapt up, his face white. 'You're not serious!'

'Just clear out of here, Monty. I told you, I'll think about it. Ring me next Tuesday or Wednesday when I'm back in town. I'll have to see my personal banker at the very least. You don't seriously think I can rustle up twenty grand on the nod, do you?'

He put up his hands in mute surrender and bowed out, leaving her to slump on the sofa, utterly wiped out. Was there to be no end to this?

Later that evening when she had calmed down, she made a tape recording of her trial effort at the spying game and viewed it on the plasma screen. Then she ran it back and gave it a second go. Monty Neville in full spate. Monty's lousy, grasping nature in Technicolor.

109

Twenty-Seven

Charlie Hilton arrived at the cottage after dark in a hire car he had picked up at the airport.

Stella had made a supreme effort: tight jeans and an off-the-shoulder top reminiscent of the style worn by Jane Russell in *The Outlaw*, a film well before even Charlie's palmy days but curiously back in vogue for clubbers, and hopefully the sort of kit to set the tone for a mini orgy in the backwoods.

Charlie was clearly on form, bounding from the car to swing Stella off her feet as she waited on the doorstep. Mood music pulsed in the background, the muted beat of a golden oldie from the Beatles softening what might have been a difficult reprise of the Paris weekend. Stella poured champagne and massaged Charlie's ego with a promising little aside about her opening nibble at Stanley Kerslake regarding the proposed Chekhov production.

'You've tackled him already? You wonderful girl!'

'Well, not exactly *tackled*. You can't reel in a crafty cove like Stanley without subtle foreplay, darling. But the ice is broken, just don't rush me.'

Later, after chicken chasseur and fresh figs in brandy, Stella led him upstairs and, under the shaded lights of the bedroom, laid out the fancy dress. By this time Charlie was in a mellow frame of mind and, after snorting a line of coke off the glazed dressing-table surface, getting into the party spirit was no problem at all. He didn't even notice the shop-soiled aroma of the extraordinary gear – or perhaps that only contributed, in his mind, to the sleaze.

They helped each other squeeze into the clothes, Charlie lacing up her overflowing corset with all the butter-fingered excitement of a novice – which she knew he certainly was not. They giggled their way through the intricacies of getting togged up and by the time the real fun began, the two performed like professional hoofers all too familiar with the footwork.

Eventually, totally wiped out by the excesses a serious romp with Charlie entailed, Stella persuaded him to crash out on the four-poster in the guest room, which he did on cue, the fancy dress now strewn about her bedroom like the discarded garments of a clapped-out old courtesan. She waited to hear him snoring like a buzz saw, then crept downstairs with the video camera to make copies.

Saturday started late and because, for discretion's sake, Charlie preferred to stay indoors, filling the day proved to be something of an Olympic love-in. Surely the man didn't expect non-stop humping all weekend, Stella thought.

In the end, once it grew dark, she persuaded him to take her into Oxford for supper. 'No one will recognize you, Charlie. Really, the pubs in the city on a Saturday night are crowded with tanked-up students only interested in pulling some nice birds before the wine runs out. Look on it as research for the Chekhov: an update on how the current young blade makes it. Anyway, I can't cook. We either go out for a plate of chips or I heat up something from the freezer again.'

He reluctantly agreed and Stella drove down the lane like the clappers. The outing took on the air of a dangerous sortie when, speeding through the village, she had to brake urgently to avoid a motorcyclist who, almost crashing into the ditch, raised a fist at her as she accelerated away.

'Bugger! That was my gardener, Jimmy Thompson.'

'Did he see me?'

'Of course not. But he knows my car and has a nose for trouble. Never mind, I was thinking of giving him the push anyhow.'

The pub grub was effective in damping down Charlie's inexhaustible ardour and back at the cottage they fell on to the sofa with relief.

'How about a jolly little video, Charlie?'

He brightened. Despite being a somewhat jaded voyeur, the prospect of a lively performance would hopefully revitalize his sagging libido.

Stella jumped up to start the video machine, filling Charlie's tumbler from the decanter and settling down beside him like a cuddly wifelet. The tape whirred into play.

Charlie laughed. 'You've got the wrong video, sweetheart. Who's this old buffer doing the burglar routine?'

Stella squeezed his arm. 'It's my electrician. He's demonstrating the surveillance equipment. Be patient, lover boy, it gets better.'

Bily Truelove's brief screen test cut out and a new scene reeled out.

'Now who's this? Your accountant? Jesus, Stella, you've got a funny idea of Candid Camera. There's supposed to be a joke, someone falling down at least, my love.' He relished what he thought to be Stella's weird sense of humour and waited for the replay of Monty's visit to get to the comic bits.

'It's my ex,' she whispered. 'He came down to see me this week. Keep watching. Charlie, it's what Woody Allen would call "Keyhole on Reality".'

As the recorded conversation spooled out, Charlie became serious. 'What an absolute shit, Stella. And you were married to this guy?'

'Years ago.'

'Why put up with a schmuck like that?'

'For Fran, my daughter. There's a dramatic teenage sub-plot in there too – I needed Monty to fill in for me so I didn't have to cancel our weekend.' The video petered out and Stella switched off the machine.

'Will you pay up?'

'Probably. After I've made him sweat a little.'

'More fool you. Just dump the guy; he deserves it.'

'Mmm. You may be right. Actually, I didn't show you that for a sympathy bid, it was more of a demonstration. Works well, doesn't it? My electrician fixed up three cameras, one down here and two upstairs in the bedrooms. I said I needed evidence to catch a sneak thief but really I was after something else.'

Charlie frowned. 'You plan to blackmail this Monty guy, pass the video on to the girlfriend, show him up?'

'No, why would I do that?'

'Spite? Jealousy? The usual female reasons.'

'I'm not that sort, Charlie. In fact, if I'm playing dirty tricks here it's for purely vicarious reasons. For a friend.'

He looked nonplussed and waited for the punchline.

'I'm a very old friend of Kate's. Your wife. You didn't know that, did you, Charlie? Kate doesn't know about us either – it's a cold war out there, isn't it? My skint ex-husband putting the pinch on me for a pay-off and Kate trying to get a reasonably fair divorce settlement from you.'

'We're two fat birds they think are ready for plucking, Stella. Don't give in to the bastards is what I say.'

'Oh yes? And what about Chaz, that useless son of yours who's been a millstone round Kate's neck for years?'

'I give him an allowance,' he protested.

'Not enough. Not enough to fuel his habit and not nearly enough to pay for rehab.'

'What's the game, Stella? Has Kate put you up to this?'

'She knows nothing about it. Kate doesn't even know we've met, let alone been what you'd call "close". No, this is all my idea. I got my technical genius here to set up a mantrap. Not for Monty, that was just my trial run. No, I wanted evidence to embarrass you so profoundly that you would be forced to agree to my terms.'

He leapt up. 'Christ Almighty! You've filmed us all weekend?'

'Not all weekend, Charlie. Just the best bits. I've got a tape of everything that happened upstairs, and a bloody laughable screening it would make. Fix you for good. I would only need to anonymously post one of my copies to a tabloid and you would be cooked. Shall I send one to your agent, Charlie, or are you open to plea bargaining?'

'What do you want? You do realize it's blackmail, Stella. You could get five years for a sting like that.'

'And the cocaine? You're clearly snorting a whole stack of snow on film, and the subsequent fancy-dress pantomime would merit an Oscar. Coke's illegal, Charlie, and if pressed

I'd say you brought it here yourself. There's nowhere on the tape that shows me partaking of the joy dust, I've checked, and if you are threatening me with a charge of blackmail, you'd find yourself with some explaining to do, even if you were willing to accept the career-busting exposure.'

He relaxed, lit a cigarette and regarded her with sly amusement. 'This is a wind-up, isn't it, darling? You had me going for a moment.'

She stepped back, suddenly afraid. 'No, Charlie, it's no joke. Do you want to hear the deal?'

He grinned, clapping his hands in derision. 'Continue, my love, this is the best night's entertainment I've had in years.'

She brushed her hair aside with a gesture of shaky defiance.

'Well, listen up, buddy, and believe me, when I first got the idea of freeing Kate from you it occurred to me murder would be the best solution, so the deal I'm putting to you is a bargain, I swear.'

She sat down, giving Charlie the full benefit of her steely concentration, and took a deep breath. 'Here goes...'

Twenty-Eight

It was eight-thirty on Sunday morning before Stella could raise her aching head, awoken by insistent knocking at the front door. She dragged herself downstairs, slowly, calling irritably, 'Wait, can't you! I'm coming.'

It was Tory.

'Good God, Stella! What happened to you? Your eye...' She moved inside and followed Stella into the chaos of the living room. 'It looks like World War Three in here.'

Stella slumped on the sofa while Tory picked up cushions

from the floor and looked around in amazement. 'Oh, sit down, do! I'll clear up later.'

'But, Stella . . . are you all right?' Tory took both her hands in her own and stared, open-mouthed, at the swelling bruise that had all but closed Stella's eye. 'It was Charlie, wasn't it? I told you he was dangerous. And trashing the place too. The man's a psycho. I did warn you, Stella. Kate said he was vicious.'

'He was looking for something.'

'And how! What brought this on?'

'I explained the deal: he had to send me a copy of his lawyer's letter to Kate upping the ante on the divorce settlement and, in return, I would guarantee a contract on a show at Bucks next spring at the latest. But I would need proof of his change of heart before the end of the month.'

Tory shook her head in confusion but pressed on, pushing aside the need for details. 'Listen, Stella, I'm driving you back to London. Get dressed, this is an emergency.'

Stella pressed her hand to her head. 'I'm OK, Tory. Really. He's gone, flown back to Paris. I'm perfectly safe here.'

'It's not Charlie I'm worried about. The police are looking for you. There's been an accident at the flat.'

Stella started up, seized with fear. 'Not Fran?'

'No, of course not. Fran's at school, isn't she? There's been a fatal fall from your roof and the police need to check whether he fell from the scaffolding or broke into your flat and threw himself off the roof terrace. They want access.'

Stella fell back. 'Oh, Tory, I really don't feel up to it. Can't it wait? When did this happen?'

'Last night or this morning, they can't put an exact time on it yet. He fell into the basement area and lay there for hours until a passing jogger found him early this morning. His driving licence was in his pocket.'

'Yes, sure, but what's this to do with me? And how did you get involved?'

'Kate rang me.'

'Kate?'

'Yes. Brace yourself, Stella. It was Chaz. He's dead.'

Stella tried to speak but words wouldn't come.

After a moment, Tory continued in hushed tones. 'It's

nobody's fault, Stella, he was high as a kite; it's just that being Chaz there's going to be one hell of a lot on the news as soon as it gets out. "Son of film star Charles Hilton plummets from Roof." Possible Suicide – all that sort of crap. The press will make a picnic out of it. You must come straight away. I'll drive you. Get dressed and I'll make some coffee.'

She pulled Stella to her feet and propelled her towards the stairs through the shambles of the room.

Dazed, Stella made unsteady progress and Tory hurried into the kitchen where, to her dismay, cupboard doors hung open, the contents spilling everywhere. 'Crikey, Charlie, with a temper like yours you should be in a straitjacket,' she said to herself.

Eventually they were seated in Stella's car, she insisting on driving, refusing to trust Tory's old banger to get them safely to London. She had disguised the insipient black eye under heavy foundation, and huge sunglasses completed the transformation.

The day was already bright, the spring sunshine sparkling off roads damp with overnight rain.

'Just for the record,' Tory ventured, 'what was Charlie looking for?'

'My video cameras.'

She laughed. 'You're joking!'

'No, seriously. He went ballistic when I said I'd got film showing him in an unflattering sequence of undress and he pulled the place apart. I gave up the tape when he got really mad and he stormed out.'

'Having beaten you up.'

'Well, a glancing blow that sent me reeling against the fireplace, but, yes, I suppose if I felt like it I could press charges. But that's all washed up now, isn't it? Chaz's death cancels everything. I'll destroy the videotape.'

'I thought you said he took it.'

'I locked a second copy in the car together with the relevant camera. Thought I was being so clever, didn't I? All a waste. Poor Chaz. And poor Kate. What did she say?'

'Rang me as soon as the police called round. They couldn't

116

get hold of you, of course, and Kate phoned me to see if you were at the cottage. I said I'd bring you in.'

'Sounds as if I'm under suspicion. Kate knows nothing about Charlie being here, does she?'

'Nothing, I swear. Will you tell the police?'

'No. The whole thing's complicated enough already. Has anyone informed Charlie?'

Tory shrugged. 'No idea. But do you think he'll admit to being at the cottage all weekend? Did anyone see him?'

'We were very careful. But I'll have to warn him to keep his mouth shut. Chaz falling off the scaffolding was an accident, no need to drag Charlie into it. I've got to stop at the next lay-by. I need to speak to Monty, he'll have to break the news to Fran and bring her home. She'll be utterly distraught, poor love. Bloody hell, why did Chaz have to play Batman on my roof?'

They pulled into a service station and Tory went into the cafeteria while Stella disappeared to make her phone calls.

'Hello, Monty. Have you heard the news? Chaz, Fran's boyfriend, has had an accident. The stupid fool got all tanked up on Saturday night apparently and attempted to climb the scaffolding outside my building. The police want to see me. I shall have to admit that he was a family friend but I really don't want Fran involved. Could you spring her from the sanatorium at school right away and take her back to your place? I'll ring the school and say you're coming to pick her up.'

'How is he? The boy, I mean?'

'Chaz is dead, Monty. It's all a horrible nightmare. I'm with a friend; we're on our way back. I'll have to see his mother, God help me.'

'Stella, are you all right? You sound terrible. Is there something you're not telling me?'

'Just do the business, Monty. I'll talk to you this afternoon. Get her home right away. I'll come and see her later. Thank goodness Tiffany is off the scene; I think Tiffany knows more about Chaz than we do. Keep Fran out of it. The police won't bother her with any questions if it's clear she had no more than a brief friendship with Chaz, but it's bound to come out. Anyway, she was away at school when he took it into his

117

head to pay a visit. I've a nasty feeling she confided in Chaz about valuables in the flat, gave him the idea it would be worth breaking in. He was a druggie, Monty, so presumably needed cash.'

Getting through to Charlie was more difficult and eventually she was forced to send him a text message. At least Charlie would be as keen as herself to keep their relationship off record. 'And I thought my life was dull!'

She joined Tory at a table in the cafeteria. 'I got through to the school. Monty's fetching Fran and keeping her at his flat until this blows over.'

'I'm worried about Kate. She's got nobody, Stella. Will you come with me? She needs us.'

'I'll have to settle with the police first. I'll pop by my place and you can take the car. I'll join you at Kate's as soon as the police have finished checking the roof terrace.'

'Is your flat the only one with access?'

'Yes. One of the other tenants, a woman, sometimes sunbathes in the nude up there if I let her, but I got a bit shirty last time after another neighbour – who lives in a house across from the gardens at the back – spotted her and thought it was me browning my tits. Cheek! The bloody woman's at least fifty and has turned herself to leather.'

'What do you think Chaz was up to?'

'Who knows? But I've got to talk to Fran. She let him into the flat while I was in Paris and showed him round. He must have got the wrong idea, thought it would be easy to break in.' She scrabbled through her bag for the car keys. 'Let's go. Oh, here, I've got a spare set of keys for the cottage. For you, Tory. They're Jimmy's. I didn't like the idea of him nosing round when I'm not there and I thought maybe you would like to use the cottage in your free time, have somewhere to go to get away from your students.'

'That's terribly kind of you, Stella. Thanks. But what about Jimmy? Doesn't he clean the house for you?'

'Yes, but I'm having second thoughts. That local police inspector, Hayes, said Jimmy needs watching. I'm hoping to get a cleaner from the village. I don't mind keeping Jimmy on as a gardener if necessary, but he is a bit creepy, isn't he?'

'Never caused me any trouble, but then I've hardly met him. It's that old farmer, Bossom, who gives me the frights.'

'Well, it's up to you. If you want to chill out at the cottage, you're more than welcome.'

'No more heavy dates then?'

'Well, Charlie's right off the menu and I've no one else in view, but who knows? Pity your Mervyn's gay, I quite fancied him.'

The mood lightened, Stella's fears allayed since speaking with Monty who had organized a quick exit for Fran to a bolt hole safe from police probing. Surely, Chaz had had scores of girls apart from his brief dalliance with Fran? Stella wondered if she had underestimated the power of love for under-age virgins, but shoved this unwelcome thought aside and concentrated on putting mileage between herself and the unresolved situation with Charlie Hilton.

Twenty-Nine

Stella parked outside her building where a police presence was already attracting the curiosity of passers-by. Church bells tolled, presumably urging worshippers to prayer. A prayer for Chaz? Was anybody passing those bloodstained railings pausing to pray for yet one more suicide in this crowded city?

Tory drove off at speed, leaving Stella to negotiate with the lone constable blocking the basement steps and fending off sensation seekers. Thankfully the body had been removed. She identified herself and, after a quick call to his inspector, Stella was allowed through. She hurried to the lift which expressed her to her penthouse apartment.

The keys worked smoothly, which was a huge relief – at least Chaz had not broken into the flat. But as soon as she

119

entered she knew she was wrong. The place had certainly been turned over, but not trashed as the cottage had been. A few drawers hung open and the drinks cupboard had been rifled – a half-empty bottle of vodka lay on the coffee table. But it all seemed more the work of a curious visitor than a thief, and Stella wondered if Chaz had been interrupted – the phone ringing, perhaps? She wandered about the living room vaguely noting the few baubles still dotted about: the minia-tures in their gold frames still in place, her enamel boxes ranged along the mantelshelf.

Abruptly she pulled herself together and ran upstairs to check the bedroom. Here was the same desultory rearrange-ment of her things. Her jewellery case was open on the dressing table, but nothing much had been taken, just Anthony's watch and a pair of cufflinks. This gave her a moment's reassurance that burglary, not suicide, had been his motive – a standard reason for a break-in that the police would leap upon.

But this temporary relief was short-lived. She knelt to recover the suitcase hidden under the bed. The natty gilt padlock had been undone, the unimaginative favourite combination – treble three – clearly aligned. Her pulse quickened. She tossed the woollens on to the carpet and upended the case. There was no mistake, the ski hat wrap-ping the remainder of Stefan's tablets had gone. Her blood ran cold.

She sat back on her heels, weak with the dawning certainty. Chaz had come for the drugs and he knew where to look. And there was only one person who could have told him. Only one person who knew the combination of the lock. Fran.

'Oh my God. You silly child. You naive darling, boasting to a boy like Chaz, showing off, thinking giving him a taster would be enough.' A user like Chaz could never glimpse such a hoard and not come back for more. And now what? The boy was dead. The burglary had been a blind. No jewel theft. No suicide. Just a sordid drugs snatch. And all her fault.

The buzzer at the front door shrilled. She slammed the suit-case back under the bed and hurried downstairs to answer the intercom. It was a police inspector, alerted by his duty constable that the owner of the top flat was back.

'Oh, come up,' she stuttered, eyeing the disorder of the rooms with dismay.

She stood by the lift and ushered the grey-haired inspector and a WPC into the living room. He noted that the unfortunate woman looked white as a sheet and directed his WPC to fetch a glass of water from the kitchen. He introduced himself as Inspector Chivers.

'This is a bad do, Mrs Buckleigh. Obviously a shock to come home to this. Sit quietly for a moment. May I look round?'

Stella nodded and sat mutely observing their rapid examination of the room. They opened one of the windows overlooking the square and leaned out, surveying the scaffolding. A scrap of fabric clung to a line of barbed wire wrapped around a pole. The girl stretched out and managed to retrieve it, placing it in an evidence bag that Inspector Chivers handed her. They spoke briefly in quiet tones Stella failed to hear, her mind whirring with the terrifying consequences of any involvement Fran may have had in Chaz's plan to filch the drugs while Stella was at the cottage.

'Er, yes, Inspector? Sorry, what did you say?'

He called her over to look at the second window. The glass was broken and the catch lifted. 'He got in through here, Mrs Buckleigh. He didn't fall from the scaffolding as we thought. I'm afraid we shall have to search the entire flat, find out what happened here. You have a roof terrace I understand? May we?'

She rose and led them upstairs and through to the terrace.

'This door was unlocked, Mrs Buckleigh. Is that usual?'

'No, but the key always hangs up here,' she said, indicating a hook over the lintel.

'Ah, well it's not there now, is it? When our enquiries here are complete we can check the keys found on the victim.'

Stella braced herself against the wall, suddenly feeling faint. 'Did Chaz die instantly?' she murmured.

The inspector's jaw dropped. 'You knew him? The lad who fell?'

'The son of a girlfriend. He came here once or twice.'

'Charles Hilton?'

She nodded.

'That's our boy. Well, fancy that. Never thought he was anything but a wired-up nutter off his head and climbing the scaffolding for kicks. Not a suicide then?'

'I d–don't think he's the type. Was there a note?'

'No, nothing like that but he was definitely high as a sputnik with all the stuff he'd taken according to our pathologist's first impression. But, yes, he died instantly. Fell off this little wall here, I reckon,' he said, pointing at the parapet. 'Thought he could fly, poor bugger. Oh, excuse me, Mrs Buckleigh, but a young bloke losing his life in a stupid prank like that is a proper tragedy; upsets me to think about. See here,' he said, taking her to the edge and pointing down, 'the scaffolding doesn't extend this far in front of the building, it's a sheer drop to the street. He bounced off the railings after plummeting down from the roof here and ended up in the basement area beside the steps.'

Stella retched, feeling the bile rise in her throat, and bolted, leaving the two of them on the terrace. She stayed in the bathroom waiting for her racing thoughts to subside. First thing she must warn Monty to keep Fran right out of it. And Pearly? Pearly might let slip that Chaz was brought here by the two girls while she was away. She must keep Pearly off the scene, prevent any loose talk. As soon as the police had finished searching the flat she would ring Pearly and tell her to take some time off. Yes, that would do it. Thank goodness Chaz's accident had been discovered on a Sunday. If he'd broken in midweek Pearly might have been the one to find him and then God knows what she would have told the inspector. Pearly, for some mysterious reason of her own, was scared witless by the police – probably something in her past, something Stella had never bothered to explore and as she came from a respectable domestic agency it was assumed her visa and work permit had been legal. The Filipina was certainly honest and hard-working, which was the important thing. She shivered.

The WPC tapped on the door, politely enquiring if she was all right.

'Yes, yes, of course. I'll be out directly.' She gazed at her face in the bathroom mirror, horrified to discover that she had forgotten to put on the sunglasses, her black eye now blooming in full Technicolor. Whatever could the hawk-eyed Inspector Chivers have made of it?

She drew a deep breath and joined the DI in the living room. The girl stood behind him, her eyes circling the room.

'Are you ready to answer a few questions, Mrs Buckleigh? Just to get the details out of the way.'

'Yes, of course. It was a shock you see. Such a terrible tragedy.'

Chivers went through the preliminaries, noting her where-abouts during the weekend, tactfully probing the nature of her acquaintance with the deceased.

'I hardly knew him, Inspector. His mother is an old friend I recently rediscovered and I suppose I met Chaz no more than twice. He invited my daughter to his birthday party, which was kind. She's only a teenager, you see, hardly of his age group. He knew where we lived, of course, but really he was hardly someone I would recognize if I bumped into him on the street.'

'Your daughter lives with you?'

'Naturally. Just us two, my husband died. But Frances is away at school. Boarding, so there was no opportunity to meet any London friends after term started.'

'She's at school now?'

'Of course. But before we go any further with your ques-tions, Inspector, I must mention that there are a couple of things which were stolen.'

His eyes hardened. 'You're sure?'

'I checked as soon as I got back. Just two things I've missed so far, both items that belonged to my late husband. Of senti-mental value . . .' she added.

He waited and, after a moment, she continued, her voice thin with anxiety. 'Some initialled cufflinks – A.R.B. – and Anthony's old watch.'

'Valuable?'

'To me, yes. And the watch is probably a collector's piece, an original Cartier.'

The WPC looked up sharply, nodding at the inspector's unspoken question.

'Items matching that description were found on the victim. He was wearing the watch when he fell. It was smashed, I'm afraid. When the body was found it was assumed the watch was his; we had no reason to believe this young man was thieving, our assumption was suicide fuelled by drugs.' He paused. 'This complicates matters, Mrs Buckleigh. Have you made a thorough search?'

'Er . . . n–no, not really. I just flew straight to my jewel case, but, as you can see,' she said, waving at the disarray, 'Chaz did search round before going up on the roof.'

The inspector stood. 'I think we had better make a thorough recce, Mrs Buckleigh. My constable will accompany you and note any observations you may have so we have a clear picture of his motives. I'm afraid we shall have to take your fingerprints – for elimination purposes. We need not trouble your daughter, but do you have a cleaner?'

'Yes, but Pearly's away, visiting her family in Manila.'

'Pity. But never mind, we shall do our best.'

Stella dutifully rose and trailed about the flat checking drawers and cupboards, confident that she had at least drawn Chivers away from the dangerous line of questioning about Fran's friendship with Charlie's son.

Poor Charlie! She had hardly given him a thought since he stormed out of the cottage with the videotape. She supposed he would return for the funeral . . . Or would he? She thrust the disturbing side issues that would arise once he was back in England to the back of her mind, and concentrated on leading Chivers' WPC a merry dance.

At the end of their fruitless tour they returned to the living room where Chivers was speaking on his mobile, anxiously relaying a description of Stella's missing treasures to whoever it was co-ordinating enquiries. When he concluded his report he turned to smile at her as she slumped on the sofa, pressing a hand to her throbbing cheekbone.

'Ah, Mrs Buckleigh. Good news then? Nothing else missing?'

She shook her head and smiled wanly.

He nodded. 'I had a colleague of mine on the phone earlier – he was my boss when I was stationed in Oxford before transferring to the Met. Coincidences never cease to amaze me, Mrs Buckleigh – believe it or not, the officer who got on to me is a friend of yours too. Chief Inspector Hayes from Renham.'

She started up. 'Roger Hayes? He phoned here?'

'No, I rang him back. He'd left a message at the station for me. Inspector Hayes had heard the news about our poor young man falling off your roof and was anxious about you. A personal friend of yours, he said . . . He called at your cottage – must have been shortly after you left this morning – intending to break the news, but, as we know, you had already been told. Did Mrs Hilton ring you?'

'Indirectly,' she murmured, her mind racing with this extraordinary interference from Roger Hayes.

'He was particularly worried about you when he looked through the window of the cottage and it looked as if it had been the scene of a violent attack. He cut through the police red tape and found yours truly was in charge at the London end of the investigation. I phoned him back just now to assure him that you were perfectly safe and helping us clear up some little details. It's a small world isn't it, Mrs Buckleigh?'

Thirty

It was after six before Stella drew up outside Monty's block of flats in Fulham. She had spent a terrible afternoon at Kate's, Tory regarding Stella with marked astonishment as she skirted round her weekend at the cottage and the subsequent run-in with Inspector Chivers. Tory insisted on staying with Kate, so Stella reclaimed her car.

'I have to get back to the flat, Katie, the police are taking the place apart. I'll pick up some things and sleep at the cottage tonight. I'll come to see you again in a day or two. Is there anything you need?'

After that she made a quick exit and sat in the car making phone calls. Pearly was at home and had heard the news of Fran's friend falling from their building. She was clearly anxious, her voice trembling with uncertainty.

'Look, Pearly, we're both best out of it. The police are all over the building and there's nothing we can do. Why don't you take a couple of weeks in Manila and ring me when you get back? The investigation should be over by then. I'll put your wages cheque in the post now and add the air fare and the bonus I usually give you for your summer holiday. OK?'

This suggestion went down a treat, and when she rang off the relief of having at least one inconvenient witness off the scene was as good as a G&T.

She rang Charlie Hilton again and got nowhere, but once the news hit the headlines the guy would surely break cover, if only to negotiate a truce and, not least, co-ordinate alibis to cover their weekend in fairyland.

Getting hold of Stanley Kerslake at his country retreat was easier, the chief honcho at Bucks basking in the status-building situation of joining the rural rich. Percivals would have been no temptation to Stanley – not nearly as glamorous as a manor house within spitting distance of the nouveau set circling the royals. He had even taken to supporting polo.

'You've heard the news, Stanley? Charlie Hilton's boy fell off my roof last night. The police are all over the flat. I'm just on my way back to the cottage for a breather but I shall have to be in town later tomorrow. Can we meet? I'm worried.'

Stanley had the sense not to probe and quickly proposed dinner next evening at Ramsay's.

'Sorry, can't do dinner, Stanley. How about your office at sixish, when the staff have gone?'

Stanley stiffened. This was not at all the laid-back Stella Buckleigh he knew. Must be something serious . . .

Stella swiftly brought the call to an end and made like an arrow to Monty's flat. He was alone, which was good.

126

'Where's Fran?' she whispered as they went through to the sitting room.

'Asleep. I gave her a sleeping pill and she went out like a light. Poor kid's keeled over completely since she heard about Chaz. And off your scaffolding, you said.'

Stella fell on to Monty's leather sofa, utterly zonked by hours of tension. 'Actually, he dived off the roof terrace. Doped up to the eyebrows, of course, but it's amazing he got that far, climbing the scaffolding to the third floor was a miracle in itself.'

'God Almighty! A drink, Stella? You look terrible. What's with the sunglasses? Not teary over Fran's trouble at school, are you?'

She took off the shades, the black eye now matured to shades of green and mauve.

Monty shuddered. 'Taken up with a bit of rough, Stella? Dangerous, and no fun at all, believe me.'

She shrugged. 'A romp that got out of hand. Don't worry, I can handle it. Incidentally, where's Morag?'

'Weekending at Lingfield – doing wedding lists,' he said with a grimace.

Stella giggled. 'Am I invited?'

'Unless you back me up, the wedding's off,' he snapped.

'Oh, you mean the twenty grand you need to make up before the roof falls in?'

'Don't be snide, Stella. It's my last chance. If I blow it with Morag I'll spend the rest of my life on the skids, even if I escape from Holland's without them taking me to court. And the Monte Carlo debt collectors are killers. But you won't let me down, will you, Stell? A loan, I promise. Once I get my knees under the table with old McDermott I'll be in clover, no need to bother you ever again.'

She sobered. 'I told you how things stand, Monty. I'm thinking about it. This bloody business with Chaz has messed up everything just now. Give me a few days. I've got to drive back to Percivals tonight, clear up the shit I left behind before a nosy copper called Hayes gets on my case. And an estate agent's coming round in the morning. I've had an offer on the cottage.'

'You're selling Percivals?'

'Possibly. The agent had a proposal from a local agricultural conglomerate last month and I've been mulling it over. Anthony bought up some parcels of land when he purchased the cottage and as a package it makes a sizeable investment. They want to combine our fields with theirs and make a commercial estate big enough to go organic. They'll probably raze the cottage and certainly bulldoze the orchard. My friend Tory scattered her husband's ashes there, so I'm not sure how she'll take it, but from my impression of Stefan I imagine being part of an organic enterprise would be just up his street. It's a spectacular offer I'd be a fool to ignore.'

'Don't rush into anything, sweetie; you're upset at present. If you sign up to sell while times are difficult, you may regret it.'

'I'm thinking of buying a place on the Riviera. I could do with a bit of sun and just lately the locals in the village have been getting nasty. Never really took to me since Anthony died. He used to butter them up, made promises about long leases on the fields and so on, which, frankly, are not sustainable.'

'What does Fran think about this?'

'Haven't discussed it with her yet. Hadn't really taken it too seriously until lately but Fran has taken against the cottage for some reason and refuses to go there. She used to love it.'

'Grown out of it, I suppose,' he said. 'At the moment she's in love with Morag's set-up at Lingfield. Horses. Must be in the blood.'

Stella frowned. 'Shall we see if she's awake?'

They tiptoed into the spare room but the hump under the bedclothes was clearly hibernating.

Stella drew back. 'Let's not disturb the poor kid. I've got to go – you can reach me on my mobile if there are any developments – but I'll be back in town tomorrow night. May I drop in about eight? Fran should have come round by then. Keep her here and off the phone if you can. I don't want her gassing away with Tiffany and I certainly don't want her rushing round to offer sympathy to Chaz's mum. Right?'

He followed her out, caught between acute anxiety about his own dire financial straits and a sensible reluctance to aggravate Stella's touchy mood.

'Thanks, Monty. You've been a saviour snatching her from school like that. I'll ring the head in the morning and offer my cringing apologies. I'm sure they'll take her back; teenage drinking's the least of the problems at a girls' boarding school, I reckon. Eating disorders kill!'

He held open the door, wondering if this new dependence on his co-operation over their daughter would work in his favour. She turned as she was about to hurry away.

'Just one more thing, Monty. I shall have to see my solicitor in Oxford tomorrow if I agree to go ahead with the sale of the cottage. It would be an opportunity to deal with another matter they've been badgering me about. May I forward your name as a trustee for Fran's fund? Anthony set up an arrangement for her – an insurance in case both of us dropped off the edge of the world – and her godfather was trustee, together with a couple of lawyers to oversee her inheritance and so on. I've no family, as you know, and the poor godfather, Alan Caister, the actor, has died, and with Anthony out of it I've been asked to reconsider the future. Would you mind? The lawyers will keep tabs on the capital and Fran won't inherit fully until she's eighteen, but in the meantime there has to be a safety net, a means of supporting her until her majority if lightning strikes twice and I fall out of the sky like Anthony. Please God, you won't be called upon to take up the reins, but it's something that's got to be sorted and you are, after all, her father.'

'Sure. We'll go over the details when there's more time. But don't forget I'm dangling by my fingertips with this debt business. I'd be no good as a trustee banged up in Wormwood Scrubs, darling.'

She grinned and pinched his cheek, secure in the knowledge that, for all his faults, Monty Neville was as besotted with their daughter as she.

Thirty-One

S tella set her alarm for seven and dragged herself out of bed to clear up the chaos Charlie had made of the cottage. In the cold light of day the mess looked tawdry, like the aftermath of a drunken orgy. She toyed with the idea of getting Jimmy in to wave a magic wand over the whole thing before the estate agent arrived at eleven, but she knew all too well that the village would wallow in Jimmy's description of the state that toffee-nosed Mrs Buckleigh really lived in. No, she would do it herself.

In fact, setting to with the vacuum cleaner and a bin bag for the after-effects of Charlie's trashing of both upstairs and down in his search for the videotape was surprisingly therapeutic, an activity totally unfamiliar to her since pushing Monty out of their marriage. Working from the ground floor up, she finally sat on the bed and stared out at the sunlit vista, to give serious thought to her plans for the day.

The estate agents' surveyors were already to grips with measuring the fields included in the sale. She could see them pacing out the sheep field with some sort of pedometer, the stocky figure of Bossom stationed at the boundary. Even from her distant vantage point, Stella could sense the man's rage. The word would go round before she had even signed the agreement that the Buckleigh woman was selling up. And inevitably the leases held by Bossom and his numerous relations, who Anthony had generously accommodated in view of the family's long-standing occupancy of the farm that Percivals had been before it was transformed into a smart weekend cottage, would have to be renegotiated.

It was the right time to go. Fran had decisively turned her back on Percivals and Stella herself felt a rising tide of local resentment lapping at the door, a resentment fuelled by the growing number of incomers who were taking over the nicest houses in Bramley Green and, according to the acrimonious backchat in the post office, converting decent farm cottages and barns and pricing the locals out of the market. At least they made their homes here, Stella mused, her own spasmodic occupancy of Percivals being, in fairness, an affront. Its reincarnation as organic farmland would, at least, be appropriate, even if the cottage itself was eliminated at a stroke from her pen.

The estate agent, a smart go-getter from town, breezed in at eleven on the dot and dumped his briefcase on the hall table without so much as a 'how d'you do'. Stella bridled, her black eye hidden behind dark glasses which, even on this sunny morning, struck an odd note within the dimness of the cottage interior.

He thrust out his hand. 'Mrs Buckleigh. A pleasure to meet you. My name's Button, Marcel Button.'

She ignored this and led him straight to her study where the correspondence relating to the sale was fanned out on the desk. They remained standing, both anxious to bring the meeting to a swift conclusion.

'There's no need for me to look around,' he said. 'My client is rather more interested in the acreage of the estate.'

'Estate's rather overstating it, isn't it?'

'Not at all, Mrs Buckleigh. A sizeable collection of fields which will blend into my client's plans very nicely. You are still happy to go ahead? The terms, if I may say so, are extremely generous.'

'This part of Buckinghamshire is much sought after, Mr Button. The price Trelawnay Holdings is offering is by no means inflated, so shall we cut through the sales talk and get down to details?'

The rest of the morning blew past like a force-nine gale and Marcel Button found himself out on the doorstep in short order. Stella agreed to see her solicitors in Oxford that afternoon and nodded through his brisk summing-up of the consortium's terms.

Stella closed the door with relief and made a pot of coffee

to clear her head. There was so much to do, so much to set in motion and so little time. It was as if her life, so predictable, so secure, had suddenly been thrown into reverse.

She decided to take a taxi into Oxford, as even the thought of driving back into London that evening to see Stanley Kerslake and to check up on Fran made her exhausted. Seeing Fran would be lovely, of course, even if the poor child was heartbroken over Chaz, but the meeting with Stanley would be tricky, no doubt about it.

The cab driver came over from Renham and was still muttering about the difficulty of locating the unmarked lane to the cottage when they passed through Thame. Stella relaxed on the back seat with her eyes closed, letting the guy vent his irritation and get it over with.

'You'll wait, of course?' she said as she alighted outside the solicitor's office. 'I shall only be half an hour. Drive round the block a bit.'

'You ain't paid me yet, missus, I'm not likely to scarper, am I?'

The solicitor's place occupied a prime spot on The High and had clearly gone through a serious makeover since her last visit following Anthony's death. She was shown through directly, but not to the senior partner's room as she expected. A door opened and Stella was suddenly taken aback.

'Rob Allinson! How nice. I'd forgotten you'd transferred from the London office.'

He drew her inside and grinned. 'Started on Monday, still making myself familiar with the client list, not helped by Mr Shoesmith's vacation. I expect you normally see our senior partner, don't you, Stella? Are you happy for me to deal with this? Simple conveyancing – I'm sure I can handle it,' he said with a deprecating smile.

'Y–yes, of course.'

'Here, take a seat. Tea? Coffee?'

'No, nothing, thanks. And if we could be quick, Rob, I've a taxi waiting. Here are the papers, all pretty straightforward.' She pushed a folder to him across the desk and he quickly glanced through it.

'I shall have to make some enquiries of course – checks to ensure all's well. You're certain you want to do this, Stella? I was astonished to hear you were leaving. Does Tory know?'

'Not so far. I haven't even told my daughter yet but I'm quite sure it's the right thing to do. Between ourselves, Rob, the cottage has bad vibes. Fran senses it and lately I've been feeling uncomfortable being alone there. It's rather off the beaten track and you know how it is once you begin to imagine funny noises, footsteps after dark, whispering in the village shop.'

'You're being persecuted?'

'Oh no, nothing like that, just a weird feeling. Intuition?' she suggested with a nervous laugh. 'The buyers plan to demolish the cottage – best thing for it – and luckily it's not grade listed so the moaners in the village can't cry foul.'

Rob Allinson was a good listener and knew when to hold his tongue. After hearing a little more of Stella's disenchant-ment with Percivals he put on his lawyer's hat again and they finalized the details.

'I'll have the papers ready for you to sign in a week or ten days if that's convenient?'

'Absolutely.' Stella half rose, her mind still distracted by the irrevocable step she was taking, and Rob straightened, assuming the meeting was at an end. But abruptly she sat down again, fixing him with a stare made disconcerting by her bruised eye.

'There is one more thing. I almost forgot. This trust fund Anthony set up for my daughter, Frances. Mr Shoesmith has been asking me to nominate a new trustee. Could you deal with it?'

'Yes, of course. I'll just ring for the file.'

While they waited, Rob took a chance and asked about Kate. 'Tory phoned Mervyn – I'm staying in the flat upstairs here for the present, but I was over at Mervyn's place last night and naturally we were shocked by Chaz's accident. Poor devil! And poor Kate.'

'And poor me,' Stella muttered. 'Falling from my roof of all things. My flat's crawling with police, I'm not at all sure when I'll have it to myself again. But that,' she said, biting her lip, 'is small beer compared with Kate's misery. What a terrible thing. I spent hours with her yesterday and God knows how she's coping with the press camping on her doorstep. The media are avid for gossip linking Chaz with Charlie Hilton, of course, and everything's being picked over. Why does it all have to be garnished for public titilation?'

'Charlie Hilton's career has been one long publicity stunt, Stella; he can't complain when the bad news gets a viewing too. It's just too ghastly that Kate has to take the barrage. I presume he hasn't surfaced in London?'

A secretary hurried in with the file and Rob excused himself to glance through the terms of the trust fund. Blimey, he thought, this Frances Neville kid's got a gold-plated future and no mistake. Stella lit a cigarette and glanced round the room, impressed by the understated charm of Rob Allinson's office with its watercolours and potted cymbidium on the windowsill.

He looked up. 'All very business-like. Your late husband made more than adequate provision for his stepdaughter.'

'Anthony was a kind and generous soul. We had no children of our own so Frances was inevitably favoured. I try to be firm but it's difficult to know where spoiling runs into real naughtiness where teenagers are involved. She's currently gated from boarding school.' She grimaced. 'A bit of a binge apparently, but I'm hoping to get her reinstated after a period of suspension.'

He waited, pen poised. 'The former trustee died, I see here.'

'Yes. My ex-husband, who has remained close to Frances since our divorce, has agreed to stand in for the late Mr Caister.' She withdrew one of Monty's business cards from her purse, scribbled his home address and phone number on the back, and passed it over. 'It's all perfectly simple, isn't it? He can come here to sign if you wish. Mr Shoesmith was insistent that there should be no further delay.'

'Leave it with me, Stella. I'll check with one of the other partners and be in touch in a day or two. Can I reach you at the cottage?'

'I shall have to stay put until the police have finished whatever it is that seems to be taking up their time at the flat, but

I'm on the move all the time. Ring me on my mobile, that's best – here's the number.' She wrote it down and frowned. 'Chaz was a difficult young man, it seems, and probably had unsuitable friends. I get the impression the police are investigating the possibility that Chaz wasn't alone. They're doing a thorough fingerprint search. The inspector hinted that they have some sort of evidence that the other person or persons made off after the accident, or even that poor Chaz fell in the course of horseplay and they bolted. It could be manslaughter.'

'And nobody else in the building heard anything?'

'The people downstairs were away for the weekend and the old lady who lives on the ground floor is profoundly deaf. I daresay the inspector's making a mystery out of nothing but I suppose they have to make sure their facts are watertight in such a high-profile case. The coroner will be anxious to get at the truth.'

'Of course. Is that it then, Stella?' he asked hopefully.

'Well, there was something else while I'm here. Would it be possible to add a codicil or whatever to the trust fund agreement, or put it in my will, whichever is the correct legal pigeonhole? I want twenty-five thousand pounds to be immediately extracted from my estate on my death and prior to probate to compensate Mr Neville for taking on this burden. I can arrange details with my banker if you require an additional cheque to augment the fund. My ex-husband is always chronically short of funds and if, God forbid, he should be called upon unexpectedly to take sole responsibility for our daughter, I would prefer there to be a financial cushion to see him able to steer Fran through any emergency without dipping into his own capital. You know how unforeseen expenses pile up – holidays and so on . . . She might want a pony to celebrate leaving school. And if Mr Neville was adequately provided for he would not have to bother the trust fund for intermediate sums not covered by the terms. Do you see my point? Monty has always shared parental responsibilities but not in any monetary way. There was never any need to claim maintenance; I have always supported Frances myself financially.'

Rob looked down at the documents and jotted notes to cover what he assumed were the aims of this unusual request, wishing he had not been pitchforked into dealing with this important client who, he felt sure, was probably too close an acquaintance for an impartial discussion on the unspoken issues of family life. And an immediate pay-off? Was this Neville guy a suitable trustee? He would have to consult Mr Shoesmith, interrupt his holiday if necessary, seeing as one of his best clients was seeking a swift rearrangement of the terms of the trust fund.

Stella escaped in just over forty minutes and was relieved to see her grumpy taxi driver parked at the kerb. He discoursed at length all the way back to the cottage on the arguments he'd had with not one, but two traffic wardens. Stella listened in silence but the ginormous tip proffered as she jumped out managed to shut him up.

Thirty-Two

The cottage seemed strangely unlived in – the result of the major tidying session that morning, Stella decided – but the sense of abandonment hung on the air like a melancholy haze.

She shivered. Her nerves were getting the better of her, no doubt about it. A cup of tea and an earful of one of Fran's pop discs would warm things up. She set the disco beat to full volume, had a shower and afterwards changed into jeans and a sweater for the drive into London that evening. The traffic on the motorway came to a total stop for twenty minutes following an accident in the fast lane and the delay jangled her nerves almost to screaming point. But she arrived at Stanley's building at ten past the hour, rang the bell and scuttled up to his office, arriving breathless at the top landing.

Stanley was waiting at his door, arms wide. He smelled of cigars and fine living, his button eyes bright with affection. He held her at arm's length, grinning. 'Hey, doll, you look great. I dig the shades, very Jackie O. Come through – I got Martha to send out for sandwiches and lattes. Knew you'd have been stuck in traffic for hours.'

She clung on like a desperate swimmer, refusing to break his embrace, as if she had found dry land at last. He pulled away and drew her through to his inner office, an opulent set-up, the panelled walls and leather chairs chosen to echo the solid comforts of his club.

They attacked Martha's takeaway with relish, Stella suddenly aware that she was famished. The coffee in styrofoam beakers was unexpected, but the quality was excellent and she guessed that Stanley had, since his shimmy up the theatrical ladder, forgotten how to brew up himself.

Finally, she broached the subject she had came to discuss.

'Stanley, I've decided to bow out. Sell my shares. Give you first option, of course. I realize it may take a little while for you to arrange, but the offer's on the table. You may prefer to form a syndicate to buy me out completely, that's up to you. I've given it a lot of thought lately and it's time for me to go.'

Stanley's eyes briefly narrowed before he rearranged his reaction to one of – what? Concern? Curiosity? Eager anticipation of taking full control of Bucks?

'Stella! You certainly know how to put the skids under a guy. I'd no idea. What brought this on?'

She shrugged. 'Just knowing that the time is ripe. Bucks was always Anthony's baby and in the not too distant future I could see myself becoming just an old nuisance to you. Bucks is in safe hands with you in charge, Stanley dear, and you certainly won't think I'm quitting like a rat leaving a sinking ship, will you? What do you think?'

He blew out his cheeks in amazement but his mind was already clicking through the permutations. Stella Buckleigh was no fool, Bucks was a sure-fire winner and if she sold out now, where else would she invest her capital? Another theatre? Hardly. Dip her toe in the rag trade? More likely. But even so . . .

'What else is troubling you, Stella? You haven't let this stupid accident from your roof frighten you, have you? The press haven't been hounding you, I hope.'

Stella lit a cigarette, her fingers shaking. 'I'm staying at the cottage, no one's interested in me yet. The problem is Chaz was, as you know, Charlie Hilton's son and the drugs aspect has got the police going. Nothing like a celebrity scandal to fire them up, especially with the media milking it for every drop of poison. Have you heard anything about Charlie surfacing in London?'

He shook his head. 'Not a whisper. What's got into you, Stella: I've never seen you so rattled. Obviously you're in the clear with the boy's death. I heard he broke in while you were away, climbed the scaffolding and got in through a window.'

She nodded. 'It's complicated by my being friendly with his mother, Kate Hilton. But that's not all. Can I use your video player, Stanley? I've got this tape I want you to see.'

He jumped up and slid back a section of carved panelling to reveal a battery of TV equipment. He took the videotape without a word and slammed it into the slot. They sat back to watch.

It didn't take long. And if Stanley had been stunned by Stella's offer to sell out, the replay of the video left the wheeler-dealing Kerslake gobsmacked.

'I recognize Charlie Hilton even in the wig, but whoa! Who's the hooker in the mask and thigh boots?'

She laughed. 'The hooker's *me*! Playtime, Hilton style.'

'You go for that stuff?' he asked in disbelief.

'No, of course not. It was Charlie's idea and it was a laugh at the time, until he got rough, that is.' She removed her sunglasses and gave Stanley the full benefit of her black eye.

'Christ! I heard he could be violent but I'd never have guessed Charlie Hilton was gay.'

'He's not gay, Stanley, I promise you. Just likes dressing up. He's bloody lucky nobody's blown the whistle on him before – it's clearly a regular hobby; his wife told me about it and they've been separated for years.'

'But the tape? Who got hold of it? Are they blackmailing

138

you, Stella? I can put a couple of my boys on to it, clear up that sort of bother in no time.'

'You don't get it, do you, Stanley? The video recording was set up in my cottage for a giggle. Charlie's got no sense of humour whatsoever and trashed my place in his efforts to bag it.'

'He attacked you?'

'Well, I didn't get this shiner playing tiddlywinks, Stanley. The thing is, Charlie thinks he's got the only tape but I made a copy.'

'Why?'

'I really don't know,' she lied. 'But you saw him on film snorting the snow, didn't you? If the police got the idea that Chaz found drugs in my flat, got high on the stuff and then fell off the roof, this is my proof that if anyone was into coke and likely to have supplied Chaz it was Charlie Hilton. I want you to keep the tape, Stanley. I think it would be helpful if you had a word with Charlie's agent and gave him a private viewing, spell out the consequences if Charlie tries to throw the blame on me for his son's accident. The boy's been a user for years, broke into my flat to steal knowing there was jewellery and some valuable bits and pieces. Charlie Hilton's a mean bastard, Stanley, kept his son on a barely basic allowance and is in the throes of cheating his wife out of a decent divorce settlement. A word from his agent would shut him up damn quick and, if necessary, you could throw in a sweetener, offer the agent a spot for Charlie on next year's programme at Bucks. Even the Chekhov script Charlie's busting to do.'

'Like hell!'

'Well, I think the pinch would come better from you via his agent. You know him, of course? Sam deLaunay.'

'Yeah, sure.' Stanley sank into deep thought for several bleak moments, his mind racing. 'And you say Charlie blacked your eye?'

'No need to bring that into it unless you have to. And please remember that his wife is one of my best friends – she knows nothing about our little affair. I just know you are the right one to handle it, Stanley, and deLaunay won't be slow to recognize the harm if shots of his client's fun and games got into the papers. What do you say?' This last was spoken with deliberation. No underlining was necessary. If Stanley played the game the full control of Bucks was in his pocket. If he refused to co-operate, Stella's unspoken grudge would scupper her offer and send her shares winging on to the open market.

He locked the tape in his wall safe and poured two stiff whiskies which they silently downed as a clincher of the deal.

Stella rose to go, smiling mischievously, leaving Stanley Kerslake to ponder the complications of handling Anthony's widow, a manipulating bitch of the first order. As he was about to speak they were interrupted by the jangle of her mobile phone.

'Excuse me, Stanley. Yes? Oh, it's you, Monty. I'm on my way. Be with you shortly.'

'No, Stella. Go straight to the clinic. The Rosemoor in Hampstead. I'll meet you there. Morag took Fran in on an emergency and they're keeping her in.'

Stella gasped. 'What happened?'

'A haemorrhage. She'll be OK but it was touch and go for a while. Morag took over, thank God. Everything's under control now but you'd better book into a nearby hotel overnight.'

'She cut her wrists?'

'No! For God's sake, Stella, get a grip. Fran's had some sort of miscarriage. Just get over here as quick as you can.'

Thirty-Three

The Rosemoor Clinic was not easy to find, especially as
Stella was unfamiliar with anywhere north of Oxford Street.
After an anxious exchange at some traffic lights with a taxi
driver, she put her foot down and luckily found a parking space
only twenty yards from the main entrance. It had started to
rain, heavy drops falling from a pewter sky.

The place was strictly anonymous, the blank facade
masquerading as just another elegant house on a quiet street.
Only the discreet brass plate announcing the single word
'Rosemoor' gave a clue to the uninitiated, and that could be
taken as a house name or perhaps, at a pinch, a private drinking
club. Stella's opinion of Monty's girl, Morag, soared. Only a
person on the inside track could have wangled an emergency
admission here.

As she hurried inside she caught a glimpse of Monty
emerging from one of the consulting rooms. She waited in
the foyer while he finished a whispered conversation with a
distinguished-looking ma n in a Savile Row suit. They shook
hands and Monty turned to pick up a raincoat slung over an
armchair in the waiting area. As he was shrugging into his
mac she hurried up to him, grasping his wrist in a painful
grip.

'Monty! What's going on?'

He looked grey, his eyes bloodshot, and impatiently shook
off her hand. 'You'd better come over here where it's quiet.
Morag's gone back to my flat to clean up. She said there was
blood everywhere.'

He pushed her into an alcove adjacent to a kiosk selling
flowers and get-well cards, and they huddled in a corner like
conspirators.

'It's been hell, Stella. That poor kid's been keeping it all to herself for weeks. She dared not tell us and only had that silly little airhead Tiffany to confide in. Says something about you and me, doesn't it?' he said bitterly.

'Don't let's get into the blame game, Monty. How is she?'

'Actually, surprisingly well now the panic's over. Morag found her flat out in my bathroom after I'd gone to work, thought at first it was her appendix or something, but clearly it was worse than that.'

'She hadn't had a backstreet abortion had she?'

'No, all quite spontaneous. Her try with the gin and hot bath routine came to nothing – where do these girls get these crazy ideas from, Stella? Personally, I think the shock of that boyfriend of hers diving off your roof probably did it. The doctor's assured me it was a natural termination and Fran's going to be absolutely fine, thank the Lord.'

'Did she tell Morag who was responsible?'

'I don't think Morag went into details. That wonderful girl acted like lightning once she realized what was going on. She knew of this clinic – her uncle's one of the consultant surgeons here – and got them to take Fran in straight away. And the joy of it is the treatment here is utterly discreet. Expensive, of course, but no one's going to know what happened. I presume you have a private doctor who can check up on Fran later?'

Stella nodded, her pulse steadying. 'Monty, how can I thank you? And Morag? It's a blessing Fran got herself expelled and was at home with you – I doubt whether the school has any experience of such emergencies.'

He rose. 'Look, Stella, I've got to go – I'm due to fly out to Ireland tonight and I can't back out. It's business. Any hope of you letting me have a cheque before the end of the week?'

She looked blank.

'Surely you haven't forgotten? That cash flow problem we talked about – it's fucking urgent, Stell! I can't keep the dogs off much longer.'

'Sorry, Monty, it's been one hell of a week but I'll see what I can do. I have to go back to the cottage in a day or two. I've legal papers to deal with and after that they're expecting you to sign the trust fund documents this week. Shall I ask the solicitor to post them to you?'

'No, I'll come down. You still with that legal firm in Oxford? If I call in there as soon as I get back from Ireland, I'll pop over to see you at Percivals afterwards, shall I? You'll be taking Fran back with you as soon as she's discharged from here?'

'Yes, of course. That sounds a good plan. Give me a call when you expect to be down – I'm still at the beck and call of the police.'

'Oh yes, the Chaz accident. Nothing fishy about it, is there?'

She raised her hands in mute surrender. 'Who knows? They're still banging about in my flat looking for heaven knows what.'

He buttoned his raincoat and they stood forlornly, like people in a departure lounge who had missed their flight. He brushed her cheek with a cold kiss and hurried off, and Stella walked over to Reception to ask the whereabouts of their new patient.

Fran looked small and very vulnerable lying in the hospital bed, her hair spread on the starched pillows, clutching the sheet as Stella burst in. She dropped on to the bed, cradling the child in her arms, tears welling up in an outpouring of relief.

'Fran, my dear, sweet idiot, why didn't you tell me?' The girl vehemently shook her head, the tears splashing from her flushed cheeks. She couldn't speak. Stella rattled on, words tumbling over and over. 'Why, darling? Why let it get so out of hand without getting help? Who did this to you?'

Fran quickly turned away and stretched across to snatch a tissue from a box on the side table. 'It's over now, Mum, let's forget it, shall we? It's been horrible these last few weeks but everything's fine now, apart from poor Chaz . . .' The tears brimmed once more and she sniffled into a tissue.

Stella pulled back, her hand to her mouth, stifling the questions that she was bursting to ask.

Fran blew her nose and squeezed her mother's hand. 'Morag's been terrific. She sorted it out, not a cross word, and I did leave Dad's bathroom in a terrible mess. It was pure luck she turned up like that after he had gone to work. She didn't seem surprised, as if something like that happened all the time – I suppose she's used to foaling horses, eh?' she added with a glimmer of a smile.

'Daddy's a lucky devil – always was. But Fran, sweetie, you must tell me, was Chaz the one . . . ?'

The smile faded. 'You mean the one who raped me? Chaz? No, never. How could he? I only met him a few weeks ago and this,' she said, obliquely looking away again, 'happened when I was sent home after that business of foul-mouthing the maths teacher last term.'

'You were raped?' Stella barked.

Fran's mouth hardened. 'It didn't start out that way, and looking back, I probably asked for it. It was a bloke I got a crush on at Christmas, a lowlife who said he fancied me rotten. I was blown away, that's why I got the tattoo – his favourite flower, he said, and I fell for it.'

'He knows?'

'About this? No, only Chaz and Tiffany knew I'd got myself up the spout, and honestly, Mum, I kept thinking it was just panic, the girls at school were always boasting about never getting caught the first time, and I'd been off my food for weeks and the anorexic bunch in the sixth form said they stopped getting the curse once their weight plummeted. I tried to shove it to the back of my mind but Tiffany pinched a testing kit from her mum's bathroom and we tried it out. I still didn't believe it but I got so crazy I told Chaz and he said he knew a mate of his, a medical student, who could fix me up on the quiet. But it would cost and I had no money.'

'Good God, Fran, are you totally naive? Why try to handle this with only a girlfriend as silly as Tiffany and a freaker like Chaz Hilton to tell you what to do?' Stella leaned forward, forcing Fran to meet her gaze. 'Has this anything to do with you giving Chaz drugs?'

Fran stiffened, her face screwed up in pain. 'Was it my fault he fell, Mummy? Don't tell Dad, but it was me who showed him all that stuff you'd hidden under the bed at home. I heard you talking about it on the phone to Tory and I guessed

144

where it was. You were never very clever at hiding things, were you, Mum?' she said with the ghost of a grin. She blew her nose again, the terrible series of events crowding in to overshadow even her current situation.

'No, of course it wasn't your fault – I was mad keeping that stuff, I should have got rid of it weeks ago. But you trusted Chaz, knowing he was into cocaine?'

'He'd been to detox – he said he was clean. When I went to his birthday party I didn't have a present and I jokingly said I'd give him an IOU, some Es I'd got at home. Showing off, really, pretending to be as streetwise as those other girls at the barbeque. Chaz said Es didn't count, they were just party poppers to get the show on the road and so when he came to the flat, when Tiffany and I were up to town from Lingfield, I showed him your little stash and gave him a few Es as a belated pressie.'

Stella sighed, assessing the terrible damage the silly girl had innocently caused. She nodded for Fran to continue and, having started unravelling the secret, it just spooled out, unstoppable.

'We talked about my needing money to pay his friend to fix things for me and Chaz laughed and said what's the problem when I was sitting on a fortune? A stack of tabs worth a mint to a dealer and he knew how to cash in. But we couldn't do anything then because Pearly was still banging about so he said the best thing would be if he came back later and staged a break-in. That way nobody would get blamed, and you wouldn't say anything about the missing drugs, would you, Mumsy? How was I to know he would get stoned and fall off the roof?'

She started to cry again, her face creased with anguish. Stella distractedly patted her hand. 'Shush now, darling, I've got to think. Have you told anyone else about this? Tiffany?'

'No one. I thought it was just his big talk, and after I'd gone back to school and Chaz didn't ring me on my mobile, I thought he'd chucked me. I was desperate. I told Tiffany nothing about his promise to get me money to pay this friend of his to sort me out but I said I was going to shift the problem myself and she said she would help.'

'Gin and a scalding bath?' Stella scornfully retorted.

'It was all I could think of. Then when I got sent home with Daddy I thought I'd have to tell someone, probably Morag. She's more on my wavelength and wasn't going to get too excited about getting me out of a jam. I think she suspected something was wrong when we were staying at Lingfield. She found the pregnancy test kit and hit the roof, but I guessed she wasn't really fooled. You and Dad treat me like a kid. At least Morag's on the ball.'

'Yes, well, I think we've said enough for now.' She rose, the difficulty of taking a parental stick to the problem complicated by the necessity to keep the lid on the Chaz connection. No point in reducing the girl to hysterics; the important thing was to impress upon her the need to guard her tongue.

'Listen to me, Fran. Stay cool. It's vital that you get well as soon as possible so we get you out of here. You had better come back to the cottage with me as soon as you're discharged and then we must talk about you going back to school. I'll say it was appendix, OK?'

Fran started to weep afresh, her cheeks now blotchy with emotion. 'Can't I go back to Lingfield with Morag? She says I can be a bridesmaid. There's going to be a marquee and everything, and I'm never going to pass those rotten exams, am I?'

Stella paled. Had she lost the girl's confidence completely? An ugly worm of jealousy turned in her stomach. 'Well, we can't go back to the flat just now, and I've business to settle. I'm selling Percivals, Fran. It's settled.'

'Good. Then me going to Lingfield would be the only solution, wouldn't it?' The logic of this was lost on Stella but it would, on reflection, be best to have Fran off the scene, at least until the inquest was over.

'I'll think about it. I'm booking into a hotel nearby for tonight. I'll come and see you again in the morning and I'll have to talk to Daddy about Morag's offer to stay with her in the country. She did invite you, didn't she? You're not making it up?'

The girl nodded energetically, her hair wild. An orderly came in with a supper tray, her black face beaming.

Stella rose and leaned across to whisper in Fran's ear. 'Now, keep all this about Chaz and the drugs between us two, Fran. It's terribly important nothing gets out about your involvement. Don't tell Daddy or Morag and, for heaven's sake, don't talk to Tiffany on the phone. Where is she by the way?'

'Her parents have taken her home. They've arranged for her to go to a crammer in Cambridge. She won't be going back to school – they think I've been a bad influence on her since we got the tattoos. How were we to know it was illegal until you're eighteen? Lots of girls I know have tattoos and the man in the body piercing place didn't ask how old we were.'

'Never mind that, it's too late now anyway. But she won't tell them about you being attacked?'

'Getting raped, you mean? No Tiffany wouldn't dare. We're in enough shit as it is.'

'Right, I'll be off. Eat up and don't worry. Everything's going to come up roses, I promise.'

She hugged her and hurried out to the lift. In the foyer she was about to rush out into the rain when a familiar skinny figure caught her eye, a girl in a plastic mac buying chocolates at the kiosk. Stella stopped dead.

'Tiffany! What are you doing here?'

She spun round, shocked and afraid.

'I slipped out. Had to see poor Fran, didn't I? I rang her on her mobile and that woman picked up. Morag? Said Fran had had an accident and was in here for a bit. No one knows I'm here – I said I was going to the flicks. Is she all right?'

'Absolutely fine, Tiffany, but seeing no one at present. You come with me; I've got to book into that hotel opposite if I can, and I need to have a serious word with you. We'll have some coffee and then I'll put you in a taxi and you go straight home, do you hear me? Fran can't see anyone just now, she'll ring you when she's back home, OK?'

The girl looked scared to death, her cheeks chalky. She always knew Fran's mother was an old cow, but why drag her into it?

Thirty-Four

Next morning Stella spent an hour with Fran. She was up and dressed in jeans and a sweater – sent in by Morag, apparently – and looking surprisingly chipper.

'Hey, look at you! So much better than last night. Sleep well?'

'Oh, they gave me some stuff. Decent of Morag to buy me some new jeans and a nightie, wasn't it? I suppose she binned my others,' she added with a sigh. Stella privately decided that Morag was a bloody miracle and wondered how this superwoman would cope with Monty's disorganized lifestyle.

Stella produced some chocolates and a bunch of teen magazines, snatching off her sunglasses to have a proper look at her daughter.

'What happened to your eye, Mum?'

Stella's hand flew to her cheekbone; she had forgotten the telltale bruises. 'Oh, nothing – just bumped myself tidying up the cottage.'

'Doesn't Jimmy do that?'

She took a deep breath. 'Actually, I'm giving Jimmy the push. I've passed his keys on to Tory. I didn't fancy him nosing round when I'm not there.' She paused. 'It was Jimmy who persuaded you to get the tattoo, wasn't it?'

Fran jolted, her eyes on stalks. 'You guessed?'

'He said something about wild roses being his favourite flower and later it clicked. A leap in the dark, but it *was* him, wasn't it?'

The girl scowled, her alarm breaking into a familiar obduracy. Her face darkened. 'For goodness' sake let it go, Mumsy. I don't want to talk about it.'

Stella knew her well enough to drop it for the present and

changed tack. 'I spoke to the school secretary this morning and I've got an appointment with the head next week. You might as well take your exams, darling, it's only a matter of weeks before the end of term. Think about it. We can make plans for September later – you might like to go abroad for a year, improve your French.'

'I can't. There's the wedding in October.'

'Ah, yes. The wedding. I forgot. Well, there's no rush to decide.'

Their exchange flowed into calmer water after that and an hour later Stella rose to go. 'I have to get back to Percivals tonight and I must go and see Kate this afternoon. Tory's staying with her but I've been too busy to go round again. Will you be all right if I don't pop back after tea?'

'Daddy's away in Ireland.'

'Yes, I know. Can you manage for a day or two? The doctor said you're to stay here till Friday. I hate abandoning you like this but there's a lot for me to arrange about the sale of the cottage. Still, I'm hoping to get back into the flat very soon. I'll phone you tonight. Anything you need?'

'I expect Morag will drop in later.'

They parted on good terms and Stella checked out of the hotel. She drove back to the flat, anxious to clear up some unfinished business.

The plastic police tape cordoning off the basement had been removed and the builders had resumed work, which was a good sign. The main door stood open, a constable seated in the hall. He scrambled to his feet as she hurried in.

'Mrs Buckleigh! WPC Atkins is upstairs, she's been waiting to see you.'

'Oh, right.' Bloody hell, did she have to account for her every movement now?

She let herself into the flat and found the same young policewoman who had accompanied Chivers before, tapping away at a laptop on the dining-room table. She got up with a rush, sending a pile of forms cascading to the floor.

'Mrs Buckleigh. Good. DI Chivers wanted to have a word with you but couldn't find out where you'd gone – your mobile was dead. He wants you to call in at the station.'

Stella petulantly threw down her bag. 'Me? Why?'

'You haven't had your fingerprints taken yet.'

'So?'

The girl looked embarrassed. 'Actually, it's just routine. One of the builders identified the bit of torn tee shirt we found caught on the scaffolding, so the chances of anyone else being with the young man when he broke in are slim.'

Stella sighed. 'Would you like some tea? I've been visiting my daughter in hospital and had to turn off my phone. I'm sorry the inspector lost touch. My fault, I just didn't think . . . I came back for some clean clothes.'

The officer smiled, a nice smile at that. 'Shall I make the tea while you pack a bag? I'll let the inspector know you're here, shall I?'

Stella hurried upstairs and withdrew the weekend case which was still under the bed. She thrust some clean undies on top of the woollens that had hidden Stefan's drugs haul and snapped shut the catches. It was important to sneak the damn case right off the premises in case the forensic boys decided to take a second look round. It was a miracle the case had not been searched before this, and although Chaz had taken all the drugs, for all she knew those clever forensic boffins could sniff out residual evidence from the other contents . . .

She ran downstairs and pushed the case under the hall table before trailing into the kitchen.

'Oh, tea! Wonderful. You must get used to finding your way round strange kitchens in your job.'

The girl laughed, passing Stella a nicely steaming cup. The doorbell shrilled. Stella jumped up but the WPC forestalled her. 'It'll be the inspector, I phoned through to say you were here. I'll let him in, shall I? He left your spare keys with me. I expect you can have them back now the flat has been checked over.'

Chivers entered with a swagger and Stella marvelled at the notion of this unprepossessing man partnering her own police contact in Renham, Chief Inspector Roger Hayes. Talk about chalk and cheese.

'Ah, Mrs Buckleigh. We've finished here, sorry to inconvenience you. Nothing new turned up and I think we can safely assume our poor young man was acting alone. No need to trouble you further, though I shall want a formal statement from you. And if you could follow me back to the station this morning, I can put a report together and expedite matters for the coroner.'

'Yes, of course. What did the pathologist conclude, or is that information on the secret list until the inquest?'

Chivers waxed expansive. That a run-of-the-mill case of a kid falling from a roof in Belgravia following a break-in should turn into a front-page story involving a film star was a real bonus. Put him on the telly for a start, a chance to be in the news on what would normally have been a very small item of media interest. He joined the two women at the kitchen table.

'In the strictest confidence, Mrs Buckleigh, the young man in question had a cocaine level of 1.36mg per litre in his body, potentially fatal, provoking a cocaine-induced delirium.'

'Good grief!'

'The toxicologist traced other substances which added up to an explosive cocktail of drugs. No wonder the poor lad thought he could fly.'

Stella gulped, visibly shaken by this dry scientific assessment of Chaz's hallucinatory death fall.

Chivers patted her hand. 'Don't you worry about all this, Mrs Buckleigh. We'll be out from under your feet now and once you've signed your statement it's best if you put the whole sorry incident from your mind.'

He stood and silently indicated to his pretty sidekick that she should get herself back in line. She jumped up and hurried off to collect her laptop and notes from the dining room.

Stella followed Chivers into the hall. 'Just one small thing, Inspector. Can I pick your brains? Rape?'

That brought him up short. 'You want to report a r–rape,' he stuttered.

'Oh no. It's not personal. But a friend of mine has a young protégée, only fifteen years old, who was raped a couple of months ago. She wants to persuade the child to bring charges.'

'How old did you say?'

'Fifteen.'

'Well, that depends. The police cannot bring proceedings without a complaint from the victim if she is over thirteen years old. It's a traumatic experience for a young girl even when the court allows anonymity. Needs serious consideration, Mrs Buckleigh.'

'Yes, of course. I'll mention it to my friend. It's a delicate situation for anyone, let alone a child, but it seems diabolical that so many of these paedophiles get away with it.'

He nodded sagely, and motioned to the WPC to get her skates on. 'Nice meeting you, Mrs Buckleigh. If I'm not at the station when you call in you can formalize your statement with my sergeant. Your house keys are on the table here.'

'Oh, thank you. I'll be right along, Inspector Chivers. Just as soon as I've finished sorting out a few phone calls.'

She closed the door and listened for the lift descending before pulling the weekend case from under the hall table and emptying the woollens into a rubbish bag to take back to the cottage. The case would have to be disposed of too, but that would not be a problem once she got everything out of London. She repacked the case with fresh clothes and locked it in the boot of her car together with the bin bag. She smiled at the constable who had moved out on to the front steps since his inspector had put in an appearance, but his curious stare was really the least of her worries.

Thirty-Five

Stella picked up a gift-wrapped bunch of yellow roses for Kate before driving to the house and, with some trepidation, rang the bell.

Tory answered. 'Hi, Stella, I've been worried about you. Come in. Kate's out but she should be back soon. Have you had lunch?'

Stella followed her into the living room and dropped the roses on a cluttered coffee table. 'For Kate,' she said, pausing to take in the comfortable disorder of Kate's normally ultra-neat home. Clearly, Tory had taken charge of housekeeping while the crisis played itself out. 'How is she?'

'Jittery since Charlie arrived on the scene.'

'Charlie's here? In London?'

'Arrived yesterday. You haven't heard from him?'

'Not a word. The skunk should have phoned me, but, then again, my mobile's been off more often than on lately. Fran's in hospital.'

'No! What happened?'

'An accident of sorts. Any chance of a stiff drink, Tory? I've just been to the flat.'

'You poor darling. Here, come down to the kitchen. You look terrible, Stella.'

Tory herself looked pretty wonderful in fact, her hair sleeked back in a ponytail tied with a silk scarf, long legs striding ahead in cut-off jeans.

Downstairs in the basement kitchen, she poured a generous slug of whisky and pushed Stella on to the sofa pulled up to the Aga where she sat clutching the tumbler, shivering with what Tory could only guess to be shock. It was odd seeing Stella all shaken up. Obviously Chaz falling from her roof had pierced her normal self-control but there must be something else. Something else had occurred since the accident to affect her so. She waited for Stella to stop shaking.

'Now, tell me. What happened to Fran?'

'She's been raped,' Stella blurted out. 'Months ago it seems, when Fran was on suspension from school for swearing at a teacher.'

'Poor, sweet kid.'

'Oh, it gets worse. Nobody knew except a dopey girlfriend at school and Chaz.'

'Chaz? He wasn't the one, surely?'

'No! But she confided in him because she needed an abortion.'

Tory fell back, her face ashen. 'Chaz put her on to an abortionist?'

'No – and you must never tell Kate about this – the shock of Chaz killing himself probably sparked a spontaneous miscarriage, though she and the other girl tried to fix the problem with various stupid efforts, so it was more likely a combination of events. Poor Fran was distraught when the news broke about Chaz. She was staying with Monty at the time, thank goodness, having been suspended from school yet again. Monty's girlfriend saved the day – got her admitted to a private clinic in Hampstead as soon as she started haemorrhaging.'

'Fran's there now? How is she?'

'Physically great. Mentally, still traumatized by it all. She's begging to stay on with Monty at Morag's parents' place in the country, and, on balance, I think it might be best for the time being.'

Tory emptied her wine glass and stared at the dishevelled figure hunched close to the Aga. Suddenly, Stella looked up, her eyes wide.

'Where's Katie? Charlie's not coming back with her, is he?'

'They've gone to identify the body.'

'Good God. Is that wise? Surely poor Chaz is all smashed up.'

Tory shrugged. 'Charlie offered to go alone but Kate

154

insisted on saying a last goodbye to the poor darling. Anyway, as Charlie hasn't clapped eyes on Chaz for three years at least, he probably wouldn't be an adequate witness. He's determined to rush the whole thing through to get himself off the headlines and stop this media circus. He's even persuaded the authorities to speed things up, so the coroner is releasing the body for burial on Friday. You will come, won't you? The funeral's to be held in York. Charlie's got a family plot there apparently, and, believe it or not, Lola Lopez, Chaz's mother, says she's coming. Can you believe it? These people astonish me. She hasn't seen her son for ten years or more and suddenly wants to get in the picture.'

'Publicity chasing,' Stella muttered dryly. 'But I can't come, Tory. All being well, Fran's being discharged from the clinic on Friday. I shall have to be in London.'

'You're leaving her there alone till Friday?'

'Got to. No choice. I'm selling the cottage, Tory. There's a pile of urgent legal papers to sign dealing with Fran's trust fund apart from the house sale. Funnily enough, Rob Allinson's handling it – he happens to be with my solicitors' firm in Oxford. Small world, eh?'

Stella's hands had steadied as she lit a cigarette and finally relaxed. Tory busied herself making sandwiches and coffee and for a pleasant half-hour they almost found themselves forgetting the current problems and chattering away like starlings about Tory's new job at the gardening school in Renham.

Glancing at her watch, Stella rose. 'Sorry, love, but I've got to go. Tell Kate I'm sorry to have missed her, but, between you and me, I'm keen to escape a face to face with Charlie in the circumstances. How did he seem?'

'Bad-tempered more than upset. Cross with the way the press have dragged his name into a hyped-up version of "Son of star in drug-fuelled death fall", and so on.'

'How is he with Kate?'

'Well, she didn't merit a black eye,' she retorted with a sly grin. 'All sweetness and light. Losing Chaz seems to have galvanized Charlie into settling all his affairs in England –

he's even been in touch with Rob, promising to finalize the divorce. Kate's quite touched by all this belated consideration and seems to think everything can be amicably settled. At least the house is all hers now, the ghastly windfall of surviving Charlie's son, so even if his temporary bout of generosity comes to nothing she can sell up here and be very comfortable financially.'

They went upstairs and Stella collected up her things and prepared to leave.

'OK if I leave my car at the cottage for a few more days?' Tory asked.

'Yes, of course. Whenever you like. You've got keys if I'm not there; make yourself at home.'

'Wouldn't you like your keys back now you're selling Percivals?'

'No rush. I must go, Tory, my car's on a meter.'

'Just one small thing. I hate to ask this, Stella, but you *did* destroy Stefan's drugs, didn't you? The ones you found in his desk?'

Stella's heart missed a beat. 'Yes! Yes, of course. My pharmacist friend took custody, all legal and above board. He has some procedure for disposing of medication handed in from bereaved relatives. Makes you wonder if there isn't rampant over-prescribing in the NHS, all these tablets and potions stacked up in medicine cupboards unused. What made you ask?'

Tory looked embarrassed. 'Oh, it's nothing. Just a niggle about something Kate got annoyed about. She's convinced herself the police have been inefficient over Chaz's belongings and mixed up stuff belonging to another case. For a start, when they showed her his things there was this ski cap, nothing to do with Chaz at all, and why should it be? A ski cap in early summer? Talk about Mr Plod and the casual way they handle things! And the stuff they found in his pockets – cocaine, Es, you name it – was stuff Kate knew he had been hooked on before, but not the crack.'

'Crack?'

'A lump of crack cocaine wrapped in a chocolate paper, she said. She swears Chaz never used crack and it struck me that one of Stefan's boys at the addiction clinic handed him just that – he showed it to me. I'd never seen crack before, you see, and I was curious.'

Stella tittered. 'Perhaps they buy it from dealers ready gift-wrapped in sweetie papers? We're out of the loop on this one, Tory, believe me. Forget it. Stefan's stuff was discreetly dealt with weeks ago.'

Tory grinned. 'Yes, sure. But you know how silly things like that stick in your mind. Go round and round in the small hours. Just as if there wasn't enough to worry about.'

'Tory, could I ask a favour? If you're free for an hour or two this week, could you pop in and visit Fran for me? She's at the Rosemoor Clinic in Hampstead, it's in the book. I can't fit in another visit before Friday.'

'Yes, sure. I'd love to. I'll ring first and see if she needs anything. You'll be at the cottage?'

'Till the weekend at least. Later I'm hoping to get back to the flat now that the police have finished turning the place over.'

She waved goodbye from the kerb and sped off, anxious to avoid a confrontation with Charlie Hilton on Kate's doorstep.

Thirty-Six

She obediently called at the police station to register her statement. It took only fifteen minutes, Chivers' sergeant clearly having more important paperwork waiting on his desk. Stella hurried out, breathing the balmy afternoon air with relief: now she could get right away and leave Chivers to pick up the pieces.

As she was unlocking her car she felt a hand on her shoulder. She spun round.

'Charlie!'

He wore a black fedora, the wide brim shading a very stern expression, his lips thin with suppressed rage.

'Don't think you can run out on me, Stella. Let's take a walk, there's a pub round the corner. We have to talk.'

'Have you been following me?' she retorted, angrily shaking him off.

'I've been dragged here by Chivers just like you. Kate went home. She's very upset, we've just been to the mortuary.'

Stella drew back. 'Tory mentioned it. I'm really sorry, Charlie. Poor Chaz.'

He took her arm more firmly this time. 'Lock your car, I'll put more money in the meter and we can sort this out.'

Stella reluctantly allowed herself to be marched to a dismal hostelry in a backstreet behind the station, the sort of shabby place she imagined Chivers might use to shake down his informants, but hardly a watering hole either Charlie Hilton or she would preferably frequent.

The pub had just reopened and an invitation to partake of the special terms of cocktail hour had yet to bring in the customers. Only one barfly had established himself and was holding a whispered conversation with the barmaid, but, as no sunshine percolated the dim interior, if Charlie planned to avoid recognition this was hardly the venue to attract any fans. He propelled her to a corner table and ordered two double whiskies. No water, no ice and certainly no cocktails.

Stella lit a cigarette to calm her nerves, wondering if Charlie had already got the bad news from his agent about a second videotape surfacing. He sipped his drink and laid his hat on the velvet banquette, eyeing Stella with undisguised malevolence.

'You can't blame me for Chaz's accident, Charlie. He was an addict, Kate's been telling you that for years.'

'Oh, can't I? How do I know how you attract your toy boys? Do you have to pay them these days, Stella? Or do nice-looking young guys get baited to your penthouse with an enticing menu. Coke? Crack? Es? Heroin? Or plain old cash in hand?'

158

'Don't be stupid, Charlie! I don't have to bribe a man into my bed and I certainly had no sort of relationship with Chaz. I hardly knew the boy, for God's sake. If he was familiar with my flat it was through my daughter, my fifteen-year-old daughter, who was dazzled by the attentions of a chap who used her to break into my property. Chaz was probably looking for something to pay off his dealer with and thought my place was an easy target.'

'But we know different, don't we, Stella? You had a supply of cocaine on tap.'

'You didn't tell Chivers that, surely?' she gasped.

He frowned. 'No. Kate doesn't know about us and shouting the odds to the police wouldn't do either of us any good. But he was my son, Stella! As soon as I heard he'd been searching your flat, the ready availability of drugs was a natural conclusion to jump to and I've been stewing on it for days.'

'Then why didn't you return my calls?'

'I had to sort it out in my head first. In the end I'm ashamed to say I chose to save my own skin and keep my mouth shut. I thought no one could possibly find out about our silly games, and dragging both of us into a legal minefield would only bring us both down.' He sighed. 'I decided to play by your rules, Stella, and signed up to a fitting divorce settlement for Kate. And then you play dirty anyway and pass a copy of the videotape, which you assured me didn't exist, to my bloody agent!'

'You gambled and lost, Charlie. I got frightened and you had more to lose than I.'

'Yes, sure I did. And how! I'm no saint, Stella, but I'm not in your league when it comes to evil double-dealing. Why bounce that tape to deLaunay? Why scotch any notion of furthering my stage career by blackballing me with Kerslake? What harm have I ever done you? Why film the weekend in the first place and then lie to me about copies?'

'Because I don't trust you, Charlie Hilton. If you even think of causing me any trouble over Chaz's death I'll blow you right out of the water, see if I don't.'

The temperature of the row might have escalated, but the

vituperative exchange was conducted in frigid undertones, their mutual hatred as wounding as frostbite.

He downed his whisky, eyeing her narrowly, assessing the power of the vice in which he was held. The icy silence grew and Stella judged their combat to be evenly matched. Charlie dare not accuse her of supplying Chaz and could never prove it, whereas she had the video which both Kerslake and Charlie's agent knew could be a killer blow to his career if ever it got out. To be seen as a sybaritic fantasist was bad but not exactly unknown in Hollywood and not insurmountable, given the right publicity spin. But to be the butt of ribald jokes would be a tag no actor could laugh off, especially one who had built his career on romantic leads.

He quickly replaced the fedora as a young crowd burst into the bar, their laughter lifting the atmosphere of the seedy surroundings like a ray of sunshine.

She rose and started to leave but he grabbed her wrist. The barmaid watched their bitter exchange from her vantage point, worrying at the niggling suspicion that the bloke in the fancy trilby was somehow familiar, a face she just couldn't put a name to. It would come to her later . . .

'Don't think you've got away with this, Stella. I haven't finished with you yet. Once the funeral's over I'll come back for you, just see if I don't.'

She laughed, pushing him away. 'Get that line from a script, Charlie? Sounds like something from that last film of yours – the one the critics panned.'

She strode out with a spring in her step, leaving him to stand aside while the cocktail hour punters shoved their way to the bar.

Stella drove back to the cottage with the devil at her heels, lucky to escape a speed trap. As she slowed down to negotiate the ruts of the lane leading to Percivals, she pulled over to let Bossom's lorry pass. He braked hard and scrambled down from the cab. She sighed, knowing all too well what the boring old fart would be on about.

She wound down the window and languidly asked, 'Yes, Mr Bossom? Something wrong?'

'This business of the surveyors measuring up my sheep

field. There's talk in the village that you're selling up, Mrs Buckleigh. Ain't true, is it?'

''Fraid so, Mr Bossom. An offer I can't refuse as they say. It's to be turned back to agricultural use – organic.' She revved up, judging how much room she had to get by.

His face reddened. 'Me and my brother would be interested in your land, Mrs Buckleigh, and the farmhouse too if the price is right. We was born there, you know.'

'So I heard. Very nice. I'm afraid it's all settled, Mr Bossom, but I'm sure the new owners would be interested to hear any proposition you have in mind. Now, if you will excuse me, I'm expecting a phone call from my daughter at seven and it's nearly that now.' He grabbed the open window, the smell of his hot breath causing her to wrinkle her nose. 'Sorry, Mr Bossom, I've got to go.'

She tried to shut the window but he held on fast.

'Just five minutes of your time, Mrs Buckleigh. You don't know about us folks, we can top any offer from any commercial farmer. I'll bring some figures round, shall I?'

'Too late, Mr Bossom. It's all settled, like I said. Now, please let me pass.'

She revved the engine and inched forward, scraping the offside on the hawthorn hedge as she forced her way past. He clung on for a moment but she sped up and managed to get through, watching in her rear-view mirror as the stout figure receded into the dusk.

Tory's car was still on the drive and the house lights had lit up on the timing device, giving the cottage an air of welcome. She lifted the suitcase from the boot of the car and hurried inside, the red glow of the CCTV camera winking away like a sentinel. Once inside she bolted up firmly and lit the fire for company. Percivals might not be her first choice of home but at least it was a safe distance from Charlie Hilton and the bloody Chivers man.

That night she slept fitfully, dreaming of being adrift in a rowing boat of all things, adrift on a dark lake under a moonless sky.

Thirty-Seven

Next morning she went to the study to make a couple of phone calls.

'Hello, Kate. How are you? I missed you when I called in but Tory filled me in with the news.'

'Yes, Charlie's managed to speed things up and he's arranged the funeral for Friday. In York. Did Tory tell you?'

'Yes. It's all been such a terrible shock, I can't imagine how you must feel, but at least, Tory says, Charlie's being supportive for once.'

'Mmm. Must have knocked him sideways. He's even agreed to my lawyer's terms and I'm to get a generous settlement which will let me make a fresh start. Oh, the roses! Thank you, Stella, it was sweet of you, a lovely thought. Tory's been an absolute brick, can't think how I would have coped without her. She's staying till Sunday. Can you come to York on Friday?'

'I'm terribly sorry, Kate, but I've arranged to pick up Fran from hospital that day. Did Tory tell you about her emergency?'

'Not really. I'll have to wait to see you to get the full story. But she is all right, isn't she?'

'Absolutely fine. Kids recover overnight having given one terrible frights, don't they? We'll get together soon, Kate. When the dust settles. I'm taking Fran to the country to recuperate and then I'm packing up at Percivals as best I can.'

'You're really selling the cottage? What a shame, just when Tory's moving into the area. But running two homes must be expensive, I bet.'

'I just decided I'd had enough of weekending in muddy

boots for most of the year. Is there anything I can do for you, Kate?'

'No, I'm being fussed over by Tory and Charlie's taken charge of the funeral arrangements. Where are you?'

'At the cottage. Did Tory mention that Rob Allinson's dealing with my conveyancing? Fancy that. Now he's transferred to Oxford he's taken over my affairs.'

'Swop! He's passed me over to a colleague of his at the London office just when my wrangling with Charlie is coming up trumps. I hope he gets the credit. Nice chap, I hope to keep in touch.'

'Well, he's likely to move in with Mervyn at the garden school eventually, so Tory will be on the spot too. Why don't you relocate to Renham if you decide to move out of London? It's a nice little market town and you did say you wanted a fresh start.'

'It's worth thinking about. Oh hell, there's someone at the door. I'll have to go, Stella. I'll ring you after the funeral and we can fix a lunch. I'm working part-time at the boutique at present, they've been so accommodating since Chaz hit the headlines. Poor lamb, he didn't deserve such a ghastly end.' She started to weep, her words blurring as she hastily broke the connection.

Stella sat back, mulling over the advisability of keeping in touch with Kate. Wouldn't her brief affair with Charlie eventually seep out? Murky secrets like that, especially those involving girlfriends, were never really buried, were they?

She thrust those dark thoughts aside and rang Rob Allinson at his office to arrange an appointment.

'Would Thursday afternoon suit you, Stella? About four? You can leave your car at the back. Mr Shoesmith's parking space is free while he's on holiday and it would save you using the park-and-ride or a taxi.'

'Great. Are the papers ready to sign?'

'The trust fund amendments have been approved by one of the senior bods here, but the sale of the cottage is still in the pipeline. But you should settle the trust fund without further delay, Stella. Mr Shoesmith left instructions for me not to drag my feet now we have finally got a new trustee.'

'Yes, sure. Till tomorrow then? Thanks Rob.'

She decided to have a little tour of the garden to try to gather her thoughts about leaving. What would Anthony have thought about it, Percivals being so special to him? Stella strolled through the orchard and finally stopped by the boundary fence to watch Bossom's lambs, now quite big but still frolicking the way lambs are supposed to do, making a bucolic picture framed by the far woods and a limpid sky. Well, Anthony was long gone, poor darling, and Stefan too. Perhaps the two of them would come to haunt the cleared fields and woods once the organic people had changed the landscape. With Percivals razed and the orchard cut down, this scene would never be the same again. She sighed, wondering if this watershed in her life had been preordained by some malevolent gods who had decided to give Stella's safe little world a volcanic eruption.

Her mood darkened as she spied Jimmy Thompson coming towards her. No point in putting it off. The confrontation with Fran's rapist was now inevitable, however much Fran might wish the whole traumatic incident dead and buried.

She caught up with him at the back door. 'Come inside, Jimmy. Leave that. We've got something to discuss.'

He wore a torn rugger shirt and jeans tucked into heavy boots. His tanned face looked solemn, the prospect of the rumoured sell-up putting his job on the line. He followed her inside, parking his boots on the step. Stella watched him lope towards the kettle, his loose, easy stride underlining the latent strength of a man conditioned to heavy work.

'Leave the kettle, Jimmy, I'm in no mood for coffee. Sit down if you like.'

Her tone rang like a warning bell but he stood his ground. 'Yeah? What's on your mind then?'

'My daughter, principally. You raped her, Jimmy Thompson, and I'll have you banged up for it.'

His face hardened. 'Silly little bint's having you on, missus. Me? I've hardly set eyes on the kid for weeks.'

'Exactly. You attacked her when she was here in the spring. She got pregnant, you fucking oaf.'

He whistled. 'Not me. Not on my baby's life, I swear it,

Mrs Buckleigh. What made you think it was me?'

'I *know* it was you. The tattoo, the wild rose, all part of your sweet talk, Jimmy.' She backed away, suddenly afraid. 'Now clear out of here and don't come back. We will be seeing the police in Renham next week, as soon as Fran's discharged from hospital, and they'll know where to find you.'

She leaned against the dresser and, for a brief moment, it seemed as if he was about to strike her. But his mouth set firmly and he lowered his fist.

'Just you try and prove it. That kid of yours is a born liar and standing up in court making accusations will take more spunk than she's ever had.'

He strode out, shoving his feet back in the boots and clumping away round the side of the building.

Stella slammed the door and locked it, her hands shaking. Was there any point in threatening the man? The chances of Fran bringing an official complaint after all this time and pinning the blame on Thompson was dicey to say the least, even if he did have a dodgy reputation with the police. Even so, it would do him good to sweat on it.

Later it occurred to her that warning him of her intention had been a dangerous move. Wouldn't it have been safer to register a complaint first and let the police handle it? With understandable rancour among the villagers at the prospect of jobs being lost if Percivals and its tenanted fields were passed to one of the agricultural big boys, her popularity in Bramley Green was probably zero without accusing one of the locals of rape.

Revenge could be ugly. If it was confirmed that Percivals was to be dismantled and the land flattened for redevelopment, Jimmy Thompson could earn much kudos from his drinking pals in the Crown if he set fire to the cottage with that bloody Mrs Buckleigh inside. Good riddance?

Stella shivered. She was letting her imagination run riot. She cheered herself up by phoning Fran, who sounded chirpy as a cricket and busting to rejoin Morag and the horses.

'I'll fetch you about eleven, OK? Then we'll do some shopping and have a nice lunch before driving down to Lingfield. I hope you know the way, I'm hopeless with maps.'

Thirty-Eight

That night Stella got a call on her mobile from Charlie Hilton. A very apologetic Charlie Hilton, his voice low and at its most seductive.

'Stella. Forgive me. I behaved like a perfect pig yesterday. I can only offer my apologies – it was the stress of seeing my boy's body all smashed up. I'm really sorry. Can we meet? At the weekend? Saturday night?'

'I shall be in London on Friday.'

'That's impossible – the funeral.'

'Oh yes. Sorry, I forgot. Actually, I may have to be here at the cottage at the weekend and would welcome some company. Are we friends again?'

'Of course. I'm flying back to Paris early on Sunday but we could get together for an hour or two when I get back from York. Say about nine on Saturday? Can't stay, I'm afraid, but it would be lovely to see you, Stella darling.'

Stella felt this last endearment sounded a little hollow after the bitter exchange in the pub. 'OK, let's do that. Nothing new has turned up, has it, Charlie? Kate hasn't found out about us?'

'No! No, of course not. Kate's still deep in despair about poor Chaz. Me, I don't register with her just now.'

'Whew. Well, that's a relief. I suppose you will try to talk me round to square things with Stanley Kerslake.'

'Well, it would be wonderful if you could, old dear.'

'Not so much of the "old", Charlie. As it happens, Stanley's keen to keep me sweet just now. I'm selling my shares in Bucks and Stanley hopes to get first option. If I say it would be nice if he could see his way to offer you a contract on the Chekhov, I think he might just fall for it. How about your agent? Does deLaunay want you to pursue this stage-struck obsession of yours?'

'Why not? You suggesting I'm past it, Stella?'

She laughed. 'Heaven forbid. And if you do pop in for a drink on Saturday night, don't come armed with a brick. My eye's still bruised from before and I won't take kindly to having my place trashed a second time. Two video cameras in smithereens – not to mention crystal glasses and a stained rug. You owe me, Charlie.'

She rang off with a gleam of satisfaction. Really, Charlie wasn't so bad. A bit of a rough house but it made a change from her nice predictable pharmacist.

The thing about Charlie was that he was such a chameleon: one minute a clubby English gent, the next pure L.A. Personally, she thought he took gobbets of old film scripts and threw them into his own chat-up lines for a bit of local colour.

Next day she drove into Oxford to keep her appointment at the lawyer's office. She was shown straight in. Rob jumped to his feet, holding out both hands in greeting.

'Stella! You're early. Here, sit down, I'll just get these letters signed and be with you in two ticks. Would you like some tea?'

'Lovely. Yes please. Parking at your back lot was such a help – I just whizzed through. Do you mind if I smoke?'

'No, go ahead. Just bear with me while I deal with this correspondence.'

Stella lit up and relaxed, pondering on the terrier-like grip in which Rob Allinson had held fast for Kate's divorce settlement. He really didn't look the part, a mild-looking young man, quite handsome but one would never imagine him swimming with the divorce-lawyer sharks.

The girl came in for the post and Rob asked her to bring some tea. 'China? Or tea bag, Stella? We cater for all tastes.'

'Weak, no milk and no sugar, but chocolate bikkies please as I'm such a favourite client.'

When the tea ceremony was over, Rob got straight down to business, reading through the brief amendments to the trust fund. 'It's just as you wished, Stella, including the top-up sum to be made available to Mr Neville if, God forbid, you pre-deceased him before Frances reached her majority.'

'Fine. Where do I sign?'

'No questions?'

'No, I know Monty too well to leave any loopholes allowing him to bleed Fran's inheritance.'

'Well, if you're happy, you sign here and here, but I'll get Suzie in to witness. OK? I've arranged for Mr Neville to countersign tomorrow.'

He rang for his secretary who obliged without so much as a glance at the blonde lady friend of their new junior partner.

'Is that it?' Stella asked.

'Absolutely. But I'm afraid I shall have to call on you again as soon as the sale contract comes to the boil. You'll be at the cottage for the foreseeable future?'

'On and off. I have to go to London tomorrow. My daughter's been ill; I'm taking her to stay with friends in the country to recuperate.'

'You too?'

'No. As a matter of fact the friend is my ex-husband's fiancée whose people have a stud farm near Lingfield racecourse. Fran's staying there with them on her own.'

'Mr Neville? He's marrying again?'

'Mmm. A nice little filly called Morag. I hope she can cope. He's not exactly the most credit-worthy character in the world but I gather she has money, so it should all work out fine – and he loves Fran to bits. Fortunately, she seems to get on well with Morag so I'm letting her stay with Morag's folks for a bit. Monty's away a lot so I gather Morag mostly lives at home with the parents at present. There's a flurry of wedding bells in the offing, so Fran is quite excited about it.'

'Sounds good. But how do you feel about it?'

'A bit dog in the manager to tell you the truth, but Fran's not a baby, I can't tie her down for ever.' Stella rose and leaned across to peck his cheek. 'Don't get up – I'll see myself out, I know you're busy.'

'You sure? Perhaps we'll meet at the weekend? Tory's coming back on Sunday afternoon. I said I'd meet her at the station and drive her over to the cottage.'

'Of course! Her car's still at my place. Yes, pop in, do – I'm dying to hear how Tory got on in York.'

Stella hurried out, breezing through the outer office, catching the fascinated gaze of two typists and the post boy. Outside, she all but collided with a tall guy wearing chinos and a denim jacket and, for a moment, she almost didn't recognize him.

'Roger Hayes! What are you doing off your beat?'

He laughed, showing teeth as gleaming as Charlie's except his had not been lavished with expensive cosmetic dentistry.

'Mrs Buckleigh.'

'Stella.'

'Stella. Great to see you. I was worried about you – thought your cottage had been turned over.'

'Yes, your colleague, Inspector Chivers, said you'd peeped in and realized there had been some partying going on.'

'Some party!'

'Yes, well, it did get a bit out of hand. Oh hell, I've just remembered. I should have brought that fancy-dress gear back to the hire shop while I was here in Oxford. Damn! It'll have to wait till next week now; I'm back to London in the morning. Hey, you look very "plain clothes" if I may say so. You working under cover, Chief Inspector?' she said with a wicked grin.

'No. I took the day off. My girlfriend's organized a charity concert for Midsummer Night and I said I'd help. She dropped me off at the printers this morning to collect the tickets and programmes and I've been doing the college circuit flogging them. You remember Pippa, don't you? You met her at Easter.'

'Yes, of course I do. The girl who works at the Festival box office. Actually, I'm off home now, would you like a lift?'

'I was planning to catch a train back to Renham but a lift would be terrific. You sure? No shopping?'

'No shopping. Do I look like such a retail junkie? No, don't answer that. I've got a parking spot at the back of this office. Come on, it's starting to rain.'

She unlocked the car and tossed the video camera off the passenger seat into the back to let him in.

'You shouldn't leave things like that in view while you're parked, Stella. It's just asking for trouble.'

She clicked her seat belt and reversed out of the narrow space. 'Yes, I know, but I'm a careless cow by nature, Roger, the bane of the security brigade.'

'Still, I did notice you'd installed surveillance stuff at the cottage. CCTV. Good for you.'

She grinned. 'You can't say I ignore your professional advice all the time then. Now, tell me about this concert.'

'It's in aid of a leukaemia charity. I thought I might twist the arm of your friend at the gardening school, see if he could sell a few tickets to his students.'

'Good idea. Read out the programme.'

He rattled through a nicely balanced programme but at the mention of a Chopin rhapsody she looked sharply across at him. 'You're playing?'

He nodded. 'The problem is a girlfriend with a wicked arm lock. Pippa's arranged for me to practise on the only tuned-up Bechstein in Renham. God knows I'm rusty as hell, but the good news is I'm cheap.'

'Congratulations. Tory will sell stacks of tickets for you – she's brilliant at it. Tory's my friend who's working at the gardening place, helping Mervyn. She's a lovely girl. If you postpone your sales talk till next week she'll be back from London. The poor boy who fell from my roof is being buried in York tomorrow and Tory's supporting his stepmother, who is naturally devastated by the ghastly accident. Still, it *was* an accident and Chivers assures me the coroner's not going to haggle over the verdict.'

'Hope not.'

She braked at traffic lights and regarded him solemnly. 'Roger. As you're in mufti and it's your day off, can I ask your advice? Off the record? As a friend?'

'You're not worried about the inquest, are you?'

'No, it's a personal matter. Roger, my daughter was raped.'

Thirty-Nine

'Shall we pull over and talk?' Hayes quietly suggested.

'No. It's all right. I think better when I'm driving.' She paused, wondering how far she could trust this policeman but, fuelled by an insupportable anger, she pressed on. 'I only found out about this a few days ago. Fran became pregnant and was too frightened to confide in any of us. I was filled with outrage, as any mother would be, and confronted the man, threatening to bring an official complaint.'

'She told you who it was?'

'I guessed. Frankly, being at boarding school for most of the year and having a limited circle of acquaintances, it wasn't difficult.'

'How old is she?'

'Fifteen.'

'And she goes along with outing this attacker?'

'Well, no, not yet, but I hope to persuade her to go to the police.'

'For whose benefit, Stella? To slake your own anger or to help your daughter come to terms with it?'

'To be fair I think she is over the worst. Fran's been in hospital.'

'A termination?'

'A spontaneous miscarriage probably brought about by the shock of that poor boy's accident at our flat. She feels bad about his death.'

'She thinks it was suicide? He was the rapist?'

'No! Chaz was a friend, but she confided in him and, being a streetwise sort of guy, she thought Chaz was the only one who could possibly help her.'

'But you've nailed the real bloke and he thinks he's likely to be charged?'

'Yes. I didn't tell him about the miscarriage. He still thinks she can prove paternity through DNA or something, which, if things had not panned out as they have, would have been perfectly possible.'

'He must be running scared. But it would be up to your daughter to bring charges; you can't act for her at her age and from my limited experience of these cases the chances of putting him away would be slim. Who shouted rape, you or your girl? He could claim he didn't know her age for a start; these teenagers can look very mature in their weekend gear. And secondly, his defence would inevitably be that the act was with her consent.'

'It wasn't! Fran admits it was possibly a misunderstanding, fumbling that got out of hand, but there's no way this oaf could claim he didn't know how old she was.'

'When was this?'

'In the spring.'

Hayes sighed, frowning at the wipers arcing across the windscreen, trying to rationalize his thoughts.

'Listen, Stella. As a policeman I wouldn't hesitate to support your desire to bring this man to justice. But as a friend I think Fran would be best served by letting it go. And you too. I know it's a cynical response and nothing can wipe out your hatred of this character, but a police prosecution would inevitably aggravate her trauma. You've had a go at this guy, scared the shit out of him, vented your fury in no uncertain terms. Isn't that enough? If you like I will speak to Fran myself and get the facts on paper, but what does her father think of your plan to persuade her to report it?'

Stella shrugged. 'I don't know. All this only came to light when she was taken into hospital. I'm fetching her tomorrow and driving her to stay with him and his future in-laws far away from here.'

He started. 'The man's a local?'

'Yes.'

He nodded. 'In that case, why does she feel guilty about the Hilton boy's death?'

172

They were entering Renham and Stella sharply enquired, 'Round here do, Roger? You do want to be dropped off near the station, I presume.'

'Yes, sure, anywhere'll do.'

She pulled into the market square and Hayes got out, pausing at the open door to lean in and try a parting shot. 'Don't rush into anything, Stella, there's no time limit. Think it over, but watch your step. Threatening some lowlife with a rape charge is big business.' He straightened. 'Let me know if I can help, but, like you said, it's my day off – our conversation is completely off the record. But thanks again for the lift.'

He slammed the door and watched her rev up to take the junction at a fair lick. That woman drives too fast, he thought, and has for so long been used to controlling events that when something like this hits her, her knee-jerk reaction is dangerous.

Stella arrived back at the cottage just as the rain stopped, leaving the sky clear-washed, the clouds like a fluffy blanket, no longer the dark pall that had overhung Oxford. She grabbed her bag and the only surveillance camera to escape Charlie's rampage, and took it inside, thrusting the wretched thing behind the books on the shelf, wishing now she had kept well clear of bloody Charlie Hilton and his weird sexual games.

Everything had seemed so simple when she had started this little adventure. She had only wanted to embarrass Charlie into coughing up for her good friend Kate and have a bit of fun on the side. But it had all gone sour. Admittedly Charlie had come up with the goods and agreed to a divorce, but the death of that boy had changed everything. Keeping Stefan's drugs as a sweetner for Charlie had seemed a good ploy at the time, but now Fran was involved and living with the burden that his death was indirectly her fault, and it wasn't. The fault had been entirely her own, and now the poor kid would never be able to absolve herself of guilt over the temptation she had put in his way by showing him a cache of class A drugs bound to dazzle the poor guy enough to try a crazy trick to get at them.

She wished now that she had refused to let Charlie come

to the cottage this weekend. Seeing him again was a stupid move. She must ring him and put him off just as soon as she had poured herself a drink and decided how to phrase it without provoking him into another attack once he realized her support for the Chekhov gig was all washed up.

But after a couple of strong whiskies and a long relaxing bath, she fell asleep on the bed and later she decided it had been a panic reaction. What was the harm in having an innocent drink with the man? And, like she had said, she could use some company.

Forty

Collecting Fran from the Rosemoor Clinic was a huge relief for both of them. Fran, subdued by the experience, seemed quieter, more matured. Stella, on the other hand, was overexcited by the move, bubbling with energy and anxious to escape.

They shopped for new clothes for Frances, including expensive riding kit and a snazzy bikini.

'Morag's people have this fantastic outdoor pool. It was too cold for Tiffany and me to try when we there before but it will be perfect now. I wish Tiff could come too.'

Stella's heart lurched. 'You kept your promise not to ring her, didn't you?'

'Yeah, sure. Don't nag, Mum. Anyway, Morag will be there and Daddy gets back late tonight. He's driving to Oxford straight from the airport, said he had some legal business to deal with and was calling in to see you at the cottage after.'

'Really? When did he tell you this?'

'He phoned from Ireland last night. Been attending some bloodstock auctions he said.'

Stella let it go, deciding to stay at the flat overnight after all, having no wish to go toe-to-toe with Monty over her refusal to cough up the twenty grand to cover his current financial embarrassment. After all, what were rich fiancées for? Bankrolling Monty to deal with expenses involving Fran was an acceptable gamble. At the end of the day the likelihood of Monty being in a position to collect the lump sum from the newly signed addition to the trust fund was remote in the extreme. Once Fran reached her majority the financial boost she had inserted would no longer apply.

Stella stayed for tea with the McDermotts, the parents charmingly smoothing a latently awkward introduction to Monty's new love. Morag was a good-looker, no question: hair with the gleam of fresh chestnuts and an outdoorsy complexion to match. No make-up and an engaging grin unfazed by the dicey combination of elderly parents, the fiancé's ex-wife and a future stepdaughter to juggle with.

Stella wondered how much the urbane McDermotts were aware of the reason for Fran's emergency admission to the Rosemoor. From their obvious approval of the potential addition to the family she guessed that a veil had been drawn over this little local difficulty, something Monty was expert at and, one might suspect, something at which Morag was no beginner either. As the McDermotts' only child, the emergence of an attractive and articulate teenager to replace Morag had been welcome and, in the right frame of mind, Fran could display a fair approximation of Monty's charm.

She arrived back at the flat at six and mooched about trying to settle down to an evening at home. Tory was probably still on her way back from the funeral with Kate and Charlie was staying on in York overnight, or so he had implied. She wondered how the atmosphere had been with Charlie's ex, Lola Lopez, on the scene, a bad enough day for Charlie without undercurrents between Lola and Kate to contend with. Irritably she decided to go to the cinema and switched off her mobile to avoid the inevitable outburst from Monty when he arrived at the cottage after being with her lawyer only to find she had skipped town. Stella decided to leave first thing in the morning and drive back to

Percivals, thus dodging any dawn rush from Lingfield to beard her at the flat. She needed time to let the stupid man cool down, to realize that as his financial backstop her day was done.

But when she returned to the cottage next morning there was a message on the answerphone: Monty Neville at full volume.

'Listen to me, Stella. I've driven over to this God-awful dump specially to see you and you've left me standing on your fucking doorstep. Typical! You could have warned me you were staying in London. I agreed to fall in with this trust fund lark and in return I expected you to keep your promise about lending me that shortfall. You knew I was desperate, you cow, and you let me breeze into the solicitor's office only to find you'd tied up the cash in a pie-in-the-sky arrangement which leaves me nowhere. You can't keep running, Stella – I'll come down again tomorrow night, so for Christ's sake give me a break.'

She heard the first few words and then left the tape to run, letting him rant on unheeded while she went to the kitchen to raid the freezer for cocktail snacks for her tête-à-tête with Charlie Hilton. Later she donned her wellingtons and took a long afternoon walk to clear her head.

That evening, just as it was getting dark, she heard a ring at the door. She glanced at her watch. Too early for Charlie. Monty? She'd have to make it short and sweet. Cruel to be kind, that was the only way to fend off congenital cadgers like Monty Neville.

'Oh, it's you again. You'd better come in, but I've no more to say, my mind's made up.'

Forty-One

It was Tory who found her. Rob parked outside the cottage on Sunday afternoon and waited while she rang the bell. It was a perfect summer day and birdsong rippled from the tree-tops like the soundtrack from an art-house movie. Tory rang again.

'Stella's not in,' she called to Rob. 'I'll only be a minute. I just want to collect some drawings I left behind. Hang on.'

She let herself in and disappeared inside, surprised to find the sitting-room lamps still burning on such a sunny after-noon. It was only on her way back that the open door of the study caught her eye. She popped her head round the door, wondering why the room was in darkness, the dimness illuminated only by a single brilliant ray of sunlight shining between a narrow gap in the curtains. Her curiosity drew her in and at that instant the full horror burst upon her like a blow to the heart, literally taking her breath away.

She moved to the end of the sofa, forcing herself to look closer. Stella lay crumpled against the cushions like a beaten child, her blonde hair darkly matted and straggling across one side of her face, masking the broken cheekbone. One eye, wide open, seemed to fix on Tory's terrified gaze, unlocking the scream that until then was paralysed by the shock. For what seemed endless moments she crouched against the wall, her screams reverberating through the low-beamed rooms, bringing Rob crashing in.

'Tory! Here, come away. Leave her, it's too late. Come back to the car!' He dragged her out and pushed her into the passenger seat where she sat shivering and gulping great rasping breaths of air.

Rob ran back inside and checked Stella's pulse. Nothing. A bare arm criss-crossed with cuts and grazes was flung out, blood-stained fingers brushing the floor. Rob touched her throat again. It must have been cold for hours. All night? All weekend?

Blood had dried into a carmine pool behind her head and one shoe lay several feet away, kicked aside in what appeared to have been a desperate struggle, a fight to the death. Stella's clothing seemed intact apart from a jagged tear at the neckline of her dress, exposing her breast. Her knees were drawn up to her chest, disclosing an expanse of thigh that Rob longed to cover with the mohair throw trapped half under the body and half caught up beneath the sofa. He gazed round the room but the dark defeated him, the chink in the curtains allowing only a spotlight on the body.

His attention was drawn back to the ringed fingers steeped in blood, and focussed on two fingernails jaggedly broken off in what must have been Stella's frantic efforts to defend herself.

Rob backed out and rang 999 from his mobile phone. He rejoined Tory, now silently weeping, and held her hand until two police cars screamed to a halt behind the car, blocking any possible way out.

Forty-Two

Four policemen exploded on to the scene, dispersing the birdsong at a stroke.

Rob jolted when a plain-clothes officer, who seemed vaguely familiar, knocked on the car window. He was accompanied by a red-headed detective constable Tory knew all too well: Robbins, the one sent to follow up the complaint about the dead sheep. She shrank back, gripping Rob's hand tighter. He extracted himself and climbed out to join the senior man patiently standing by.

He flashed his ID card. 'Detective Chief Inspector Hayes,' he said flatly.

Rob introduced himself, adding, 'Yes, of course. I remember you taking Stella aside in that restaurant at Easter. She was a friend of yours?'

'Acquaintance. Now, before we go inside, may I have a run-down on your arrival here, which was – when?'

'About three thirty. I'd picked up Tory from the station and—'

'The young lady in the car?'

'Yes. Victoria Blum, an old friend of Stella's, they knew each other at school. She works at the gardening school in Renham, has a cottage on the estate. Tory had left her car here a week ago when Stella drove them both to London. There had been an accident.'

'Yes, I heard about that. A man fell from Mrs Buckleigh's roof terrace. Go on.'

'I stayed in the car while Tory went in to collect some stuff of hers she'd left behind.'

'Ms Blum has keys? Or were keys hidden outside?'

'No. Stella gave her the gardener's keys in case she wanted to come over when Stella was away.'

Hayes nodded, listening intently but keeping a wary eye on the female slumped miserably in Allinson's passenger seat. He directed his sidekick, Jenny Robbins, to sit in with her and motioned his witness to continue.

'Tory went in,' Rob continued, 'and I put the radio on, thinking she'd be longer that a few minutes, but almost immediately she started screaming and I dashed inside.'

Hayes nodded towards the lighted interior shining through the open door. 'You touched nothing, either of you? Put on lights? Moved anything?'

'The lamps were already on in the sitting room but Tory had gone into the study, which was almost totally dark, and discovered Stella had been attacked. It was obvious she was dead, though I did check her pulse after I'd shoved Tory back in the car.'

'You came back?'

'Yes. I had to make sure, but there was nothing I could do except ring for the police.'

'Now, Mr Allinson, you're certain you disturbed nothing? Touched nothing?'

The uniformed men were getting restive, anxious to get on with the job. Just then two more cars drew up and three men emerged from the first, carrying various items of equipment Rob could only guess were forensic stuff. Hayes excused himself to speak to the driver of the second car, leaving Rob to stand about like a spare tyre, wishing he could get back to Tory, who was clearly still very distressed, holding her head in her hands, her long dark hair spilling over her face. The policewoman had her hand on Tory's shoulder and was muttering away at the poor girl as if trying to bring her round after a motorway smash-up.

Hayes returned. 'We shall have to continue this conversation later, Mr Allinson. Could you call in to the station in Renham tomorrow morning at ten and sign a formal statement? And Ms Blum, too, if she is up to it. I can send my sergeant to drive her in; her car will presumably stay here for the present?'

Rob agreed and hurried back to Tory. The red-haired constable jumped out and, after a thumbs up from Hayes, allowed Rob to claim the driver's seat and manoeuvre into the lane to drive back to Renham.

Hayes took the doctor inside, admitting he had yet to examine the crime scene himself. 'Good of you to come so promptly on a Sunday afternoon, Doctor.'

'No problem. Emergency call outs come with the territory.' Doctor Flanagan was a red-faced countryman, stocky and of a cheerful disposition, unfazed by his role as police doctor even in the unlikely event of a brutal murder. 'I'll need some light,' he said, peering anxiously into the gloom of the study.

'I'll get the SOCO boys to rig up an arc light – I don't want to disturb the scene too much before they've had a chance to go over it.' Hayes hurried out.

Once the room was floodlit the extent of the victim's injuries seemed garish, unreal, the clear evidence of a struggle dramatized by all the blood. Hayes stood aside while the doctor gently felt the cold skin, closely examined the eyes and tested for rigor mortis. He straightened. Staring down at the body as it lay sprawled on the sofa, Flanagan was obviously disturbed by what must have been a frenzied attack.

'Been dead for some hours, probably since yesterday evening between eight and ten at a rough estimate. Do we know this lady, Chief Inspector?'

'Stella Buckleigh. Been weekending here for several years but normally resides in London. A widow. Any idea about any sexual contact?'

Flanagan shook his head. 'The pathologist's examination will supply all the information you need, but as her clothes are more or less intact I would guess not. A feisty young woman. She didn't give up easily.' He repacked his bag and made for the door. 'Keep me informed, Inspector; I'd like to know what the pathologist makes of it. A nasty business. Killed by heavy blows to the head, most certainly. She lived alone?'

'I believe so. I warned her about security and she sensibly took steps to safeguard the property, but so far there's no evidence of a break-in, so at present we must assume she admitted her attacker.'

The photographer took over from the doctor and took video footage of the scene. Hayes made a quick tour of the house before admitting the SOCO team to do their work. It all seemed reasonably undisturbed upstairs, the bedrooms tidy, no clue to any other person staying over. The girlfriend who had found the body, Vicky Blum – or was it Tory? – would be a useful witness. Pity there were no near neighbours to observe the comings and goings from Percivals, Stella Buckleigh being a prime subject for conjecture in a village like Bramley Green.

While the SOCO team were nit-picking their way through the cottage, Roger Hayes contented himself by going through paperwork from her desk. Stella was, he had to admit, a tidy sort when it came to accounts, her business correspondence all neatly placed in individual folders, colour-coded and dated. All the documentation was concerned with Percivals and he concluded a similar filing system must exist at the Belgravia address. A legal file bulged with current business, presumably affairs Stella had been attending to when he had bumped into her in Oxford on Thursday. He scanned the latest document and then put this aside, keen to keep an eye on the SOCO findings, if any, and to make sure they took any fingerprints remaining about what, at first glance, would seem a thoroughly dusted set of rooms. Was there a cleaner? And when had Stella reclaimed the keys from that gardener of hers, Jimmy Thompson, the dodgy customer she would have been wise to keep well outside the house? Perhaps his warning had prompted her to sack the bloke. Hayes sighed. It was a difficult situation, not helped by the fact that her occupancy of Percivals had become less frequent since her husband had died. But who could blame her for that? A nice enough country place, but lonely, and from what he heard Stella Buckleigh had not endeared herself to the locals.

He must get back to Dennis Chivers, the man who was investigating the apparent accident at Buckleigh's flat. Yes, check to see if there were any links with that other suspicious death. Funny sort of coincidence . . . And unfortunately, the fifteen-year-old daughter would have to be questioned about her relationship with the poor stiff. He searched through Stella's address book and jotted down some phone numbers. Several featured frequently on her telephone bill and he settled down to trace the ex-husband. It didn't take long.

'Hello, is that Mr Neville? Stella Buckleigh's former husband? My name's Hayes. Detective Chief Inspector Hayes, Thames Valley Police. I'm afraid there's been an accident at Mrs Buckleigh's cottage. Percivals. You know it?'

'Yes, of course. What's all this about, Inspector?'

'Your daughter is Mrs Buckleigh's next of kin? There is no one else?'

'Only me. Why? What's happened?'

'I suggest you meet me tomorrow. Would four o'clock be convenient? At the mortuary in Oxford. I can arrange for a car to meet you at the railway station. In the event of no other relative close enough to register an identification, your assistance would be invaluable, sir.'

'Good God, man! What are you saying? Stella's dead?'

'Yes, Mr Neville. My sincere sympathy. I'm afraid I am unable to comment further at this stage as the investigation has only just begun, but someone will have to break the news to your daughter. I suggest you confine yourself to confirming that there was an accident at the cottage, and I assume there is someone who can look after her in your absence. She is still with you? I shall need you here for some time I'm afraid.'

Monty replaced the receiver with shaking hands. Stella dead? It was impossible. And this inspector pulls him in for questioning straight off, no messing? His mind ran in frantic circles trying to establish his last contacts with Stella. Bad news, there was no doubt about it; his motives for wishing Stella dead and buried would be difficult to refute since that financial amendment had been added to Fran's trust fund.

Forty-Three

Jenny Robbins knocked on the door of the sitting room. 'Sir. Any chance of making some tea? The SOCO team have finished in the kitchen and we're all parched.'

Hayes looked up from the bumph he had extracted from the dead woman's files. 'Yeah, sure. Milk and no sugar for me. By the way, Robbins, where's Sergeant Bellamy?'

'On holiday, sir. Majorca. Won't be back for a fortnight.'

'Damn! I need someone who can break down the CCTV footage with me. And there's a video camera the lads discovered hidden behind some books which might identify possible suspects. Is Sergeant Buller up to scratch on technical stuff?'

'Not unless it's under the bonnet of a vehicle, if you ask me. But I've done the advanced IT course, sir,' she said brightly.

He frowned, unwilling to admit that working with this perky redhead in place of reliable, stolid Bellamy was not first choice. But speed was vital and, short-staffed as they were, it looked as if Robbins would have to do. At least she was enthusiastic.

'Right, do a tea round for starters and I'll think about it.'

She returned with a mug. 'Only Earl Grey I'm afraid, sir, but the poor lady was kind enough to put out a plate of savouries – OK if we polish them off?'

Hayes perked up. 'She was expecting someone then. Wine?'

'Champagne in the fridge and flutes and table napkins all laid out on a tray. Untouched. Either her date never turned up or he got frisky before they got round to the drinks.'

He sipped his tea, grimacing at the thin brew. 'Blimey, Robbins, this stuff tastes like cats' piss. Any coffee?'

She stiffened. 'I'm not a tea boy, sir. Shouldn't we be pressing on with the videos? Terry found an unmarked tape in her underwear drawer. Could be interesting.'

Hayes stacked Stella's files on the coffee table and allowed Robbins to play the videotape. It was sod's law, Bellamy being on leave just when he needed some familiar back-up. Getting on with this girl with her touchy reservations about PC duties would take some getting used to for a start, but he'd let her have her head at least while he was so short-handed. With half the investigation taking him to the victim's London stamping ground, he was going to need solid team-work at both ends.

They settled to watch Stella's dry run with her new surveillance equipment, Hayes impatiently fast-forwarding Truelove's caper, recognizing an amateur performance for what it was. The film went blank for a moment before continuing with a replay of Monty Neville's urgent request for a loan.

Hayes and Jenny Robbins sat riveted to the screen, the effect electric. Why had Buckleigh done this, a secret filming of her ex putting the bite on, and obviously not for the first time?

He curtly instructed Robbins to run it again and, as an intro-duction to a key player in the case, they got a real insight into a relationship far from dead. Hayes suddenly jumped up and rifled through the legal papers he had just put aside. 'Ah, I thought something fishy was hiding under all this legal jargon.' Without further elucidation he snatched the tape from the machine and bagged it up with the trust fund agreement on which, it would seem, the ink was barely dry.

Jenny Robbins irritably followed her boss outside, where he engaged the senior SOCO investigator in an urgent conversation. She stood by, waiting to be included. At last he registered her presence and barked, 'Right, constable. Follow me and take notes while this officer and I run through the CCTV footage. And I want no interruptions.'

The reel seemed to be faulty or possibly tampered with. As Hayes' brief examination of Stella's accounts disclosed, the Truelove bill had yet to be paid and the equipment had certainly been installed within the month. Perhaps there was a complaint. A delay in her usual swift settlement of bills owing to a malfunction yet to be corrected? He would have to question Truelove.

'The tape should have continued without a break. See here, Inspector,' the SOCO officer insisted, 'it starts off OK and then, three-quarters of the way through, it gets a blip, cuts out and then starts up again before blacking out entirely. Wait here, sir, I'll take a dekko at the camera outside.'

Hayes watched the stuttering film more closely, wishing he could identify the players. Robbins, peering over his shoulder, perked up. 'I know that bloke, sir. The one standing at the door with the bundle under his arm.'

He stopped the tape and peered at the figure illuminated under Stella's porch light. A man in a pork pie hat and sports coat. Portly. Middle-aged at a guess, but the picture would need to be enhanced.

'You recognize him?'

'He's a local farmer, sir. Bossom. He said the dog that was here at Easter had savaged one of his lambs. It was settled privately, though the owner swore it wasn't her animal that caused the damage. Mrs Blum, sir, the woman who found the body, it was her dog Bossom was accusing.'

Hayes watched the full sequence. According to this, the farmer called to see her Saturday afternoon, limped up to the door, rang the bell, got no answer and drove off. She could have been dead already, though that didn't tie up with Doctor Flanagan's estimate.

'The tape goes off course here, sir. If you run it again the other man who knocked on the Friday – that's the day before Bossom came calling – that strip of film runs *after* Bossom's appearance. I think what's happened is the film was in the middle of a rewind having reached the end of the tape when Bossom turns up, reactivates the sensor and it goes off at half-cock, leaving the remainder of the film on tape but in the wrong sequence.'

Hayes looked doubtful but had to admit she was probably right.

'The Friday caller looks suspiciously like the ex-husband we clocked on the tape that Buckleigh secretly filmed herself, wouldn't you say?'

Jenny nodded enthusiastically and at that moment the SOCO man, Jennings, reappeared, insisting they follow him outside.

The CCTV camera was fixed high up under the eaves to a post supporting the porch and Jennings had brought out a set of steps to have a good look at it. 'See here, sir, if you get up close you can see that the sensor's been taped over. Nothing scanned from here since whatever you saw on the machine.'

'No wonder the bloody thing malfunctioned. Come in here, Jennings, and look at this.'

They trooped back inside and earnestly sat through two more reruns of the clip, its frequent blanks and false starts finally settling into a sequence Jenny Robbins could spell out in her notes.

'Neville, the ex-husband, turns up Friday and finds her away. Bossom arrives Saturday afternoon and also draws a blank. Either she wasn't answering the doorbell or was off out somewhere. We'll have to ask round, see if anyone saw her Saturday afternoon. Then the damn camera gets nobbled and we see nothing more. What beats me, Jennings, is how did the saboteur tape over the sensor without being filmed doing it?'

Jennings hurried back outside, followed by Hayes and a scurrying Jenny Robbins intent on missing nothing.

'See this, sir?' Jennings had clambered over a raised shrub border and approached the porch from the rear. 'If the bloke took it carefully he could blank out the sensor from behind and the lady in the house would know nothing about it. He could then ring the bell knowing he hadn't been filmed.'

'We'll have to see if the pathologist can put a closer estimate on the time of death but, yes, you're right, Jennings, the CCTV isn't much help if it backed up on itself while in the process of rewinding, filmed a short sequence of the farmer then later blanked out. On the face of it this Bossom character was the last one at the scene, but was she already dead?'

'But all we've got here, sir,' Robbins cut in, 'is two people who knock at the door and go away. The Friday guy was well off the scene before she was murdered and Bossom was a genuine caller.'

Hayes was beginning to feel badgered. 'Well, there's the video camera we found behind the books, which may put someone else in the frame. She had that video camera in her car on Thursday. I saw it myself.'

Robbins' eyes widened, wondering if the boss was too close for comfort on this case.

'Bag up the CCTV, Jennings, and take it back for a closer look; we may be able to save something.' He thumbed through his notebook and tore out a page. 'Here, take this, it's the name of the electrician who installed the equipment. Ring Truelove and see what he's got to say. Ask him why Buckleigh suddenly wanted to upgrade security. Have you checked the other CCTV at the back?'

'I'll get straight on to it, sir. Getting a fix on callers is a real break, isn't it? Don't expect it outside commercial properties as a rule.'

'The marvels of technology,' Hayes dryly commented, wishing now he had kept up with the latest IT stuff. Having that redheaded firecracker, Jenny Robbins, on his back wouldn't leave any room for errors.

Forty-Four

The search continued, the cottage and outbuildings invaded by men tearing the fabric of Stella Buckleigh's life apart.

Hayes forced himself to attend to the paperwork taken from the desk while he waited for the pathologist to arrive.

Jenny Robbins scuttled about the rooms like an eager bloodhound while the rest of the team searched the grounds and tried to select individual tyre tracks in the muddy yard fronting the stable block. Rain had scuppered any chance of obtaining any clear patterns and with at least two visitors arriving and departing over the previous days, their efforts were desultory to say the least.

Robbins bounced into the sitting room hugging a black plastic bin liner.

Hayes looked up. 'Yes?'

'They found this by the bonfire site, sir. Jumpers, nice ones too, too good to burn.'

'Perhaps she was saving them for a jumble sale,' he replied sourly, 'or to take to the charity shop. Women's stuff I presume?'

'Yes, sir, but cashmere and designer labels, not bog-standard twin sets.'

Hayes shrugged. 'Put it in the scullery, Robbins, I can't deal with a rag bag while there's all this paper to go through.'

She stood her ground. 'That's not all, sir, there's a whole pile of glitzy stuff upstairs and not the sort our fashionista would wear. Too big for a start, and there's also wigs and a tart's kit.'

Hayes laughed. 'Oh, I know about that. It's fancy dress gear hired for a party. Didn't get a chance to return it, poor cow. I'll take a look at it later, from what I hear the partying got a bit rough.'

Robbins backed off, wondering what it took to get at this guy. She stalked out, dragging the bin liner across the floor and dumping it in the utility room. She decided to trawl through Buckleigh's phone messages on the answer machine and this time struck gold.

Hayes flung down his notebook when she appeared again. 'What now?' he barked.

'You've got to hear this, sir. Her ex blasting off when he found he'd come all the way here and she'd stood him up. It must have been Friday when we saw him arrive on the security camera. He threatens to come back!'

Hayes tensed. 'Well, let's get on with it. Where's the phone?'

He listened in silence to Monty's incandescent outburst. He couldn't blame the poor guy. Having toed the line at the lawyer's office in Oxford and come over here to have it out, he finds her gone. Staying in London he suspects. Was she? And did Neville's temper stay red-hot, enough to make him drive down here a second time, to put in serious mileage to vent his fury?

'Get the tape out of the machine, Robbins, I'll need it when I interview Neville in the morning.' He dipped into the legal file again and reread the terms of the trust fund. 'Sounds pretty generous to me,' he muttered. 'A bung up front to spend on the kid's little extras. What more did he want?' Clearly, the guy was in a serious financial jam and expected Buckleigh to bail him out pronto, and all he got was the prospect of a pay-off if he became solely responsible for Frances. But surely that wouldn't drive him to murder? Depended what was at stake, he decided, wishing now he had summoned Monty Neville straight to the interview room in Renham, no messing. Still, he wasn't going anywhere, was he? Not with a lump sum inches away now the poor woman was dead and the conditions of the trust fund nicely in place. A word with the lawyer, Allinson, would clarify the legal position.

But jumping on the first likely suspect was not an option, not till after the pathologist had put in an appearance at any rate.

189

He wandered outside to collect his thoughts, surprised to find it was almost dark, the black outline of the woods on the skyline almost melding with the heavy clouds, warning of more rain overnight. Jennings caught up with him and the two men paced out the stable yard, skirting the ramshackle 2CV, which he presumed was Tory Blum's car.

'We've pretty well finished here, sir. All right if we pack it in? I want to have a go with that security equipment when I get back. There's a technical nerd who I can call on first thing in the morning, see if we can enhance the footage and flush out any taped-over evidence.'

Hayes nodded. 'Right. I'll be in by eight and I want to call a briefing for the whole team, get the interviews shared out so we can see what's on the cards.'

A uniformed man hurried up. 'The pathologist's arrived, sir.'

'Be with you right away.' He turned to Jennings. 'See you in the morning, Sergeant.'

Doctor Blandish was one of the younger recruits to the Home Office forensic brigade and someone unfamiliar to Hayes. He caught up with him at the front porch and they shook hands and had a brief discussion about the crime scene.

'You knew the victim personally, I gather.'

Hayes looked up, visibly startled. 'Well, slightly. Who told you that?'

Blandish grinned. 'Funny how these rumours get about. One of the officers saw you in her car a few days ago, being dropped off in Renham.'

'Ah, yes, well . . . She gave me a lift from Oxford. It was my day off,' he added for no good reason at all and wished, as soon as he'd said it, that he had kept that little snippet to himself. It looked bad. As if he was putting himself about more than a chief inspector should, even on his day off.

They trooped inside and Blandish quickly got down to business. Hayes stood just outside the study watching with interest a swift assessment of the attack, hoping the doctor would supply a few pointers.

At last he rose and shed his protective clothing.

'Run-of-the-mill battering. Dead for eighteen hours at least. No weapon to hand?'

'No, Doctor. Not so far.'

Blandish repacked his instruments and made a phone call. 'You're releasing the body to the mortuary?'

'I'll have a better view of things in the lab. I'll see you there, shall I? In about two hours? I've arranged for the body to be taken to Oxford; the facilities are better and I assume you have no objection.'

'None at all.'

They stood in the narrow hallway and Blandish glanced around with interest. 'Nice place this. The lady lived alone?'

'She had a daughter but it was mainly used as a holiday cottage, for entertaining friends mostly. Mrs Buckleigh lived in London.'

Blandish frowned. 'Makes your job no easier, Hayes, checking out both venues.'

'It's a tricky case, complicated by the extraordinary co-incidence of the death of a young man falling from the roof of her London flat only a week ago.'

'Suspicious?'

'A drug-fuelled accident. Our victim here wasn't at home, so on the face of it there's no link.'

Blandings grimaced. 'Well, I don't envy you, Hayes. Let's hope the lady had no important family connections – nothing like protective relatives for jamming up an investigation.'

He waved him off, feeling the weight of the issues Blandish had not spared him. Robbins bobbed up out of the darkness having been with the uniformed squad now standing discon-sonately in the yard.

'Organize a team to stay overnight, Robbins,' he said gruffly. 'The rest of you can push off home. Briefing eight thirty at the station, but the crux of the investigation will be set up in the village as soon as possible.'

He stalked back inside, stiff with irritation, and sat for another hour examining Stella's accounts and rerunning the Monty Neville videotape.

Having raised no fresh leads he stretched and casually exam-ined the bookshelves, generally a pointer to the character of

191

the householder. Stella was not, it would appear, much of a bookworm, the titles stacked neatly in rows mostly blockbusters of the sex-and-shopping genre, apart from a couple of Harry Potters which might, or might not, have belonged to the kid. He rummaged through the shelves, idly filling in time until the overnight watch team had been set up.

It was with surprise that he discovered the video camera put back behind the books, the top-of-the-range piece of equipment he had last seen tossed on to the back seat of Stella's car and presumably replaced in situ after the police search of the sitting room. Robbins came in with a mug of coffee and a plate of sandwiches, placing the peace offering at his elbow with a shrug. 'Thought you'd need this,' she said stiffly.

'Yeah, thanks, Robbins. You off?'

She eyed the camera in his hand with avid interest. 'You just found it?'

'Let's give it a whirl, shall we?' he said with a grin.

Forty-Five

The briefing next day had a distinctly Monday-morning feel to it, the assembled team snatched from their own cases to work under Hayes, their new DCI, and a man already noted for a curt manner with backsliders. They waited in sullen silence, their feet shifting impatiently as the clock ticked on.

Hayes was behind closed doors with the superintendent, another short-tempered bugger, but at least someone they were used to, someone familiar with the local scene. Hayes' reputed career failure as a pianist had done him no favours. Had he been a failed footballer, now that would have been a different story entirely.

Superintendent Waller was not letting Hayes have free rein

on this one. The lady – Stella Buckleigh? – was not the sort to swim in his particular pond and, despite having apparently lived in Bramley Green for at least eight years, her name struck no chords at all and he was a man who prided himself on having a nose for every VIP within a twenty-mile radius. But then weekenders didn't count, did they? It was a pity, Waller thought, the woman had not croaked in her London pad. She had no business bringing all this trouble down here, no business at all.

'And you'd met this Mrs Buckleigh, Hayes? Come across her how, exactly?'

'Her late husband sponsored a music festival my girlfriend was involved in. I met her once or twice and—'

'Socially?'

'Well, yes, but I hardly knew her, sir, just someone I bumped into occasionally.'

'Pity,' Waller replied sourly. 'If you'd hobnobbed with this victim a bit more we wouldn't be in the dark about her fancy friends for a start. Good-looking, was she?'

'I would say so,' Hayes said guardedly. 'Someone used to getting her own way, it seemed to me, but perfectly civil. She was about to sell the cottage, the sale was already agreed I understand.'

Waller laughed bitterly. 'Just our luck to catch the dirty end of the stick then. You'd better play your cards right, Hayes, I don't want any shit on our doorstep, no accusations of sloppy policing, eh? What's the agenda?'

Hayes outlined his proposed interviews and sketched in a résumé of the Hilton lad's death from Stella's roof, which did nothing to lighten Waller's forebodings. And the replay of the videotape showing Charlie Hilton's high jinks put the lid on it with Waller.

The phone rang and the super dismissed Hayes with an irritated wave of the hand as he started to put the commissioner in the picture.

Hayes hurried into the briefing with renewed energy. Getting a bollocking from Waller even before the investigation got into its stride was par for the course, and, if anything, gave a frisson to his attack on what was shaping up to be a fascinating mystery. What the hell was Stella Buckleigh doing installing this security equipment all of a sudden? And taping high jinks with her cross-dressing paramour too? A premonition of violence? Blackmail?

He addressed the team standing in front of a display board to which he added names and connecting arrows as he coloured in details of the victim's background. Their eyes glazed with the proliferation of information Hayes insisted they digest, only Jenny Robbins alert to the details. Sergeant Buller sat stolidly in the front row, eyeing the DCI with respect, recognizing the kudos at stake if they managed to nail the killer before more experienced murder squad officers were called in to take charge.

'I shall be taking a statement from Buckleigh's solicitor shortly; he was one of the couple who discovered the body. Later, her ex-husband will be joining me at the mortuary to make a formal identification and to explain his current relationship with the deceased. DC Robbins has been taking notes and will fill you in on the details before you start door to door enquiries in Bramley Green. Remember it's a small village and the locals may be prejudiced against incomers like Stella Buckleigh, so don't be too influenced by biased opinion. Have an open mind, lads, it lets the fresh air circulate. Sergeant Preston has divided up duties and will co-ordinate operations from here. I don't have to emphasize the necessity to keep in touch and to take accurate notes of any information relating to Buckleigh's past and present activities and any men friends seen about with her recently. We are particularly interested in where she may have gone on Saturday afternoon. Was she in the village shop? Was she seen walking across the fields? Meeting anyone? Keep your ears open for gossip, however unimportant it may seem. Nosy neighbours are in short supply here; the location of the crime scene was secluded and, apart from CCTV footage, we're feeling our way in the dark.'

He waited for questions. There were none. Puzzled, he watched the men disperse, a trio lingering to question Robbins at the back of the room and a knot of unsettlingly morose officers closing in on Preston, a senior man but hardly of the calibre of Detective Sergeant Bellamy.

After typing up his notes on his laptop, Hayes called Sergeant Buller and Jenny Robbins into his office.

'You're up to speed on the current state of play, Buller? We're short-staffed already and it's a bloody nuisance Bellamy swanning off to Majorca just when we need every man we can lay our hands on.'

Buller was a stocky, middle-aged copper normally allocated technical duties, a qualified motor mechanic with an easy manner, which put him in good stead with the locals but whose swift grasp of any investigation Hayes was less certain about. Teaming him with the hawk-eyed redhead, Robbins, would be best, Buller's even temperament diluting the sharp approach of the little madam who, it was generally agreed in the canteen, would soon be climbing the promotion ladder.

'I want you two to shake down this farmer character, Bossom. Robbins, you've met him before, you said – something about Buckleigh's dog killing one of his lambs?'

'Yes, sir, but the dog belonged to her friend, though Mrs Buckleigh settled with Bossom so there was no further action.'

'Right. Well, go softly. Bossom was last seen at the cottage on the CCTV before it was nobbled. But don't let on that the sensor was later taped over, I've got my own ideas about that. Find out what he was up to calling at Percivals on a Saturday afternoon. Was it by appointment? Was he angling for more compensation? More sheep savaged? OK?'

After a rerun of a copy of the CCTV reel for Buller's benefit, Hayes dismissed the oddly mismatched pair and played Monty's message recorded on Stella's answermachine. The bloke was definitely ticking about her nifty sidestep over the expected loan, something Hayes would need to clarify with Allinson, get him to explain the conditions of the trust fund.

The trouble with this case, he decided, was the number of men Stella had double-crossed. Firstly, she had promised to bail out Monty Neville and then had given him the slip when he had arranged to see her on Friday after signing the trust fund agreement in Oxford. Secondly, she had secretly filmed embarrassing footage of her lover, the purpose of which was not altogether clear. Thirdly, she had threatened a man – at a guess the gardener, Jimmy Thompson – with a charge of raping her teenage daughter. Hardly a series of endearing relationships, was it? And yet, to him, she had seemed a charming person – beautiful, a loving mother and generous to her friends.

Hayes decided that the one who really knew what made Stella tick wasn't her lover, or her ex-husband and certainly not her sexy gardener, but her girlfriend, Tory Blum, the unfortunate soul who had stumbled upon her blood-soaked body.

Forty-Six

B uller drove Jenny Robbins to the Bossom smallholding, filling her in with a mild commentary about the history of Bramley Green, a village which had so far escaped the spread of commuter housing serving the expanding demands of Aylesbury and Thame.

'Nice little place, saved by the agricultural belt which has kept the developers at bay,' he said. 'One shop, a school for little kiddies that's on the verge of being closed down, a church likely to be rounded up into a group of other parishes any day now, and no pub.'

'Sounds ripe for a shake-up if you ask me,' Robbins tartly retorted.

'Well, the local families are a bolshy lot, including Bossom and his brother, a gamekeeper on the Williams' estate.'

'Bossom's just a tenant?'

'So it seems. Must have got the shits with this sale of Buckleigh's place, I bet. Chances are he'll be looking to renew his tenancy with the new people.'

They pulled off on to a muddy track which led to a well-appointed farm cottage with outbuildings. Mrs Bossom, a stout party in a flowery apron, opened the door and cheerfully directed them to the tractor shed where they found

Bossom tinkering with his pickup truck. A red Fiesta occupied a tin-roofed lean-to tacked on to the side of the cottage.

'Mr Bossom?' Buller pleasantly enquired. 'I've seen you down at the Crown in Sawston on darts nights. I'm Sergeant Buller and this is our lovely constable, DC Robbins.'

Jenny glowered.

'Aye, I know the young lady. She was handling my complaint about that bloody wolfhound.'

Bossom leaned against the door of the truck, wincing with a stab of pain.

Buller's eyes narrowed. 'Trouble with the truck, Mr Bossom?'

'Dratted thing's always breaking down.'

'Let's have a look, shall we?'

Robbins stood aside, exasperated by this pointless delay. But Buller peered under the bonnet, quietly dissecting the problem with Bossom. 'You sit in, sir, and turn the engine over when I raise my hand.'

Robbins watched the old man climb awkwardly into the driving seat and waited while they ran the vehicle through its paces. Finally, Buller slammed down the bonnet, all smiles. 'Reckon that's done it, Mr Bossom, but take it easy on the clutch, you've been a bit heavy on it, see.'

Bossom got out, the extent of his lameness all too apparent. 'It's this bloody hip of mine. Give me gip, Sergeant. Been on the waiting list for months. They keeps putting me off. It's enough to make me drive the blasted truck through the front doors of that hospital.'

Buller laughed. 'Don't reckon you much of a ram-raider, sir. But I can see your point, must be very hard trying to keep working with pain like that.'

Bossom had visibly relaxed, his florid features wreathed in smiles. 'Come in and have a cup of tea, Sergeant. What was it you wanted?' He grabbed his walking stick and set off.

Robbins sloped along behind and irritably checked her watch. At this rate Buller's interviews were going to take for ever.

The cottage was warm and smelt deliciously of baking. Bossom sat heavily at the kitchen table, leaning his stick against the dresser, and invited them to sit themselves down.

'Nice stick, that,' Buller observed. 'Don't often see crafts-manship like that these days.'

'Belonged to my grandfather. Carved it hisself.'

Buller nodded. 'Worth a bit, I bet. But,' he said, sipping his tea, 'we mustn't sit here enjoying ourselves. It's about Mrs Buckleigh.'

The wife hurried in with a plate of warm scones. 'Goodness, yes, poor lady,' she said breathlessly. 'Attacked in her own home. Whatever next?'

Bossom scowled and she swiftly retreated. 'Aye, so I heard on local radio this morning. Terrible thing.'

'Now, Mr Bossom,' Jenny cut in, impatient with all the chit-chat. 'You have been noted as having been the last person seen on the premises on Saturday and—'

'Last seen? Who says?'

'You were recorded on Mrs Buckleigh's security camera at four o'clock.'

'Was I? Well, if you say so, but I wasn't the last, was I?'

'The killer was, you mean,' Buller said patiently.

'Well, of course he bloody was. I called to see Mrs Buckleigh in the afternoon but she weren't there. Her car was there all right, so I suppose she was having a kip or keeping her 'ead down as regards the neighbours.'

'She was avoiding you?'

'P'raps. Funny woman, thought herself a cut above the folks round here.'

'Did you have an appointment?'

'Me?' He shook his head, bushy eyebrows meeting under a lowering brow. 'No, I just wanted a quick word about another of my lambs with its throat torn out.'

Robbins piped up. 'A second sheep killed?'

'Aye. I would have taken it off straight away but I had no boots with me so I went back later. Mrs Buckleigh was red-hot on dead animals in her field, reported me to the cruelty people one Christmas, got no idea at all.'

'You didn't like her?'

'Couldn't stand the woman, tell you the truth but, fair's fair, she always paid her dues.'

'She accepted responsibility for the dead sheep?'

'First one. We come to an agreement, but this last one was a bit over the top and I wanted to speak to her about it.'

'So you went back later?'

'Only to pick up the sheep from my field, I weren't dressed for chatting up the toffs.'

'What time was this?' Buller asked.

'Blimey, I don't keep my nose on the clock all night. After me tea, but, like I said, I didn't go right down the lane, I pulled off into the field and picked up the animal. You can see it if you like, it's still in my trailer.'

Jenny Robbins wouldn't let it go. 'But the sheep killing wasn't caused by her dog, was it, Mr Bossom?' she insisted. 'And the chance of a second attack from the same dog was unlikely, wasn't it, seeing as it was only visiting at Easter when you made the complaint the first time? Had you considered it might have been a stray? The dog warden in Renham picks up loose dogs every day of the week.'

'Not round here he don't. Once a sheep killer gets a taste for it he'll come back, run for miles if need be, you mark my words. And that dog was like a bloody mastiff.'

Buller gently steered the conversation into calmer water. 'So you called at Percivals on Saturday afternoon and drove straight off. And later you skirted the cottage to pick up the dead sheep and didn't see Mrs Buckleigh at all. Were the lights on?'

'Yes.'

'And you didn't go round the back to see if Mrs Buckleigh was in the orchard?'

'No, I went straight home. I'd already been up at the Crown for an hour for the darts match. I met my brother and we had a pint.'

'You were in the team?'

'No, just Sam.'

Robbins jotted down a few notes and finished her tea.

Buller took the hint. 'Right then, I think that'll be all. Thank you for your time, Mr Bossom.'

They left Bossom morosely gazing out at the empty vista

beyond his kitchen window and drove off at speed, scattering mud across the yard.

'Poor sod's in a right old state with that hip of his,' Buller remarked. 'No chance of *him* climbing up to the CCTV to tape it over.'

'I suppose not. Still, he admits to a poor relationship with the victim, doesn't he?'

'Him and the rest of the village, Jenny. And he was her tenant; always a tricky job keeping in with the landlord, especially when she's a townie like Mrs Buckleigh. I remember her old man, a very nice gentleman, very polite, in and out of the Crown with his actor friends when he first moved here. Bought his round at the bar and decent with the tenants, so I've heard. OK if I drop you off at the station? I fancy a nice bacon butty at the Crown myself. Call it neighborhood good relations.'

'Being matey with the locals? But that doesn't include giving free servicing to clapped out pickup trucks though, does it?' she retorted with a grin. Jenny liked old Buller, he was what everyone that banged on about missing a village bobby had in mind. But hobnobbing at the pub wasn't going to advance a murder enquiry, was it? With people like Buckleigh's crowd in the frame, the killer was the sort for whom Stella had put up cocktail snacks and champagne, not barflies clustered round the dartboard at the Crown.

But she was wrong. Buller's hour at the pub proved to be the first lead. He drove back to Renham with a grin like the Cheshire Cat, and bounded straight up to Sergeant Preston's desk.

'Blimey, Ted, you smell like a brewery.'

Buller dropped heavily into a seat and banged the table. 'Ferreting round the district takes time, Mick, lad. And here's a nugget for you. The landlord at the Crown – the nearest pub to Bramley Green, as it happens – gave me the tip they had a real dust up in the bar Saturday night. That fella, Thompson, the odd-job man who worked for Buckleigh, busted in about ten o'clock with this chainsaw. Blind drunk an 'all, so Wesley says.'

'With a chainsaw?' Preston gasped.

Buller laughed. 'Wanted to sell it, Mick, not mow down the punters. Practically brand new it was, said he'd bought it from a mate at this autocross he'd been to all Saturday.'

Preston looked sceptical. 'Bought it?'

'That's what Wesley thought. Pinched obviously. Thompson never bought stuff fair and square in his life, Wesley says. "Fell off the back of a lorry" as they say. Well, Thompson gets a load of crap from the blokes in the bar and loses his rag and throws the thing at the wall, narrowly missing this nice couple sitting in the corner. Got bundled out into the car park by two of the darts team. Turns out his old lady had walked out on him, gone to her mother's after getting a visit from Mrs Buckleigh that afternoon. Gave the girl all his wages and extra in lieu of notice – a great bundle of twenties, more housekeeping that she'd seen in years – and says Jimmy's to keep clear of Percivals or she'd call the police.'

'Thompson spilled all this in the car park?'

'Straight up. But that wasn't all of it. To cap it, Buckleigh spells it out to Jimmy's wife that he'd screwed her daughter! Fifteen-year-old! Fancy that! Bloody cow lied through her teeth o'course, sheer bitchiness if you ask me. The boys who'd bundled him out calmed Jimmy down and loaded the chainsaw on to his motorbike and he weaved off up the road home. They felt quite sorry for him at the finish, told Wesley what had gone on and Thompson ends up favourite with our poor bloody victim cast as an evil-mouthed witch.'

'But why would she lie to his wife – make up a story like that about her own kid?'

Buller shrugged. 'Search me, Mick. These people have some funny ideas and no mistake. Where's Hayes?'

'Gone off to the gardening school to interview the lady who found the body. You want to put a report in about this story about Jimmy Thompson?'

'Yeah, why not? Up to Hayes to follow it up or not, ain't it? Where's my so-called associate, Ginger Robbins?'

'Latched on to the DCI to see Mrs Blum. Reckons she's met her before.'

Buller raised his eyes in disbelief.

Forty-Seven

Hayes used the brief respite on his way to the gardening school to shake down Jenny Robbins about her interview with Bossom.

'Nothing much of interest, sir. He confirms he was calling at the cottage on Saturday afternoon to talk to Mrs Buckleigh about more sheep killing, and mentioned that her car was there. He seemed to think she was avoiding him.'

'I bet she was – guessed the old duffer was trying to up the ante on the compensation. Being rich didn't do her any favours, did it? People always trying to fleece her for as much as they could get.'

'You mean Monty Neville?'

'He's the worst, but she was her own worst enemy in some ways, thought she could always buy her way out of trouble. I'm going to see her business partner in the morning, a big noise in the theatre world called Kerslake. Ever heard of him?'

Robbins shook her head. 'No. Movies are more my thing.'

'Talking to her solicitor prompted me to widen the net.'

'Mr Allinson? The one who reported finding the body?'

'Mmm. He outlined the terms of this trust fund set up for her daughter. Very generous. Over-generous, I would say, as regards to her ex-husband, and Allinson went as far as he dare as Neville's lawyer to agree. But like I said, Stella Buckleigh liked to buy her way out of a tight corner and some people took advantage.'

'Did Allinson suggest you spoke to this business partner of hers? No money troubles there surely, sir?'

'Christ no! The late Mr Buckleigh had the Midas touch and his wife was no fool, but apparently Allinson received a phone call at his office first thing, from Kerslake. He had heard about the murder and wanted to check on the situation regarding ownership of the theatre they ran. Buckleigh was the major shareholder but was already planning to sell out to Kerslake and naturally he was worried about the deal going sour. Allinson wouldn't comment further but hinted a word with Kerslake would throw more light on our victim's London friends.'

They drove through the wide gates of St Osyth's Manor, now transformed into a residential gardening school, the sign attached to the lodge directing visitors to the main house.

'It used to be a hotel, sir,' Robbins said, 'but the new owner's spent a bomb bringing it up to scratch inside, I've heard, and gets his students to put in the hard graft of landscaping his gardens. Brilliant idea, don't you think? Getting his students to pay good money to fix up the grounds for him?' She giggled, her ponytail jiggling as they emerged to stand at the front entrance.

Mervyn Stott came to the door himself and held out a hand.

'Chief Inspector Hayes, I think we've met before if I'm not mistaken?'

Hayes brushed this aside and introduced Robbins as they were shown into the panelled hall. Sounds of activity filtered from a conservatory opening off the refectory, the tables already set for tea.

'I've come to see Mrs Blum,' Hayes insisted. 'How is she, Mr Stott?'

'Bearing up.' His response was muted, the man's normal bonhomie diminished by anxiety. 'She insists on working but I'm not sure she's up to it yet. Finding Stella all bashed up like that takes time to accept. And, of course, it's not long since her husband died. A heart attack, poor man, a quick release for him but a devastating blow for Tory. A lovely girl. She's taking students through a botanical drawing class but they're due for a tea break. May I offer you folks some refreshment?' he asked, his eyes darting towards a group emerging from the library. Stott greeted them warmly and led Hayes through to meet Tory who was pinning up watercolours on a display board. She visibly blanched as Hayes crossed the room, her cheeks ashen against the fall of dark hair.

Mervyn backed away, murmuring, 'Will you excuse me? Can I send in some tea, Tory?'

'Y–yes please. That would be nice.'

She wore a yellow smock over jeans, her tall figure slight as a wand. She smiled, offering Hayes a seat, Robbins hovering in the background, missing nothing, her gaze sliding around the room with interest. All three seated themselves by the window and Hayes paused only briefly before plunging into the business in hand, guessing that the sooner the job was done the tension Tory Blum clearly suffered would lessen.

'To recapitulate, Mrs Blum. Your full name and address for our records, please.'

Tory's voice was surprisingly firm, though her fingers twisted nervously as if to rid her hands of an invisible stain. Jenny scribbled away in her notebook.

'And your relationship with Mrs Buckleigh?'

'We were friends at school but only became reacquainted recently. Kate traced me on the Net.'

Jenny's eyes lit up. 'Really?'

Tory smiled. 'Stella insisted we got together at the cottage at Easter and things snowballed from there. It was indirectly through Stella that I got this job.'

'So you were only close for a few months?'

'Yes, I suppose so. But we slotted together straight away, as if there had been no years in between. But Kate and Stella were comfortably off and had lead quite different lives from me so it was kind of them to be there for me when Stefan died so suddenly.'

'Kate?' Jenny cut in, her pen poised.

'Kate Hilton, her husband is the film actor, Charlie, you must have heard of him.'

'Yes, of course,' Hayes said doubtfully. 'And his son? The boy who fell from the roof?'

Tory glanced away, her eyes hooded. 'That was an accident. He broke in and stole a few things and then . . . then fell . . .' she added lamely.

'I know this is difficult for you, Mrs Blum, but we have to build up a picture of Stella's friends,' Hayes said firmly. 'Her boyfriends? You shared confidences about her private life?'

Tory looked down, frowning into her lap. At that moment a girl came in with a tea tray which she placed on the window seat between them. Tory thanked her and busied herself pouring tea and offering sugar and milk, the interruption bringing a brief respite.

'I must ask you, Mrs Blum, to cast your mind back to any confidences Stella shared with you. It is very important we catch her killer and the strong possibility is that he was a close friend of you both. Can you help us?'

Tory stared out at the sunny vista, her mind in turmoil. At last she spoke. 'There was a man. But it was complicated. It was a secret between us. He was related to a friend of ours who never found out about their affair. I'd hate to bring her any more grief on top of everything else.'

Hayes took a shot in the dark. 'You mean Kate? Your friend whose son died at Stella's flat. You know why he was there?'

She looked up wildly. 'Oh no! I wasn't talking about Chaz. Stella wasn't attracted to young men, Chaz was more like her daughter Fran's boyfriend. It was his father, Charlie.'

'Charlie Hilton?' Robbins gasped, unable to stop herself.

'And you're sure about this?' Hayes barked.

'Absolutely. She stayed with him in Paris and later Charlie spent the weekend with Stella at Percivals.'

'She told you all this?'

'In confidence. I can't believe Charlie would hurt her; it was a little game of hers – I think she had the idea she could make him do things.'

'In confidence, did Stella Buckleigh admit to a drug habit? That she had access to cocaine for instance?'

Tory stiffened. 'Stella didn't do drugs, she was much too careful of her looks to dabble in something like that. You found drugs at the cottage?'

Hayes let this question hang in the air and insisted they get on with taking her statement. Jenny Robbins' sharp brain went clickety-click and it was only on the drive back to the station that she dared to voice the conclusion that now seemed to have been staring them in the face.

'I thought you said you were a movie fan?' Hayes chivvied.

'Didn't recognize Charlie Hilton in drag, though, did you, Robbins?'

Forty-Eight

Hayes dropped Jenny Robbins off outside the station. 'Can't stop – got to be in Oxford to meet Neville at four o'clock.'

He found Monty Neville in the waiting room at the mortuary, a cheerless Valhalla at the best of times and the scene of sorrow for those left behind.

He hurried in. 'Sorry to keep you, Mr Neville – very good of you to come so promptly. How is your daughter?'

'In a terrible state. I've left her with my fiancée's people at present – I've no one else. Fran clings to Morag, they seem to have formed an alliance against the world since all this happened. Any news?'

'Not so far, but we have a few leads. Shall we proceed? I realize that this is an ordeal for you. I'm sorry.'

They were admitted to a viewing room where the light was uncompromising and the smell of disinfectant something Hayes would never get used to.

Monty Neville dealt with the situation stony-faced, his composure a relief to Hayes who was all too aware that the broken figure lying on the gurney was a travesty of the lovely Stella Buckleigh. They went out, Hayes steering his witness to a side room.

'Before you go, Mr Neville, could I have a statement from you? You were seen visiting the cottage on Friday.'

'That's right. It had been arranged, but Stella wasn't there. Her car was missing so I assumed she had stayed in London. I had been to the solicitors' office in Oxford.'

'You were angry.'

Monty looked harassed. 'Well, yes, as a matter of fact, I was bloody furious. We had things to talk about, financial details concerning Frances' trust fund.'

'May I ask you to listen to this?' Hayes produced a small tape recorder and played Monty's message from the answer machine.

He shrugged. 'That just about sums it up. Stella had promised to lend me a substantial sum to tide me over a sticky patch and when I got to Allinson's office it turns out the money was to be tied up in legal rigmarole connected with the fund. Pie in the sky, Inspector. No use to me at all. Do you blame me for losing my rag like that? Stella and I rubbed along as best we could because of Fran but she was a very manipulative woman. Cruel, in fact.'

'But to put it bluntly, Mr Neville, she had bailed you out before.'

'Often enough. The business I'm in, horse racing and betting shops, is volatile, Stella knew that. She turned nasty on me because I had found someone else – you know what women can be like.'

Hayes slipped the tape recorder back into his pocket. 'But things have gone in your favour now, haven't they? Now that you are the major trustee, you do, so I understand from Mr Allinson, qualify to claim the twenty-five thousand pound personal payment Mrs Buckleigh agreed to be made immediately available to you to cover incidental expenses running up to your daughter's majority, at which point your duties as trustee would cease.'

Neville's face darkened. 'You're not insinuating I had anything to do with Stella's death, are you?'

'You were furious enough on Friday to threaten to come back, were you not? And desperate. Your fiancée knows nothing of your continuing dependence on your ex-wife?'

'The cash-flow problem would have been settled even if, as a last resort, I had to appeal to my future father-in-law for a loan.'

'Hardly getting off on the right foot though, is it? Can we have your assurance you did *not* return to Percivals to pursue this quarrel?'

Monty braced himself, balancing the odds that this detective had the answers to all his questions before he posed them.

'Well, actually, I did go back. Sunday morning. I'd been away in Ireland and my daughter had just got out of hospital so it was impossible for me to leave Morag alone for the weekend. But I left early Sunday morning and drove to Percivals to make a final appeal to Stella to keep her word. Frances had spoken to her mother on the phone on Saturday and assured me Stella was staying in the country, so I took a chance on catching her unawares, dropping in unannounced so she couldn't dodge the issue like she had on Friday. But she wasn't there. Her car was round the back but there was no sign of her so I had to push off back to Lingfield – there was to be a family lunch and Morag had invited some cousins over to meet me and to discuss the wedding arrangements. There was no way I could hang about for Stella so I drove straight back. Then later, of course, I got the terrible news and it's been a nightmare ever since.'

'But, let's be frank, Mr Neville, the nightmare started before your ex-wife's death, didn't it? She told me, in confidence, that Frances had been raped.'

'She told *you!*'

'She asked my professional advice about bringing a case. I advised against it, for your daughter's sake. Did Mrs Buckleigh tell you she was hoping to institute charges again the man?'

Monty looked utterly shocked. 'No.'

'And did Frances tell you who this man was?'

'No. She refused to discuss it even with Morag. My daughter can be stubborn and even Stella knew nothing about any rape until Fran was in hospital.'

Hayes relaxed. 'We shall have to leave it there I think. While we are examining your ex-wife's relationships, I have to ask this: did you know of any lovers?'

'Stella didn't share her secrets with me.'

'So you know of no affair? No current man in her life?'

'I suggest you ask her girlfriends. It's the sort of thing women chat about, I guess. And she was very close to friends who stayed at Percivals over the Easter weekend. Fran knows them.'

'I'm afraid I shall have to interview your daughter, Mr Neville.'

Monty leapt up. 'That is totally unnecessary. Entirely out of order! Fran's in no state to be put through any third degree. And about what? I strongly object to any rape investigation and I'm sure my daughter feels the same.'

'It is necessary for us to co-ordinate with the investigation of the Hilton death. Frances may have information linking the young man's accident with her mother's murder. We have evidence that Mrs Buckleigh was in the throes of an affair with Charlie Hilton, the father of Fran's boyfriend.'

'Good God! That's all settled, the inquest is to be next week, an accidental death, no question. The stupid fellow was half blind with a concoction of drugs and booze. It's a wonder he could stand, let alone keep his balance in any roof-terrace caper. It was in all the papers.'

Hayes closed his notebook. 'Nevertheless, I shall need a signed statement from you, Mr Neville. I suggest you come back to Renham station with me now and list your move-ments over the weekend. We shall also require a formal acknowledgment of your reasons for calling at the cottage not once, but twice, in your efforts to persuade Mrs Buckleigh to lend you a considerable sum of money. You can catch a train back to London from Renham this evening.'

Hayes escorted Monty to the car park and they drove to Renham in silence. Later, when his witness had departed to catch his train, Hayes settled down with Sergeant Preston to check through the results of the day's investigation.

'Sergeant Jennings left a message to say he'd spoken to the electician who installed the security cameras. No joy. The bloke swears his stuff was top class and any malfunction was down to the lady herself who must have messed up the CCTV tape, being a bit green with the new technology. Mr Truelove did say the videos were a try-on, to catch a domestic she had said. Petty pilfering. Didn't sound right to me – shelling out on all that surveillance equipment just to catch the cleaner pinching cigarettes or helping herself to any spare cash lying around.'

'Oh well, win some, lose some. Anything else, Sergeant?'

'Not a lot, sir,' Preston admitted. 'Buller's was the only break – we at least know that our unlucky lady spent Saturday afternoon walking to the village to pay off Thompson's wife.'

Hayes reached out for the file and scanned Buller's report.

'It's the chainsaw incident that worries me,' Hayes reflected. 'Give me ten minutes and then ask Buller and Robbins to be in my office.'

He rifled through the accounts from Stella's desk and pounced on a receipt just as Robbins and the burly sergeant knocked at the door.

'Ah, Buller, sit down, mate. Good work here,' he said, tapping Preston's file.

Robbins looked puzzled. 'The fracas in the pub Saturday night? Thompson going berserk in the public bar?'

'Yes. Thompson toting a chainsaw. Who says the country's boring? Selling it, he claimed. An item he had bought that very afternoon from a biker at the autocross?'

'Well, that's what the landlord said,' Buller insisted.

Hayes passed over a receipt. 'This was paid for by our victim just before Easter. Cash purchase from Limparts Hardware in Aylesbury. Know it?'

'Big outlet, best-quality gear, sir.'

'Right. Now, the chances of our unemployed gardener getting his hands on an expensive piece of equipment like that are not great, would you say? I want you to get a warrant and go to Thompson's house straight away before he's had a chance to pawn it. Search the premises for stolen goods – take a couple of men with you. You might strike lucky, but in any event bring back the chainsaw and put Thompson through the wringer for proof he bought it like he says. Check the reference number with Limparts against this receipt. If Thompson stole the chainsaw from Buckleigh's shed he was probably on the premises during the fatal weekend, wouldn't hang on to it any longer than necessary.'

Buller half rose but Hayes motioned him to stay put. 'And Robbins, I want you to ferret out his wife. If she's still at her mother's, the post office will put you on the right road. Nothing goes on in a small place like Bramley Green that doesn't get filtered through the village shop. And when you find Mrs Thompson, very gently ask her if Buckleigh called in on Saturday afternoon to give her Jimmy's wages. Don't panic the woman – keep everything low key – she'll be all nerves as it is waiting for the police to check up on Buckleigh's movements. You'll have to question her about the accusation of rape. Give her plenty of time but don't let her off the hook with that. If her mother's sitting in on the questioning she may want to put the boot in with her no-good son-in-law. A nice sympathetic ear, OK? Then, as if as an afterthought, slip in something about the chainsaw. Did she see it in the house before Saturday? Did she see it at all? If he says he bought it that afternoon she would have scarpered with his wages well before the showdown in the pub. Put in your reports with Preston first thing and if you get any aggro from Thompson, Buller, arrest him on suspicion of handling stolen goods.'

Robbins leant forward. 'This rape business, sir. You don't believe it, do you? That Buckleigh's kid was attacked?'

'I do. Stella Buckleigh discussed it with me personally and was definitely in a mood to take it to court if the girl agreed.'

They found themselves shunted out in double-quick time before Robbins could ask more, the question of the nature of the governor's friendship with the dead woman far from clear. Buller impatiently strode off, his anxiety to jump on Thompson before the chainsaw vanished blanking out any side issues about the DCI's social connections.

Robbins followed, closing the door firmly behind her.

Hayes decided to catch up on his own love life before it was too late.

'Hi, Pippa! Darling, I've been up to my eyes here. You've heard? Well, I think I need a bit of pampering tonight.'

'Oh, yeah? And what about the piano practice? This concert's only a few weeks away, Roger.'

'Christ, you sound like my old piano teacher. "If you don't practise, Roger, you'll get nowhere." Dear old Mossy.'

'Well, she was right.'

'Everyone needs a bit of relaxation – even you, my sweet. How about a Chinese and a couple of videos? You still a member of that video club? I fancy something romantic. Why don't you get a pair of Charlie Hilton films to put us in the right mood?'

She snorted in derision but agreed to play along with his wild fancies just for once.

They were well into the second film when Hayes' mobile rang. Pippa grimaced. He extracted himself from their cosy embrace and went into the hall to answer it.

'Yes?'

'It's Robbins, sir. I was getting some petrol at that big place just outside Renham and having a bit of a josh with the regular girl there, Shirley Phillips. She was just bubbling with excitement about this birthday card.'

'Come on, Robbins, get on with it.'

'Apparently she was on duty Saturday night when this celebrity bowls in. Over the moon she was. Guess who? Charlie Hilton! She told him it was her birthday – a blatant fib but she's quick on her feet that girl – and ran over to the racks, picked up a card and asked him to write in it for her.'

'You checked? It's kosher? He features on their security camera?'

'It's been run back since the weekend. Sorry. But there was another guy working in the petrol station that night who backs her up. I've bagged the card, promised to get it back to her soonest.'

'Did he sign for his petrol?'

'Paid cash.'

'Pity. Never mind. Excellent work, Robbins, I'll go over it with you when I get back from London tomorrow. Bag it up, there might be fingerprints, don't want the guy swearing he was off the planet at the weekend.'

'I doubt there'd be anything useful, sir. Shirley's been showing off this birthday card to all her customers.'

'Well, book it in with Sergeant Preston, OK? What time was this celebrity call?'

'About a quarter to ten, she says, but we could budge that ten minutes either way.'

'Right. Well, cheers, Robbins. Don't you ever take a night off?' he added with a chuckle.

When he got back to the film Pippa had fallen asleep and

lay across the sofa in all but a coma. Hayes didn't blame her: Charlie Hilton's brand of passion was not the sort to have you foaming at the mouth, even on film.

He left a note on the coffee table and quietly let himself out.

Forty-Nine

B efore he set off to make his appointment with Kerslake, Hayes put through a call to his former colleague, DI Chivers.

'Hi, Pete, how's tricks? Better class of crime in Belgravia, I bet.'

'Same villains, bigger heists,' he countered.

'Any chance of a window in your schedule, mate? We've got two cases which overlap. I expect you heard – the Buckleigh woman's dead.'

'Yeah! Hasn't rocked my investigation so far, but you think there might be a link with the Hilton accident?'

'Possibly. I've got to be in Soho by eleven. How about a beer and a sandwich when I get through?'

'Is this official, Roger?'

'Not yet. But I'd like to compare notes, OK by you? I've got the keys to her flat if you're interested.'

'My investigation's already passed to the coroner's officer,' he said defensively.

'No harm in showing me round though. What do you say? Shall I give you a bell when I've finished in Soho and we can meet outside the Buckleigh building?'

Hayes rang off, suspecting that his one-time partner, newly transferred to the Met, was an unwilling participant in a re-examination of the crime scene now that, as far as Chivers was concerned, the file was in his out tray.

Stanley Kerslake greeted the DCI affably, though he had to admit this ascetic-looking copper was hardly the sort of flatfoot he was expecting. They settled down in his office without too much preamble.

'Any idea who killed Stella Buckleigh, Mr Kerslake?'

Stanley stiffened, his notions of a police investigation loosely based on the civilized dialogue between characters in *The Mousetrap*.

'No! of course I haven't. Some local riff-raff I imagine. That cottage of hers was far too remote to be safe. Never understood it myself – no social life at all in a dead end like Bramley Green. It was Anthony's choice, of course. Strange fellow. Astute as a bag of monkeys when it came to a business deal, but choosing a weekend place out in the sticks like that? Utter madness. Stella was selling up you know, fancied a nice little flat in Monte Carlo.'

'Mrs Buckleigh was also thinking of bowing out of your joint theatre project.'

'Who told you that?' he snapped.

'I'm a detective, Mr Kerslake, information comes in from all sides.'

'I bet it was that bloody lawyer, Allinson, tipped you off. I hardly need to emphasize to you, Chief Inspector, that speculation in the money market could badly influence the value of Stella's estate.'

'Frankly, sir, the deal is of no importance to my line of enquiry and any confidences you may wish to share with me are strictly background information, which is why I sought a private discussion, Mr Kerslake. You see there are aspects of Mrs Buckleigh's lifestyle about which you may be extremely helpful.'

Stanley offered Hayes a cigar from an elaborate humidor before lighting up himself and filling the room with the pungent aroma of rich Havana.

'In what way, Mr Hayes?'

'Concerning Mrs Buckleigh's private life. I've brought with me a videotape of a recent situation played out at the cottage. May I run it?'

Stanley's eyes glittered. 'If it's that bloody silly lark with Charlie Hilton, I've seen it. Stella gave me a copy.'

Now it was Hayes' turn to sit up. 'Really? The cross-dressing party?'

'That's the one.'

'Why did she pass a copy to you?'

Smoke drifted around Stanley's head as he lazily puffed away the seconds while considering how far it was necessary to shop Charlie Hilton. In the course of Stanley's confabulation with Charlie's agent, deLaunay, they had agreed that Hilton's reign as a movie heart-throb was, in any event, on its last knockings and, if anything was to be salvaged, keeping a lid on Charlie's little hobby was essential.

Stanley humorously raised an eyebrow. 'You don't take that sort of thing seriously, do you, Inspector? Stella was a minx. She'd been having a romp with Hilton and no harm had been done until his son broke into her flat and fell off the roof. That put an entirely different complexion on things. The videotape shows Charlie snorting coke and Stella was afraid she would be linked with the boy's supply, which the police investigation might point to the reason Chaz was busting into the apartment.'

'Did you ask her why she secretly videoed the party games in the first place?'

'I did. She wouldn't say. I suspect it was thought up as a practical joke and later, after Chaz died, she decided to keep it as some sort of insurance. Stella didn't do drugs and didn't trust Charlie not to imply under questioning that she was the one who supplied the stuff to put Charlie in the party mood. She was terrified of getting involved and asked me to put his agent, deLaunay, in the picture. She hinted that if Charlie threatened to drag her into the Chaz investigation on a drugs link she would hand the videotape to the media and that, as I need hardly spell out, would be curtains for his career. Incidentally, where did you come across Stella's copy?'

'In the cottage – we ran the video camera and caught several interesting vignettes of Mrs Buckleigh's private life.'

'Really? So Charlie wasn't her only victim?'

Hayes let this pass. 'So you played along with her request and debated a rescue package with Charlie's agent?'

'The carrot was a role in a future production at Bucks Theatre. Charlie wanted to prove himself as a stage actor and deLaunay thought it would be a wise career move. As a major shareholder, Stella had a say in production and she intimated that if Charlie kept his nose out of the police investigation of his son's death she would support his hopes of starring in a Chekhov play.'

'Chekhov!' Hayes spluttered.

Kerslake blandly continued. 'It was all panic on Stella's part, of course. Why would Charlie wish to flaunt an affair with her and involve himself in a possible counter accusation of drug taking? Or worse, supplying, if the bloody video came out and Stella felt vindictive.'

'Well, Chaz was his only child, Mr Kerslake. Any man would want revenge if he thought his lover was involved with the boy in some way. Do you think she had access to class A drugs?'

'Absolutely not! Stella wouldn't know where to start, and let's not forget she was a clever woman with a child of her own to consider. Protecting Frances was her main concern; Charlie Hilton was just a fun thing that went off the Richter scale. Dumping a bloke like that wouldn't concern her for a moment. Stella was the last person to be star-struck, believe me.' He paused, eyeing Hayes with steely intent. 'I'll tell you something, though, that kid of hers was in real trouble, much deeper than the usual teenage stuff. Stella got an emergency call from her ex while she was here in the office with me. Frances had been taken to hospital and Stella's immediate response was to ask if she'd slit her wrists. How about that? Only fifteen and her mother thinks she's tried to top herself.' Stanley dabbed at his mouth, clearly affected.

'So what's your impression of Charlie Hilton, Mr Kerslake?'

Stanley leaned back in his leather chair and drew on his cigar. 'Not much as an actor. I wasn't keen to get pushed into this Chekhov play idea but I needed to keep Stella sweet. Screwed me to back her if any dirty linen got into the papers, but if I played my cards right with her I'd be in a position to run Bucks on my own terms, buy her out and blow off the jackals who've been circling Bucks ever since Anthony died.'

216

'Do you think Hilton murdered her? Revenge? Self-preservation? She was a dangerous enemy by any calculation.'

'Wouldn't put Charlie in the killer bracket myself, though he *was* violent. Gave Stella a black eye after that fancy dress party got rough. Ask around. Stella's shiner was blacked out with Jackie O shades for a week.'

Hayes rose and shook hands across the desk. 'Thank you for your time, Mr Kerslake. I hope I won't have to bother you again. Where is the videotape now?'

'DeLaunay has it. Do you want his address?'

'Please. But perhaps you could warn him to keep it in his safe. We wouldn't like stuff like that to leak out, would we?'

Stanley scribbled down an address and phone number and passed it over.

'I shall have to interview Mr Hilton. Any idea where I might find him?'

'You'll have to ask deLaunay. Last I heard he was filming in Paris.'

Out in the street once again Hayes tried to put Kerslake's comments in context. In fact, as opinions went, Stella's business partner had added only to a suspicion that Stella's freakish control over the men who had had the misfortune to swim in her muddy pool was awesome. He phoned Pete Chivers and was feeding the parking meter opposite Stella's apartment as the police car drew into the kerb.

Hayes slapped him on the shoulder, grinning. 'Long time no see, Pete.'

'Not long enough if you're here trying to rubbish my investigation,' Chivers retorted with a wintry smile.

They rose to the top floor squeezed into the coffin-sized lift. Hayes unlocked the main door and they stepped inside, the stench of decaying lilies in a vase of stagnant water wafting round the flat like miasma from the grave.

Fifty

Hayes and Pete Chivers had just sat down with their lager and ploughman's when Hayes' mobile shrilled.

'Hayes.'

'Buller here, sir. Thought you ought to know we've got Thompson in custody.'

'On what charge?'

'He took a swing at Terry Bell when we tried to search his house.'

'Right. Leave him to cool off, I want to have first shot at that bastard. Has he admitted anything?'

'No. But we found the chainsaw and the hardware suppliers are looking at it now. Robbins buzzed over to Aylesbury straight off to try to get a tie-in with Mrs Buckleigh's receipt.'

'Good work, Sergeant. I'll be back as soon as I can.'

Buller coughed. 'Sooner would be best, sir. The superintendent wants a word.'

Hayes stifled an expletive and rang off, Chivers' amused expression doing nothing to sweeten his mood. 'Trouble, Roger?'

'Not a problem. It was just that I had hoped to drive down to Lingfield this afternoon and talk to the daughter. It'll have to wait, my super's on the rampage. Can't keep his sticky fingers out of it.'

Chivers frowned. 'Take my advice, mate, and leave the girl alone. A vulnerable witness presents a sackload of difficulties. Why involve yourself with the kid? She was away at school when the Hilton boy broke in and, from what I've read, miles away when her mother copped it.'

Roger shrugged. 'Can't help feeling she's being ring-fenced

218

and, apart from the two deaths, I have a shrewd suspicion that the man we're holding on the assault charge was a rapist.'

Chivers whistled. 'She says she was raped? The daughter?'

'Stella Buckleigh admitted it to me but the girl won't name the man involved.'

'Funny thing is, I had my doubts about that. Her mother told me her friend was interested in bringing a rape charge and when I ask her for details, it turns out the victim was a teenager. She pretended she was asking out of interest, never said anything about her daughter. You sure?'

'The father's not co-operating and the girl's only just out of hospital so I suppose you're right – asking awkward questions when her mother's just been killed would almost amount to police brutality,' he said wryly. 'But you know how it is, Pete, unless you get your witnesses while they're still in shock the chances are they get amnesia.' He tossed down his beer and put on his jacket. 'No evidence of drugs at the flat, was there?'

'Not a sniff. The mixed bag stuffed into the Hilton guy's pockets was all we found. The inquest's due next week.'

'Is his father attending? The film bloke.'

'No idea, but I doubt it. Seems he pretty well lost touch with the lad in recent years and left the stepmother to shell out for at least two detox programmes. Expensive waste of time if you ask me; users like Chaz Hilton rarely give up till they've either run out of funds or come to a sticky end.'

'Well, Hilton junior certainly did that. I'd better push off back to Renham, Pete, and see what I can squeeze out of our number-one suspect.'

Hayes' debriefing by Superintendent Waller was short and not at all sweet. They sat opposite each other as if preparing for an arm-wrestling match.

'Well, Hayes?'

'Not much, sir. I've got a lead on Charlie Hilton's movements on the fatal Saturday but we may have to persuade him to return from Paris.'

'Fat chance!'

'He was definitely seen in Renham that night and had previously landed a fist on our unfortunate victim.'

'Proof?'

'Her business partner's willing to put his name to it and I imagine even the ex-husband would notice a black eye.'

'You think Hilton killed her?'

Hayes played it cool. 'Well, he *was* in the locality, which is not exactly on the celebrity beat, and probably suspected Buckleigh was involved in his son's drug habit. I'd like to get a sniffer dog to run over the cottage. OK?'

'All sounds very wishy-washy to me, Hayes. You've come up with nothing else?'

'Not so far, sir. I took a look round Buckleigh's flat while I was in the area. In the company of the investigating officer, DI Chivers.'

'You're not interfering in a Met case, surely?' Waller snapped. 'We're not stamping our shit all over their crime scene, Hayes, so forget it.'

Hayes closed his mouth and put away his notebook. 'All right if I check with the incident room, sir?' his said with barely concealed irritation. 'Sergeant Preston's co-ordinating lines of enquiry.'

Waller nodded bleakly, leaving Hayes to bolt to his own room. He closed the door and lit a cigarette, running his eyes down the list of suspects. Putting Charlie Hilton in the frame was a long shot but what did he know? These actor types were trained to put a gloss on things, but being seen at a service station on the Saturday night was not exactly pin-pointing the man at the murder scene, was it?'

The problem was the CCTV camera being taped over. Anyone could have come and gone after Bossom's visit without being recorded. And he only had Monty Neville's word for it that he was tucked up at Lingfield all Saturday.

'By the time I get the chance to interview that jammy bastard he will have half a dozen alibis lined up,' Hayes mused. But, at the end of the day, Neville was the only suspect who had a practical motive: twenty-five thousand quid in his pocket just when he needed it. Nearly as good as winning the Lottery.

He called in Buller to go over the arrest of Jimmy Thompson. All as one might expect – an alleged thief objecting with his fists and boots to a search of his house.

'Robbins is just back from Aylesbury, sir. The hardware people confirm that the chainsaw is the one they sold to Mrs Buckleigh. A new model, just out, and the only one they've sold so far. Worth a bob or two, even at a boot sale.'

'How rough did you get with Thompson? I don't want any flack about undue pressure being put on a prisoner.'

Buller's mouth tightened. 'He wants to see a solicitor.'

'OK, we'll play it by the book. As soon as his brief turns up let me know and we'll take him through his story. In the meantime, line up a sniffer dog to go over that cottage.'

Buller's eyes widened. 'Might take a while, sir. I'll ring the airport, see if they can come up with something.'

Hayes spent the next hour going through the statements – no mean task, Robbins having cornered a whole bundle of witnesses, including the landlord of the Crown, who was willing to testify about Thompson's efforts to sell the chainsaw in the public bar that night. Her report from Patsy Thompson was less revealing, the girl clearly worried about her husband's reaction to her co-operation with the police. She had seen no chainsaw in the house, nor any other tools that might have been brought back by Jimmy. However, she admitted that Stella Buckleigh had visited and made an accusation that Jimmy had attacked her daughter. Patsy didn't believe it. Well, she wouldn't, would she? Not now she had had time to get over the shock.

Hayes went to the door and called Jenny Robbins to come through. She wore a navy-blue tee shirt and jeans, her hair a flaming halo in the light streaming through his office window.

'Sit down, Robbins.' He tapped Patsy Thompson's statement. 'Apart from the facts, what was your impression of the woman?'

'Shy, nervous and struggling between her mother – an overbearing sort who had nothing good to say about Jimmy – and a waning desire to leave home. I'd say she'll be back with Jimmy just as soon as she dares. She's got two kids, one barely six months old, and the prospect of life as a single mother living in her mum's house must seem a poor alternative, even if Jimmy isn't exactly God's gift as a husband.'

'At least she got her hands on his wages.'

'A month's pay in lieu of notice, plus a week owing. Pretty generous for a mother who suspects him of raping her daughter.'

'Buckleigh may have picked on the wrong guy, of course. Her girl's keeping his name to herself and Monty Neville wants to brush the whole thing under the carpet. The super's against any probing in that direction – it's political dynamite trying to shake down a child without her father's co-operation. Anyway, it's a side issue in this investigation, merely a stick to beat Jimmy Thompson.'

'Can I sit in on the interview, sir?'

Hayes pulled a long face. 'Jumping the gun, aren't you, Robbins? Incidentally, when do you take your sergeants' exam?'

'September.'

Hayes reread Patsy Thompson's statement, the silence growing between them. 'OK. But keep your mouth shut. Jimmy's been in interview rooms a dozen times; he's not going to respond to wild shots from an amateur.'

Robbins took this as a yes and hurried out before the DCI changed his mind.

Fifty-One

Tory phoned the police station and got permission to remove her car from Percivals. It seemed like a good opportunity to take Moses for a long walk and she set off across the fields, picking a bunch of buttercups and daises en route and tying them into a bunch with a ribbon from her hair.

Arriving at the cottage, she was surprised to find that the police presence had been rigorously scaled down, only a constable in a panda car blocking the lane from curious trespassers and a second man on duty at the door. She explained her mission, keeping Moses on a tight rein, and was directed to wait outside while he fetched the sergeant.

Buller emerged and, after ringing for confirmation from Hayes, escorted her to the stable yard where the 2CV was still parked.

'Nice little motor that,' he said with a smile. 'Not the prettiest car on the road but ideal if you've got a dog like that.' He patted Moses who responded with an effusive flourish of the tail. At that moment a man with a spaniel joined them and Buller pulled him aside for a quiet word.

Tory waited, and after a few minutes Buller and his colleague rejoined her. 'Was there something else, miss?'

The dogs sniffed each other with enthusiasm.

She held up the flowers. 'I wondered if it would be all right if I had a walk round the orchard? I wanted to say goodbye to my husband – his ashes are scattered under the trees and once the cottage is sold I shan't be able to come here again.' Tory nervously bit her lip.

Buller, a pushover when it came to damsels in distress, decided to chance it. 'OK, miss, but mum's the word. My boss likes to keep a crime scene secure, if you see my point.'

The man with the spaniel piped up. 'It's all right, Sergeant, Buster needs a run, I'll accompany the young lady if she's agreeable.'

Buller relaxed. 'That's a good idea. But don't let the dogs near that sheep field, mind. The farmer's had another sheep savaged at the weekend and he's looking for someone to blame.'

'A second sheep?' Tory gasped. 'He complained about a dead sheep at Easter and blamed Moses, who wouldn't hurt a fly.'

'Just keep to the orchard, all right? I'll see you both off if you let me know when you're leaving. I shall be inside.'

Tory nodded and walked off with the man she assumed to be a plain-clothes policeman.

'I'm Victoria Blum,' she said, setting the pace. 'I found the body, but I expect you knew that.'

'No, I didn't. I'm with Customs and Excise – the best option they had at short notice. Buster's a sniffer dog, we're usually working at the airport.'

'Really? How interesting. Would it be all right if I let Moses off? He's a very friendly dog.'

'Not a sheep-killer then?'

'Never! That old bloke was just hoping Stella would accept responsibility again – her boundary fence was broken down before. Tell me about Buster. A lot of training, I bet.'

'He's a valuable asset in our line of business.'

'But why are you here? Stella didn't do drugs.' Tory paused and laid her bouquet under a tree. The blossom was almost over, petals drifting down like confetti.

'I'm not allowed to say,' he replied. 'She was your friend? The dead woman.'

'Oh yes, we'd known each other for years.'

'Then I'm sure you're right. But Buster never makes a mistake and he sniffed out some women's clothing that was bagged up in the house. It must have belonged to someone else. Your friend brought people from London to stay, I expect.'

Tory paused, frowning, then hurried on, calling to Moses before replying as casually as she could, 'I suppose so. I've been living in Suffolk until recently. When my husband died, Stella helped me find a job in Renham. I'd been looking forward to living near her but she suddenly decided to sell up here – her daughter turned against the cottage. Teenagers are like that, aren't they? I know I was. All of a sudden they're only interested in shopping and boys. A quiet place in the country can be boring at that age.'

He whistled for his dog who bounded back, Moses tagging along. 'I'll have to get back to work. Nice meeting you, Mrs Blum. Are you leaving now?'

'I'd better. I don't think the sergeant wants me here unescorted. Thanks for being so kind. I don't think I shall be back again.'

Buller watched the two cars drive off and phoned through to Preston to let him know that the Blum car had been removed. 'Any developments, Mick?'

'Hayes wants you back as soon as the sniffer dog's off site. Any evidence?'

'A ragbag of stuff Robbins left in the utility room – she'd better make out a report on it.'

'Hot?'

'Pretty niffy according to the spaniel. The dog's specially trained to pick up on cocaine apart from everything else, so the forensic lads will have a lead. I'll bring it in straight away.'

'The DCI wants you to sit in on the Thompson interrogation. His solicitor's banged up with him now.'

'How's Terry?'

'He'll live. An uppercut enough to rattle his teeth but the doc says he's OK to work, which puts him in the police medal class with the super while we're so short-handed. I'll tell the DCI you'll be about fifteen minutes, shall I?'

When Buller got back to the station, the mixed bag of woollens was immediately grabbed for the forensic lab. Preston wasted no time in shunting him down to Hayes' office.

'Struck gold, I hear?'

'Not what you'd call a stash, sir, but according to the dog handler they've picked up traces of snow spilled in the bag. Could the bag have been contaminated?'

'Absolutely not!'

'Well, we'll just have to see what turns up but it don't look like anything much according to this bloke from Customs and Excise.'

There was a knock at the door. It was Jenny Robbins. 'The solicitor's ready when you are, sir. It's Mr Limpney – you remember him from before? He's got to be in court in an hour he says.'

'Does he, by God? Then we'd better jump to it and wheel out our suspect.' He turned to the sergeant. 'You arrested this guy, Buller, make sure he's not changed his tune about the chainsaw, eh? I've reluctantly agreed to let Robbins here sit in – these redheads can be very persuasive,' he added with a grin.

The three trooped out and assembled in the interview room, Robbins stationing herself at the door. Jimmy Thompson was already seated, his lawyer – a skinny, middle-aged man with thinning hair – regarded Hayes with respect. The tape recorder was set in motion and Buller uttered the preliminaries. Thompson looked as if he'd been up all night, his dishevelled clothing and bleary eyes robbing him of his usual air of defiance. Hayes noted that there were no obvious signs of anything which could be described as contusions, though he had no illusions about the firm treatment meted out to a bruiser who threw a punch at a constable.

'Now, shall we get down to details, Mr Thompson? This chainsaw. Before you answer, may I remind you that the suppliers have identified this particular model as the one sold to Mrs Buckleigh?'

'I just borrowed it, didn't I? She bought it for me to use and I took it back to my 'ouse to saw up some logs.'

'And when was this?'

'Can't remember everythin', can I?' he retorted.

'OK, let's move on. After "borrowing" your employer's equipment, why were you offering it for sale at the pub last Saturday night?'

Thompson glanced at his solicitor, who nodded.

'She owed me, see. Me wages.'

'Why was that? Because you had been sacked?'

The solicitor nodded again and Thompson let fly. 'That fucking cow went round to my 'ouse and told my old lady a pack of lies about me. And when I got back from the autocross I found out she'd buggered off with the kids. Left me! Gone off to her mum's, and all that woman's fault.'

'Your wife left a note?'

'No, Patsy's writing's none too good. I phoned her on her mobile and she told me about these lies she'd been fed.'

'Did she say Mrs Buckleigh had given her cash? For your work?'

'Yeah, and she weren't parting with it neither. It was Norah – her mum – put her up to it, so there was no point in going straight round there till Patsy cooled off. She'll come round soon enough.'

'But you needed the money?'

'Bloody skint, I was.'

'You told the landlord you'd bought the chainsaw from a mate at the autocross,' Buller barked.

Thompson refused to answer.

'I'm getting confused here, Jimmy,' Hayes put in. 'Tell me again. You borrowed the chainsaw when?'

He shrugged, saying nothing.

'Perhaps you "borrowed" it,' he said meaningfully, 'after you got back from your day out and found out Mrs Buckleigh had had words with Patsy? Any man would lose his rag coming home to find his wife had walked off with his wages, taking his kids, and believing a stack of gossip spewed out by a spiteful employer. You thought Mrs Buckleigh owed you, didn't you, Jimmy? And you bombed over to Percivals on your motorbike to have it out with her.'

'No way!' he shouted, half rising from his seat. Limpney grabbed his arm and persuaded him to sit down.

'You were seen,' Buller quietly put in. Hayes glanced at his sergeant whose stolid features were unreadable.

'Seen?' Thompson muttered. 'Who by? That bloody old fool Bossom been shouting his mouth off?'

Hayes remained silent. Buller continued to focus on his target and Robbins swallowed hard, Thompson's retort of 'Seen?' reverberating in her head.

'Saturday night,' Hayes continued. 'Bossom saw you in the lane Saturday night.' It was a flyer, but worth a try.

'I weren't in the bloody lane Saturday night. I cut through the woods on my bike.'

'So you *were* on your way to face off Mrs Buckleigh Saturday night.'

Thompson had started to sweat, moisture glistening on his upper lip. He glanced at Limpney, who remained stony-faced.

'Well, in a manner of speaking...Look, if I admit to taking the chainsaw – she owed me, Inspector, make no mistake about it – do I get off the assault charge?'

Buller's hollow laughter echoed in the bare room. 'For punching a constable, Thompson? Come off it, mate. You'll have to spell out more than that to get consideration and don't you know it!'

Limpney intervened. 'May I have a private word with my client, Chief Inspector? I think we can simplify all this.'

Hayes agreed and they discontinued the tape before trooping out. In the hallway Hayes turned to Buller. 'What's all this about being seen?' he whispered.

The sergeant looked decidedly sheepish. 'Worked a treat

though, didn't it? If he was there Saturday night he saw *something*, and theft of a chainsaw is small beer to Thompson. He's hoping nothing's going to come out about the real reason he got his cards, is he?'

'The rape,' Hayes muttered.

At that moment Limpney called them back. They sat down and reactivated the tape recording.

'My client wishes to change his plea.'

Buller cautioned Thompson and they settled down to hear his new story.

'OK. I did take the bloody chainsaw after I got back and found out Buckleigh had blown me out with Patsy. I got stuck into a bottle of whisky and after stewing on it for a couple of hours I decided to pay her back. I shot over to the cottage and took the saw from the shed. End of story.'

But Buller wasn't going to let it go. 'End of half the story. What about being seen? What about the security camera?'

Thompson laughed. 'Don't come that old malarkey, Buller. I was never clocked on her bloody CCTV.'

'Oh no? What makes you so sure? How was anyone to get near the cottage without being recorded? Fly there, did you, Jimmy?'

Hayes was getting tired of this and Limpney was glancing at his watch, worried about his appointment in court.

'You was the clever bugger who taped over the sensor, wasn't you, Thompson?' Buller spat out. 'Come on, lad, stop pissing about. As soon as we get the full story we can see how to spell it out on the charge sheet.'

Thompson closed his eyes. 'What about a fag?'

Hayes leaned across the table and offered his pack and a box of matches. Limpney nodded at his wretched client and they all waited for him to continue.

'Right. Straight up. Just after eight I decided to cash in. I shot over to Buckleigh's place and left my bike in the woods. I climbed up the bank and cut out the sensor from behind with some black plastic tape I'd brought from home. I'd worked out how to do it before – don't like sneaky tricks like CCTV at the best of times. Who was she trying to nab?

Poachers? I lugged the chainsaw back to the woods just in time before the old geezer comes up the lane.'

'Bossom?'

'Yeah. Silly old fart fancied he could get her to let him stay on, keep his fields and that. Didn't know that bitch like I did; no way was she going to change her mind.'

'And you say this was eightish?'

''Bout that.'

Buller impatiently cut in. 'Well, we know about Mr Bossom's visit. He was collecting a dead sheep from his field – he's already told us that.'

'In his little old Ford Fiesta? You're out of your tiny mind, Sergeant. It wasn't his pickup truck and there was no way Cissie'd let him stuff a dead sheep on her nice clean upholstery.'

Hayes stayed silent, letting Buller wind up the interview. He accompanied Limpney to the car park.

'I shall have to consult my superintendent about charges, Mr Limpney. Your client's co-operation is much appreciated. I'll ring you as soon as possible.'

They shook hands on it, the solicitor eyeing Hayes with the shrewd appraisal of a poker player.

Hayes returned to his office where Buller and Jenny Robbins joined him.

'He's not exactly what you'd call a reliable witness, but he's all we've got. I want you two to get back to Bossom and make some excuse to see this dead sheep he's on about. Robbins interviewed him before when the first sheep got savaged so he's not going to be too surprised if she tries to follow it up.'

'But he's made no official complaint, sir,' Robbins insisted.

'Well, just say it's new regulations from the Ministry. Red tape. We have to follow up these things for their records.'

Buller knew what Hayes was getting at. He smiled, his florid features taking on the semblance of a Toby jug. 'Right you are, sir, we'll get out to Bossom straight away.'

Fifty-Two

The superintendent was in a jovial mood.

'I hear you're mounting an investigation into the case of the dead sheep, Hayes,' he said with a chuckle.

'Just tying up a few loose ends, sir.'

'Well, don't waste any time on it, lad. We've got far more important problems as you well know. What's the score?'

'I got through to Charlie Hilton's agent and tracked him down in Paris. But deLaunay's confident Hilton will come back for an interview, if only to clear the air. I managed to speak with Hilton on the phone myself and I was surprised to find him so co-operative. Agrees he drove down here on Saturday night – he'd been in York for the boy's funeral the day before and Stella Buckleigh had invited him to the cottage for drinks.'

'What time did he say?'

'Got there about twenty past nine but she didn't open the door. They had quarrelled over his son's death and the meeting was so they could kiss and make up, but although the lights were on and her car was parked outside, there was no response. He said he knocked several times and shouted up at the bedroom window in case she had dozed off, but after five minutes' banging about he decided she'd changed her mind and didn't want to see him after all. He was pretty bitter at the time he said, and as he had made a special detour to effect this reconciliation thought the least she could have done was to phone and save him the journey. "Stella was like that," he said. "Thought nothing of treating her men like dogs. Ask that ex-husband of hers." His exact words, more or less.'

'Can't say I'd blame her leaving him on the doorstep if he

230

trashed her place like you saw when you looked in the windows the week before.'

'*And* he blacked her eye, don't forget. But what if he'd felt so furious he'd forced his way in to have it out with her? He would have discovered her body and found himself in deep shit. The doc estimated she was already dead before nine.'

'We can't guarantee a time of death though, Hayes, not that accurately. Are you saying you don't think he killed her?'

'If he did he was a cool customer, joking with the girl at the service station just after half past nine. We've no witness who saw Hilton enter the cottage that night and Monty Neville says he wasn't there at all on Saturday.'

'But you are checking Neville's alibi?'

'Just as soon as I've tied up the Thompson business.'

'He's still in custody?'

'Yes, but we shall have to charge him soon, sir. Limpney's on his case. I'll leave the interview tape for you, shall I, sir? I thought we could just charge him on the chainsaw and let him loose on bail and see where he leads us. We can always pick him up later if the rape charge goes ahead. Buller and DC Robbins have gone over to Bossom's place now to check him out – he was on the scene Saturday night, according to Thompson.'

Waller frowned, suspicion curling in his gut like dyspepsia. Hayes wasn't giving him the full picture, was he? Hayes would never have been his choice. The commissioner dumped him in Renham after some business in Oxford with that other officer who got shunted into the Met. What was his name? Chambers?

He pulled himself up short and dismissed his DCI with a curt, 'Well, you'd better get on with it, Hayes, you're not going to get anywhere with this murder hanging about here.'

Buller and Jenny Robbins arrived at Bossom's cottage just after three. The late spring had come into its stride at last, the rising temperature bobbing in the highs like a bottle out to sea with an SOS message. Several chickens scratching about in the dust scattered as the police car drew up. Mrs Bossom's cheerful face popped round the kitchen curtains

231

and she beamed, waving them in. The door was open, the sunshine forming a speckled pathway through the mote-laden air.

Buller's heavy footsteps clumped inside, Robbins lingering for a moment in the yard, estimating the extent of the small-holding. It wasn't much of a place, no more than two or three acres, and all the animals farmed out in tenanted fields, spread about the district like orphans. Not a lot of scope for a decent living, she guessed and, if Bossom rented the cottage, his tenancy would depend on the whim of the new landlord – a grim prospect for a man nearing retirement. In practical terms old Bossom and his wife would be better off in a council house like Jimmy Thompson.

She hurried through to fall in line with Buller, who was already seated at the kitchen table, a mug of tea steaming in his hand.

'Mr Bossom's having a bit of a lie down,' he explained. 'Did his back in heaving that dead sheep on to the trailer.' He shook his head sympathetically and turned to the wife. 'When did you say it was, Mrs Bossom?'

'That day you came here before. He left it till late, after his meeting in Thame. Now when was that?'

'Monday.'

'Yes, that's it. Getting too old for heavy work like that. I keep telling him, but will he listen?' Cissie's ample chins shook with indignation.

'Well, we don't want to disturb him, Mrs Bossom, just need to have a look at the sheep, all right? Since that foot-and-mouth scare we have a duty to check on all dead animals. Can't be too sure – disease like that can spread like wildfire.'

She was appalled. 'Oh no, Mr Buller, we've no disease in our flock. That sheep bled like a stuck pig it did, poor thing. I told Harry to leave his overalls in the trailer till I got a chance to put them through the washer.'

'Still there, are they, Mrs Bossom?'

''Fraid so. I've been run off my feet since Harry took sick, what with the chickens and my baking order for the farmers' market on Thursday.'

'Good home-made bread, Jenny,' he said, turning to

Robbins. 'My wife runs over there every week. And you do all the farm work between you? No help?'

'Things aren't that bad as long as Harry's not laid up with his hip. Then I have to keep an eye on the sheep for him but I can walk over to Percivals, it isn't far. I can't drive that filthy truck, but at this time of the year sheep don't need feed, and water's on tap.'

Buller finished his tea and he and Robbins strolled outside, the bright sunlight smiting a blow after the dimness of the cottage. They had a quiet word behind the barn, Robbins agreeing to check the Fiesta while Buller sought out the dead sheep. After a few minutes she hurried round to the back of the tractor shed where Buller had found the trailer covered with a tarpaulin.

He turned. 'Found anything, Jenny?'

'You'd better come and look at this, sir. The car was unlocked so I had a good nose round. This tweed jacket was in a bag in the boot. It looks as if it's got bloodstains, quite a lot, no stains inside the car though.'

'We'd better ask Mrs Bossom about that, but livestock farming's gory work. There'll be a reasonable explanation. I found the overalls, caked up with blood like she said, but my problem is that if he didn't pick up the dead animal till Monday night like she said, and it had been dead all weekend, where did all that blood come from? The poor beast wasn't bleeding for days, was it? I'm going to ring the vet in Renham, get him over here smartish, get him to have a look at it.'

'What about Bossom? He said he picked up the sheep on Saturday night and that's when Thompson saw him in the lane.'

'Leave him be. Take the jacket in and show her, without making a dog's dinner out of it, Jenny. Get the story. Keep her talking while I wait here for the vet. I don't want either of them around while he's making his examination. If she asks, tell her it's routine procedure, the vet has to verify for the Ministry that the sheep died from injuries not disease, OK?'

Jenny hurried back to the cottage, her mind churning with

the least of their worries: what the super would have to say about vets' fees incurred without permission.

Buller must have spun a good yarn to the vet, Tim Chichley, who arrived in a shower of spinning wheels within fifteen minutes. Buller stubbed out his cigarette and drew him round to the trailer and, pulling off the tarpaulin with a flourish, spelled out the problem.

'And Bossom says this poor beast was savaged by a dog? Not having me on are you, Ted? Not another sighting of the mythical black puma, eh?' he said with a laugh, cuffing the sergeant with a muscled forearm.

Chichley climbed on to the trailer and gently rolled the sheep on to its back. It had been savaged all right, its head almost severed. The vet spent ten minutes searching for other injuries and finally climbed down to join Buller. He pulled him into the shed.

'It's not like you said, Ted. No claw marks, no tears and, as far as I can see, not an ounce of flesh eaten. That sheep had its throat cut, no more than two strong slashes, it must have died in minutes. Are you thinking what I'm thinking? Some evil bastard killing livestock for kicks? I had a horse stabbed to death last year and after a couple of similar slashings they set up a vigilante group and caught the devil literally red-handed. I hope we're not getting a copy-cat nutter round here, are we?'

'Don't think so, Tim. We had a previous complaint from the same farmer at Easter time, but that was a hungry stray's work – the dog warden nabbed the likely culprit soon after. One of the villagers spotted a dog running off with blood all round its muzzle after her kid's pet lamb had been killed. Let's have a look.'

Buller climbed on to the trailer, followed by Chichley, and it was agreed that the killing had been carried out with something like a butcher's knife.

'Efficient and humane,' Chichley observed. They attached the trailer to the back of the vet's vehicle and he drove off back to the surgery, leaving Buller to bag up the bloodstained overalls and stack them in his car before joining Robbins in the cottage.

Cissie Bossom was clearly distressed, watching the vet's departure with acute anxiety.

'Don't you worry, Mrs Bossom,' Buller encouraged. 'It's nothing bad, no foot-and-mouth symptoms. Your flock's perfectly safe. Mr Chichley thought you'd prefer the carcase off your land, what with all this hot weather we're having. I explained it's been lying in the trailer since Monday and your hubby's been too poorly to deal with it himself.'

She relaxed. 'Oh, that's all right then. Frank will be grateful it's been taken care of. But we won't get a bill, will we, Mr Buller? Vets' bills are sky high these days.'

'No fee, Mr Chichley said. Glad to be of service.'

Robbins stifled a grin, the sergeant's ad-libbing never ceasing to amaze her. 'Mrs Bossom's explained about the jacket in her car, Sergeant. It was on its way to the cleaners in the village. I said we'd pop it in for her on our way through as she's tied up here with her husband off sick.'

'Yes, of course. What happened, Mrs Bossom?'

She frowned. 'My Frank can be so thoughtless sometimes. He put on his best jacket to go to a Farmers' Union meeting in Thame on Monday night and thought he'd pick up this dead sheep on the way back. He forgets to do up his overalls and gets his nice jacket stained lugging the animal on to the trailer. No brains at all.'

Buller nodded knowingly and made his farewells. Back in the car he became deadly serious. 'The jacket's in the boot, I hope?'

'Yes, sir.'

'And I've got the overalls. We'll get the forensic lads to check on the blood, though after seeing that poor beast with its throat slashed I'm not surprised it was a bloodbath. But why slaughter the animal himself and try to lay the blame on Buckleigh's dog?'

'Not hers. I keep telling you. It's the friend's dog he blames – Mrs Blum's mutt.'

'What, that great tail-thumper? That's never a sheep killer, Jenny, not in a million years.'

'Well, it worked first time, didn't it? We don't know how much compensation Mrs Buckleigh paid out at Easter. Perhaps

Bossom thought he was on to a good wheeze and decided to kill one of his lambs and try it on a second time.'

'But he didn't fetch it till Monday evening, did he? That's what his wife said. And he already knew that Stella Buckleigh was dead; he'd heard it on the news even before we got there on Monday. And why put on his best jacket to go to the Farmers' Union meeting and travel there in his filthy pickup truck when he had a perfectly respectable Fiesta sitting at home?'

'He could have killed the sheep days before he picked it up. Or she could have got the dates mixed up,' Jenny put in. 'Cissie doesn't strike me as being a mastermind. He says he went to Percivals on Saturday after the darts match and she says it was Monday after the FU meeting.'

'And either way he was driving the wrong car or truck for the job.'

'Well, we'll just have to wait for the results of the blood tests on the jacket and the overalls and let the DCI pick the bones out of it.'

Fifty-Three

After listening to Buller's account of the afternoon at Bossom's smallholding, Hayes decided to see the dead sheep for himself.

'Get the clothing straight over to the lab, Buller, and keep this part of the investigation strictly to yourself. I don't want any loose talk leaking to any interested parties in the village. Is this vet discreet?'

'I told him to keep his mouth shut – anyone in the know would panic if word got round that a foot-and-moth epidemic was on the cards.'

'Where's Robbins?'

'She's trying to get hold of the F.U. Secretary to see if

Bossom's story holds up about attending the meeting on Monday night. I've had words with the landlord at the Crown – on the face of it just checking up on Thompson's performance at the pub Saturday night. He confirms his statement about Thompson offering the chainsaw to any willing bidder but doesn't want to make a complaint about him chucking the thing about in the public bar and causing ructions in the car park. Thompson's a bit of a local hero; they gloss over his naughty ways mostly because he grew up in the village and so did Patsy. The locals stick together like glue, sir. We're lucky to get to hear about the incident at all.'

'Did you see Bossom?'

'No, he was in bed upstairs. If he heard the vet arriving he kept his head down.'

'Right, Buller, until the results come back from the lab we'll just keep mum, OK? No need to put Sergeant Preston in the picture for now; we don't want to loosen up on the other suspects. Has Thompson been released on bail?'

'Yes, sir. Mr Limpney drove him home an hour ago. When I left the pub after speaking to the landlord, I did a sly recce over at the council estate and saw Patsy Thompson putting washing out, so it looks as if all's forgiven.'

'Let's hope he behaves himself then. Thompson's a key witness and him admitting to blacking out the CCTV about eight o'clock on Saturday gives us some idea of the timescale.'

Hayes reluctantly decided it was time to put Superintendent Waller in the picture and knocked on his door. The room was airless, the windows hermetically sealed against the bright sunlight.

'Good work, Hayes. I hear you've solved the mystery of the dead sheep.'

Hayes obligingly smiled, wondering how Mrs Waller coped with all this quick-change bonhomie and intense irritation. He had met her once at a retirement party. A nice enough woman, a good deal younger than her husband and rumoured to have a teenage son from a first marriage. Hayes was still shell-shocked from his ex-wife's tantrums and regarded the softly spoken Mrs Waller with approval. She deserved better, not that the Super was the worst boss Hayes had ever had. But that was a time he thought of as the Dark Ages of his life. Pippa was a gift from heaven: perky, passionate and not in the least possessive. Perfect.

He roused himself to endure more jibes before bringing Waller back to the Buckleigh case. 'The scenario as I see it is as follows, sir. Friday night our victim is away – probably staying at her London flat. Maybe she wanted to avoid her prearranged meeting with her ex, Monty Neville. He arrives in a filthy humour having been to Oxford to sign legal papers only to find no target. He has to content himself with an angry message on her answer machine.'

'You've got the tape?'

'Yes, sir, all tagged with the other evidence. Mrs Buckleigh returns to Percivals on Saturday and prepares drinks and nibbles for her date with Charlie Hilton that evening. In the afternoon she walks to Thompson's house and spills the poison about her daughter's alleged rape to Jimmy's wife.'

'But you've got no corroboration from the girl or her father?'

'Not yet, sir. I plan to drive over to see Neville in the morning.'

Waller nodded.

Hayes continued. 'Just to lay it on thick, Buckleigh hands all his wages to his wife, a no-no in Thompson's book. Patsy probably never knew how much he earned and must have got used to getting her housekeeping doled out, no questions asked. Robbins has been to see her and says she's a timid little thing, batted between her mother and her bloke, who considers himself cock-of-the-walk in the village.'

'But he's got a record, hasn't he?'

'Yes, sir. Murky. But Patsy seems to accept it and he is a good-looking guy, if you fancy a bit of rough.'

'D'you think Mrs Buckleigh fancied it? Jealous of his attentions to her daughter, say?'

'No. I've met Stella Buckleigh a few times and, apart from the fact that she turned nasty towards Charlie Hilton once he got too rough, she was a snob, probably treated Thompson like some sort of peasant, useful about the house but totally unsexy to a woman like her.'

'I understand she let him do the housework at the cottage as well as the gardening.'

'Yeah! Funny arrangement, but he must have been good at it because she wasn't one to suffer fools gladly. She reclaimed her keys smartish once she'd decided to get rid of him – passed them over to her friend Mrs Blum, which is how she got inside the cottage Sunday afternoon and found the body.'

'Hang about, Hayes! We've skipped Saturday night and that was when the murder happened. Got any sequence on paper yet?'

'Can't swear to every hour but it goes roughly like this. While Buckleigh's out visiting Patsy in the village, Frank Bossom is recorded on the security camera calling at the cottage about four o'clock. Says he wanted to discuss the dead sheep. When he finds out she's not there he drives off back home and is not seen again until he meets his brother at the pub that evening. There was a darts match and the brother says Bossom was with him till about eight. Thompson arrives home after a day out at the autocross and discovers his wife's scarpered to her mother's with all his wages. He talks to her on her mobile and she says she's not coming back because Mrs Buckleigh has said Jimmy raped her daughter. Fireworks! Thompson, who's already had a skinful, decides to go thieving at Percivals to make up for his lost earnings and has worked out that if he's going to approach the place without being seen, he's got to immobilize the security camera.'

'The CCTV.'

'That's right. He's brought some parcel tape and manages to blank out the sensor from behind, which leaves him free to steal the chainsaw from the shed without being filmed.'

'Not such a thicko after all!'

'Trouble is, once Thompson's fixed the camera we don't know for sure who came and went after that. Bossom admits coming back later to pick up the dead sheep, but that wouldn't involve calling at the cottage first. Thompson says he saw Bossom's car in the lane about eight thirty or thereabouts and—'

'Coming or going?'

'Going back. Which would fit in with him collecting the sheep like he said. Monty Neville swears he was at home all day Saturday and when Charlie Hilton turns up just after nine the woman is probably already dead.'

'Or was she? For all we know she opened the door to Hilton and he beat her up for putting the boot in, as far as his career goes, by exposing the embarrassing video footage to his agent and possibly blackmailing him.'

'She didn't need his money, sir! Stella Buckleigh was rolling in it; blackmail wasn't her game.'

'Control then. You said Hilton told you she treated her men like dogs. A woman who had a fixation about being in charge, who hated her sexual partners.'

'You've been boning up on your psychological profiling homework, sir,' Hayes said with a grin.

Waller felt the ground shifting under his feet and muttered irritably, 'All right, Hayes, you've had your little joke, but where do we go from here?'

'Next thing I'm off to see the vet and hopefully interview Monty Neville on home ground in the morning. It looks as if I might manage to have a word with this teenage daughter of his. She's been in hospital you know, sir, and we've all been too polite to ask why.'

'An abortion?'

'Quite possibly.'

Waller shook his head, anxious as a hunted fox with the hounds baying at his heels. 'Dangerous, Hayes. Don't try to shake anything out of the kid without observing every rule in the book. If she really has been ill you could trigger a relapse, and even asking her the time of day would be taboo without her father's permission. Who's looking after the blood test results when they come in?'

'I'm keeping that aspect of the investigation under wraps. Only you and I, Sergeant Buller and Robbins are in on it. I thought you might like to handle it yourself, sir. I should be back by six and Bossom's not going anywhere. I'm just popping over to the vet's to view our other murder victim: the dead sheep.'

Fifty-Four

Monty refused to see Hayes at home so it was agreed that they should meet at his office in Belgrave Square. Hayes decided to take the train in the hope that he would be back in Renham by lunchtime.

For a man reputedly on his uppers, Monty Neville had acquired a cushy set-up at Holland's, one of the leading bookmaking firms with outlets all over the country and a spotless record in the horse-racing world. His office commanded a view over the treetops in the square and if his career had been, as Hayes guessed from the urgency of his cash-flow predicament, on the skids, Stella Buckleigh's sudden death had come in the nick of time. Hayes was taken to the top floor by a messenger boy all decked out in a fancy uniform like a bellhop.

He was taken aback to find Monty's fiancée, Morag McDermott, in attendance. She continued to sit on a sofa at a safe distance from the main action as Monty rose to greet his unwelcome visitor. He introduced Morag, who coolly shook hands. She wore leather trousers and a tweed jacket, an odd choice, Hayes thought, for such a warm day. At a guess Morag McDermott was, unlike Stella, totally uninterested in fashion, her unsophistication possibly the secret of her appeal to Monty.

'You may speak freely, Chief Inspector. Monty has told me the whole story. I can't think why he didn't tell me before, money being the least of our worries while Stella's killer is still at large.'

Monty brought out a chair for Hayes and seated himself next to Morag. She patted his hand, never taking her eyes off Hayes, who felt almost at a disadvantage. 'You have no objection to me taping this interview, Mr Neville?'

241

'None at all.'

Hayes produced a small recording machine and placed it on the coffee table between them.

'Miss McDermott's remark about her anxiety about the killer being at large intrigues me. You're worried about your daughter's safety? That she has information which might be dangerous to the murderer?'

'No, of course not,' Monty blurted out. 'Frances has nothing whatsoever to do with this tragedy.'

'I beg to differ, Mr Neville. Your ex-wife spoke to me herself about the alleged rape. Shall we stop avoiding the issue? Has Frances told you who attacked her? Before you answer, I have a witness who was one of the last to see Mrs Buckleigh on the day she died and she states a name was given – the name of her husband in fact, a man we have as a prime suspect.'

'Stella was guessing,' Morag insisted. 'Fran confided in no one, not even her mother. She refuses to identify the man even to me and we have developed a special bond since . . . er, since . . .' Her words petered out like a blocked tap.

'Since the abortion?' Hayes suggested.

Monty jumped up. 'There was no abortion, and my daughter's medical records are strictly confidential.'

Hayes raised a conciliatory hand. 'Calm down, Mr Neville, we're just seeking a guideline here and it would be important if your daughter pointed her finger at a certain person. Rape, especially of a minor, is a very serious offence and if Mrs Buckleigh threatened to bring it to open court as she was seriously minded to do, a desperate man might have a motive for – to put it crudely – shutting her up before she persuaded Frances to report it to the police.'

Morag rose. 'All this is irrelevant, Chief Inspector. Fran will *not* be dragged into this. I've come here purely to confirm that Monty was nowhere near that cottage on Saturday – he was at Lingfield all day and on Sunday we were joined by friends at a family luncheon party. I have already typed out a statement and signed it to that effect.' She produced an envelope from her bag and handed it over, dismissing Hayes with a steely look he had not encountered since being thrown out of his piano lesson by an irate Miss Moss all of thirty-five years ago.

Monty showed him out with a stiff apology. 'Sorry if things got a bit heated in there, old man. Morag's a stickler for procedure.'

They descended in the lift and Monty stood in the reception area, his aplomb sorely dented. 'Look, Hayes, I know what you're thinking, but Morag's a gem at heart, really she is. She made me tell her everything and got her pa to write a cheque immediately. Saved my bacon. I'll pay him back, of course, just as soon as the lawyers sort out that emergency payment Stella fixed up for me. Don't worry, I won't steal Fran's inheritance, but bringing up a girl who's been used to the best in life's no picnic. I've arranged for her to go to a crammer in Felixstowe just as soon as she's feeling better. A new start.'

'Sounds great. But I'm afraid meeting you here was not a good idea. I may have to insist on further questions at the station, Mr Neville.'

When he got back to Renham he found the superintendent in Hayes' office poring over the Buckleigh files and statements. He glanced up.

'Don't mind me, Hayes, just seeing if there's anything been left out. Any progress with Neville?'

'I've a signed statement from his fiancée confirming his alibi. All day Saturday boxed up at Lingfield.'

'And that was it? You wasted the whole bloody morning shoring up that cringing bastard's alibi? I've been running the videotape his ex-wife made of Monty Neville's performance and listening to the foul-mouthed message he left on her answering machine. The man's nothing but a full-time cadger, Hayes. I bet he's battened on to another rich woman already.'

'Just in the nick of time, too. His fiancée's well caked up and has all the right horsy connections. Her father's coughed up, which saves a lot of embarrassment all round. I tried to get Neville to let me talk to the daughter about this rape business, but we've only got Stella's wild guess that Thompson was the man.'

'But Thompson's a big bloke, Hayes, the only one in the

frame who strikes me as strong enough to beat the daylights out of the victim.'

'Wouldn't take that much force if the weapon was heavy enough. Could have been a woman even.'

'The fiancée?' Waller conjectured, his eyes alight with the possibility of a fresh lead.

'Well, Morag McDermott's a strong healthy girl and jealousy's a powerful weapon.'

'She could have heard Monty's confession, brooded on his ongoing relationship with his ex and stormed off down to the cottage herself on Saturday night to have it out with her. That'd mean Neville's backing her up, that he knew she'd gone off somewhere Saturday night and put two and two together.'

Hayes held up his hands in surrender. 'It was only an idea, sir, and a pretty wild one at that.'

A knock at the door put the lid on this little mental excursion and Buller hurried in, surprised to see the super behind Hayes' desk.

'A result, sir – er, sirs. The blood on the overalls is sheep's, no question. But the stains on Bossom's jacket are sheep's blood an' all. It looks like Cissie was right.'

'Cissie?' Waller barked.

'His wife, sir. She said he got his coat messed up when he went to fetch the dead animal.'

Waller groaned: another dead end.

Hayes' determination hardened. 'Bring him in.'

'What? On what evidence?'

'It just doesn't smell right to me, sir, and we can't reconcile the two versions. Was he at Percivals' field Saturday night *and* Monday night? Either or both? As a long shot we still have the blood residue the pathologist extracted from under the victim's nails. Did anyone see scratches on Bossom?'

'None of us saw the bloke,' Buller admitted. 'He stayed upstairs in bed.'

Fifty-Five

After Bossom had been taken off for questioning, Jenny Robbins hung back with his wife. Cissie was in a terribly agitated state, dabbing her eye with the corner of her apron. Robbins steered her back inside and seated her at the kitchen table where she sat immobile, staring at the clock on the wall.

'All right if I make us a pot of tea, Mrs Bossom?'

Getting no response, Jenny filled the kettle and hunted out mugs and spoons.

'You mustn't take on so, Mrs Bossom. It's only routine. The inspector has to find out exactly who was near the cottage that Saturday night and your husband may have seen something which he hadn't thought important at the time.' She placed a strong brew in front of Cissie, who roused herself and attempted a shaky smile.

'But Frank wasn't there,' she pleaded. 'He was at the pub with Sam. Why drag the poor man off to the station like he was a criminal?'

'He'll be back soon, don't worry. Would you like someone to come and sit with you this evening? Or can I give you a lift into the village?'

'No thanks, dear, I'd rather wait up for him here. He's not well, you know, hasn't been hisself for days. Gets confused in his mind.'

'Well, it's easy to forget things. That's why the inspector wants to go over the timetable. Mr Bossom went to the pub to meet his brother that night and then he went back to the sheep field in the Fiesta?'

'Never! Couldn't take the car in the field, could he?'

'But he said he went back to fetch the dead animal.'

'Oh, no, dear, that was Monday, the day he got his best jacket all messed up.'

'But I thought the sheep had been dead for days. The vet said it wouldn't still be bleeding on Monday.'

'Wouldn't it? P'raps getting it in the trailer set it off again . . .' Cissie's mind was clearly elsewhere, her anxiety about Bossom's interrogation clouding an already limited attention span. She sipped her tea.

Jenny softened her tone. 'I know how you must feel, Cissie, but perhaps you could put the record straight for him. Try to remember. On Saturday afternoon he went to see Mrs Buckleigh but she'd gone for a walk to the village. OK? So he went back later?'

'Oh no. Frank went to the Crown for the darts match. He met his brother, Sam, and came home about nine. I was just finishing a bit of ironing in the scullery and he went straight upstairs to bed. Called out to say he didn't want no supper, his hip was playing up.'

'You didn't see him?'

'No, lovie. If he's feeling bad I generally leave him be and sleep in the spare room so as he's got plenty of room to spread out in the double bed upstairs. He's a martyr to that hip, you know; be a blessing when he gets the dratted operation over with.'

'But he was well enough to go the Farmers' Union meeting on the Monday and pick up the sheep afterwards. It must have been very late.'

'Yes, it was. Can't imagine how he heaved that poor beast into the trailer in the dark. But he's an awkward beggar once he gets an idea in his head. 'Twas after midnight before he got in.'

Jenny refilled Cissie's mug and leaned across the table, all ears. Cissie Bossom clearly had little experience of anyone hanging on her words, and Jenny wouldn't have been surprised if there had been scant notice paid by Bossom himself, a man's man as they would call him when such inattention to 'her indoors' was more acceptable.

'Tell me, Cissie, do you recall what he was wearing on Saturday night?'

'For the darts' match?' She brushed a strand of grey hair behind her ear. 'Oh yes, it was drizzling, I remember that. I'd just gone out to shut up the hens and he waved to me as he was getting into the car to go to the Crown. His blue anorak,' she said firmly. 'The one with the hood.'

'Right. I know this sounds silly, Cissie, but could you show it to me? In case the inspector needs to check who the person was that was seen driving past in the lane near Percivals on Saturday evening – must have been someone else, you said, seeing as he came straight home from the pub.'

Cissie rose and, sprightly for a woman of her age, hurried upstairs to their bedroom, Jenny Robbins close on her heels. The old woman shuffled through the row of coats and skirts, a meagre selection, mostly belonging to the man of the house.

'Not here,' she said. 'He usually hangs up his best things in the wardrobe, but we'll see if it's with his other stuff on the back of the door in the scullery.'

It took Cissie a good ten minutes to search for the anorak but nothing turned up. She looked worried. 'Wasn't he wearing it, dear? When the sergeant took him off to the station?'

'No. Just his shooting jacket, the one with all the pockets.'

Cissie nodded. 'That's right. Well, it fair beats me, we'll just have to ask him when he gets back.'

'He may be some time, Cissie. Why don't you let me drop you off with a friend? I'll ring you when the interview's over, shall I?'

Cissie's anxious state of mind reassured itself. 'Do you think that'd be best, dear? I could go over to my sister's if that isn't out of your way. I can't drive, you see.'

'No bother. Here, put your coat on, it looks as if it might start raining again. I'll lock the back door for you. What's your sister's phone number?'

Cissie jotted a number on a pad and bustled about shutting up the chickens before they drove off. Having deposited her at a council house not far from Thompson's place, Jenny doubled back to the cottage and did a second, more thorough search of the wardrobes and cupboards. No anorak. It was only when she scouted the area behind the barn that she discovered the bonfire site.

247

With infinite care she sifted the ashes and uncovered the remnants of what had once been a handsome garment. Not much remained and it took a good half-hour before she was satisfied that what was recoverable was safely stowed in an evidence bag. She only hoped it was worth the effort. Jenny did lock the back door this time and went out via the front, speeding back to Renham in the panda car.

She caught Sergeant Preston just as he was about to go off duty and dumped the evidence bag on his desk.

'What's all this?'

'Burnt offerings for the lab. Could you send it over straight away? I'll speak to the DCI later. Still at it, are they?'

'Keeping Bossom overnight, poor old sod. Between you and me, Jenny, I reckon the governor's overstepped the mark here. Still, he did get the doc to give Bossom the once over before they shunted him into the interview room.'

'Did he take a blood sample?'

'Eh? What for?'

She shrugged. 'Just an idea. I'll scribble some notes for your file, shall I? An interview of sorts with Bossom's wife. I wish those two would get their act together. I can't decide whether they're both confused or just acting up.'

'Old folks get muddled,' Preston said defensively.

'Well, I think I'll call it a day. I shall be at home if there's a panic but I don't think Cissie Bossom's evidence amounts to much.'

In the interview room, Hayes was facing the same inconsistencies, but Buller, patient as Buddha, persisted in his slow, relentless interrogation.

Fifty-Six

Hayes was getting nowhere with Frank Bossom and when he insisted on having his solicitor present it was a relief to curtail the interview. Unluckily for the old man, his lawyer was not immediately available and he agreed that further questioning could be put off until the morning. Bossom's ready acceptance of this postponement was something of a surprise, despite the man's insistence that only his own lawyer would do even if that meant that an overnight stay in a police cell was unavoidable. Hayes wondered if the crafty old codger needed time to get his story straight, the normal response to an extended interview being uncooperative at the very least.

Hayes left instructions to make the old man as comfortable as possible and hurried off to phone the superintendent at home.

'Any joy, Hayes?'

'Not so far, sir, but he's certainly playing it cool. DC Robbins recovered an anorak from his cottage that's at the lab. I'm hoping they'll pick up something but the thing's been burnt so it's unlikely to give us anything positive.'

'What did Doctor Flanagan make of Bossom's state of health? Not likely to croak under all this questioning, is he?'

'He checked his blood pressure and I got him to listen to the old man's chest only because I wanted the doc to have an excuse to have his shirt off. Bossom's got scratches on his neck all right, but says he got snagged on barbed wire climbing into his sheep field.'

'Climbing? I thought this bloke was disabled?'

'Well, hardly crippled if he can haul a dead sheep on to his trailer.'

Waller was not happy. 'Is this another one of your wild guesses, Hayes? What about Charlie Hilton? He sounds a much safer bet and can be pinned down to the area at the time Buckleigh was killed.'

'I'm on to it, sir, but getting him back from France won't be easy unless we have evidence that he entered the cottage. There are no positive sightings of him nearer than Renham and he sticks to his story that he got to Percivals a bit late and, on the face of it, Buckleigh refused to let him in. I assume his agent's anxious to keep him out of England if possible – there's been enough bad publicity since his son fell off the roof and Hilton's definitely said he's not attending the inquest.'

'And you can't crack the ex-husband's alibi?'

'No. Well, not yet anyway.'

'What about Thompson? He was there all right, admits blacking out the CCTV and being on the spot within the timescale Doc Flanagan sets the murder.'

'Thompson's out on bail. He says he saw Bossom's Fiesta in the lane when he was cutting through the woods on his motorbike on the way home with the chainsaw. He was fighting mad about his wife bunking off with his pay packet and spent an hour after the theft on Saturday night getting tanked up before deciding to get rid of the saw as soon as possible.'

'Then he went to the pub and got thrown out trying to sell it?'

'That's right, sir. Ten o'clock or thereabouts.'

Waller sighed, now more certain than ever that Hayes was barking up the wrong tree with Bossom. 'And a weapon, Hayes? Found no weapon yet?'

'No, sir, but a heavy beating like the victim sustained blurs any clear indications. It could have been anything – even something he found at the scene and took away with him. There was no bloodstained poker conveniently lying about.'

Waller caught a whiff of sarcasm there and decided to cut it short. 'You'd better come up with something soon, Hayes. What time's Bossom's solicitor booked in?'

'Nine o'clock. He wants a private discussion with his client first, of course, so I'm assuming we shall get our suspect into the interview room about ten.'

'I'll be there. Do you know this solicitor? Local man, is he?'

'Rayner. Has an office in Renham. Never met him myself, but perhaps you've come across him.'

'Not professionally but he has a good reputation, mostly conveyancing and commercial work. Would have thought a potential criminal case was well out of his league.'

'Good.'

Waller rang off but found it impossible to pick up on the European Cup match that Hayes had interrupted.

'Bloody man's off at a tangent again, Betty,' he complained. 'I think I'll have to take over before the commissioner kicks us in the balls with a specialist murder squad.'

Hayes spent the next hour mulling over the questionable statement Robbins had extracted from Mrs Bossom. He scribbled down a possible sequence of the comings and goings at Percivals during the fatal weekend and bitterly concluded that, for a remote country cottage, the place had a proliferation of visitors all converging within the estimated time of the murder. And all that new security equipment had done Stella Buckleigh no good at all, had it?

Next morning, Hayes and Sergeant Buller settled in the interview room with Frank Bossom and his solicitor, Rayner. Superintendent Waller had got himself a front row seat in the adjacent viewing room and Jenny Robbins stationed herself with her notebook at his shoulder.

Hayes curtly introduced himself to Rayner and waited for Buller to switch on the recording equipment and pronounce the formal preamble to questioning. Bossom looked calm, his stolid features unreadable. He sat squarely before his inquisitors, gripping his walking-stick, alert as a terrier at a foxhole.

'Shall we start with Saturday afternoon, Mr Bossom? You were seen knocking at Mrs Buckleigh's door about four o'clock.'

'Got no answer, did I?'

'What then?'

'Went home. What else was I supposed to do?'

'And the purpose of your call?'

'One of my lambs, a second one, had been savaged. Mrs

Buckleigh's orchard runs along the boundary fence. I wanted to speak to her about it.'

'She accepted responsibility for a lamb that was killed over the Easter weekend?'

'Denied it but we come to an agreement.'

'She compensated you financially?'

'Fair's fair, and I still say that great mongrel what was staying there did the damage.'

'So when another animal was killed, you decided to call on Mrs Buckleigh again. When did it die?'

'Can't say for sure, I don't check the flock every day, but no question the poor beast had its throat torn out.'

'The vet has examined your animal, Mr Bossom, and agrees it was savaged, but not by a dog and not before the weekend.'

'Well, he's wrong.'

Rayner looked sharply at his client who remained obdurate.

Sergeant Buller chimed in. 'Its throat was deliberately cut, Mr Bossom.'

Bossom gripped his walking-stick. 'Well, there was such a lot of blood it looked to me like a dog kill. But if you said it was done in by one of them village louts, I'd believe you.'

'Another thing puzzles me, Mr Bossom. All that blood, you say,' Buller patiently continued. 'Your vet reckons it died later than Saturday, Monday for instance. Your wife says you picked up the dead sheep Monday, after your F.U. meeting.'

Bossom let out a loud guffaw. 'You don't want to take no notice of Cissie, Sergeant. Got a mind like a sieve that woman.'

Buller nodded encouragingly but Bossom's mouth clamped firmly shut.

Hayes took up the enquiry. 'Shall we go back to Saturday, Mr Bossom? What followed your abortive visit to Percivals in the afternoon?'

'Nothing much. I poked about with my truck which 'ad been playing up, and after me tea I went over to the Crown to watch the darts match. I met my brother, Sam, he'll tell you.'

'And you didn't take the truck?'

'No, the Fiesta. Like I said the pickup was dodgy; your sergeant here kindly put it right for me later.'

Hayes glanced at Buller, who nodded.

'So you drove to the pub in the car and stayed for a pint or two. And when did you leave?'

'Blimey, that's a tall order. When I'd had enough, I suppose. Wasn't over the limit if that's what you're getting at.'

'You went straight home?'

'Not straight off. You trying to confuse me, Inspector? No, like I said, first off I went back to Percivals to sort out the dead 'un.'

'Your red Fiesta was seen about eight.'

'Course it bloody was. Didn't I just say I went to see to the carcase?'

'Not in your nice clean car, you didn't,' Buller put in. 'Not a speck of blood inside – I checked it over myself. And how would you drive into the muddy field on a wet night in that little runabout, I ask you?'

'I didn't. I parked in Percivals' yard and cut through her orchard. Climbed over the fence and tore my sleeve on the dratted wire, I did.'

'And the sheep was dead?'

'Yes. I left it till I had the truck.'

'But you admit being at Percivals that Saturday night?'

'No chance of dodging all that bloody security caper of hers, was there?'

Rayner looked restive, his eyes darting from Buller to Hayes and back to his client who, for an old man who had never been subjected to police questioning in such a way before, was holding up well.

Hayes avoided eye contact with Buller, both acknowledging that Thompson's tampering with the surveillance had pushed Bossom to confirm his presence, a fact he could have denied had he known it had been disarmed.

Hayes hung on in there. 'So you went to your field after the darts match to collect the sheep? That's what you said originally.'

'Did I?' Bossom's eyebrows raised in mystification. 'Must have got mixed up, Inspector. I *meant* to pick up the sheep but being as I wasn't dressed for the job – no overalls or boots on me – and seeing as I had no truck with me neither, I must have decided to leave it. The sheep weren't going nowhere, were it? And providing Mrs Buckleigh hadn't spotted it, one day was as good as another.'

'You didn't like Mrs Buckleigh, did you?'

'Snotty bitch. No country woman for sure.'

'Shall we continue? You are saying now you eventually picked up the sheep Monday night?'

Rayner cut in. 'Excuse me, Chief Inspector, but is all this relevant?'

'I'm afraid so, because—' Hayes broke off as a knock at the door preceded Sergeant Preston with an urgent note. Hayes irritably tore at the envelope as Preston made a quick exit. Bossom lit his pipe, regarding the two policeman seated opposite with amusement. Rayner sat stiffly at his side, his confusion at his client's convoluted story gaining momentum.

Hayes brightened and Buller restarted the recording.

'And what were you wearing to check on your flock Saturday night, Mr Bossom?'

That floored him. He laid his pipe on the ashtray and ponderously blew his nose on a large striped handkerchief. Hayes relaxed, waiting for a response.

'Can't remember,' he said gruffly.

'No problem. Mrs Bossom remembers clearly. Women do, don't they? Notice things.' He paused. 'I suggest you wore a blue anorak.'

Bossom thought for a moment. 'Er, yes, Cissie was right. I burnt it.'

'Burnt it? Why?'

'Like I said, it got snagged on the fence wire. Ruined. So I put it on the bonfire.'

Buller looked anxious. 'Saturday night? You tore the anorak Saturday night?'

'That's what I said, didn't I?'

Hayes cut to the jugular. 'I have here a report from the forensic laboratory which has matched bloodstains on the remains of your anorak with those of the dead woman. How do you explain it?'

'Lies. All lies!' The old man's features suffused with rage and he attempted to rise.

'Please sit down, Mr Bossom,' Rayner entreated. 'I'm sure there is an innocent explanation.'

Bossom slumped, bravado suddenly swept aside.

'Did you go in?' Buller gently enquired. 'Discover the body?'

'You caught me on that security camera by the front door?' he croaked.

'As it happens, no, but that's not important. You can't deny forensic proof, Mr Bossom. Shall I tell you what I think?' Hayes waited while Bossom fingered his pipe, staring down at the table, waiting for something. What? Waiting for a plausible explanation to come to him?

Hayes launched into his scenario. 'It's a complicated business, killing someone, isn't it, Mr Bossom? Much more difficult that killing a sheep. No one could plan such a wretched scheme. As I see it, you called on Mrs Buckleigh in the afternoon, got no answer, and fumed about it all evening. You had a serious grudge, didn't you? Not about a sheep at all, was it? The grudge festered and after a few beers at the Crown that night you decided to have another go at cornering the woman and, instead of driving home, you pushed on up the lane. Bad luck was, Jimmy Thompson saw you and when the murder was discovered you remembered the CCTV must have pinned you to the scene, so you invented this cock-and-bull story about calling on her to talk about a second dead sheep. Right so far?'

Bossom remained slumped in his seat, apparently taking in nothing.

Buller joined in, eager to add his faggot to the fire. 'The vet swears the sheep must have been killed no earlier than Monday. And all that blood you got on your sports coat got there after the F.U. meeting, when, in your rush to get the job over with, you didn't do up your overalls properly and the poor beast spattered blood everywhere.'

Hayes took over. 'You killed the sheep yourself, didn't you, Mr Bossom? To substantiate your alleged reason for calling on Mrs Buckleigh on Saturday night. What happened?

Remember anything you say . . .' Hayes continued with the caution, aware that Rayner was well out of his depth, a useless support for the poor, wretched Bossom.

Fifty-Seven

'I've lost more sleep over killing that lamb than finishing *her*. Never butchered one of my own flock before; fair broke my heart. But I did it quick, poor animal hardly felt a thing – but all that blood. . .' Bossom looked up, his rheumy eyes fixed on Hayes, the recollection of the slaughter seeming to agonize afresh with the telling. But he continued, his voice firm.

'I don't care what happens to me now. It's all over, but I tried my best. What you people don't understand is what Percivals means to us. Sam and I was born there you know, my dad worked for Grandpa Percival and us boys were all set to follow on. But we was dealt a wicked blow when our dad died, TB it was, a killer all them years ago. Still, Sam and I worked on for the old man and we all lived at the farm expecting to end our days there. But the silly old fool left everything to Uncle Bert, a bloke with no interest in farming, who had run off to sea as a lad. When he come back to claim Percivals we thought we would go on as usual, me and Sam working the farm, Mum having the place to herself after a lifetime grafting for my grandfather, a hard man if I say so meself. He made this stick,' Bossom added, holding up the roughly carved handiwork with pride.

Rayner touched his arm. 'Are you sure, Mr Bossom? You don't have to say anything you know and—'

Bossom rounded on him angrily. 'Don't interrupt me, man! Let me have my say if it's the last thing I do. People should know they can't treat us like dirt – like *she* did.'

'Mrs Buckleigh?' Buller gently put in. He turned to focus on the sergeant, his stubborn determination drawing him on. Hayes motioned Buller to back off and waited, leaving the old man to plot his own destruction.

'Yes, Mrs bloody Buckleigh,' he spat out. 'I was prepared to beg, get on my knees if need be, but she wouldn't listen. Wasn't asking for a hand-out, was I? Sam's got a nice little nest egg and Cissie and me don't live like royalty. We had enough between us to pay.'

'To top the Trelawnay Holdings bid?' Rayner blurted out incredulously.

'No, of course not! But their surveyor who was measuring up my sheep field told me they wasn't interested in the farm-house, only the land. They'd be demolishing Percivals, the orchard, the lot, and parcelling it up with the rest of the estate. Fair knocked me sideways. That place is our heritage, what right had that woman to put it to the bulldozers? But after I'd thought a bit and had a word with Sam and the bank manager we decided it was all to the good. If the buyers only wanted the fields and Mrs Buckleigh was willing to sell off Percivals as a separate lot, we stood a good chance of buying it back. Even with no acreage it would be something to pass on to our sons.'

Bossom blew his nose, shaking his head when Buller suggested a cup of tea might be in order. Hayes sat rigidly to attention, refusing to allow a break. Rayner shrugged, knowing that the tide had turned against his client and a fierce undertow of resentment was carrying him beyond help.

'You approached Mrs Buckleigh with a business plan?' Hayes prompted.

'Got all our accounts in apple-pie order and I tried to see her Saturday afternoon but she weren't in. Her car was there so I decided to try again later. There wasn't much time, you see, the sale was already in the hands of the lawyers. But you was wrong about a grudge, Inspector. I was quite sure I'd get her round to my way of thinking. It didn't matter to her what they did to Percivals, did it? If she saw my point and we had enough money to square it with Trelawnay Holdings it could all work out for everyone – save them the expense of clearing the land and give us back what should never have been sold off in the first place. Sam and I had been waiting for a chance like that for forty years, ever since Uncle Bert chucked us out.'

'But Mrs Buckleigh wasn't interested?'

'Wouldn't even hear me out, the arrogant cow. I knocked at her door that night, all my facts and figures under my arm, and if I hadn't pushed my way in she would have left me out on the doorstep. Anyway, having got my foot in the door she said she'd give me five minutes and we stepped into her office. To give her her due she listened while I spouted all the figures, then she pushed the sale agreement under my nose. "Too late, Mr Bossom, you're wasting your breath. And if you think what you're offering is a decent valuation, think again. Now clear out, I'm expecting a friend." Her exact words. "Clear Out." She tried to push me out and I stumbled back and accidently tripped her up with my stick. She went sprawling and bashed her head on the corner of the desk and fell on to a settee. And seeing her there, blood trickling from the cut on 'er 'ead, her face all ugly, looking at me as if I was some sort of mad bull that 'ad broke into her smart cottage, I just lost it. Went for her with my stick, hitting her over and over again. Who was she to treat me like that? It was *our* place, *our* land, *our* inheritance – not for her to throw us off.'

'You killed her?' Hayes persisted.

'Bloody right I did, and glad of it too. Like I said, killing the lamb's been on my conscience, but people like *her*, people with no roots in the countryside, have no rights, no rights at all.'

'I shall have to take your stick, Mr Bossom, hand it to the sergeant please. We'll find you another.'

He reluctantly handed over what could only now be regarded as the murder weapon. The old man smiled. 'Grandpa Percival would have cheered you know: using his old stick to defend our rights.'

Hayes rang for a constable to take Bossom away. Rayner, considerably chastened, followed his client out.

Hayes regarded Buller with satisfaction. 'Thanks, Sergeant. Good work.'

'What do you think, sir? Manslaughter? It wasn't premeditated, was it? You could almost say he was provoked . . .'

Hayes shrugged. 'Not our problem, Buller. Now, I think we deserve a pat on the back from the super. That little firecracker, Robbins, came up with the anorak in the nick of time. Real teamwork.' He beamed. 'Still, there are the scratches on his neck – bet you the blood samples from under the victim's fingernails will put the seal on it.'

Buller reluctantly agreed.

'Do you think the brother, Sam Bossom, was in on it, Buller?'

'No. He's a quiet bloke. Gamekeeper. I'd put my money on our Frank thinking he could pull this off all by himself. Crafty old bugger. Tells a good story though, the defence will have plenty of folks on his side in this – an old farming family the victim of a greedy agricultural conglomerate and an unsympathetic woman who some would say deserved a beating.'

Buller hurried out.

Hayes packed up his file and put through a call to Pippa.

'Hi there, sunshine. Guess what? I'm putting in for some leave.'

'Piano practise?'

'If you're really nice to me I might even fit in an encore – how about *The Minute Waltz*?'

'Now you're just showing off!' she retorted. 'Anyway it generally takes at least a minute and thirty seconds, hardly more than a gesture.'

'You're never satisfied are you, darling? Anyway, I'm in a mood to celebrate. Any ideas?'

Fifty-Eight

Stella's funeral was scheduled for mid-June. Morag had arranged for the service to be held at a tiny church in a village with a decent hostelry within walking distance. Stanley Kerslake offered to host lunch and assembled a dozen theatrical friends to support Stella's final departure. This was just as well as the mourners were few, the select band standing in the country churchyard subdued but tearless, apart from Fran who stood, white-faced, supported on either side by Monty and Morag.

Tory and Rob Allinson stood apart at the edge of the interment, sunlight glancing through the trees, dappling the sombre scene. Flowers were heaped around the carpet of false turf that was now draped over the rough mound, and the mourners started to drift away, hustled by Stanley towards the inn.

Stanley waited for Monty to catch up and drew him aside. Morag, with Fran firmly in tow, gravitated towards the vicar.

Stanley moved in on Monty. 'You're OK about this little lunch aren't you, old chap? I don't want to seem to be pushing in.'

'Absolutely fine! A very generous gesture, Stanley. You've been a good friend all these years, kept an eye on poor Stella since Anthony died.'

Stanley shrugged, a shadow of confusion clouding his eyes. 'That business of Charlie Hilton's son breaking into her flat . . . Accidental death was the coroner's verdict. Fair enough. But between you and me, Monty, Stella getting herself involved with Hilton and that wife of his – Kate, wasn't it? – still worries me. A friendship going back years, so I'm told.'

'Kate and Stella were at school together. With Tory,' he quietly added, nodding towards the couple lagging behind, examining the heaps of flowers. Rob Allinson looked discreetly suave in black suit and tie, Tory pale as death. Morag gripped Fran's arm as if she was afraid the girl might make a run for it, yet managing to continue a smooth conversation with the vicar.

'I had a long talk with Tory, Stanley,' Monty confided. 'It seems Stella had this lunatic idea she could manipulate Charlie Hilton into a decent divorce settlement for her friend – Stella's brief affair with the mean sod being all part of the scam. Stella was holding out the carrot of a starring role for Charlie at Bucks, a kick up the backside for his flagging film career. I expect she tried to coax you to come round to her way of thinking? What happened about that, Stanley?'

He frowned. 'Well, we let it go through. The publicity about his boy hadn't done Charlie much harm, and there was a certain amount of sympathy for the bloke, kids into drugs not being exactly an unheard-of problem these days. His agent persuaded me that Charlie can still pull in the punters, but we scotched the Chekhov idea.'

'Chekhov! Charlie Hilton going legit?'

Stanley grinned. 'These guys hanker for professional kudos like it was the Holy Grail. We've agreed on something lighter, less demanding: *Blithe Spirit*. Reckon it'll be a sell-out; Charlie still has shedloads of charm and his agent and I put it to him that Noel Coward was more his style.'

'Where's he now?'

'Scarpered back to Paris, "filming". Keeping his head down if you ask me.'

'And Kate? He came through with the divorce settlement?'

'Very generously. His agent, deLaunay, and I put the screws on him but he'd already agreed acceptable terms before Stella was killed. Drowned in sentimentality was his version, but we impressed on him we wanted no back-sliding, no recriminations in court to cloud his stage debut next year.'

'I thought Kate would be here, being such an old friend.'

261

'DeLaunay wangled a job for her in L.A. The last thing Charlie needed was Kate stirring up any media interest so soon after Stella's murder and the death of his son. DeLaunay leaned on a producer he knows to come up with a contract for her to do some research – an English woman with experience, tailor-made for Kate – and she was eager to get away, so shunting her off to Hollywood made sense all round.'

'Experience?'

'She used to work in films, apparently, and Charlie assures us Kate's well satisfied with the divorce settlement and is not the sort to turn nasty now she's got this chance of new life for herself. You'll have to excuse me, Monty – you'll be joining us in the pub later?'

'Sure. I'll just wait for the girls to catch up.'

Stanley hurried off to join the rest of the lunch party, leaving Monty to gaze around with a nagging feeling of remorse. Fancy poor Stella ending up in this quiet churchyard. So far from home. It seemed sadly inappropriate for a beautiful woman who had been so vibrant, so citified, so sure of herself. And now here she was, shunted aside to lie amid all these villagers with whom, if any sort of afterlife existed, she would have absolutely nothing to talk about.

He brushed aside this weird notion as Tory hurried forward, leaving Rob Allinson to join Morag.

'Such a beautiful day,' Rob murmured, smiling at Fran clamped like a prisoner between Morag and the vicar and clearly reluctant to leave the graveside. The vicar remarked on the hastening progress of the funeral party towards lunch, and the three waited, in awkward silence, for Monty to rejoin them.

But Tory seemed intent on a private word with him herself as they slowly walked back to the group.

'Monty, I wonder if you could spare Fran for a while? I'll bring her over to the pub in a bit if that's all right.'

Morag nodded and Monty touched Fran's arm. 'OK by you, darling? Stay a little longer if you like.'

Frances raised a tearful face and pulled away to stand by Tory, glad to be excused from Stanley's pre-lunch drinks at a guess. Morag and Monty linked up with Rob and left with the vicar, relieved that the worst was over.

Tory touched Fran's shoulder. 'My dog's in the car. Shall we take him for a bit of a run?'

Fran agreed with a desultory nod, her misery like an unshakeable burden. They released Moses from Tory's ramshackle vehicle and he bounded off up the lane, following the two of them through a farm gate and into a meadow bright with wild flowers. Fran trudged alongside, her dark mood intractable, the silence heavy between them.

Without glancing at her, Tory quietly said, 'You know you don't have to carry this burden on your own.'

Fran stumbled, staring at Tory who took her in her arms, firmly gripping the thin shoulders in a fierce embrace. Fran had lost weight, her tear-stained cheeks no longer the chubby features of three months ago. Tory whispered urgently into Fran's hair, holding on as the words tumbled out.

'Stella was my dearest friend and a wonderful mother, Fran. She had such love for you and didn't mean to leave you shackled by the secret.'

'What secret?' Fran croaked, her mind racing.

'About the drugs. She told you never to tell anyone, didn't she? But, sweetheart, Stella never meant you to live under that shadow for always. I guessed, and I could have made her share the secret with me before poor Chaz died. It wasn't your fault, Fran. Really it wasn't. It was mine. Do you know where your mother got those drugs from, the ones Chaz found in the flat?'

'Not exactly. But I heard her talking to you on the phone about it. She promised to get rid of them, didn't she?'

'I needed to believe her because I was too wrapped up in my own sadness to be firm. It was *my* fault, darling. The drugs were to do with my husband's work at an addiction clinic. He was a doctor . . . The important thing for you is to forget your pact with Stella about keeping it a secret – she wouldn't have wanted you to spend the rest of your life blaming yourself for Chaz's accident. It gradually dawned on me what must have happened at the flat that night. Stella would never have dared to share the secret with a known user like Chaz and there was only one other who could have found out, and that was you.'

They started to walk on, following Moses' erratic forays into the hedgerow. Fran's pace quickened. 'But it *was* my fault, Tory. You don't understand. I found out about the drugs hidden in the suitcase and I knew the lock combination. It was me who showed Chaz where they were. He said he could sell them and pay for an abortion for me. Did you know about me being raped?'

Tory brushed this aside. 'That's all old history, Fran. Forget it, you're fine now and starting a new part of your life. It will be difficult without your mother, but you have Monty and Morag and the wedding to look forward to. Don't burden yourself with guilt; Stella just wanted to shield you from the police investigation when you swore never to tell anyone about the drugs. Promise me,' she insisted, gripping the girl's elbow. 'Promise me, Fran, you'll put all that behind you. It was selfish of me to let Stella tidy up after Stefan. It was *my* responsibility, and if anyone is to blame for Chaz's accident it was me, not you and not Stella.'

'Does his mother know all this?'

'Absolutely not. Kate has to make a new life for herself and I shan't ever speak of this again, either to you or to anyone else. I've lost Stefan and have to learn to live again. Your life is just beginning. Secrets are dangerous, never forget that.'

Fran had started to weep tears of relief. They clung together in the sunlit meadow for a long moment, oblivious to the cavortings of Moses who was madly circling as they broke apart to run back, laughing, to Stanley's party.